Ottilie Liljencrantz's
The Viking Adventures
Volume 2

Ottilie Liljencrantz's
The Viking Adventures
Volume 2

The Vinland Champions
The Ward of King Canute
and
A Viking's Love
and Other Tales of the North

Ottilie A. Liljencrantz

Ottilie Liljencrantz's
The Viking Adventures
Volume 2
The Vinland Champions
Randvar the Songsmith
and
A Viking's Love and Other Tales of the North
by Ottilie A. Liljencrantz

FIRST EDITION

First published under the titles
The Vinland Champions
Randvar the Songsmith
and
A Viking's Love and Other Tales of the North

Leonaur is an imprint
of Oakpast Ltd

Copyright in this form © 2014 Oakpast Ltd

ISBN: 978-1-78282-385-8 (hardcover)
ISBN: 978-1-78282-386-5 (softcover)

http://www.leonaur.com

Publisher's Notes
The views expressed in this book are not necessarily those of the publisher.

Contents

Ottilie A. Liljencrantz	7
The Vinland Champions	9
Randvar the Songsmith	119
A Viking's Love and Other Tales of the North	279

OTTILIE A. LILJENCRANTZ

Ottilie A. Liljencrantz

Ottilie A. Liljencrantz was born in Chicago in 1876, the daughter of Gustave A. M. and Adeline C. Liljencrantz. On her mother's side, she was a descendant of the Puritans; on her father's she could trace her lineage from Laurentius Petrie, an Archbishop in Upsala, a disciple of Martin Luther, and a translator of the Bible in the sixteenth century. The first ancestor to bear the family name was Count Johan Liljencrantz, Councillor of State and Minister of Finance, who was ennobled for his valuable services to the Kingdom during the reign of Gustavus III.

She received her education at Dearborn Seminary in Chicago, graduating in 1903. While her health did not admit of a college course, she took a postgraduate course in literature and was always a persistent student in that line. She showed a marked literary taste at an early age. She said:

"I was brought up on Longfellow and Bret Harte, as well as on the myths and sagas of the North, and wrote my first story at the age of seven, a tragic love story, which was a great deal funnier than anything I have ever written since."

While yet a schoolgirl, she wrote a number of plays for amateur theatricals, and some short stories. Her first book, *The Scrape that Jack Built*, was published in 1896, but the tales of the North, with the daring exploits of its heroes, were alluring, and she made a thorough and exhaustive study of Northern literature Paul Du Chaillu's *The Viking Age*, *Frithiofs Saga*, Rasmus B. Anderson's introduction to Norse Mythology, and nearly forty other works of the same character. Among these should be specially mentioned *Havamal*, which comprises the sayings of Odin and is regarded as the laws of the Vikings, and from which quotations appear at every chapter in her two great historical novels, *The Thrall of Leif the Lucky* and *The Ward of King Canute*.

Her writings are all morally wholesome, for both the virtues and the vices of her Viking heroes are those of their own times. In the eyes of a Viking, the slaughter of an enemy was not a crime, but a noble and righteous deed; and on the other hand, he would cheerfully lay down his life for a friend.

Ottilie A. Liljencrantz had a most charming personality, and she was an honoured member of "The Little Room," "The Chicago Woman's Club," and of the "Lyceum Club" of London.

She died in Chicago on the seventh of October, 1910.

The Vinland Champions

HIS EYES SHOWED FIRE, WHILE HIS VOICE WAS ASLEEP

Prologue

It happened first in the history of the New World lands that the Northman Biorn Herjulfsson saw them when he had lost his way in journeying to Greenland. But he lacked the adventuresomeness to go ashore and explore them.

Then Leif the Lucky, son of Eric the Red of Greenland, heard of the omission and set out to remedy it. He rediscovered the lands and went upon them and named them, after which he built booths at a place he called Vinland and passed a winter there.

Next, Leif's brother Thorwald Ericsson came over the ocean; but his luck was less for he was shipwrecked on one cape and killed on another, and his men returned disheartened.

He was followed by the third brother, Thorstein; but this expedition had no success whatever for they spent a whole summer in wandering in a circle that landed them finally upon the west coast of Greenland itself. And here Thorstein died of a plague, leaving his young wife Gudrid to return to the hospitality of Leif at Brattahlid.

The explorer who came next and who did the most was Thorfinn Karlsefne of Iceland. While he was visiting at Brattahlid he married Gudrid, the widow of Thorstein, and she—together with others—talked to him so much about the new lands that he resolved upon settling them. In the spring of 1007 he set out from Greenland with three ships heavily laden and came to Vinland and wakened the sleeping camp to new life.

This story begins on an autumn day in the second year of Karlsefne's settlement, and on board the little ship called the *Wind-Raven* which he had sent out at the beginning of summer to explore the eastern coast.

Part First: The Brood of the "Wind-Raven"

Chapter 1

Concerning Alrek of the Viking Camps

For four days the *Wind-Raven* had drifted blindfold in a fog, and now the fifth day had dawned with no prospect of release and the explorers were hard put to it for amusement. On the after-deck the helmsman had sought comfort in his ale horn; spread over the benches below, the two-score men of the crew were killing time with chess games; and the twenty-odd boys who completed the company had turned the forepart of the ship into a swimming beach around which they sported with the zest of young seals. On the murky waves their yellow heads bobbed like so many oranges. The forecastle swarmed with them as they chased one another across it, their wet bodies glimmering moth-like in the grayness. And the first two benches were covered with those whom lack of breath had induced to pause and burrow in the heaps of clothing scattered there.

The centre of the group of loungers was a brown-haired brown-eyed brown-cheeked boy relating with a grin of appreciation a story of Viking horseplay. The laughter which applauded him ceased only when a lad with a sword approached and set the laughers to dodging thrusts.

"Your noses are as blue as Gudrid's eyes," the newcomer scoffed, sprinkling them with tosses of his dripping red mane. "Rouse up, Alrek of Norway, and have a bout with me to set your blood to moving."

The brown-eyed boy looked around without enthusiasm; and from the others rose a disparaging chorus:

"There are more chances that you will set your own blood to running—" "Hallad once had the same belief in—" "Perhaps the water has blurred the Red-Head's memory so he thinks it was he who won the dwarfs' sword last winter."

The Red-Haired became also the Red-Cheeked; he was overgrown and undisciplined and his temper appeared to be hung as loosely as his limbs. " If you allow him to think," he cried, "that we twenty Greenlanders are afraid to fight him because he was bred in a Viking camp while we are farm-reared, I will challenge him where I stand." He was swelling his chest as if to devote his next breath to defiance, when he was prevented by Alrek of Norway himself.

"I will not fight you, but you may have your way about fencing," the young Viking consented, rising leisurely and laying aside his cloak of soldier scarlet. Emerging from its folds, it could be seen that besides his brownness he was distinguished among his companions for the soldierly erectness with which he bore his broad-shouldered thin-flanked young body, and the compactness of the muscles that played under his burnished skin with the strong grace of a young tiger's.

While he dug up his dwarf-made weapon from the mound of his clothing, the Red One ran up to the forecastle and kicked clear of ropes and garments a space in the centre; and the loungers hitched themselves around to face the deck, and joined in elbowing off the swimmers as they came splashing in to see the sport.

Sport it unquestionably was at the beginning, for the camp-bred boy set the tune to a tripping measure that made the graceful blades seem to be kissing each other. Back and forth and up and down they went as in a dance, parry answering thrust so evenly that the ear grew to anticipate the clash and keep time to it as to music. But presently this very forbearance nettled the farm-bred lad so that he broke the rhythm with an unexpected stroke. Passing Alrek's guard, it opened a red wound upon his brown breast. He accepted it with a grimace as good-humoured as his fencing, but his opponent was unwise enough to let fly a cry of triumph. Alrek's expression changed. The next time the Greenlander made use of that thrust, his blade was met with a force that jarred his arm to the shoulder. Under the hurt of it, he struck spitefully. Alrek answered in kind. Slowly, the even beat gave way to jerks of short sharp clatter, separated by pauses during which the two worked around each other with squaring mouths and kindling eyes.

With the beginning of the clatter, a short old man called Grimkel One-Eye and a long young man known as Hjalmar Thick-Skull, sitting at chess behind the mast, had put down their pieces to listen. Now, the discord continuing, old Grimkel left his place and strolled forward to the forecastle steps. Spying blood spots on the Greenlander's white shoulders, he made Alrek of Norway a sign of warning. But the Viking boy did not even see him.

Over the spectators such stillness had fallen that the scuffle and slap of the bare feet upon the boards sounded with sickening distinctness. The indrawn breaths made a hiss when, more swiftly than eye could follow, Alrek's blade described a new curve which the other's sword could not meet. To save himself from being spitted, the Greenlander was forced to leap backward. Leaping, his back came against the gunwale with a crash which told that further retreat would be impossible. From the watchers burst a cry, but no recollection relaxed the terrible intentness of the young Viking's eyes as a second time he drew back his arm to speed that lightning stroke. The Red One's rashness would have been his bane if the old man had not sprung upon the deck and caught Alrek's elbow.

"Do you remember that you are playing?" he growled.

If he needed an answer he had it in the savage force with which the boy tore himself free, and the fierceness with which he whirled, before the meaning of the words came home to him so that he lowered his point.

"You guess well," he muttered. "I had altogether forgotten." Half angrily he turned back to the Greenlander. "Why, in the Fiend's name, did you not remind me?"

Though much blood from his scratches was on the Red One's body and little was in his cheeks, he still tried to swagger. "I am no coward," he proclaimed. But on the last word his voice broke so hysterically that Grimkel thought it the part of kindness to interfere, and did so, his kindness masking as usual under gruff severity.

"You are a fool, which is worse," the old man snapped, pushing him roughly down the steps, while with his head he motioned those below to disperse. "Go put on sense with your clothes. Get dressed, all of you. If you do not do as I tell you, you will feel it." When he had shaken his fist at them once or twice and finally seen himself obeyed, he turned back where Alrek stood drying his weapon on a cloak he had thrown around him. "You! Listen! I have a warning I want to speak to you."

"You would do better to warn the Red-Head against stirring me up again," the young Viking returned, still half angrily; but the One-Eyed heard him as a rock hears a wave-splash.

"Before now, I have reminded you that your father was an outlaw—"

"That you have!" Alrek assented. "Six times have I heard the tale since I touched Greenland, though I lived eight years in the camps without hearing it once! In Norway, men remember only that my father was the bravest of the earl's Vikings."

"In Iceland, they remember that before he became a Viking he was an outlaw," the old man went on imperturbably, "and so like your father are you in looks that every eye is watching to find his unruliness in you. Now what I would tell you is that if you do not bridle this Viking fierceness, you will ruin yourself with Karlsefne."

The boy uttered a sudden short laugh. "Is it possible that I could get less honour with him?" he jeered; and polished awhile in tight-lipped silence. At last he straightened to meet the other's gaze and his eyes showed fire, while his voice was deep with resentment. "I am

Karlsefne's brother's son, but I get less praise from him than his thralls. He notices his dogs more often than he notices me. It is difficult to know what he expects of me. I believe that he hated my father."

Grimkel rubbed his bristly chin upon his palm. "It cannot be said that Karlsefne has a fondness for outlaws. So great is his love for the law that he was called 'the Lawman' before ever the chiefs who came with him on this expedition chose him to be over-chief in Vinland. Yet neither can it be said that he hated his brother. While they were young their love was great toward each other; and when Ingolf, your father, broke the Iceland law, Karlsefne gave half his property to pay the fine. And when Ingolf died, Karlsefne brought you into his following—"

"Where he shows every day that he holds me in dishonour for being his brother's son," Alrek finished.

The old man spat over the gunwale with explosive impatience. "Simpleton! He holds you neither in honour nor dishonour—yet. He but waits to see which you will earn."

Slowly, understanding dawned in the boy's face; turning away he stood kicking at a pile of walrus-hide thongs coiled on the deck before him.

Grimkel concluded his plea earnestly; "You cannot say that this is unfair. It lies with you to take whichever you want. For my part, I believe that you will do him credit in every respect. It is because I believe this, and because I loved your father in the days when he was your height and I taught him spear-throwing, that I speak."

After a while, Alrek said gravely, "I take it as very friendly of you."

He said nothing further, finishing his rubbing in silence and in silence descending the steps, but his advice-giver needed no more than one eye to see that at last he understood the difficulties of his position.

Chapter 2

In Which the Boys of the "Wind-Raven" Consider the Chances of Finding a Skraelling

Meanwhile, something was happening aft. Over his horn the helmsman discovered that a thin place in the fog vail was wearing into a hole, through which could be seen a low coast ending far ahead in a cloud-like hill.

"The Cape of the Crosses!" he broke the news, and the word was caught and tossed along like a ball.

"The Cape of the Crosses! The last point we must touch at!" the men cheered as they hurried to get up sail and put about for the opening door.

And the twenty lads, busy settling beltfuls of knives over tunics of deerskin, plunged into such eager anticipation of the joys of the landing that it was no time at all before they were scuffling with the Red One, whose smarting wounds made him particularly perverse. By the time Alrek had got into his tunic and buckled on the beautiful weapon that gave him his nickname of "the Sword-Bearer," he was obliged to weather a storm of nutshells in order to join the group. It took all the persuasion of the stout comely fellow called Erlend the Amiable to bring them back to peaceful discussion.

"We were talking of going ashore tomorrow and considering about whether there is any good chance that Skraellings may be there now," he explained, when he could make himself heard.

The subject attracted Alrek. Strolling over to the Amiable One's bench, he stretched himself upon it and made his head comfortable on Erlend's gay blue cloak. "Now it had fallen out of my mind," he mused, "that it was here that the inhabitants killed Thorwald Ericsson, when he went up on land and found three boats with three men hiding under each—"

"What is your tongue wagging about?" Ketil the Glib interrupted. "It was not those men that killed him; he killed all of them but one, who escaped in a boat. It was the host which that one brought back that shot arrows into him until—" He was interrupted in his turn by a piece of sailcloth which the red-haired boy threw over his head.

"Gabbler! He knew that story before you had chipped the shell," the Red One snubbed him. "Go on, Alrek, and say whether you think it is to be expected that we will see any."

The Sword-Bearer shrugged his shoulders. "You should have the best judgment about that, Brand Erlingsson, for you were visiting your brother Rolf at Brattahlid when Thorwald's men brought back the tidings of his death. You know whether or not it is their belief that Skraelings live on the Cape."

The Red One—who, it appeared, answered also to the name of Brand Erlingsson—replied earnestly. He said that Thorwald's men did not believe that the creatures lived there, but that they inhabited the mainland and only visited the Cape for clams or something; that the Cape was no more than a thin land-neck, that ended in a kind of cross-bar composed of a beach connecting two hills; and that it could not possibly have anything of interest on it; whereas, if they could go on to Keel Cape—

But there the shell shower recommenced, amid a protesting chorus; "Do not let him get started—" "End his noise!" "He is always sputtering!" And Strong Domar extinguished the last sputter by a wild whoop as he tossed up his cap in celebration.

"However it stands, our chance for catching some there on a visit is as good as Thorwald's! Luck be with us!" he shouted. Whereupon he tossed up his neighbour's cap—being much given to good-natured jests of the fists—and the jubilee would have been general if it had not suddenly been discovered that Alrek was slowly shaking his head on its blue pillow.

"Why not?" they paused to demand.

When he had taken his full time about chewing and swallowing a mouthful of nuts, he told them; "Because we lack Thorwald's energy at the helm. He went ashore so soon after he cast anchor that the men on the Cape did not have time to get away. We shall remain quiet a whole night after we come to anchor. If it should happen that any Skraellings are there, they would have plenty of light to see us by, and the whole night to escape in. Little danger is there that the Weathercock will break the Lawman's order to keep peace with the inhabitants; but if Karlsefne is to be any better off about news of them, he will find it needful to put a shrewder man at the steering oar."

The celebration died in midair; no more chance was there of denying the argument than of remedying the fact. What comfort they could get out of blaming the helmsman, they took; then returned one by one to a gloomy munching of nuts from the store under the benches. In the lull, Brand of Greenland found opportunity to vent the rest of his dissatisfaction.

"Neither will any good come to us out of these trips, while the Weathercock steers!" he burst out, shaking the hair from his bright impatient eyes. "These five months, we have gone ashore only when there was no chance for adventure to result from it; and so have I tired of this trough that I could gnaw the edge of it as a horse gnaws his stall! Sooner than I shall make another voyage under his leadership, I will paddle back to Greenland in a skin-boat!"

The fact that they all agreed with him did not prevent them from jeering through their mouthfuls. Even his loyal younger brother, Olaf the Fair, showed a merry face under his yellow curls.

"You speak too small words! Say that you would build a dragon-ship and have sole power over it," he mocked,—then scrambled discreetly out of reach as Brand turned on him.

"Well—I *could!*" the Red One defied the universe. "King Half owned a ship and headed a band when he was no more than twelve winters old—"

Jeers cut him short. "King Half! He will liken himself to Olaf Tryggvasson next!" "You great donkey, you!" "No—calf, with the milk of his kinsman's dairy-farm still in him!" cried the unoccupied mouths, while the full ones grinned broadly.

Only Alrek, smiling up at the sky, said whimsically; "Give me leave to travel with you when it is built, Champion. I should like to be on a ship that would come and go according to my will. For one thing, I should like to go ashore tonight to see Thorwald Ericsson's grave. The Huntsman told me once, when I laughed at his magic, that if ever I stood beside a grave in the noon of night I should know what fear was. It has long been in my mind to prove him a liar, but no other grave than Thorwald's is in the new land. If we were on your ship now—"

"What is to be said against swimming?" inquired Gard the Ugly, from the bench where he sat weaving fish-nets,—for it was a trace of the thrall blood which was in him, that, although he was free, his great hands were always busy with some service.

"Hallad, Biorn's foster-son, used that expedient once,—and it can not be said that he is of a bold disposition even if he did go with the Huntsman this summer. I am willing to try it. We can slip overboard shortly after it becomes dark, and spend the time before midnight in ranging over the beach,—I would give a ring to get the knots out of my legs! Will you do it?" Pulling himself up lazily, Alrek sat a while gazing ahead where a second hazy mass, seemingly as far away as the horizon itself, was rapidly pushing out from behind the Cape.

"Why not?" he responded at last. "Only, the swimming part is not to my mind; I find that deerskin dries on me less easily than on deer. Because of what has been told of the shallowness of the harbour, it is unlikely that we shall anchor very near to land; so it is my advice that we take the small boat. We can lower it with little trouble, if there is no moon, while the men are aft drinking their ale."

He rose as he spoke, and Gard leaped up also and clapped him on the back in token that it was a bargain; at which the scoffers quieted into a semblance of interest, and Erlend regarded him with amusement.

"Suppose it does not happen that you get a chance to tell the Huntsman of your experience?" he suggested. "I think it altogether unlikely that he will return from his trip to the south country. Will the entertainment be worth the exertion?"

Alrek gave him a poke between his well-padded ribs. "A man must risk something if he wishes to avoid getting fat," he answered. Whereat the Amiable One came in for his share of gibing; and during it, Gard put his arm through the Sword-Bearer's and drew him forward to look at the land.

The land was worth looking at, certainly, as it revealed itself bit by bit through the mellow haze of the sunset. Skimming toward it in the path of a breeze, it was not long before the sickle-curve of a harbour had drawn out from behind the Cape. Then the inner of the Cape hills looked out from its hiding place beyond the seaward knoll. Next, a streak of white beach unfolded itself between them. Finally the whole began to take on colour, gray giving way to grayish green and brown and red, while the cold gleam along the water's edge warmed into faint yellow.

So it lay motionless and soundless in the waning light, the sun fading from it in a drowsy smile, as the helmsman ordered the sail to be lowered and the anchor to be heaved overboard, and the little ship settled into her berth with a groan of satisfaction.

Chapter 3

Relating How One was Found on the Cape of the Crosses

A means to while away a long evening,—that was how the pair looked upon the trip as they rowed away from the ship's stem while the crew chatted over their ale horns in the torchlight of the stem. Dreamily enjoying the boat's motion and the rhythm of their oars, they swung through the dusk in contented silence; and only once did their thoughts reach the point of speech.

"He is knowing in all kinds of weird matters, your countryman the Huntsman," Alrek said, reminiscently. "Do you remember the time that he was lost in the unsettled places south of here, and, after looking for him far and wide, we found him lying flat upon a rock, mumbling at the sky? He said he was making *stanzas* to Thor, and that it was an answer when a whale came ashore the next day—"

"If that is the cheer which Thor has to offer, may I never eat at his house!" Gard grunted. "So starved was I that I ate a piece the size of my heady and—excepting the time of my first storm at sea—it has never happened to me before to be so sick! If Thor gives the Huntsman no better help where he is now, it is likely to go hard with him. It is said that the south country is more full of Skraellings than a goat of fleas. He was a headstrong fool to go there with no more than three men and one small boat."

Alrek lifted his shoulders indifferently. "If he never comes back, the sea will be no Salter for my tears," he answered; and relapsed into silence which was not broken until their nearness to land obliged him to ask a question about the steering.

If there was a moon, it had stayed sulking somewhere behind something, leaving the world in a dusk which was equally far from light and from darkness. Through the gloom they had been able to steal off with the boat in chuckling security; now its glimmer was still sufficient to guide them to a landing-place upon the pebble-strewn sand, which ran like a shelf around the base of the seaward hill. Beaching their boat they clambered up the slope, tripping more than once over the fist-big stones which studded it, before they entered breathless and laughing into the grove that crowned the crest.

"Who cares about seeing, so long as he can feel earth under him!" Gard cried. And all at once he had dropped upon the leaf-covered ground and was rolling over and over like a horse just freed from a tight girth, while Alrek stretched his cramped muscles in a somersault.

Something in the fragrance of the damp leaf-mould seemed to intoxicate them. Presently, both were whirling on their hands; and from that they went to jumping, and from jumping to wrestling. The shadows had grown a finger's length before they sank down to get their breath.

As the grove was nowhere very thick and the sea gale had winnowed the leaves, they had not looked about them long before they made out the objects which gave the Cape its name,—the two rude crosses of dead bleached wood rising in the centre of an open space by the sea. Around it, fanlike pine-boughs swayed heavily, and that was all there was of motion; and the only sound that broke its stillness was the splash of waves on the sand below. Between the Crosses, a low mound rounded black against the gray water. Their hearts gave a little throb as they distinguished it—Thorwald's grave! Amid a chattering throng out in the sunlight, those words had not conveyed much; but here— here they took on meaning. Rising silently, the lads groped their way between the pines until they stood beside it.

Into Gard's voice there came a note of awe. "Thorwald said this cape looked to be a fine place to live in; I wonder how he likes it to be dead here? Strangely still must it seem to him after the battle-din of his life! And strange feelings must have been in his men's minds when they sailed away and left him here, the only white man on this side of the ocean."

"He must have found it lonesome to lie here by himself for four winters," Alrek said very gently. "Surely, if he hears our voices, his heart must welcome the sound. I tell you, Gard, I think I should not be sorry if we found him sitting on his grave when we came back at midnight. If we should tell him that we are his comrades' sons and relate to him all the news, it may well be that he—"

Gard's hand fell on his arm. "Hush!" he entreated. "I do not care what anyone says on shipboard, but here—! Suppose he should be listening and take you at your word! Brand says that sooner than go into a witch's den as Leif's Englishman did, he would allow his arm to be hewn off,—and a witch's temper is more to be depended upon than the temper of a dead man. I am not eager to grasp his bony hand, if you are. Let us go down to the beach—But first, I want to find that knife I dropped. Will you feel around that bush-clump where I came down at the last leap, while I look over the slope where I stumbled?"

"Certainly," Alrek consented; and picked his way over the uneven ground to the spot where a clump of sumacs fringed the edge of the hill-crown as it sloped down to the beach. Just before he stooped to feel for the knife, however, he paused to look around.

Seaward, on his left, shone the far-away torches of the ship, a streak of brightness on the gray. Below him stretched the beach, its farther end lost in the looming shadow of a tree-crowned hill—he blinked and leaned forward and blinked again. Out of that shadow, a light had seemed to open on him like an eye! It did not come from the ship; he glanced over his shoulder to reassure himself. It came from the hill across the beach, a dim unwinking eye which up to this time some obstacle had hidden.

For an instant he thought of ghost-fires, and cold trickled down his spine; then came a recollection that smote every nerve like a cry,— the Skraellings! Some had been trapped and had not yet escaped, and it was going to fall to him to get sight of them! To succeed where all the rest had failed! To be the one to give Karlsefne the information he wanted! What wonder that all recollection of the knife—even of Gard—was wiped off his brain like breath-mist off a shield; that he was obliged to press his nails deep into his flesh to get a grip on his excitement!

"I shall wreck the chance if I go about it hotly," he admonished himself. "It was Karlsefne's strong command that we do nothing to offend them. I must steer it so that I see them without their seeing me,—and it is unadvisable to be too slow in acting, either, or they will have made their escape!" He put his body in motion even while his mind was debating, but it did not render him less cautious. He did not let a finger of him stray beyond the shadow of the pines, nor did he venture upon the beach until he saw his way clear before him.

The only objects that offered shelter were the low hummocks, crested with tufts of wiry grass, that stretched in a broken chain between the heights. From link to link of this he crawled, unobtrusive as a serpent; and when the links were wanting and gaps of glimmering sand lay before him, he ran crouching with the light swiftness of a fox, holding his breath in expectation of arrows hissing about his ears. None came, however, and at last the shadow of the second knoll and its spreading tree-crown fell over him like a canopy. There he paused to listen.

Once, an owl wailed tremulously from a distant tree; and once, it seemed to him that he heard brush crackle as under a stealthy tread; then all was silence and the swish of breaking waves. Laying hold of a gnarled root that reached down like a writhen arm, he drew himself noiselessly up the slope. Where it flattened to the crest, a clump of sassafras shoots made a fragrant screen. When he had listened and found the quiet still unbroken, he ventured to peer between the sprouts.

So long did he remain there without moving that the insects he had startled began walking over him in restored confidence. The little nook was empty. Except the patch of embers and a litter of clam shells, there was no sign to prove that living things had ever been there. As a final test, he hung his helmet upon his sword and showed it cautiously above the bushes, and the decoy drew no arrows from the thicket beyond the fire; the spot appeared to be genuinely deserted.

It is not too much to say that his disappointment brought him near to tears. "They must have run away as soon as darkness fell," he muttered. And pushing into the open, he sent the shells flying before a savage kick. "What Troll's luck!"

As the words left his lips, the flying shells uncovered a peculiar bowl-shaped basket woven of reeds. He stooped to it curiously; then, even as his fingers closed on the rim, he took another step forward, staring at the bushes that hedged the further side of the open space.

"It appears that someone has plunged through here in a hurry," he told himself. "The branches are bent as if—Odin!"

There was no need of finishing his thought. His eyes had the answer before them, a shaggy figure crouching among the bushes, so motionless that it might have passed for one of them. An instant he also stood motionless, staring back at the eyes that he could feel without seeing; then Viking training flashed two thoughts to his brain,— that the creature was aiming at him from the darkness, and that he must lose no time in advancing. Clutching his sword-hilt, he sprang forward.

After that there was no chance for reflection. For a second the blade stuck; and in the delay a copper-coloured arm shot out and fastened on his wrist, while the other copper-coloured arm brandished a stone hatchet over his head. With his left hand he caught that arm and held it off; and they swayed, panting, in the firelight that gave him his first glimpse of the foe all sailors yarned about,—the bristling black hair and wide-rimmed beast-bright eyes, and the skin of unearthly hue showing under the animal hides of the covering. Under the copper-coloured skin, the muscles were like copper wire. Strong as he was, Alrek could not twist aside that wrist above his head.

He gave up trying, presently, and limited his efforts to freeing his sword-arm. Putting all his force into the wrench, he succeeded at last in loosing it and shooting forth his weapon—and that was all that he had to do! At the bare sight of it, darting glittering from its sheath like lightning from a cloud, the Skraelling uttered a yell of terror, dropped the hatchet from his hand and his hands from their hold, and flung himself backward into the darkness. There was a crackling of brush, the spat of bare feet upon sand, and then—silence.

Gradually the Sword-Bearer's amazement gave way to amusement. "He thought it was magic,—here is a joke of the Fates!" he breathed. "If Thorwald had but shown them steel, it is likely that he could have put the whole host to flight! Never could I have wrested the hatchet from him. Now it is likely that my kinswoman Gudrid will open her eyes when I show her this!" Bending over the embers, he examined the weapon with deep interest; the edge was knife-sharp. "It would have cleft me as if it cut cheese!" he muttered; and was laughing in somewhat unsteady congratulation when the sound of feet scrambling up the slope straightened him to greet Gard.

For a space the Ugly One stared about him, blinking in the firelight; then the eagerness of his swarthy face gave way to bitterest reproach.

"You scared them away before I had a chance to see them? "he cried. "Slipped away, because my back was turned, and got all the sport for yourself? Never would I have believed it of you! Never—"

Alrek threw up his hands in honest compunction. "Gard, I beg of you to forgive me! It is the truth that when I saw the light, I forgot that you were alive. And I feared the Skraellings would get away before I could see them. I intended only to creep up and look, without—" He broke off and stood with his mouth open, staring at the other.

Involuntarily, Gard whirled to dart a glance over his shoulder; and finding nothing, cried out, sharply; "What ails you? Have you got out of your wits?"

Alrek regained his self-control with a short laugh. "I think I have," he answered. "Do you know another thing besides yourself that I forgot? I forgot Karlsefne's command to keep the peace."

Chapter 4

Wherein the Sword-Bearer is Further Reminded that He Has Broken the Law

The return to the Wind-Raven was even fuller of thought than the departure from it had been; though once Gard broke out in lamentation:

"If you had only allowed me to have part in the fun, *I* should have remembered."

Although his shoulders remained square-set against the gray of the night, Alrek's silence was so full of scepticism that the other blushed and hastened to speak of something else:

"Why are you so bold as to tell of this? It seems to me sufficient to say only that you found the hatchet on the ground."

"The Weathercock must be warned," Alrek said briefly. "Do you not see that this Skraelling may bring back a host, as happened to Thorwald?"

Apparently Gard saw, for he did not speak again. The silence lasted unbroken until they glided under the ship's prow, and a chorus of suppressed greetings came down to them.

"Hail, explorers! What luck?" "It seems that your stay was short—" "Was Thorwald lacking in hospitality?" the voices laughed, while the hands reached down to pull them aboard and assist in raising the boat.

When at last the pair stood on deck, however, the tune changed. "Now there are tidings in their faces!" cried the boy who, from the quality of his temper, was known as the Bull. "News! Let us have it out of them!" Whereupon the group made a fence across the way, every picket in it crying, "Give up your news!"

Gard waved them off crossly. "I have none," he growled.

Alrek gazed back at them as though they really were boards in a fence. "Where is the Weathercock?" he inquired of the Amiable One. "Has he drunk the wits out of him yet?"

"Such as they are, I think he has them still about him," Erlend answered. "But will you not tell us—"

The Sword-Bearer shook his head as he pulled away from the other's ringed hand. "The jest is not good enough to bear two tellings. Come after me if you want to hear it." Whereupon the line instantly became a column, marching at his heels as he walked aft.

On the after-deck, the helmsman who was known among his followers as the Weathercock, was droning a song over his ale horn. He was a fat bald-headed man with a heavy doughlike face and a grizzled beard that bristled like wiry beach-grass from his plucking at it while he sang. His listeners greeted the appearance of the lads with much cordiality; but he took the interruption very ungraciously indeed.

"It may well be that the reason boys always come at the wrong time is because there is no right time for such hindrances," he snapped. "Which of you wants what of me?"

The oncoming wave fell back a little, leaving the Sword-Bearer stranded before the helmsman. He said, saluting, "I want to tell you that when you go upon the Cape tomorrow you must go in war clothes. I have been ashore and seen a Skraelling; and I think he has gone to call his people to arms."

"What!" cried all the men in chorus; and those on the outer edge leaned forward, palms curved around their ears. Only the Weathercock sat squinting in a dull man's attempt at sharpness.

"What kind of jest is this?" he sneered at last.

Alrek drew the stone hatchet from his belt. "One of the proofs that it is not a jest is this."

There were more exclamations, while a dozen hands snatched at it; but old Grimkel bent forward and pinned his eye upon the Sword-Bearer.

"How did you get it?" he demanded. "You did not fail to remember—"

The boy's lips curved into a rueful smile as he met the look. "I remember now," he said slowly, "and I remembered up to the time I saw the Skraelling. But when I came upon him suddenly—"

"You attacked him?" It was the helmsman who screamed that, his doughlike face reddening to the very nose-end.

Alrek regarded him with critical brown eyes. "You prove a good guesser," he said politely.

From all sides went up exclamations of dismay; while from the Weathercock went up smoke and flames as though Hekla itself had broken loose.

"You—you—you-good-for-nothing-wolf's-whelp-gone-mad!" he sputtered. "What do you mean by standing there so quietly when your mad-dog temper has brought discredit upon my leadership which would otherwise have got me great fame with the Lawman? One thing after another, worse and worse, will be caused by this! The Skraellings may be surrounding us even as we speak; and we shall be forced to share your disobedience or else get. killed—or, it may be, both fight and get killed, since when Karlsefne finds how his orders have been regarded—But the first result of this will be that we will not go ashore tomorrow nor any other time—Ale! Faste! Hjalmar! Up with the anchor and out with the sail—"

As cries of protest arose, he beat them down with his short fat arms. "You shall not set foot upon land, you pack of ravening curs! Not until you get to camp,—and then I hope you will have reason to wish—Ah, to think that when we get to camp I must tell this instead of the report I had expected to give!" He struck his fists together until it seemed as if he might forget the Sword-Bearer's free birth and lay them on him in blows. "Why did I not remember that you had outlaw blood under your fair speaking, and keep you under my heel! But you shall pay for your liberty now. You shall be tied with walrus thongs and thrown into the foreroom, and kept there without food or drink until we reach Vinland! Take him hence,—do you hear my words? Lodin! Grimkel!"

He broke off to tug at his belt, which unwonted exertion was rendering distressfully snug; and in the interval the protests of the young Greenlanders burst forth anew, expressing unreservedly what they thought of him for taking away their chance of going ashore. When he turned on them, his thick neck rumbling volcano-like, they even gave back curse for curse; until—what with their racket and his bawling and the running to and fro of the sailors—the after-deck of the *Wind-Raven* presented a lively appearance.

The only quiet person on it was the culprit. Saluting with ironical ceremony, he yielded to the touch of Grimkel's hand upon his shoulder; and they proceeded to the little room under the foredeck, which served on extraordinary occasions for a dungeon and on ordinary ones as a storeroom for bales of fur and ale-casks and kegs of salted fish.

"If I could learn to feed my stomach through my nose, I should not starve however long I stayed here," Alrek observed with an expressive grimace as they entered.

The hand on his shoulder shook him roughly. "You deserve to starve," the old man snapped. "I have the heart to pound you! After I had warned you how the Lawman is holding you in the balance!" He jammed into its bracket the torch he carried, and sent a barrel out of his way with a thundering kick.

Somehow, the heat of his elder's concern moved the boy to an affectation of unconcern. Holding out his wrists for the rope, he replied that if Karlsefne had been watching him for two years, it was time he found out something.

Grimkel jerked at the thongs with a growl for every knot. "You will find out something when you come before him! Have you got it into your mind that you have prevented him from fulfilling what lies nearest his heart? Since the time when he was making ready for his journey at Leif Ericsson's house in Greenland, he has counted on strengthening the settlement by making friends of the Skraellings; and planned to get knowledge from their experience of the country, and riches by trading with them. And he has condemned Thorwald's shortsightedness in attacking them, and commanded how they should be received with gifts and fair words—Oh, it is impossible that the Fates will allow a wise man to be balked by a boy's folly!"

"If it is impossible why do you trouble yourself over it?" Alrek suggested; then went on to request that the hatchet be carefully preserved for him.

Grimkel, bending over to fasten the ankle-bonds, straightened stiffly in awful silence. But before his exasperation could escape through his lips, a waking thrill ran along the *Wind-Raven's* spine; a voice called him to lend a hand with the sail, and he was obliged to wheel and stamp away.

With him went the torch; so that the darkness of the foreroom became a black wall, upon which a gray square like a patch showed where the low doorway opened into the night. Gradually, the outside hubbub died away until the only sound that came in was the creaking of ropes and the sail's dull boom.

Left to himself, the boy left off feigning; and turned and grappled with his trouble. Breast to breast they struggled, while the gray square melted shade by shade into cold light; and when the square was gilded by the morning sun, they were struggling still.

Trying to shake off his thoughts, the Sword-Bearer flung his fettered body about in a kind of frenzy. "If I stay three days like this, I shall go out of my wits!" he cried to himself. "To lose all my chance with him is bad enough, but to sit here and think about it—! I shall become mad if I cannot move about and forget it for a while!"

Chapter 5
Through Which the Storm Giant Blusters

A stooping black shape against the sunshine, Hjahnar Thick-Skull came through the doorway and began to paw over bales and boxes in search of extra oars.

"Your luck is great, young one," he remarked. "You would not be sitting quiet if you were outside. Perhaps you think, because you see sun through the door, that the whole sky is like that; but you should see the clouds ahead of us! The only thing equally black is the Weathercock's face since he finds that he must put into the Keel harbour after all. And on top of it the wind has failed, and he has commanded all hands to the oars—"

Rising to his fettered feet, Alrek held out his bound hands. "Here are mine! Take your knife to the knots."

The Thick-Skulled gaped over his shoulder. "Why—why—he did not mean you."

"Have I not hands?" the Sword-Bearer demanded. "With a troll's strength in them this morning! Certainly he meant me."

He strove to speak carelessly while his fingers were twitching, but some breathlessness must have betrayed him. Scratching his tow mane and staring as he scratched, Hjalmar began slowly to grin. After a little, Alrek laughed also and spoke in frank appeal:

"Do me this good turn, shipmate, that I may stretch myself some while. If he did not mean me, yet might you easily have mistaken him. You can tell him so when he makes a fuss,—it is not likely that he will notice me until the storm is over. You know it is a saying that '*the wolf allays the strife of the swine.*'"

After a while, the Thick-Skulled stooped, grinning, and laid his knife against the thongs. "Behold what a good thing it is to have a reputation for dullness!" he said. "But see to it that you bear me out by giving good service at the oar."

The Sword-Bearer stretched his arms with a sigh of relief. "Only let me get at it!" he breathed, and plunged into the air like a fish into the water.

True enough! Though sunshine lay bright on the *Wind-Raven's* decks and blue sky was above her, before her—like the entrance to another world—sagged a canopy of slate-coloured clouds. Swollen with rain, they hung low over the shore-line of forest and dune and darkened all the distant water save where, here and there, streaks of white gleamed like monsters' bared teeth. Full of ominous warning was the calm that had fallen on land and sea, robbing the sail so that it hung like a live thing gasping for breath.

"If he did not put into the harbour he would be likely to share the fate of Thorwald Ericsson, and be cast ashore in the same place, and likewise with a broken keel," Alrek commented after a look at the sky; then laid hold of his oar and bent himself almost to the bottom of the boat in the relief of spending his energy.

Perhaps his appreciation of a small favour touched the Fates in their woman hearts, for presently they extended it. When the *Wind-Raven's* brood had brought her safely behind the wooded bar that lay across the harbour mouth like a screen in front of a door, the helmsman gave out word that since they were plainly storm-bound for the night, at least, they would not deny themselves the comfort of a camp on land, but would proceed immediately ashore. Ashore! the Sword-Bearer could scarcely believe his good fortune, until Brand dared to lean over and poke him in congratulation.

"I knew the Old One would take care not to have his fat jolted," he whispered; "and he can not leave you behind. Your luck will last until we come back again."

"Until we come back again!" Alrek repeated as though it were a toast, and threw himself resolutely into the work of the hour.

There was field for action. They had barely reached the shore and found refuge in a hollow below a wooded knoll when the tempest burst upon them, rushing through the forest with a swelling roar that rose above the thunder of the breakers. After that every minute of the day was a battle—a fight over the tent canvas which the wind threatened to pick up and carry off like a kerchief with all of them hanging to it in a fringe; a skirmish for fuel through forests into which sand from the dunes beyond was rushing like yellow swarms with biting mouths; a contest over the fire, blown out or struck out with lances of glittering rain; a struggle to hear or be heard through the thundering downpour, to see the very food in their hands through the suddenly fallen darkness—a battle between giants and pygmies!

Exhausted yet exhilarated, as after a day at the sword-game, the band fell over from eating to sleeping. When the lightning tore apart the darkness and disclosed the deserted ship reeling in terror upon the twisting black water, they only laughed and burrowed deeper, falling asleep to the thunder of breakers booming along the shore as to a lullaby from a mother's lips.

The ocean was still booming when they awoke, late the next day, and the wind was still blustering in the tree tops. The leader, with his mind reaching out toward Vinland fires and Vinland fare, cursed peevishly; but the juniors of his following greeted the delay with open rejoicing.

"Here is our chance to see the land!" Brand cried, shaking out his ruddy locks like fiery banners. "Let us take it before anything gets it away from us. I will wager a ring that I will beat any one to the top of this steep!"

So promptly did they respond that although he won his wager, the next boy was only a step behind; and none of the twenty was more than a pace in the rear. Once on the crest, they streamed, whooping, into the grove of oak and pine and sassafras which they had seen from the water, lying along the bay shore like a ragged rich-hued mat.

Raggedness showed more plainly than richness, upon a nearer approach, though nothing could take away the beauty of colouring where pines spread their ever-living green over the windy crests and the oak trees on the slopes had turned yellow and russet and red without losing a leaf. But it was no such forest as Vinland boasted; compared with Vinland trees the growth was stunted and there was not enough underbrush to give it even the wildness of a thicket,— only tangles of rose briar and berry bramble where the ridges sank into hollows cupping reed-fringed ponds. Perhaps the best that could be said for it was that its endless undulations kept curiosity awake. Passing over them was like breasting billows; one gained a height only to behold another deep.

After a while, it stirred Alrek to restlessness. When it was suggested that they should stop at one of the ponds for a duck hunt, he objected.

"Who knows what the next ridge may be hiding?" he said obstinately. "Let us find out first what lies before us."

"What but the ocean?" Erlend asked in surprise. "That can not be far away now; the sand wastes between the trees are getting much wider."

But Alrek was already moving on, dealing blows of his hatchet at the trees on either side of him. "Do as you like," he answered over his shoulder. "I shall not stop until I come to the end."

Erlend sent him a glance of surprise; but the others had caught the fever of his mood so that they dashed after him in a cheering charge.

Their run did not keep up long, however, for the walking was momently becoming harder. In the next hollow the pond had been smothered beneath a sand blanket, and the bushes were strangling in sand. In the next there were no bushes at all, only mats and tufts of wiry grass. On the slopes the trees became fewer, the sand piled between them like drifted snow; in one place it had buried a clump so that only their tops showed, bush-like, above the creamy surface.

"There you can see what kind of place this would be to set up a landmark," Njal of Greenland observed, pointing at them. "In twenty years more it is likely the whole forest will be covered and the man who comes then will say that we lied because we told of trees being here. I doubt if we would be able to find much of the keel that Thorwald set up—"

"Then do not let us spend time looking for it," Alrek finished. And so completely had his mood taken possession of them, that they consented without argument; plodding on doggedly over the dunes that had become like yellow snow-banks, bare of a single tree, rounding in absolute baldness against the gray of the sky.

Gradually, feverish expectancy grew in them all. It was as though the vast shifting mass were a living monster, whose depredations they had seen, whose lair they were now approaching. They stopped in a hushed group when the last dune revealed the beach sweeping down to the water. The scarred and furrowed ocean was another monster, still growling and showing his tusks at the wind giant.

Northward, the ocean was all they saw. Westward, they saw it over a yellow waste as the dunes sloped down to the Cape point. Southward, lay the land over which they had come; beyond it, the bay in which their ship rode at anchor. Eastward, unbroken drifts, unspotted beach—their silence ended in a cry:

"Yonder! Yonder is something washed ashore!"

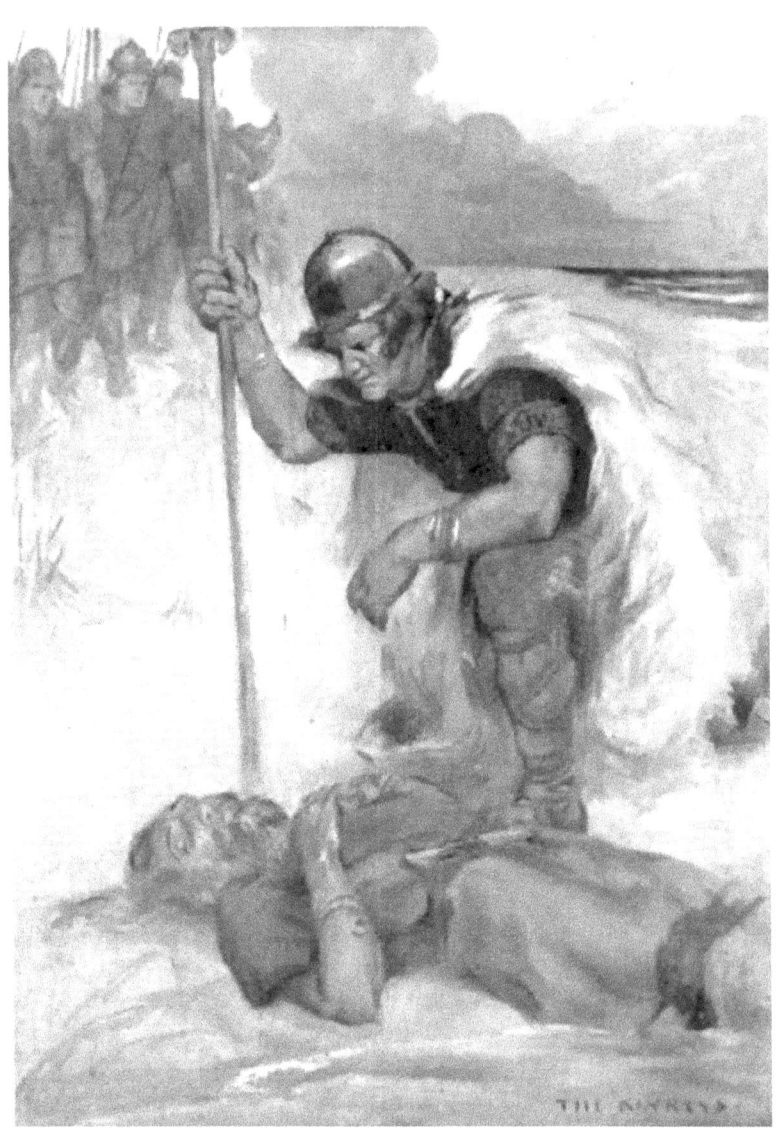

Neither sound nor motion was on his blue lips.

All saw it, so plainly did it show against the sand,—something dark and motionless which the waves had flung up there out of their way. So large did it loom in the strange light that, as they went plunging and floundering toward it, some declared it to be a whale; and others, an overturned boat.

But the light on the Wonderstrand is a wondrous light. When they had raced over some hundred yards of beach, the dark object—instead of growing larger—dwindled suddenly from whale size and boat size to the size of a human body. Involuntarily, they slackened their pace and a whisper went around: "It is one of the Skraellings, overtaken by the storm!"

Only Alrek shook his head and pressed forward. "That is no animal hide wrapping him," he said.

A dozen yards more brought him to the side of the stark form; he bent over it—and remained bent as though petrified with astonishment. When the others had reached him and looked, their voices went from them in a cry of amazement:

"The Huntsman!"

And the Huntsman's gigantic figure it was, sea-drenched and wave-battered, kelp snarled about his feet, starfish tangled in his hair. As he had lain upon the rock that winter day, so he lay here upon the sand,—flat on his back with his hands clasped over his breast; though now his eyes were closed, and neither sound nor motion was on his blue lips.

Doubting their senses, the explorers stared at him and then up and down the shore. Never was scene more yawningly empty; between the sweep of sand and the stretch of water he lay as though fallen from the sky.

Chapter 6

About the Strange Find on Keel Cape

"I would give much if he had not died until he had told us how he came hither," Gard remarked, presently.

"And what he was employing himself about in the north of Vinland when he set out to explore the country south of it!" Brand cried; while the Glib One added:

"Yes, and how it went with Hallad and the others he had with him!"

Then they became aware that Erlend's handsome brown face— three shades browner than his hair—was turned toward them in reproach. "It may be that Alrek will get the belief that a Greenlander's loyalty to his countrymen is somewhat shallow," he suggested.

In those days, disloyalty to a comrade was held a contemptible thing. Two of the three reddened; and Brand bent his tongue to apology.

"He knows that we care as much as any one. Eric of Brattahlid had the Huntsman for his steward, because they found pleasure in talking evil together about Christianity; but that was all the friend I ever heard of his having. It is understood that we will do him the favour to bury him, however."

Gard the Practical rubbed his ear. "That will not be easy unless we carry him far inland," he said. "If I am not much mistaken, this sand will move about like snow,—and I have heard that if dead men come uncovered and sleep cold, they are wont to get up and walk around to warm themselves."

A dozen of them crossed themselves involuntarily; and the Strong One squared his magnificent shoulders.

"Quickly will I proclaim my choice to carry him to the bay!"

"That would best be left unsaid until we see how heavy he is," Alrek advised. "Raise his other shoulder, Domar, and let us see how— One thing is that he is not yet stiff. Wait! What is this on his neck?" With his finger, he followed a cord running from the grizzled beard across the motionless breast to lose itself in the shelter of the rigidly clasped hands. "It is a deerskin bag."

"I know he did not have it on when he went south!" Harald Grettirsson cried, excitedly.

And a chorus added; "Here is something of importance!"—"Something of value!" "To think of it then—" "Yes, to grasp it when he was drowning!"

Sitting back on his heels, Alrek gazed down at the figure curiously. "He has grasped the bag too close to move, but it would be possible to pry a finger into the top and see what is inside,—if you would allow it? He is your countryman." He glanced inquiringly at them as they stooped around him, their hands grasping their knees.

The Greenlanders looked down at him; then around at one another; then Brand spoke under his breath; "If you dare—"

"Dare?" Alrek's mouth curved disdainfully. Picking out the cord-ends from between the chill palms, he undid the knot that fastened the mouth of the bag and inserted a thumb and forefinger. "A chain," he said as they closed upon something; then, as they began to draw it out, "What a chain!"

All echoed him: "*What* a chain!"

For it was of shining gold, set here and there with a rough-cut gem; while its girth was that of his largest finger, and it unfolded itself coil after coil to the length of his arm. What a keepsake to bring out of a waste peopled only by wild men! Devouring it with hungry eyes, they drew closer; and Rane Thin-Nose put out a hand to feel of it, at the same time sending an apologetic glance toward the rigid face.

As he did so, the drawn eyelids rose slowly and silently as curtains; and the Huntsman's small evil eyes looked back at him. Rane's hand was withdrawn as though it had encountered fire; and the circle fell back, screaming. Even the Sword-Bearer was startled enough to drop the chain, as the eyes rolled in his direction and remained turned on him in a baleful glare.

Through the blue lips came a voice, so faint that it seemed to be one of the smothered voices which cry through the roar of the surf; "You would rob me?"

At that the circle rallied indignantly, shouting, "We would *not!*" "It was our intention—" "You need not reproach us for—" "We thought—"

"Put it back."

Alrek hesitated, his face colouring with resentment. Then he asked himself of what use it was to argue with a piece of driftwood, and gave up justification with a shrug. While the rest spent their breath wrathfully, he complied in silence. When the last knot was tied—and not before—the eyes left him to roll around the circle.

"Swear—" the voice said faintly.

Before the glare they shrank in spite of themselves, fluttering like birds around a snake; until Erlend said, with quiet haughtiness:

"There is no need for us to swear that we will not rob you."

The voice was so faint that they barely made out the words; "Swear—to keep it secret. On the edge of your blades!"

"I suppose he has the right to ask it," Erlend gave judgment after a while. "It was his secret and we thrust ourselves in. It seems to me that it is his right?" He looked at the Sword-Bearer with questioning eyebrows.

No one ever disputed the decisions of the Amiable One in matters of honour. Alrek answered by unsheathing his sword, with another shrug of his shoulders.

Drawing each a knife from his belt, they grasped them by the blades so that the sharp edges cut red grooves in their bare palms. Holding the knives aloft thus, they spoke the oath together; the Huntsman's eyes telling them off, one by one. When he had come to the last— little Olaf the Fair twisting his face to keep back tears of pain—his eyes stopped and settled slowly into their unwinking stare; but that they were less dull than fisheyes, his stark figure would have differed little from the myriad fish bodies strewed upon the sand.

Though they rattled their weapons blusteringly in putting them up, a kind of panic chill crept over the band. The stare was so awful in its dumb evilness; and the scene was so weirdly desolate,—the stretch of bleak sky, the sweep of naked shore, and the breakers' unending boom out of which stifled voices seemed trying vainly to call. The lad who was called the Hare—alike for fleetness and for timidity—voiced the feeling in a quavering outburst:

"Let us leave him! I do not believe he is alive at all. I believe a troll hides in him and uses his mouth to speak with. I know evil will come of this. Let us leave him." He plucked nervously at Alrek's coat. "Come on!"

Alrek was strung high enough to be irritated by the clutch. "Keep off!" he ordered, jerking himself free. "It is no lie about you that you are cowardly, if you would desert a shipmate!" Then regaining possession of his cloak, he regained possession of his temper, and spoke quietly; "If we get some big branches and make a litter with our mantles, it will not be difficult to get him to the bay. It seemed to me that you were all eager in having him alive to tell you news?"

If it had not been for that hope, it is doubtful if the twenty would have toiled to bring such a burden over the sand-hills; and it is certain that the sailors had this end in view as they rubbed the Huntsman's limbs and poured ale down his throat. Had they been polishing a knife or oiling a lock, they could scarcely have been more business-like or less tender.

"As soon as he gets strength to talk he should be able to tell tidings worth hearing," they said to one another when at last they left him rolled in skins and went about their preparations for returning to the ship, a rift having come in the gray toward the west.

The main difference between their attitude and that of their juniors was that they felt merely dislike for the Huntsman, while for the one-and-twenty he had the fascination of fear. To them, his eyes were twin demons keeping guard from their cave doors over the treasure bag below. It is safe to say that they never lost him out of their minds through all the bustle of going on board and resettling themselves, as they awaited a surer sign of the Storm King's reformation.

With the sunset, the rift in the gray widened. Thrym, the giant who herds the clouds, drove the hulking masses northward, lagging from their own weight. In the clearing west, the sun dropped golden behind a jagged bar; and while the rosy glory of it was still in the southern sky, the moon looked out of the east. To a rousing cheer, the *Wind-Raven* shook out her storm-beaten plumage and skimmed away over the silvering waves. The change was so grateful that Alrek was able to shake off depression one time more; while the loungers on the benches were noisy with satisfaction.

"Never was there a better time to experience the Wonderstrands!" they jubilated afresh, as the curving stretch of shining dunes pushed itself into their vision.

Passing that curve was little less than an experience; for the bend of the shore made it ever appear as though a cape lay just ahead, yet the cape ever receded as they approached, a flying point that could never be caught.

"Certainly it makes the world seem a place of strange wonders!" Faste the Fat marvelled, when they had sat a long time watching it in silent fascination. "It makes one curious about everything. If the Huntsman would only speak now and tell us what he has seen, this would be a good time to amuse ourselves with a tale."

"How do you know that he has seen anything?" sneered a harsh voice—harsh for all its faintness—from the pile of skins upon the forecastle.

They wheeled so eagerly that the ship rocked under them. "Are you ready to tell the tidings you have seen?" "Will you tell us about—?" "Tell about the south country, Huntsman." "Did you see any Skraellings?" "No, tell us first how you came here—" "Yes, your adventure—" "Yes, yes!" "We beg of you—" "Go on! Go on!"

They were all speaking at once now, boys and men, and their greed proved their downfall. For, the clamour reaching the helmsman on the afterdeck, he descended with unusual agility and waddled toward them.

"If you are going to talk to anyone, you talk to me, your chief," he commanded; "and tell me what you have done with the boat and the men I lent you."

The Huntsman's manners gained little at sight of his superior. "I do not see that *I* have done anything with them," he answered sullenly, "because the boat went to pieces on a sand-bar and Rann drew Svipdag and Black Thord down to her. It is seen that I saved you the best man of the three."

"Four men were in the boat when you started out on that foolish trip," the helmsman caught him up. "Biorn's foster-son is worth speaking about; what have you done with him?"

The blood settled in the Huntsman's sunken cheeks as water in a hollow. "Is the boy of so much importance that I must carve his rune on a separate stick?" he snarled. "What else could he be than drowned? Is it likely that Valkyrias came down for him? I think you are a fool. If Freydis, Eric's daughter, had not married you for your wealth and sent you out here after more, you would never have had manhood to set foot on a ship. *You* my chief! You can think what you like; I will not answer you another word." He flung himself over on his face in one of the black sulks no man had ever yet sounded; his officer's threats might as well have been addressed to the mast.

At last the fat helmsman was forced to pause to take in breath, standing puffing and glaring and tugging at his belt. And it was this unpropitious moment which his roving eyes took to remind him of Alrek's existence. The Sword-Bearer felt the gaze when it fell, and shut one eye in an expressive wink at Brand; nor were his forebodings without foundation.

The helmsman let his recovered breath go from him in a snort. "You! What are you doing here? Did I not order that you should be shut up for the rest of the voyage?"

Alrek unclosed his eye to gaze out of the pair in respectful surprise. "I?" he inquired. "Was it not your intention to free me when you ordered all hands to the oars?"

Before the Weathercock found adequate words he had stamped three times in uncouth capers of rage; when he did find them, however, they came with such force that they burst the buckle off his belt.

"Go back!" he wound up in a bellow. "Go back, and do not dare come forth again until I haul you before Karlsefne. If I were your chief, I would hang you!"

For once, exasperation got the better of Alrek's soldier training. He looked the fat figure up and down as he arose. "You would not need to take the trouble," he retorted. "If you were my chief, I would hang myself."

He heard applauding laughter from his mates as he walked away, simultaneously with a roar from the helmsman, and after that a confusion of sounds; but his mind was too full of bitterness to leave any room for curiosity. It roused him with a start when the solitude in which Fat Faste was reinstalling him was disturbed by a second consignment of captives,—Brand with torn clothes and flashing eyes; at his heels, little Olaf striving to quench a bleeding nose as he panted with unquenched partisanship; back of him Gard the Ugly, made uglier by a swollen lip; and behind the three. Strong Domar, a purple lump on his forehead and breathless delight in his voice as he shouted the explanation over the others' heads:

"I knocked him down, Alrek, as sure as I stand here! He tried to cuff Brand for laughing at you, and I laid him flat before Lodin could lay hold of me,—and he will have to come before Karlsefne with a black eye! Think of it!"

Apparently Alrek did think of it, for he stared for the space of a minute before he spoke. "You struck your chief!" he repeated at last.

The Strong One chortled with relish. "*And* blacked his eye! It will be shut tight, I know it will,—and he thinks so much about making a fine appearance before the Lawman! And maybe his nose will swell also, and—" He broke off abruptly as the meaning of Alrek's expression came home to him; and his freckled face reddened. "Now I forgot that you are soldier-bred. I suppose that in the earl's camp they would not call it a jest to knock down a chief?"

The Sword-Bearer leaned back on his bale of fur with a long-drawn yawn. "They would not be likely to call it anything," he said drily, "for it could not happen there at all."

As he said nothing more in congratulation, it was rather a sulky group that the torches left to darkness when the last walrus-hide knot was tied.

Chapter 7

Concerning Thorfinn Karlsefne, the Lawman

And that night was as long as two nights; and the sunrise into which it melted lasted until noon; and the day which finally grew out of that sunrise had no end whatever! Apparently, the Weathercock had managed to tie walrus thongs around Time's ankles also.

Glimpses of banks, caught through the doorway, showed when they turned from the highroad of the ocean up the river-lane which led into the Vinland bay; but the banks kept on unravelling like witch's weaving that has no end. They had turned their attention from watching the landscape to robbing a fish keg, when the drone of voices on the deck above broke suddenly into shouts:

"A boat! Coming from behind that island!" "Who—" "— thralls, the two in white—" "But the man in blue?" "Karlsefne is wont to wear blue—" "By the Hammer, I believe it is the Lawman himself!"

If cheers rose from the forecastle, silence fell on the foreroom. Eager as they were to reach camp, to run upon this portion of it in midstream was little less than startling. The face of every Greenlander confirmed Domar's fervent gasp:

"Now I am thankful that Karlsefne is not my chief!"

Into Alrek's quiet came a kind of constraint. "Other men wear blue mantles," he suggested. "Hold your tongues and listen."

Crouching on rope-coils and piles of fur, they held their breath as well as their tongues while they tried to separate the tumult into meanings; the scuffle of feet on the deck above was like a blur over all other sounds. But finally the feet rushed down the steps; there was a lull in which could be heard the sound of oars backing water; then, through the quiet a new voice, deep and kindly:

"Greeting and welcome, friends! Tell me before anything else if you are all here, sound and whole?"

The prisoners' mouths shaped one word as they gazed Into one another's faces: "Karlsefne!"

How thinly and sputteringly the Weathercock's voice fell on their ears after that! "All here, Lawman! And all sound,—saving this eye of mine which has met with a mishap of which I will tell you later."

Very likely he rambled on with his wonted long windedness, but the five eavesdropping in the foreroom heard no more. The throng that had surged forward receded noisily; and through the rift the prisoners had a glimpse of the gunwale and a sinewy blue-clad form rising beside the fat helmsman like a tree beside a bush, a towering mightfull figure with a face of rugged beauty framed in locks of iron gray. Even after the rift had closed up again they crouched motionless, staring at the shifting backs and straining their ears for tones of that deep voice, until—jangling through it like clattering pottery—came the helmsman's lament:

"But ask not what success we have had Lawman, for I will tell you without delay that the plan you had most at heart has been marred past mending! By no fault of mine, but through the bloodthirstiness of your brother's son; who has not only thrown your commands aside, but has kindled outlawry in the heart of every boy on board, who would otherwise be obedient to my—"

Brand got on his bound feet—no one knows how—and on them got to the door.

"That is not true, though you or others say it!" he shouted; and when his leader stopped out of sheer amazement and everyone turned, gaping, he followed his voice through the door. "We endure him altogether against our will. To obey him is a disgrace to all with manhood in them. Domar made his eye black—"

"Yes, that is true," bellowed Domar. Followed by Gard and little Olaf, he in his turn worked his way to the door, where a sudden lurch of the ship caught them and rolled them in a struggling heap almost to Karlsefne's feet; when the crew began to laugh and the Weathercock began to accuse and the rebels began to deny.

Looking after them Alrek's lips curled in soldier scorn; that gave way to amusement when the clamour ended abruptly at a single word from the deep voice, and he had a glimpse of Brand's fiery locks drooping like captured flags. But after a moment, he turned and stretching his bound arms across a cask, hid his face upon them.

"Whatever they do, they can not serve him so badly as I have done. Certainly I can find no fault with his act if he hangs me up like a sheep-killing dog, for little better has my service been," he murmured; and lay there with his face hidden until the jar of Hjalmar's heavy foot brought him suddenly upright.

"Karlsefne sends for you," the Thick-Skulled announced in his wonted roar; then, coming close to cut the thongs, he spoke in hoarse whispers; "Hear great wonders! Your luck has not quite shown its heels, after all. It has happened that the Lawman also has seen the Skraellings! The day after you met the one on the Cape, a host of them appeared before the Vinland booths,—to see, it is likely, if the others had your mind toward them. But Karlsefne made so plain his good intentions that they went away after doing nothing worse than stare. And yesterday they came again, with bundles of fur which they traded with much friendliness. It is his belief that they also have young fireheads among them so that they understand how little value is to be put upon—"

Stretching out his freed arms, the Sword-Bearer gripped Hjalmar's hand to the point of crushing. "You make my heart merry in my breast!" he breathed.

"Yes, certainly; I am in high spirits also," Hjalmar assented, returning the pressure. "It is an exceedingly useful thing for you. But see to it that you bear yourself boldly as a hawk; and keep it all the time before his mind that no real harm has been done."

Alrek began suddenly to laugh. "It may be that I would better tell him that he owes me thanks for sending the Skraellings to him?"

"That might have no small power," the Thick-Skulled responded gravely; and Alrek laughed again, as he caught at the huge shoulder to steady himself in rising upon his stiff legs.

If the shoulder had been Grimkel's, the mouth belonging to it would have advised differently. During all the time that the helmsman was bewailing the evils to come out of such rashness, and Karlsefne was courteously explaining how luck had warded off such evils, the old seaman's weather eye had scanned the sky of his chief's face with deepening gravity. Now his speculations broke out into words.

"If the boy tries to make light of his disobedience because it ended luckily, the Lawman will spare him neither in words nor deeds," he muttered to himself; and the impulse came to him to try to push through the crowd pressing him mastward and impart this prognostication to the Sword-Bearer. But even as he moved to carry out his kindly intention, the boy's erect red-cloaked figure appeared in the doorway of the foreroom and it was too late to do anything.

Though his dress of blue was merchant garb and the staff in his hand was a farmer's symbol, the face of Karlsefne was the face of a law-giver. Above the beard of iron gray his mouth showed firm-lipped as a mouth of stone, and the gaze of the steel-bright eyes under the bushy brows was such as none with guilt in their hearts might sustain. Meeting it, the Sword-Bearer's eyes fell and the blood was drawn to his cheeks, and he came forward and bent his knee before the Lawman.

Hard as measured steel were Karlsefne's measured words: "For a long time I have been watching to know whether you deserved favour or starkness, and held my hand from you lest it deal unjustly. I thought, long ago, that I smelled hot blood which would one day break out and sweep away all bounds. Now that day has come, and the worst things I have thought of you are proved the true things."

As he bowed his head under the rebuke, Alrek's teeth cut a blood-line on his lip; but he attempted no defence. For the space of a second it seemed to Grimkel that the Lawman's face showed surprise.

Yet his voice was even sterner when he spoke again. "They are no less true things because good fortune has enabled me to ward off the damage which would otherwise have been caused by your deed. If you are at all versed in camp ways, you know that this happening does not make you any less liable to punishment."

Rising from his knee, the young Sword-Bearer faced him without fear. "My fate is for you to decide over, kinsman, according to your pleasure," he said with soldier submissiveness.

Then there was no question whatever about Karlsefne's surprise. After a moment's silence, he spoke slowly; "I think it best to hear first from your own mouth about this happening."

"I have no excuse why you should withhold your anger from me, yet I would not have you believe that I wished the thing to happen," Alrek answered. "When I set out for the light, my one thought was to get honour with you by finding out the news you wanted; and I think I should have remembered your order if the Skraelling had been where I first looked for him. But after I had given him up I saw him suddenly, hiding in the shadow; and something in me cried out that he was aiming and—and I have not been wont to jump backward when I saw a foe. Yet I ask you to believe that I wished least of anything to hinder your plans."

A while the steel-keen eyes probed him; but he did not flinch. "That is not in every respect as the helmsman relates the story," Karlsefne remarked at last.

"That is very likely," Alrek replied, "for the helmsman knows nothing whatever about the matter." Whereupon the helmsman let his stored-up breath go from him in a snort.

A dozen seamen endeavoured suddenly to hide laughter under fits of coughing; but the Lawman said gravely: "Nevertheless, I now see that there is truth in the other things he told me about your behaviour toward him;" then turned away and stood a long time pondering, his hands gripping his silver-shod staff, his half-closed eyes resting on the group of gaping boys. And gazing at them, he seemed to forget the Sword-Bearer in a new problem.

"Here are more rebels," he said to the helmsman, with a sweep of his staff. "Little order will there be in camp if they are turned loose on it in no better state of mind. How is it your intention to deal with them?"

The Weathercock shifted his weight peevishly; he was tired of standing; and his mind was upset within him; and he wanted besides to get back to his ale horn. "Since they are free-born, it seems that I can not even give them the flogging they deserve," he snapped, "but if they were thralls, I would drown them."

"It may be then that you would be willing that I should offer them to come under my rule? "Karlsefne suggested; and went on to say more in an undertone.

Astonishment opened the helmsman's eyes at first; then, slowly, he wrinkled into a fat smile. At last he reached out and grasped Karlsefne's hand.

"If you will rid me of the twenty plagues, who are turning me thin, I will feel as though you had given me twenty marks of gold," he declared. Whereupon the Lawman turned to the group of blank faces.

"Now this is my offer to you," he said, "that you part from the rest of the Greenlanders and form yourselves into a band and build your own booth and choose one of your own number to rule over you,"

The faces lighted in ecstasy,—then gloomed in unbelief. Brand spoke for all when he inquired timidly:

"Is this a *punishment?*"

"It is not a reward," Karlsefne answered; and for a moment his gaze sharpened so that the Red One winced under it. "If I did not believe that it is because you know no better that you act thus, there would be hard things in store for you. I take this way to show you why lawfulness is needful. Yet is there no trick to it; all I have promised shall be fulfilled,—and more. You shall have your own table if you can furnish it; your own boat if you can build it; in every way like men—"

They thought his pause the end, and burst into jubilant chorus; "It will not take us long to know what to answer to this!"

But he raised his hand for silence. "Answer nothing until you have heard the whole. If you form yourselves upon the manner of men, so must you also bear men's burdens. You must furnish your share of hunters and fishers and of workers in the fields; and you must do your share of guarding against outside foes or lawlessness within. Even as Thorvard, here, and Snorri and Biorn, answer to me for the behaviour of their following, so must your chief answer for you—"

"Yes! Yes! "they cried eagerly.

But he lifted his hand again; his measured tones became like tolling bells. "Think well! I speak not in jest. If you accept, I take you in grim earnest. You may not have men's liberty without men's care, and I shall hold you like men to your word though the matter cause death itself. Think well!"

They did pause; his manner was impressive enough to insure that. But in a moment. Brand flung back his red locks daringly.

"Much should we lack in manhood if we would refuse a fair offer! Take our word!"

Every one of the twenty echoed him wildly. "Take our word!"

"It is taken," Karlsefne said gravely; then bent his gaze on the Red One. "It appears likely that you will be the chosen head, since you seem always to speak for your comrades?"

Brand flushed with delight. But before he could answer, Domar spoke bluntly:

"I do not see in what Brand is above the rest of us Greenlanders. I raise my voice for Alrek Ingolfsson."

"Alrek Ingolfsson, by all means!" Erland seconded; and Brand joined him generously.

In another moment, all were shouting, "Alrek! Alrek!"

Plainly, this was something the Lawman had not expected. "Alrek?" he repeated in surprise. "Yet I do not know that it would not be a punishment to answer for such a band" Turning, he looked again where the Sword-Bearer stood with folded arms, awaiting his sentence.

Perhaps with mouth firm-set and troubled eyes he looked more than ever like his father. Old Grimkel's watchful gaze saw the Lawman's hardness break up like Greenland ice before a warm land wind. Taking a slow step forward, he laid his hands upon the square young shoulders and looked long into the brown young face.

"Since you left in the spring," he said, "a son was born to me, but I swear I do not love him more than I love you when that look is on you, bringing back my brother and my boyhood and the time before our ways parted." His voice softened to very grave gentleness. "Since you did not mean offense toward me, I will take none; and you shall accept this chief ship and use it to prove what nature is in you. All I have of love and honour lies ready for your gaining,—it will not gladden you more than me if you are strong enough to take them. Will you accept the test?"

He held out his hand, and the Sword-Bearer grasped it in both of his and looked him full in the face, his eyes in a golden glow. "I accept the test,—and I give you thanks for it from the bottom of my heart," he said.

Part Second: Alrek's Champions

Chapter 8

At the Hall of the Vinland Champions

"Whether you think so or not, I know that Gudrid would not keep milk in a fish-pail," the Bull's voice rose above the racket.

There was not a little racket to surmount, for it was rising time at the new band's new booth. In the high-seat that had been built for him midway the length of the hall, the red-cloaked chief occupied the interval before breakfast with rune-carving; but that was the only employment which was being carried on in silence. Whistling boys were lacing their high boots along the benches right and left of the high-seat; grumbling boys were just turning out of the bunks behind those benches; jeering boys were throwing bedclothes at the sluggards, and disputing boys were clattering bowls and trenchers on the tables which stood on either side the fire. One of these table-boys was the short and chesty Bull, sniffing hostilely at the milk he was pouring; and the head of the division was Brand, the long and loose-jointed.

Over a platter of cold venison, he frowned on his scullions. "Gudrid has nothing to do with this house," he snubbed the faultfinder; then, in peremptory aside, "Olaf, keep that door shut! Do you think it is warm outside?"

"Do you think that anyone who eats your cooking needs to be told that Gudrid did not do it?" retorted the Bull, refusing to be snubbed.

A sigh came out of Erlend's handsome mouth as he looked up from hunting a lost button among the pine branches of the floor. "Ah, Gudrid! After that last meal she invited me to take in their booth, eating here has been like living on seaweed!"

Brand's frown took on an edge of scorn. "Fussers! Go and live in Gudrid's house! It may be that she would allow you to crawl into the cradle with the baby. Yesterday the grumbling was because I put my head out of the door to look at a dog-fight and the bread got a little burned. If I were as womanish as the rest of you, I would braid my hair and put on skirts!"

Still bending over his rune-carving, the young chief spoke with a drawl: "Here is something worth a hearing! Is it in truth your opinion that there is the most manfulness in you? "

Surprise took the head-cook a little aback; then defiance took him a long way forward, flourishing his red mane. "Yes, I think so. You also found fault with the bread, for all your Viking training. I think I am the most hardy man here."

When Alrek's knife had cut another rune upon his stick, he straightened deliberately. "Yesterday," he explained, "Karlsefne gave the chiefs the advice to pick out each week five men who should have it for their sole service to keep the camp in fire-wood—"

A prolonged groan interrupted him; of all the burdens of housekeeping, fuel-getting weighed the most heavily.

"—and he bade me send the hardiest man in our booth. I intended Domar to go, but now I see that Brand Erlingsson is the man to do it."

"Hail to the chief!" yelled Strong Domar. And Brand's flame of defiance sank in ashes of sulkiness; and from the others came shouts of laughter.

"He will wish he was back at kitchen work!" "Tree-chopping is the least interesting—" "And the weather is such that wood lasts the shortest time—" "Still Karlsefne is lacking payment—" "Never will we get to cutting timber for the ship!"

The Hare made a pettish flourish with the knife he was using to trim away the rags from his garments. "Who wants to prepare for anything so far in the future? Why will you, Olaf, open that door? What I should be glad of is a chance to exercise myself for the spring games. Since we began this way of living, I have not had one race worth talking about."

"I should be thankful if we could get a chance to go north where the big game is," Erlend said with a disapproving glance at the empty walls. "All the booty we have to show is the Skraelling hatchet, and Alrek has the habit of carrying that in his belt. Many hunting journeys will be required to make this booth equal to the others in outfittings. Let your eyes run over it and then think of Karlsefne's!"

Thinking, they were silent for a little, gazing around at the great room which even in the fire-glow showed so baldly white with newness. Karlsefne's walls were decorated with bears' heads and eagles' claws and antler-racks of shining weapons; and Karlsefne's benches were covered with rich furs, and his high-seat had velvet cushions stuffed with eider-down.

"Alrek, when is it your intention to take the time to get furnishings?" Erlend besought.

The chief shook his brown head steadily. "Not until we get out of the debt which we got into to build this booth," he answered, and closed the opening discussion by putting aside his rune-stick and rising. "Now it seems to me that you are all looking too far into the future. I should be content if I could get something to eat. Who has gone after the fish? And what is the reason that he is not back again?"

As head-cook, Brand answered him, though sulkily: "Gard has gone after the fish, and it is high time that he was back again."

"That is what I have been trying to do, look for him," little Olaf the Fair spoke up for the first time, in aggrieved tones. And secure at last from interference, he flung the door open to the nipping January wind. "No, I see nothing of him—but I do hear the snow crunch!"

"It is certainly time," Brand blustered.

Nevertheless he bent his lank length over the fire with recovered good-humour; and greater alacrity came into the movements of those who were not yet dressed, while those who were, turned toward the door, gibes at each tongue's end.

The nature of their greeting changed, however, when Gard the Ugly had stamped into the room and they saw the size of the catch swinging at his side. Waking, their sleeping appetites cried out in alarm:

"Only three!" "Go into the hands of the Troll—" "—gone long enough to get thirty!" "What in the Fiend's name has come to the fishing?"

Tossing his fish to the clamouring cooks, Gard was a long time pulling off his fur-lined gloves before he answered: "Nothing has come to the fishing."

"What has come to *you* then?" Brand demanded.

After a while Gard said gruffly: "I forgot to take any more."

"*Forgot!*" echoed the chorus; and Erlend laid his plump hands on the Ugly One's shoulders and shook him good-naturedly.

"Are you asleep?" he inquired.

Gard pushed off his brown cloak and with it his questioner. "Since I can feel your grasp, I am not asleep. I think I have seen Hallad's ghost."

"What!" cried the chorus; and Domar, mistaking it for a joke, burst into his uproarious laugh. He stopped abruptly when he found that he was alone, and Gard spoke without further interruption:

"It happened that the first set of lines I stopped at had been robbed, so I was obliged to go across the river, which is what makes me rather late. Over there I had pulled up three fish when I heard a noise on the bank and looked around. Some evergreen trees hang down their branches there, and they are white with snow; he had on a white cloak that mixed him with them, at first. But suddenly I saw him looking out at me, as near as that bowl. His eyes were very wide open, and his face was white as milk. It may be that he would have spoken to me, but I did not wait to see."

"And therein you showed sense," Domar breathed in sympathy. But again he was on the unpopular side, for Ketil began to hoot:

"If you had waited, it is most likely you would have found out that you are a simpleton. Why should Hallad be dressed in white like a slave? He wore green when he went on his death-journey. Is it likely that Ran keeps new cloaks for drowned people?"

"Certainly, I think you are asleep after all!" Erlend laughed; which was the signal for a flight of chaff until Brand at his fish-fork endangered the peace by scoffing:

"I think you are lying."

To have said that to some of the band would have been to bring on a fight to the death, and many caught breath apprehensively before they remembered that this was one of the points about which Gard's thrall-blood gave him feelings different from theirs. He answered without resentment:

"I am not apt to lie when nothing is to be gained by it. I call Thor as witness that I have spoken the truth!" His oath he directed toward the chief, who had returned to his high-seat and from there listened intently to what passed.

But in the very act of nodding, Alrek Sword-Bearer broke off to ponder; and in the midst of pondering, he began to grin. "If you want to know my belief," he said, "it is that you saw the Weathercock's thrall, Tunni."

Instantly the chorus seconded him. "That is certainly the truth of the matter!" "Their hair is of the same colour—" "—the branches hid its shortness—" "and explains the slaves' cloak—"

"And explains why his look was fearful," Alrek added, "if, as I think, it was he who robbed the lines to save himself the trouble of going farther. He would think his hide in danger of a flogging—"

"Which it will get!" roared Gard; whereupon the chorus redoubled its delighted jeering.

This one time, however, the Ugly One's patience had a limit. Gradually his swarthy face turned mottled red; slowly a gleam came into the dull eyes above the high cheek-bones. Suddenly his voice rumbled through theirs: "If any of you tell this so that outsiders make derision, you will feel the edge of my knife."

They knew then that they had gone as far as was safe. When each one of them had spoken one gibe more to show that he dared to, there was a lull, of which Erlend the Amiable took advantage to make a tactful suggestion.

"I shall think those fish are ghosts if I do not get some of them between my teeth before long," he observed. And lo! ghosts and threats were, of a sudden, things of the past.

"Get to your places," commanded the head-cook, sweeping them aside that he might place before his chief the first portion of the crisp and rosy dish, savoury with garlic and sweet with its own freshness.

There was an eager scrambling of feet, a joyful clattering of brass-hilted knives, a flurry of half-spoken requests; and after that all noise gave way to a pleasant munching sound, enforced now and then by a contented sigh or a long-drawn "Ah—h!" of satisfaction.

A mumble of applause greeted the Bull when, having licked the last morsel from his fingers and pushed back his bowl, he looked around to say, stretching: "I should like to see the man who could make me go back to the old way of living!"

Chapter 9

About the Huntsman and the Boy Who was Drowned

To keep such a band supplied with food was an occupation in itself.

"Certainly I begin to believe there is truth in the things women say about a boy's stomach being like the bottomless horn which Thor tried to drink dry" Brand jested. With his week of fuel-duty far behind him and a day's hunting immediately before him, it was a light heart that beat under his deerskin tunic as he followed his chief and the Ugly One out of the booth door.

On the threshold the hunters paused to call back in mock admonition: "See to it this time that the meat is hung where the dogs can not get it—" "Watch Njal, if you do not want the cheese cut with the garlic knife—" "Put a bone in the Bull's mouth! If the Skraellings should come while he is bellowing like that, they would get more scared than they were at Karlsefne's bull."

Then Brand shut the door upon the counter-chaff, and the three began to burrow for their *skees* in the pile beside the house.

Trees—such trees as Greenland never dreamed of—rose snow-laden behind the booth, and before it a sweep of snow-buried meadow sloped away to beaches of white sand; for the little settlement was built across a neck of land that reached down between a river and a great lake-like bay. But the lads went neither forward nor back when at last they were shod for the trip, but turned to their left and moved across the camp toward the river bank.

It was so early in the day that no wind had yet arisen to stir the fleecy snow-blanket which the night had spread, and to look up a sunbeam was to look up a track of swirling star-dust. From the provision shed next their booth the first camp dog to leave night quarters had only just emerged, yawning, and dragging his hind legs after him. Passing the great log-built sleeping houses with gray banners flying from every smoke hole, they caught a rattle of dishes and a hum of jovial voices which told pleasantly of the breakfast hour. Farther on, they overtook the thralls carrying the pails of milk to the dairy, and had—for a wink of time—a glimpse of Gudrid herself. Looking out to hurry the milkers she stood an instant in the dairy door, tall and straight and deep-bosomed, carrying her baby on her hip as though he were a doll. For all the white matron's cap upon her sunny locks, her face showed young and flower-fresh as she turned to smile at them. When they had lost sight of her, Brand spoke reflectively:

"Women are as helpless in hardships as a rowan tree in the open; but if they must be in the world, let them be like that."

"It is a good thing to be in a country where there are but seven women," Gard assented.

What Alrek would have said no one knows; for they reached just then a corner of the last booth, and rounding it, encountered Karlsefne returning from an early search for a favourite hound which he now carried in his arms, badly torn by fighting.

As he was coming out of the snow-mantled grove, so he might have been coming out of the finest trading booth in Norway, so splendid were his garments of blue, so rich the silvery furs that bordered them. On the iron of his hair and his beard and his bushy brows, the morning light was sparkling like rime frost; and a glint of kindly humour lighted his deep-set eyes as they fell upon the approaching three.

"I salute the Chief of the Vinland Champions and his men!" he greeted them. "We old bones need to look to ourselves when young blood is on the trail so early."

Drawing up his soldierly form in salute, the Sword-Bearer replied that young blood had need to stir early when it had young appetites to provide for.

"That is true," the Lawman assented; then added politely: "Yours is certainly a hard-working household, chief. I hope your debt to me does not lie heavy on your shoulders?"

Involuntarily the Champions of Vinland exchanged wistful glances, and their chief paused to consider his answer.

"Why, the truth of the case is this," he said at last. "It is only a little time that is left over after we have got the food and fuel which are needed to keep us going; and since we have to spend that time in working out our debt to you, there is left no chance whatever to employ ourselves with accomplishments or skin-hunting. That some have found this hard can not be denied, yet it should not be thought either that our knees are in any way weakening under us."

"Ah?" said Karlsefne, and stood a while stroking the head of the hound that had just strength enough to lick his hand. Presently he spoke with much graciousness: "It is an old saying that *'necessities should be taken into consideration.'* Let us therefore look upon the debt as paid. In a short time to come you will find your hands full with ship-building. I expect that your boat will stand to Vinland's aid and strengthen us greatly, when it is ready."

So unexpected was the turn that for a time it took their breath away, but at last their chief recovered enough of his to answer gratefully:

"To let the matter rest so would be a great help for us, Karlsefne. If we do not serve Vinland well, it will not be for lack of trying."

"That is well-spoken, as was to be expected from you," Karlsefne made courteous return; whereupon they shook hands all around with the ceremony which becomes a dealing between chiefs.

After they had parted from the Lawman, however, and were skimming through the grove which was the back dooryard of the little settlement, dignity gave way to delight. Reaching the trail that zigzagged up the bluff, they streaked down it cheering, and cheering slid far along the sparkling track of the river.

Though black rifts yawned here and there in the middle of the stream, the ice within a hundred paces of the shores was as solid as a rock and as smooth-carpeted as a floor, a shining temptation to any with red blood in his veins. From sliding they went to racing, cleaving the air like swallows. There is no knowing when they would have stopped if they had not been halted, on turning a bend in the river, by the sight of smoke curling up from behind in a low white bank ahead of them.

In the same breath Brand cried: "Skraellings!" and Gard cried, "Dwarfs!" At which Alrek repeated the last word with lifted eyebrows:

"*Dwarfs?*"

Somewhat shamefacedly, Gard explained himself: "I said that in jest. It came into my mind how Biorn Herjulfsson's men used to think that this land was inhabited by them. But the rocks are not large enough here. It is more likely to be Skraellings."

"It is most likely to be some of our own hunters," Alrek dissented, "but it lies on our shoulders to investigate. We will leave our *skees* on the ice and creep close to the bank and listen; the tongue they speak, and their voices, will tell us something. If they are Skraellings, remember to behave well toward them, but on no account allow them to get hold of your knives. Karlsefne would blame the man strongly who should give them a weapon."

The plan was simple enough to carry out, for the shore was flat at the river's edge. With a sudden freak of perverseness, Brand decided that doffing his *skees* was unnecessary, and edged his way up sidewise, the six-foot runners threatening more than once to trip his neighbour. But they did not have to get very close to hear, as the place was still and the voices loud.

Their first expression was disappointment, for the language spoken was nothing more novel than Norse, and the voice was the hoarse one of the vagabond Greenlander known as Faste the Fat.

"—they are contented with no better excitement than hunting," he was saying.

"And to get only such wealth as is to be got from trading with Skraellings," added the grumble of Ale the Greedy.

In the faces of the eavesdroppers disappointment began to give place to curiosity.

"Better two followers like you than twenty cinder-biters," returned a third voice, harsh and sneering for all the flattery of the words. "I have not brought my news forward in the hall because I do not want the chiefs to take the power out of my hands. I have told only men who—"

Snap! Snap! Recognising the Huntsman, Brand had moved involuntarily; and his cumbersome foot-gear came in contact with a bush and the dry twigs broke. Before the lads could more than straighten, the giant form of Thorhall appeared at the top of the bank, his knife bare in his hand.

"Prying again!" he snarled, in his small eyes so evil a look that Gard's fingers began instinctively to shape runes against charm-spells, and Alrek's deliberate voice became fiercely swift as at a challenge.

"A man must be doing something which he expects to have pried into who makes his council-hall in the wastes," he retorted. "We thought the smoke must be from a Skraelling cook-fire, and crept up to see."

The Huntsman tossed his knife back to its case, and his anger sheathed itself in contempt. "If a man in the wastes is unable to escape the meddling of fools, what would he not have to endure who remained in camp?"

To that there did not appear to be any satisfactory answer; and as he remained standing with folded arms, plainly awaiting their departure, there did not seem to be any adequate reason for staying. The only revenge they could take was to move away in the most deliberate manner possible and mutter scathing comment to one another, feeling all the while his eyes like knife-blades in their backs.

"It has something to do with that bag of his." "He is trying to get another ship-load of fools to accompany him south—" "If he thinks the Weathercock will lend him another boat—" "None but the scum will listen to him—" "I wonder if Ale and the Fat One were ashamed to show themselves?" "Let us turn around suddenly when we get to this bend and see if they are not all looking after us."

Agreeing, they reached the bend and turned,—but it was a day of surprises. Though each boy would have taken oath that he felt that gaze on him as he wheeled, neither Huntsman nor followers were anywhere to be seen. And as they stood staring, Gard uttered a smothered cry and flung out his arm in another direction, toward the middle of the stream.

Through a broken place in the ice not twenty paces away, two claw-like hands were reaching up; as the trio gazed, a head followed, covered with carrot-yellow hair which hung in dripping points about two starting eyes set in a ghastly blue-white face. Finally a white-cloaked body raised itself over the edge of the ice and stood before them.

Whether it would retreat or advance none waited to see. With a yell of "Hallad!" Gard was off up the river at a deer's pace, the others at his heels. When he came to another place where the bank was flat, he turned his long toes up it and plunged into the forest, the others still following.

Guiding six-foot runners in and out between trees, however, is less easy; and before long they were forced to moderate their speed. As soon as they did that, Alrek's wonted coolness was able to overtake him. He stopped disgustedly.

"We are simpletons to run. Hallad would do us no harm."

Gard devoted the only breath he had to triumph: "You do not claim that it is Tunni, now!"

"It is Hallad," the Red One agreed in a gasp. "If we could cut off his head and put it between his feet, that would make him rest quiet."

The Ugly One shook his black mane. "You forget that a wave-covered man can not be dug up again. It is said to be a sign that they have been received well when drowned men come back after their death; yet Hallad has scarcely the look of one who has been well entertained—"

"He was always wanting something different from what he had," Brand sniffed.

"However that is, it is unlikely that he has come back to make trouble," Alrek said. "That is only done by men who were unruly before their death. Hallad had less spirit than a wood-goat when he was alive. I think we were fools to run."

"If you had been that kind of a fool on the Cape of the Crosses, you would have made more by it," Gard muttered in rare resentfulness,— though he was not rash enough to speak so that his chief could hear him.

The Sword-Bearer on his side knew better than to ask over. Instead he said: "This is the first time I have been in this part of the country. I wonder what kind of game they have here," and moved leisurely away where a treeless space left a white page crossed and recrossed with woodland runes.

Preferring to discuss their last adventure before they sought a new one, the other two sat down to wait for him. But they were hardly settled before his whistled call brought them again to their feet.

They found him kneeling beside a trench-like trail, testing with his bared hands the condition of the snow that had fallen back into it.

"If this were a five days' journey north, I should declare them elk tracks," he said. "Snorri of Iceland shot many a one of them up there, last winter, which he thought greatly superior to any we have in Norway. I would give my head for another elk hunt." He remained gazing at the trail in pleased retrospection, which moved the two Greenlanders to say enviously that they had never seen an elk.

"You will find it sport when you do," the Sword-Bearer assured them. Then he came out of his musing and arose, once more Alrek the Chief, brief and purposeful. "They can scarcely be less than deer's, however; and they were made this morning. It is easier to find tracks than to find what made them, as it is one thing to sight land across drift-ice and another to land on it; but we shall have poor luck if we can not get our meat out of this."

Instinctively they fell again under his leadership, straightening as he rose and turning their runners in the direction he was facing.

"Certainly the snow could not be in better condition," Brand gave tacit assent, and reassured himself of the safety of the quiver at his back.

"I knew that we should have luck today, because I heard a wolf howl last night," Gard added, with a hitch to his belt.

Then they glided away, single file, under the white arches spanning the white aisles.

Chapter 10
Through Which the Champions Chase Vinland Elk

Through the forest and out like flitting shadows, pausing only to make sure that the trail they were following was fresher than any of those which crossed it. Over a pond and across a bog and zigzag up a hill,—they had not grazed a stone or snapped a twig; it seemed that every stride must bring them in sight of the game. Then, on the other side of the slope, Alrek blundered. Descending at lightning speed, he turned his head to look behind, and in so doing unconsciously straightened his body ever so little from the required bend. In a breath he was seated on the snow while his *skees* finished the coast without him, at the bottom dashing noisily against a stone. Instantly, from somewhere in the white distance, came like an echo the sound of crashing timber, a sound which passed so quickly that if only one had heard it he might have doubted his ears.

All three had heard it, however; and the two who reached the bottom still shod looked scathingly upon the third as he came plunging down, breaking through the crust to his knees wherever it covered a hollow.

"I advise you to tie yourself on," one of them jeered; and the other one gibed: "Would you like to hold to my cloak in going down the next hill?"

If he would, the Sword-Bearer did not admit it; but it was something that he was reduced to silence. They swung after him in high feather when he was once more on his runners and off across the valley.

Beyond the next rise there was a plain, fringed by a thicket; and there in the packed and trampled snow and the gnawed branches and peeled bark they found yet more tangible proof of what they had lost.

"We should have got a herd if nobody had spoiled it," Gard grunted.

Before Brand also could voice his reproach, Alrek—darting here and there among the trees in search of the new trail—uttered his low whistle and was off like a hare. Like hounds after hare they were after him, and Vinland trees looked their first upon real *skee*-running.

Speed, not silence, was the object now. More than once their iron-shod staffs rang sharply against the rocks as they thrust out the poles to change their course, rudder-like. Finding coasting too slow now, they took the last half of each hill at a leap. And when a plain stretched its smooth surface before them, or a frozen pond or a marsh, their speed was the speed of a deer at his best.

And now the hunted were far from their best. The holes which their sharp hoofs had at first cut so cleanly through the crust were becoming haggled. Farther on, the trail itself that had been so straight began to show the wavering of the panic-stricken. At last the hunters came to a place where a wisp of bloody foam stained the white. Only a rigid economy of breath kept back a cheer, and they put the energy saved into fresh speed.

A jump over a pile of boulders, a spurt over a low knoll, and there in the open space beyond was the prey, six panting froth-flecked creatures, stricken staring with terror.

"But what in the Troll's name are they?" cried Gard and Brand together, at sight of the huge, shaggy, ungainly bodies with antlers like shovels and enormous noses like nothing they had ever seen in their lives.

At the same instant Alrek answered them with the glad cry: "Vinland elk!"

The next instant he had added a command to halt, checking his own advance by a thrust of his *skee*-staff into the snow, and following that act by casting it aside and swiftly unslinging his bow: "Be on your guard! They have not deer's tempers."

Even as he spoke, the bull in the lead flung up his mighty antlered head and, while the other five moved on, wheeled and faced the foe, like a chief covering his people's retreat.

Alrek paid him the tribute of an admiring murmur, but the withdrawal of the five set the Greenlanders wild with exasperation.

"Charge him!" "Finish him!" "Get him out of the way!" they cried savagely, and started forward even before their arrows were on their bowstrings.

The only thing they knew clearly after that was that the Vinland elk did not wait to be charged. Gard, who was a length ahead, had suddenly a glimpse of eyes like balls of green fire; something which had looked as fixed as a boulder became, lightning-quick, a hurtling mass descending on him, and he had a vision of terrible sharp-edged forefeet that could mangle a man to jelly.

Dropping his weapons, he turned to run, but lapped his *skees* and fell headlong. Falling, he uttered a hoarse cry as he saw Brand's hastily aimed arrow bury itself harmlessly in the animal's flank. Then, as he rolled backward, he caught sight of Alrek and regained hope.

Only the Sword-Bearer's brown cheeks, flaming crimson, showed his excitement; the rock beside him was no steadier than the arm that held his bow. Drawing back the string with all his strength, he sent an arrow through the shaggy neck where it joins the body; and the great beast fell forward on his knees and died without a quiver.

As the animal sank, Gard arose, breathing curses on his own awkwardness while he snatched up his scattered weapons, his eyes fixed greedily on the five disappearing over a ridge. And Brand cried fiercely: "There is as much ahead, and more besides!" and leaped forward. And Alrek plucked forth another arrow and drew himself up to spring over the dead forester lying high before him—drew himself up and then paused and hesitated, gazing down at the mighty shape. As nobly warrior-like as he had made his desperate charge, so nobly warrior-like he lay in his death, a leader who had given his life to save his people.

Slowly the young Viking stretched forth his hand. "Stop!" he ordered.

Poised in midair, as it were, they looked over their shoulders at him, crying impatiently: "What is the matter?"

This time the Chief of the Champions gave his gesture authority. "Come back. To kill them also would be a low-minded act. He took his death-wound to save them. We have all we need. Come back."

An instant they balanced there, gazing at the white ridge over which the last dark form was disappearing. Then the obedience bred in the bones of Gard the Thrall-Born turned him back to his master.

"You are the chief," he muttered.

At the same time Brand the Red made up his mind. "Though you should spend all your breath, you would not hinder me from going!" he cried, and sprang forward.

The arrow which Alrek had drawn forth was still in his hand; in the grasp of his other hand was his bow. Fitting the shaft on the string, he spoke his warning:

"It is unlikely that you will do any hunting for some time if you do not come back."

As a flame to a dry leaf, so was a threat to Brand's temper. Hissing defiance, it flared up, and he redoubled his speed.

Above the creak of his *skees* he heard at the same instant two sounds,—Gard's voice crying: "Would you kill him?" and the twang of Alrek's bowstring. Then his right arm dropped at his side with an arrow through it. His chief had foretold truly that he would do no more hunting for some time. It was as much in rage as pain that he caught at the shaft, cursing.

Gard's relief took the form of boisterous laughter; but the Sword-Bearer, as soon as he could make himself heard, spoke gravely:

"If you think you paid too much for your big words, you have only your own foolishness to thank for making the bargain."

Coming slowly back to them, still holding his arm, Brand's face was as white as it had been that day on shipboard; but there was no less of a swagger in his bearing. "Who says I paid too much?" he panted. "I shall say what I choose though you shoot into me every arrow of your quiver. I find no fault with the bargain!"

Alrek's gravity yielded to one of his short sudden laughs. "Now if you are satisfied, it is certain that I am," he said, and studied the Red One with twinkling eyes. Amusement was still alight in them when he stepped forward and held out his hand, yet there was also in his manner a new cordiality. "It has never happened to me before to meet a sprout to equal you," he declared. "I foretell that I shall certainly kill you sometime, but I promise that I will carve nines about you afterward."

"How do you know that it will be you who does the rune-carving?" Brand retorted; but at the same time he yielded his palm with flattered willingness. A little later he even yielded his wounded arm that the hand which put the shaft in might cut it out again.

Twilight never gathered in upon a more contented party than these three weary hunters, sprawled luxuriously on the fragrant heaps of evergreen boughs around the leaping fire, fed to repletion on the daintiest food they knew, pouring their hearts out in discussion of the day's adventures. They fell asleep wrangling over the placing of the antlers on the booth wall.

Chapter 11

Telling How Trade With the Skraellings Came to a Mysterious End

The antlers were finally hung over the high-seat, while the hide made a blanket for the bunk below, and the effect was so imposing that every Champion went fur-mad as soon as he saw them. For a month afterward, it took all the chiefs authority to keep the fuel pile supplied and cooks at their post. Every lad not told off—and told sternly off—for public service or private drudgery, spent his days in ranging the country in search of spoil, and his nights in dreaming of hunts wherein each dead tree should turn out to be the den of a hibernating bear which he would slay with valorous ease and bring home to deck the high-seat, even as Leif the Lucky had done before him.

The way in which they did finally come into possession of a bearskin, however, was really more dream-like than their dream.

Nothing could have been more peaceful than the beginning of the happening, in the women's room of Karlsefne's booth. Loafing after the noonday meal, Erlend the Amiable had stretched his plump length over the cushions of a bench. At one end of the fire, the long-kirtled forms of Gudrid and her women moved to and fro before their looms. At the other, where the firelight lay brightest, the Sword-Bearer was playing wolf with the baby,—a game evoking so much rumbling growling and squealing laughter that presently it took precedence of the conversation.

"You are spoiling him. Kinsman Alrek," Gudrid said, looking around the edge of her loom with a smile which belied her reproach.

The prettiest of the bondmaids gave her braids a pettish flirt. "That is so," she confirmed. "Yesterday, when it happened that I was at the door trying to talk to Hauk Votsson, I was obliged to turn around and growl between every two words or the child would have deafened us. I do not know what Hauk thought of me."

"If you wish, I will ask him," Erlend offered,—a piece of flippancy which cost him his comfort, as to save his ears he was obliged to take to instant flight around the looms.

But Alrek, sitting back on his heels, shaking back his long hair, remained intent upon the cradle. "It is the greatest fun," he said, "to see the cub try to frown at me. His eyebrows are like the fuzz on a chicken, yet he tries to make them look like his namesake's, before a laugh gets the better of him. Watch now!"

Small Snorri had been there but seven months; he was still wonderfully new. The maid and Erlend left their chase, and Gudrid came from her loom, and together they watched breathlessly the knitting of the downy brows above the blue eyes, and the slow dawning of the unwilling smile, brighter and brighter, until in each soft cheek a dimple broke.

"He is going to be in every respect like his father!" Gudrid cried, falling on her knees beside him. And she was smothering him with kisses, and the others were looking on sympathetically, when the door was flung open before little Olaf the Fair, rosy and breathless.

"Where is Alrek?" he panted. "I want—Oh! Alrek! What do you think I have seen?"

"Hallad?" shrieked the three bondmaids together.

"Skraellings! Black as crowberries. Crossing the open space west of here. With big packs on their backs. I was up in that tree by the wheat-shed, watching for Brand to slip on the slide I had made to get revenge on him for cuffing me, and—" His voice was lost in the babble of exclamations that came from the bondmaids and from the men peering around the hall door.

Gudrid rose from beside the cradle with a gesture of authority. "Too much noise is here. Since Karlsefne is away it behoves us to be especially careful how we behave. Run, someone of you, to the Icelanders' booth. I know that Snorri is not there, but if it happen that Biorn is, ask him to get a following together and stand ready to receive the wild men. And since it is likely that they will want to buy the same dairy wares as before, Melkorka, you may have charge—but there! Tch! Your heedlessness is such that you would give them three times as much as they required. I shall have to portion it out myself. The child I will leave with you, Roswitha—No, you would forget him if a man so much as looked through the door at you! Kinsman!" She laid a white hand on Alrek's brown one as he would have moved past her. "He is more fond of you than of anyone, and I would trust you before a hundred girls,—so long as you keep his fingers away from that hatchet in your belt. Will you not stay with him the little while that I must be in the dairy?"

Stay with a baby while the long-looked-forward-to trading went on without him! Frowning involuntarily, the Sword-Bearer hesitated,— and during that pause the Fate who was spinning his life-thread sat with suspended breath, so much hung on his answer.

It can not be denied that it came somewhat grudgingly when it did come. "Why—if it *will* be a *little* while, kinswoman," he stipulated, turning back.

Gudrid waited to hear no more; with the last word she was off, sweeping the maids like chaff before her. Erlend and Olaf had long since vanished; and now the men could be heard clattering out of the great next room that was their headquarters.

From the green behind the booths came the clamour of barking dogs and the thud of running feet accompanied by excited voices, now far away, now just outside the door. Gradually the scattered chatter blended into a hum; the hum rose higher and higher; then fell suddenly in a hush so deep that it seemed to the Sword-Bearer he could hear the pat of bare feet and the rustle of boughs put aside; and his fancy conjured up a picture of dark forms with bright-eyed shaggy heads bent under shaggier packs, emerging single file from the white depths of the forest. Directly after, the sound of strange guttural voices speaking words he had never heard told him that some part of his vision was correct.

"Oh, you great hindrance!" he sighed to the tyrant in the cradle.

But as even while he complained, he obeyed the command of the chubby fists by picking up the soft little body as gently as a woman would have done, and tossing and dandling it in his strong brown hands as no woman could have done, the tyrant was in no way cast down but clung to him confidingly, catching his breath with squeals of delight and winding up by burying both fists in the brown mane with a rapture of gurgling laughter.

So Gudrid found them when she came in, the colour of haste in her fair face; and her smile was very lovely as she took her baby from his guard.

"Whether you are like your father or not, Alrek my kinsman, you have a good disposition," she said; then went on swiftly: "I hurried because I want to remind you of something. I beg of you, do not forget that Karlsefne has forbidden any weapon whatever to be traded to the hatchetmen, no matter what loose property they offer for it. Do not forget, or let your men forget."

Alrek's glance reassured her. "I will remember," he said quietly.

"Then go quickly! They have only just opened their packs." She gave him a little shove, but she might have saved herself the trouble for he was out of the door at a bound.

Coming out into the gathering was like coming upon some strange new-world fair. Everywhere over the white of the snow-covered earth, against the gray of the snow-filled sky, the Northmen's gay cloaks made rings of bright colour around the dark fur-clad forms of the wild men. Everywhere the sounds of fair-time had vanquished the stillness of the forest,—the hails of eager barterers, the boasts of jubilant purchasers, even the familiar din of fighting dogs wherever a Norse hound and one of Skraelling breed were able to find a spot free from interfering boot-toes.

On the step before the dairy door, the yellow heads of the three pretty bondmaids showed above a hedge of bristling black locks; the love of trading, so long denied, getting the better of any fear they might have felt of their uncouth customers. As Alrek looked, Roswitha with one hand delivered a cheese ball into a copper-coloured palm and with the other drew in a magnificent wolf-skin; while Melkorka, her saucy Irish face twinkling with mischief, ladled curds from her bowl into the gaping mouth of an enormous Skraelling, standing before her with half-shut eyes and an air of solemn content.

"If only we could build cows as well as ships out of timber!" the Sword-Bearer wished as he watched them with a grin.

He was brought out of his reverie by the appearance of a shadow on the snow at his feet. Though he had not heard the faintest sound of an approach, he looked up to find a wild man as dark as the shadow and almost as tall standing at his side. Over the Skraelling's left shoulder and arm was hung a bearskin which took the Viking's breath to look at; his right arm he was stretching toward Alrek's sword, a glitter of indescribable craftiness in his beady eyes. It was so like the stories that the Irish monks told of the wiles of the Evil One that Alrek's recoil had in it even a touch of superstitious fear.

"No," he said severely. "No!" And without further parley, he turned and hastened in the direction in which Brand's red locks glowed between the gray of cap and cloak, like fire amid ashes.

"I want to know at once that you have remembered not to trade them any weapons," he demanded with an urgent hand on the Red One's arm.

Once Brand would have shaken off that hand resentfully; now he looked around with affectionate impudence. "Which are you the more anxious to know,—that I have remembered or that I have not traded?" he parried.

The Sword-Bearer let his hand fall with a breath of relief. "Since you can make light of the matter, I know that no harm has been done; if you had been disobedient, you would have hurled the news at me

SHE LADLED CURDS FROM HER BOWL INTO THE GAPING MOUTH.

like a spear. I trust you to keep on remembering it."

Brand made him a salute of mock deference. "I will heed your orders in this as in everything," he mouthed the formal phrase of submission.

"Now I hope you will do better than that," his chief returned; then hailed the Hare, scudding past, and bade him summon every member of the band to immediate council.

When at last they were all before him, and he had obtained from them individually an assurance that the order was still unbroken, he delivered the command over again with all the weight he could bring to bear.

They received the reminder as insult added to injury.

"I do not think I stand in need of telling when already for my poorest spear I have refused three wolfskins!" the Bull cried, wagging his yellow head; while Ketil the Glib mocked openly:

"Behold the caution! Lose no time in punishing Erlend who has traded them a brooch with a pin as long as my finger."

Even small Olaf sniffed rebelliously. "If I had known *that* was all you were going to say, I doubt if I would have come. I thought you were going to offer us your red cloak to trade with."

"My red cloak?" Alrek repeated.

Forty eyes fastened themselves wistfully on the garment, while at least ten voices answered: "Of course it is not to be expected—" "Yet you could buy the most costly furnishings—" "They would like it better than curds even—" "Njal got the finest gray fur only for a kerchief with one stripe of red." "Think if this were cut in strips!" "Another cloak would keep you equally warm—" "Karlsefne would give you a king's mantle for the asking—"

Shaking his head, Alrek folded the stained drapery to him with both arms. "You show too much generosity! I can tell you that you would not get this though it would buy all the fur in Vinland. My father gave it to me at the time of my first Viking voyage; while one thread holds to another, I shall wear it." Then he unfolded his arms with a gesture more encouraging. "But it may be that we shall not fare so ill, for I have hit upon another plan. I have a suit of feasting-clothes of red velvet—"

Not one of the twenty waited to hear more; after the Hare the band was off like the tail after a comet. The Sword-Bearer considered himself lucky that he reached the booth in time to secure one sleeve for his own ventures.

After that the trading was like trading in a dream. Even after the first recklessness had passed and they had cut the velvet into strips no wider than their thumbs, the same sizes of skins were given in exchange. Erlend, the first to run out of purchase money, was made custodian of the spoils; and the rapidity with which the pile grew behind him in what remained of the short afternoon was enough to heat cooler blood. By the falling of twilight, Alrek announced the whimsical determination to try if he could not capture the bearskin itself with what remained of his red sleeve and the foot of a red stocking which he had found.

Because of the failing light, quenched early by a gentle fall of snow, the trading had ceased before he started. Here and there, where light streamed out through open doors, the forest men stooped in groups, packing for departure all wares not previously bound around their heads or bestowed in their stomachs. From group to group he went without finding the tall Skraelling, until suddenly he caught a glimpse of him passing the last door in the line, the door of their own booth. It looked as though the great skin was still draping his shoulders, so Alrek started leisurely toward him and reached the wheat shed this side of the Champions' booth. Then he slipped on Olaf's slide and fell, striking his head against a great oak root.

That was the last thing he remembered,—and he did not remember that for some time. The next thing he was conscious of was sitting in his high-seat in the booth, in silence and alone. The flickering firelight that showed him the stretch of empty benches revealed gradually to his bewildered eyes a dark huddled shape on the white surface of the table in front of him. What it was or how it got there, he knew no more than what he was doing there himself. He wondered dully if the Huntsman could have put a spell upon him, until—like a wind-breath through a fog—came the recollection that a sailor had once told him of having had a similar experience, and that it had been caused by striking his head in falling through a hatchway on the ship. Moving his head, the Sword-Bearer found it as sore as an unhealed wound, and that part of his problem was solved. But where had he been, and why was the booth empty at this time of day? It was a relief to have the door open upon Gard's hulking long-armed figure, powdered with glistening snow.

When the Ugly One had taken three steps beyond the threshold, he saw the chief in the high-seat and stopped with a loud exclamation.

Alrek grinned faintly. "Your surprise is no greater than mine. I should be thankful if you would tell me how I got here. No," as Gard made a gesture of unbelief, "I declare myself in earnest. I suppose I fell and struck my head somewhere. Do you know where I have been? And why the booth is empty?"

When he had come around the fire and looked curiously at the Sword-Bearer, Gard's doubts were laid. "The proof of this is that the left side of your face is scratched and dirty," he said. "It is likely that you fell on Olaf's slide. You were going in that direction, the last I saw of you. I forgot you after the screech."

"What screech?"

"The yell that started the Skraellings, of course."

"What Skraellings?"

"*What* Skraellings!" Gard echoed; but Alrek's memory had stirred.

"I remember! They were here trading. I came out of the women's house and saw them—" He got upon his feet. "Are they gone?"

Gard began to laugh. "You *are* addled! I should have thought the racket sufficient to wake Thorwald in his grave. It is certain that they are gone! At the first note of the yell they dropped their packs and plunged into the woods, howling like trolls. What frightened them this time, no one knows. Erlend and Brand followed, and also some of the other men of the band, but the creatures seemed to melt and vanish. The men are only just coming back. That is why no one is here yet to get the meal."

Coming down to the fire, Alrek kicked the logs about, partly to mend the burning, partly to vent his irritation. "Never have I heard of a fall so foolishly timed. I could give my head another knock—What is this? Fur?" He stretched his hand toward the table. "A bearskin? What a—*the bearskin the Skraelling offered for my sword?*" Memory came back like a rush of fire, lighting the dark corners of his mind, flaming from his eyes as he turned upon the slouching figure. "How did it come here?"

Gard began to speak with unwonted swiftness: "It is true, I forgot to tell you that I bought it myself. You must recollect that things were not so dear at the end of the trading. I gave only a piece of your tunic and—and my ring with the red stone. I would not have parted with that ring for anything less. He liked very much to get it, and put it on his finger as soon—" He broke off as Alrek's hands fell upon his shoulders, forcing him down on his knees where the fire could light his face. For the moment they were neither comrade and comrade, nor chief and follower, but master and thrall.

The Sword-Bearer's low voice seemed a hiss between his teeth. "Swear to me that you gave no weapon for it! Take oath on the cross of my sword hilt!"

Gard reached out even eagerly. "I take oath on the cross, so help me Frey and Njord and Odin!"

After a while Alrek's hands relaxed their grasp. It was some time before his eyes loosened their hold, but at last they also released the Ugly One and fell away, back to the fur. "It is good that you are able to swear to it," he said grimly.

Brushing from his knee the ashes into which he had been forced, the Ugly One grunted. "Do you think I am a fool like Brand? Even if I did not care for your orders, would I not be apt to heed Karlsefne's?"

"It is a good thing that you do," the chief said again.

Chapter 12

In Which the Champions Feel Their Importance

Smiling, Gudrid drew out the head she had thrust through the booth door at Erlend's urgent invitation. "It is as splendid as can be in every way. I do not wonder that you want to give a feast to display it."

A little consciousness was in Erlend's laugh as he shut the door and walked beside her through the grove. "It is not altogether to display it," he protested. "In a few weeks the spring games will be held; it is the custom of every one to give a feast at that season. I tell you we are going to show some great feats. We exercise ourselves every afternoon. They are practising now in an open place which the chief found in the woods. That is where I am going."

Pausing, Gudrid drew higher on her hip her accustomed burden, a bundle wrapped in white rabbit-skins from which looked forth a little rosy face. "Is Alrek there?" she asked. "Then I think I will try my luck in that direction, if so be they will allow a woman to come near?"

"I think they will not mind your coming if you go right away again," Erlend concluded after some consideration.

Apparently she felt equal to the risk, for she entered with him the broad trough-like path trodden through the snow of the grove. "I go only for a walk," she said. "We have been too much shut in the house, the child and I, since that frightful trading day."

It seemed to the Amiable One that she shivered as she spoke, so he observed politely: "It is a bad thing that you were made sick by it. Melkorka says that you even saw a ghost."

"Melkorka blunders much in her speaking and blundered twice as much in her hearing," Gudrid answered. "I said only that I got so full of fear that I expected to see ghosts. Sitting alone in the house with the child, it came into my head what might happen if the Skraellings should turn an evil side, with Karlsefne away and that good-natured Biorn not expecting evil. And the more I thought, the stranger the noises outside seemed to me and the stranger shapes the shadows took, until once I was so sure that one was a Skraelling stealing in upon me that I bent over and covered the cradle with my body,—and just then came that cry!" She pressed her hand to her ear at the recollection.

Erlend smiled indulgently. "Now did you think it so terrible? It is likely that one of them looked into the cattle-shed and saw the bull—"

The glance her blue eyes sent over her shoulder silenced him even before her words. "It would be a strange wonder if you could tell me news about it! Was I not here at the time the bull frightened them? I heard how they screamed then, and it was as different from this screech as day from night. In this cry there were death-sounds and no life-sounds. My foster-mother, Halldis, was knowing in weird matters. I know of what I speak, though all men think otherwise. And I know enough to wish to forget the mishap. Let us not talk of it any more. I wish to enjoy this fine weather."

It was a day to be enjoyed. Beyond the network of brown branches the sky was dazzling blue, with here and there a fleecy cloud. Dazzling white, snow lay in the curves of the boughs and filled the hollows of the ground; though on the ridges where the bright sun touched, the brown earth showed through. Everywhere, the wind was moistly, sweetly fresh.

"I do not wonder that it makes you kick up your heels like young horses," Gudrid laughed, when she came at last to the level treeless space in whose middle six Champions leaped and wrestled, while ten more lounged at one side, applauding or hissing the wrestlers as their critical judgment decided.

At sight of Erlend, the ten waved their hands in careless greeting; at sight of the kirtled figure of Gudrid, they sat up in unmistakable disapproval; and a long lean wrestler with a mane of red hair stamped petulantly when he was obliged to retire from the field to the bordering trees where his tunic and cloak awaited him.

"Though no more than seven women are in Vinland, a man can not get away from them though he go into the heart of a wood," he sputtered.

"Hush! She will hear you," muttered Gard, who stood beside him; whereupon the Red One's voice rose in exasperation:

"I do not care whether she hears me or not! Will you keep to what concerns you? I have told you before this that I am able to pay the price of my deeds."

From under the tunic he was about to pull down over his head, Gard looked at him irefully. "And I have told you," he retorted, "that one can not always tell what the price of his deed will be."

"I do not care *what* it is!" bellowed Brand.

Harald Grettirsson turned on them with a grin. "What ails you two that you have done nothing but quarrel since the trading day? Cool off a little," he jeered, and suddenly ran into them so that they were jostled off the high ground into a hollow and sank in snow up to their waists. Foreseeing vengeance, Grettirsson took promptly to his heels, and the desertion of the three completed the interruption begun by the appearance of Gudrid's blue hood.

Gudrid took her departure with tactful promptness. "Now you need not trouble yourself to hunt for fine words," she forestalled the somewhat embarrassed greeting of her young kinsman. "I am well versed in the Viking laws about keeping women out; we have no other intention than to go directly back, the Frowner and I."

Cordial as his relations with his kinswoman were, the chief could not ask her to alter her decision; but he reached out and took the bundle off her hip. "The Frowner is not a woman," he corrected. "I think he will like the noise better than the rattling of his string of shark's teeth. I will see to it that he comes to no harm."

The mother yielded him doubtfully. "But do you know for certain that you will?"'"she demurred. "If he should get his hand on the hatchet in your belt—"

"Why, he would be able to do more than I can," Alrek finished for her. "I have been unable to find my hatchet for weeks."

Gudrid consented to smile. "I took for granted it was there. Then I will certainly leave him, for I should like him to be outdoors some while longer. I will send a thrall—a man-thrall—to fetch him."

But it came about that small Snorri Thorfinnsson was returned to his mother by no such humble individual. With the shortening of the light and the lengthening of the shadows, Karlsefne the Lawman came through the wood on his way campward from a day's outing. Coming out in the open where a dozen Champions were fencing with a mighty clash and clatter, he would have apologised for the intrusion and kept on his way; but reaching the tree before which the red-cloaked chief sprawled on a great rug, drawling comment, he heard from the rabbit-skin bundle at the chief's side a squeal of laughter which brought him to a standstill.

"What have we here?" he asked in surprise.

Rising to greet him, Alrek looked down at the bundle with a laugh. "It is likely that your son is going to make a Berserker, Karlsefne," he answered. "The more noise the swords make, the louder he laughs."

The smile dawning on the Lawman's lips faded as his glance passed from the rabbit-skin bundle to the rug on which it lay. After a little he said gravely: "This is an unusually fine bearskin which you have, my young kinsman. I want to ask if it is the one the Skraellings brought, on that last trading day of which so much has been told?"

It was so plain that the same misgiving was in his mind which had first risen to Alrek's, that the Sword-Bearer breathed a prayer of thankfulness that he had lost no time in making sure of Gard's good faith. He replied readily: "It is the same one, Karlsefne. One of my men had such luck in trading that he bought it when the price was lower than it had been."

"Nevertheless, I should like much to know what he paid for it," said the Lawman.

"Willingly," answered Alrek the Chief. "He paid a large piece of the red cloth which we had been trading with, and a ring with a red stone. The Skraelling liked the ring so well that he put it on as soon as he bought it."

The Lawman's gaze became less unswervingly direct; presently its sharpness was softened by a twinkle. "Now if all the Northmen of the new lands continue to show such merchant talent, Vinland will soon be as great a trading place as Iceland," he laughed.

Then, as if to remove any lingering doubt of his friendliness, he added that their taste in selecting a practising place was excellent; and that it appeared that they were doing good work in it; and that, if they would allow it, he should be glad to remain a while and look on. When permission had been graciously accorded, he sat down on the rug between the chief and the rabbit-skin bundle and showed himself the most inspiring audience the band had ever performed before.

Under the stimulus of his applause, Njal the Jumper achieved a mark a finger's length higher than any he had made before; while Brand the Wrestler felt such power swell in his great limbs that for a time he seriously considered the idea of challenging Karlsefne himself. Later, he was glad that he had not, for when they stopped to rest and came and stood around the bearskin, Karlsefne borrowed Alrek's dwarf-made sword and rose up, towering and sinewy and straight as a pine, and showed them some feats that he had learned in the East,—the real East where the sun is so hot that all people are as brown as roasted fowls, and the rich eat snow for a luxury. Baring a knotted arm as lean as a spear-shaft, he did things that furnished them fireside gossip for the rest of the cold weather.

When at last he had set the Frowner on his shoulder, and he and the Champions had parted in a glow of good-fellowship, Erlend said warmly:

"Biorn Gudbrandsson is an open-handed chief, and Snorri of Iceland is shrewder than most men; but the one surpassing others in high-mindedness and knowing everything is Thorfinn Karlsefne, I think it an honour to our feast that he has consented to come to it."

Chapter 13
Giving the Reason Why the Skraellings Fled

It happened, however, that Thorfinn Karlsefne did not get back from his spring exploring trip in time for the games. Inspecting all the self-sown wheat-fields and natural vineyards in the vicinity, he had been gone a week; and the light of the momentous day had faded into twilight and the dusk in its turn had melted into moonlight, silvering the forest like a frost, before he came through it with his men.

Meeting a ray of light from the last booth in the line and catching from the same source a faint note of revelry, he spoke smilingly to his partner, Snorri of Iceland: "I recollect now that we have missed great happenings. It is likely that if the light were good enough we should find heads and limbs strewed like pebbles over the plain."

"What witches' stuff this moonlight is!" Snorri laughed in return. "As you spoke, it almost seemed to me as if I saw an arm down there." He nodded his head toward the ravine along whose brink they were walking; and old Grimkel, behind him, followed the motion with his one eye and grunted:

"I see what you mean,—yonder where the moon strikes. It has the look of an arm."

Still moving forward, Karlsefne also glanced down into the black pool of shadow. From the dark slope, something like a snag stood out so that the moonlight caught it and gave it a weird resemblance to a human hand with fingers wide-spread in the air. Looking down at it, he came slowly to a standstill. Presently, while the chat behind him ceased in surprise, he grasped a wiry bush on the brink and let himself over the edge until he could touch with his staff the dark mass from which the snag stood out.

Using the staff like a pitchfork, he flung off the layers of sodden pine branches heaped there and bent to look again. Then he saw that the reason it looked like an arm was because an arm was what it was, lean and brown, outflung from a stark body lying face downward in the brush.

Those waiting above heard his voice rise awfully from the shadow: "It is a Skraelling who has been murdered! Fetch torches!"

Waiting for the lights to be brought, the men stood looking dumbly at one another and at the snag-like arm, in every mind the same thought. Once Karlsefne's deep tones interpreted their silence, tolling heavily through the darkness:

"I do not know who has done this deed, but I know that in slaying this one man he has taken the lives of more men than tongue can number. If ever the Skraellings come again it will be to make warfare, and to save our lives we shall be forced to take more of theirs; and so it will go on through ages yet unborn, until a white face—which I had striven to make a sign of friendliness—will become to the wild men a token of bloodshed." A moment his voice rang out in terrible wrath: "Behold how the heedlessness of one man can overthrow the wisdom of a hundred!"

Daring no answer, they awaited in silence the arrival of the torches. But when at last the lights had been brought and handed down, and they had descended after them, at least four spoke at once:

"It is the Skraelling who offered the bear's hide!"

"By Odin," cried a fifth, "I saw him walking in this direction shortly before the time of the scream! He must have fallen over the bank and lain all this while under the snow that was coming down."

"What has become of the hide, however?" pondered Hjalmar Thick-Skull, before memory recalled to him whose booth the great skin was even now gracing as its chiefest treasure.

"It must be that they bought it just before he was slain," Grimkel struck in hastily.

But the Lawman took the torch from him and held it to each brown hand in turn. "No ring with a red stone is on any of the fingers," he said.

Immediately after, Hjalmar, holding the other torch, uttered an exclamation: "Here is what slew him!" and they all crowded forward to look,—and looking, stood dumfounded.

The Thick-Skulled said wonderingly: "Now I have several times heard it said that men believe Brand the Red gave the Skraelling a weapon for the skin, but no man guessed that a weapon had been given in this way,"

Chapter 14

Showing How Disgrace Came Upon Alrek the Chief

It was as though all the troubles of Vinland were gathered around that dark heap in the ravine, and all the pleasures were gathered around the Champions' hospitable fire. Built of juniper fagots whose sweetness blended with the fragrance of the pine branches carpeting the floor, it filled the air with the spicy aroma of Yule-tide; and Yule-tide cheer was on the long tables on either side the hearth, and Yule-tide mirth was on the faces above the board. Every leap of the flames revealed some new treasure of claw or hide or antler; and at each admiring tribute from their guests the Champions' hearts swelled with pride, so that they were obliged to relieve the pressure by echoing at the top of their lungs the song Rane was singing to chords from a home-made harp. The only flaw in their content was that Karlsefne was not there to see their glory. When an uproar among the dogs outside announced the arrival of a guest, they left everything to fix eager eyes on the opening door.

The form that strode in out of the moonlight was Karlsefne's, followed by Snorri of Iceland, but the breath they had thought to spend in cheers went out in gasps as the dancing firelight showed his face. Stopping just within the threshold, he stood gripping his silver-shod staff in both hands before him, like a bar in the way of his wrath.

From the high-seat, the young chief saluted him with troubled mien: "We bid you welcome, Karlsefne, and take it as an honor that you have come. I hope your journey has been according to your pleasure, and that nothing has happened which you dislike? "He made a sign that Erlend, in his feasting clothes of blue-and-silver, should act as master of ceremonies and conduct the distinguished guest to the seat prepared for him.

The Lawman did not appear to heed the invitation. "I give you thanks for your greeting," he said, "but I will not conceal it from you that something has happened. Before this feast goes any further, I want to put some questions to your men."

From some instinctive foreboding, Alrek glanced hastily across at Gard. Finding the Ugly One's dark face as lowering as a storm cloud, while Brand's beside him was aflash with excitement, the trouble in the young chief's eyes deepened. Yet he answered steadily: "You are overchief in Vinland, Karlsefne, and must have your way about everything. Yet will you not first take the seat of honour—"

"I will accept no hospitality here until this matter is cleared," the Lawman grimly cut him short; then turned upon the Ugly One. "I want to ask Gard Eldirsson what he paid the Skraelling for the skin yonder on the high-seat?"

As he had given it each time before, Gard muttered his answer, without looking up: "I gave him a piece of red cloth and a ring with a red stone in it. He liked so well to get the ring that he put it on his finger as soon as he got it."

Crack! the staff Karlsefne was gripping broke under the strain; it seemed that his voice also must break from his control. "It was not seen that he wore it today," he was beginning; when Brand arose, pushing back his goblet and bowl with a loud clatter.

"If what you mean is that you have met that Skraelling and seen a knife in his belt instead of a ring on his hand," he said, "I will spare you the trouble of asking further by declaring that I traded it to him myself. Gard lies when he says that he bought the skin. It happened that from behind a tree he saw me give the weapon; and because he expected that Alrek would slay me for daring it, he sought to save trouble by making up the ring-story before I got a good chance to tell what I had done. I gave him no thanks for it, as I do not lack the boldness to stand behind any deed I do. I held my tongue only because I could not speak without bringing him into trouble. Now I will hold it no longer, and you may do what you like when my chief is through with me." He flashed his leader his glance of affectionate insolence, and grinned at the look he got in return. But before Alrek could answer, Karlsefne spoke:

"You would have me believe that your chief does not know of this matter?"

The Red One tossed his long locks with a flourish which suggested that he was enjoying the excitement of the moment. "No more than the bench before you," he answered. "He himself had started out to make an offer for the skin, but he slipped on the ice and muddled his wits so that he did not even hear the yell or know how he got into the booth, until he found himself there with the fur before him—"

"Was it you who brought the fur into the booth?" Karlsefne interrupted him.

But Gard took the answer out of Brand's mouth: "No, it was I who did that. When the wild men began yelling and running, I saw Brand drop the skin and run after them; and I picked it up and brought it into the booth before I followed him. When I came back, Alrek was sitting there and asked me where he had been." He turned toward the high-seat as though he would address a word of apology to him who sat there, but the pause was shattered by an unpleasant laugh from Snorri of Iceland.

"I call Loke as witness," he ejaculated, "that though I have dealt with men in France and men in England and all that are nearer than those, I have never seen given such a running-over measure of lies!"

"They are like saplings drifted ashore that one picks up for their good shape and finds to be worm-eaten," Karlsefne responded; and the violence of the anger he was holding back shook his towering frame and vibrated through his deep voice. "Yet should it be kept in mind that these two lied in order to assist a comrade. Only Alrek Ingolfsson lied for himself."

In his place Alrek the chief arose, his lips forming a question; but Karlsefne stayed it with uplifted hand.

"I will make it plain that I do not wish to tempt you to further falsehood. I tell you openly that I know you to be the man who slew the Skraelling—"

"Slew?" repeated Alrek Sword-Bearer.

And "Slew!" cried the chorus of Champions; then divided into scattered cries: "It was his death-yell—" "They took it as a warning—" "The next time they come, it will be in warclothes."

Hearing this last. Brand hammered the table with his fist. "Now I know who killed him!" he cried joyfully. "It was Thorhall the Huntsman! More than anything else he wanted to break off trade with the Skraellings and stir the camp to discontent—"

"Now your tongue goes faster than your mind," the Iceland chief interrupted him. "That trading day the Huntsman spent with me, setting traps in the wood far north of here."

Brand shot his arrows desperately: "Then it was Ale the Greedy!

Or Fat Faste!"

But from the quarter where the Greenland guests sat, rose resentful cries: "Faste was off all day fishing with me—" "I myself saw Ale in the group before the Lawman's door!" "You take too much upon yourself!" "Remember that the spoils were found in your booth!"

The Red One stood with empty quiver. And Gard left his place and went and laid clumsy hands upon the Lawman's cloak.

"I swear that it was not Alrek but I who brought the skin into the booth. I take oath that I am telling the truth this time," he said.

"*This* time!" the Lawman repeated, so that the blood was rasped into Gard's swarthy face.

"Nay, it was to help Brand that I lied before," he pleaded.

"And this time it is to help Alrek!" Karlsefne finished. "Learn, boy, once and for all, that you can not spend your wealth and have it also in your pouch. Learn now and forever that your word buys nothing when the pouch of your honour is empty." Casting him off as he would have spoken further, he turned upon the red-cloaked figure of the Sword-Bearer, standing rigidly erect before the high-seat. "Too long, Alrek Ingolfsson, have you hidden behind this shield; show now the boldness which should be in your blood. That you lied because you wished to keep my good opinion, I can guess. That you fell not upon the Skraelling treacherously nor yet in greed of his property, I do you the justice to believe. It may even be that he gave provocation to your mad temper by seizing your weapon. I expect that you will acknowledge yourself guilty and submit to me."

Their glances clashed like blades as Alrek turned his high-borne head.

"You can decide over my life, but I will never acknowledge that," he said. "May the gallows take my body if I knew aught of the happening until your own lips told of it. I say, moreover, that it is unjustly done to accuse me of it only because others have juggled with the truth and because it looks as though mine were the hand which had brought the spoils hither."

That, at least, did not lack boldness. Flinging the broken staff from him, Karlsefne made a stride forward; the veins of his forehead swelled out white against purple. "This case has not yet been fully tried," he said. "I have not told that those are my only reasons. Another proof is this, which my own hand took from the Skraelling's head into which it had bitten so deeply that not even his fall down the bank had dislodged it." From his belt, where his cloak had hidden it, he drew forth the stone hatchet, discoloured with dark stains.

To Alrek of Norway it was like a trick of magic; his jaw fell and he recoiled against the high-seat. "My hatchet!" he breathed.

Then the sheeted lightning of Karlsefne's eyes was loosed upon him. "Tempt me with no more defiance lest I forget that I am a Lawman and strike you dead where you stand! Recollect that I also am of Viking stock, and tempt me not! Come down from the seat in which you were never worthy to sit; put off the cloak whose soldierliness you have disgraced; unbuckle the sword you cannot be trusted to wear."

It was as though the Viking blood in Ingolfsson were a tiger that had been wakened by a blow. Straightening with a terrible inarticulate cry, he leaped to the floor and over the fire, his sword gleaming in his hand before they knew he had drawn it.

But the Lawman's mightfull figure neither gave back nor moved; the blaze of his eyes neither weakened nor swerved. Tiger-like, the boy's eyes wavered and fell aside; he halted, uncertain.

Karlsefne's voice was as the voice of thunder: "I am over-chief in Vinland."

The flesh defied, but the soldier-drilled spirit heard. Slowly, Alrek put up hands that shook from passion and unfastened the clasp on his shoulder. With a soft sound the drapery fell and lay like a blood-pool around his feet. Slowly and yet more slowly, he changed his hold upon his weapon and extended it as it had never gone before—hilt forward.

Receiving it, the Lawman finished the sentence amid deathlike stillness: "Hereafter, wear no colour of soldiers, nor carry any more weapons than the beasts whose uncontrol you show. You, Champions of Vinland, get you another chief." Signing to Snorri to open the door he left the booth, the Icelander following.

Spellbound, the revellers remained without sound or motion, until Brand flung himself at the feet of Ingolfsson, thrusting into the brown hand one of his own knives.

"You foretold that you should kill me some time," he whispered, and bared his breast for the blow.

Those who saw the eyes the Viking bent upon him, believed that he would do it; it was seen that his fingers closed upon the haft. Then suddenly they thrust it from him with such force that its owner was thrown backward.

"Keep away," he said hoarsely. "Keep away!" With hands flung out to keep them off, he walked past them; and the door opened upon him and the night swallowed him up.

Part Third: The Huntsman's Prey
Chapter 15
About the-Fire-That-Runs-on-the-Waves

Where an arm of the big Vinland bay met a narrow river so far inland that it was hard to tell when bay ended and river began, the band of Vinland Champions was at work. Before the invasion of their young voices, the stillness of the primeval forest had taken flight; and the age-old trees had fallen victim to the greed of their young hands even as the old-world cities were falling before the might of the young North. On the river bank, sweating in the June sun, some of them were toiling to bring a great log down to the stream which was to float it on to the building place. Along the edge of the clearing, others were busy lopping from the fallen monarchs their green crowns. And the song of axes, ringing from the depths of the cool shade, told of conquests still in progress. This last task, however, was so nearly completed that in the intervals of their work the choppers talked of the untrimmed logs as though they were already in the form of a ship.

"What we stand in need of is red paint for that hull—" "If Gudrid will only make the sail—" "—so long as we get gilding for the dragon's head, I do not care—" "The dragon's head will be a weapon in itself!" "I expect the wild men will run at sight of it!" "There will not be many to equal this ship when it is done."

Lowering his axe to moisten his palms, Brand cast his bright impatient eyes around severely. "If ever it is done," he supplemented. "At this rate, it is the summer which will be finished first. If we had worked as we should have done, it would be completed now."

"Then why did you not work as you should have done?" laughed Ketil the Glib."

And Erlend, pausing to take a gauzy fanged fly off his neck, observed: "Certainly I think you ought to be the last one to make a fuss. Every time I have told you off to work on it, you have preferred to go hunting, or even help Karlsefne's men with the fence."

"What difference what I prefer?" the Red One retorted. "You are the chief; it is your duty to see that work is done as it is necessary."

The difficulty of answering that, left Erlend rubbing his plump neck in silence; and in the pause Brand returned to work, swinging the axe over his shoulder with a forcefulness which brought it near to smashing the head of a man who had just appeared in the underbrush behind him.

"It is my advice that you see what you are doing," the man spoke in a harsh voice which they recognised.

It was but faintly that Brand was apologetic as he glanced around. "Why do you creep up like a cat if you are not willing to risk something?" he inquired, and aimed another stroke.

But for once Thorhall the Huntsman did not dismiss them in contempt. Breast-high in saplings he lingered, regarding them with curiosity; when he had swallowed the irritation attendant upon dodging, he spoke politely: "My excuse is that if the leaves had not muffled my steps, I should have missed hearing tidings of great interest. I ask of you to tell me what all this is about a ship?"

"How does that concern you?" muttered Gard the Ugly.

Erlend, however, lowered his axe readily. That there should be any one willing to listen to the ship-plan who had not already heard it as many times as he would endure, seemed too good for belief. Feigning that his axe edge needed attention, he drew out a sharpening-stone; and while he plied it, he talked happily.

The ship, he said, was to be so long and so wide, with a fore-deck to shelter the provisions, but nothing so womanish as a cabin. The mast was to be that pine-tree yonder, and the sail was to be woven by Gudrid, Karlsefne's wife—that is, they were going to ask her to do it for them—and he thought the colours would be red and yellow, and the name would probably be *The-Fire-That-Runs-on-the-Waves*. It sounded very well as he told it; gradually Brand's blade also became silent, and Ketil and Harald and half a dozen others crept nearer to listen with kindling eyes that now and again shot triumphant glances at the Huntsman.

It was something of a triumph to make him who was usually so sneering listen so respectfully. When the recital was finished, he was even flattering,

"Certainly you are foremost among youths in energy! Where is it your intention to voyage when the fire is built?"

Gard, who alone had kept on working, gave his tree a resounding blow. "How does that concern you?" he demanded a second time. "You will not be invited to take the steering oar."

Now anyone can see that it is bad manners to insult a man who is complimenting you. Eight glances fixed the Ugly One angrily, while

Erlend spoke in mild reproof:

"What is the need of talking in that way?" he asked him; then, to the Huntsman: "If the ship is done before the summer is, we are going against the Skraellings. It comes like a piece of luck that there is enmity between us; otherwise I do not know whom we could fight."

"Since it is unadvisable to do what we want and fight Karlsefne," Brand added vindictively; and there was a murmur of acquiescence.

The Huntsman's eyes, trained to detect prey in the very darkness, went from one to another of the young faces. "Now that is a strange way to speak of the Lawman," he remarked.

The answers rose in his face like a covey of birds: "How else would you expect us to speak" "—after the way he behaved toward Alrek Ingolfsson—" "I think he deserves worse words—" "To my backbone I hate him!"

Parting the sapling screen, the Huntsman came out and seated himself on a prostrate tree, as though he found the field worthy of his attention. "Yet it is a foolish way after all," he began, "for only see how Alrek's bane has been Erlend's good fortune—"

The Amiable One's handsome brown face flushed. "We have given no thanks on that score, nor shall give any," he answered hastily. "I have seen Alrek only once since the day that bad luck overtook him, and then I dared not speak to him; but the first chance I get, I shall offer the chiefship back."

The murmur which greeted that was almost a cheer; only Thorall made a sound of dissent.

"Now do you act after the manner of boys rather than of men," he said. "Pity Alrek Ingolfsson you may if you will, but in so doing you should not undervalue the leader you have got in his—"

"Now what trap are you baiting?" grumbled Gard, at the same instant that Erlend interrupted.

"I beg of you to leave that and give us instead your advice how the Skraellings may be found. You, more than any other, know the secrets of the south country."

Some of the band drew breath rather quickly as their chief said that, and looked to see the Huntsman rise in offense; but again he surprised them. Re-crossing his legs and settling his broad back against a stump, he did nothing worse than to sit gazing away at the sunshine of the open. His voice was still amiable when at last he spoke:

"It would be useless to deny that many wonders may be told of the south country. I will begin by telling you that it contains bigger game than Skraellings and—his hand strayed to the deerskin cord looping his neck and ending in the breast of his stained green tunic—"and more valuable things than furs." He paused to cough, and no one moved for fear of breaking the spell. He recovered himself with a covert smile. "It may be that I will even do better than telling you. What should you say if I would show you the paths that lead to the treasure? I have some thought of going south myself this summer—"

Gard answered with an unexpectedness that made them jump: "I should say that we were rabbit-brained if we allowed you to lead us anywhere! Because Erlend is caught with your chaff, it is not proved that you can trap us all. I would not follow you a pace. To your face I tell you that I believe it was your hand that slew the Skraelling, though your body was further off than could be seen by a raven hovering in the sky!" He broke off and began making rune-signs with his fingers, as the small eyes turned toward him.

But it was not the Huntsman's anger which he had to reckon with, but the resentment of those who feared to lose a tidbit from their watering mouths.

"Hold your tongue!" "You know that is an old woman's story—" "For what purpose should you interfere?" "You are not all of us!" the mouths growled, while the elbows belonging to them made themselves felt admonishingly in his ribs.

Erlend spoke with unprecedented severity. "You have no right to show enmity toward a man who is behaving well toward you. You may take your choice either to go off by yourself or else sit down and keep quiet like the rest of us."

Nine times out of ten, Gard would have subsided in sulky submission; but this was the tenth time. Moving toward the bush whereon his cap and bow and quiver hung as on a rack, he sent the Huntsman a glance of such hatred as springs from fear.

"I choose the best company," he said; and gathering up his things, he slung his ax over his shoulder and slouched away. Those at work in the clearing refrained from addressing him when they saw the expression of his swarthy face; and those toiling on the river bank agreed with polite alacrity when he deigned to growl in passing that the day was unbearably hot.

It was, moreover, easier to assent to that remark than to deny it. Far and near, blue water and green land were ablaze with sun. When the Ugly One had forded the river and ploughed through the treeless meadows where Karlsefne's cattle stood knee-deep in the reed-fringed pools, his linen clothes were wet on his body; and he gave up a vague plan to spend his unexpected holiday in fishing.

"There will be fewer chances of the juice drying in my skull if I go to that wood place where the red berries grow," he decided, and struck across the grove toward the camp to leave his burden in the booth.

The camp was not so easily entered as of old, for now there rose around the twelve huts a fence of mighty logs with sharpened tops; and at each of the three gates there stood a man on guard. Yet neither was the watch strict enough to justify the precautions of Strong Domar who chanced to hold this post. With his joyous bellow, he promptly barred the passage with his spear until the newcomer had answered a catechism that began by asking his age and ended by demanding a list of the things he had eaten for breakfast. The Ugly One's patience had run as dry as the Strong One's power of invention, by the time he was permitted to make his exasperated entrance. Repulsing a pack of affectionate hounds, he stamped across the clover-sprinkled grass and would have stamped into the booth if he had not glimpsed through the open door a figure that had come to seem, almost as much as Hallad's, to belong to another world,—the gaunt form of Alrek the Exile, rummaging in the chest which had been his treasure-box in the days of his prosperity and still remained reverently untouched. Evidently he had known that at this hour the booth would be empty, for there was no watchfulness in his ears; he neither heard nor saw when his comrade stopped on the threshold and stood gazing at him.

It seemed to Gard that he had never seen so great a change in any one. From the unkempt brown hair to the black cloak that hung about his heels in rusty rags, he was as different from what he had been as November from June. His face showed the change most of all, for no glow of red was left in the brown, and his eyes were like cinders out of which the fire had died. From Gard's throat there burst suddenly a dry sob; and before the Swordless could move, his one-time follower was kneeling before him, clutching at his tattered cloak.

"Alrek! Come back and let me make it up to you. I cannot sleep at night with thinking what I brought upon you. I beg you to come back!"

When he had stood a while looking down at him, Alrek spoke with suppressed scorn: "Are you still trying to spend your money and keep it too? You do not want to bear the burden of your deed, yet you knew when you slew him that someone must suffer for it—"

"I slay him? I did not! I did not! I only told that lie—"

"So that I repeated it and became also a liar. I would not believe you though you swore with your hand on the Boar's head. You tried to take back the weapon which Brand gave, and the Skraelling resisted and you struck—with my hatchet which you had found where it dropped when I fell. I tell you I would not believe you though you took oath on the Cross. Let go my cloak and get away from me. If you had more than a dog's wit you would know better than to talk of making it up to me; you would know that I am disgraced forever. Let go my cloak before I kick you away as I would a dog." Freeing himself, he was gone. Gard reached the door only in time to see him pass out of the gate, Domar eagerly saluting; then the forest took him again into its silent keeping.

Thrusting his hands through his belt, the Ugly One leaned against the casing and spoke heavily to the hound that had left a noonday nap to come and fawn upon him. "It is likely that we have low minds as he says, Fafnir.... Yet, for all he says, we are faithful.... We do not lay it up against a friend if it happen that he ill-use us...." Seeing the bristles begin suddenly to rise along the hound's spine, he looked up to find Thorhall the Huntsman swinging past over the grass. He finished with a sound very like the one coming from the dog's great throat: "And both of us can tell a foe when we see him!"

Chapter 16
Proving that Alrek's Empty Hands were Full of Power

"A sail is not a small thing to ask for," Gudrid observed,—then raised a finger hastily as Erlend would have pleaded his cause. "You will put me in the most disobliging temper if you wake the child! As far off as the table I heard him crying, and came and found that it had happened as I suspected, that Roswitha had slipped out and left him. And he would not be quieted unless I got a cord and looped it around his feet and let him hold the ends and play at driving horses while he went to sleep!" She laid a hand on the Amiable One's silken sleeve, and another on the arm of Brand Erlingsson, and drew them gently off the dangerous ground out into the great back dooryard where the four households of Vinland sat in that contented idleness which follows the evening meal.

Roundabout the grassy space the stockade rose in grim foreboding; but the three gates opened wide upon shadowy grove and silvered meadow, and their three guards left their posts at will to bandy jests with their comrades at the long tables under the trees. Over the juice of the Vinland grape the men were lounging contentedly, while the cook-fires sank into red embers, and the moon sailed up from the tree-tops and floated free in the blue above them.

"It is certainly a night to bewitch one into promising anything! You choose your time well," Gudrid said with a little shake of the sleeves she was holding.

Brand moved his arm away abruptly; there was a limit to the liberties which even one who was asking a favour could endure. Erlend, however, was always affable.

"That will be seen if you grant our request," he answered. "It could not take you long, Gudrid, if you are such a weaver as you consider yourself. And I promise you that you should not lose by it, for we would bring you back a fine present from our journey. The ship is well begun now. We delayed about the sail as late as possible in the hope that Alrek would come back and do the asking for us. We know that his favour is no less with you because trouble has come on his hands."

Gudrid's face lost some of its wonted sweet serenity. "Alas, my kinsman!" she sighed. "I wish my favour could do something useful for him. I can tell you that even the child is full of longing for him. Time and again, when he hears a step that is like Alrek's, he turns his eyes toward the door and cries when it is not his kinsman who comes in."

The three walked a little way in silence; Erlend frowning perplexedly at the ground, Brand kicking the heads off the clovers in the sullen discomfort which this subject always aroused in him. Presently Gudrid came slowly to a standstill.

"I am going yonder to speak with Jorund, Siggeir's wife," she said. "I do not say that I will not do your weaving for you, but I must see first how it goes with my dairy work. In the meanwhile, I wish you luck with your undertaking."

"That is no worse than a promise," Erlend returned blandly, "for if you do in truth wish us luck, you will help us all you can." And they departed from her in high feather to tell their comrades of the boon granted.

Standing where they had left her, Gudrid pondered a while whether she really would cross the grass to the spot where Jorund and the two other Greenland women gossiped beside a doorstep, or whether she would go into the booth where Karlsefne sat with his chiefs over a chart. There was a matter of cheeses that she particularly wished to discuss with Jorund, and yet it would be interesting to hear whether the Lawman had seen any trace of Skraellings in his trip that day. Considering, she put a hand up to finger her amber necklace, as was her habit, and made the discovery that it was not there. She took her hand away with a gesture of impatience.

"Now will Karlsefne laugh at me, for he has always said that this would happen if I allowed Snorri to play with it! I remember that it was by the river, where I sat with him this afternoon. I gave it to him to bite, and then it happened that he dropped it to reach out for the boat which Biorn was rowing past; and Biorn called to me, and I forgot to pick it up again. Tch! What a stupid business! It is in my mind to slip out and get it before anyone notices that it is gone. The exact spot is known to me."

Going over to the western gate, she looked out toward the shining river. Less than a dozen trees dotted the space between her and the little knoll on the bank where she had rested, and the moon made it almost as bright as day. She gathered up her trailing kirtle with prompt decision.

"Any Skraelling small enough to hide in those shadows, is not big enough to be afraid of," she said, and passed out quickly with her firm light step.

That anything besides Skraellings might lurk in the shadows, she seemed to forget. Reaching the bank, she sent one look of admiration out over the radiant river, then bent her gaze to the foot of the tree among whose roots her fingers were swiftly feeling. To look up into the branches she had no thought whatever.

Yet not ten paces from her, Death lay along a bough,—Death in a tawny body with eyes like fire and a tail like a serpent, noiselessly lashing the air as the graceful form crouched for a spring.

The first warning she had was when a voice she knew spoke sharply from the shadows before her: "Lie down on your face!" The catastrophe came only a breath after the warning. As she threw herself forward, something leaped over her and met something else in midair. There was the jar of heavy bodies striking the earth, a crackle of breaking twigs, and the silver stillness was profaned by a horrible sound of snarling and long-drawn gasps.

Clutching at the tree-trunk, she tried to pull herself to her feet; but the two struggled on the very skirt of her robe and held her pinioned. Only over her shoulder she caught a glimpse of the giant cat, where it lay on its back, clutching in its claws the boy who knelt on its lashing body with no other weapon against the gaping jaws than his bare brown hands. It seemed to her that she shrieked, and it is certain that she swooned; for the next thing she knew, she lay on her face in the grass with Alrek bending toward her.

"It is over," he said briefly, and dragged a heavy weight from her skirt.

Pulling herself to her feet, she leaned dizzily against a tree, staring down at the strange monster that had the shape of a cat and the size of a hound.

"You choked him" she whispered.

The Swordless One nodded. "There was no other way. Last week I saw him leap down upon a deer and suck the blood from its throat. I thought then that my hands on *his* throat would be my only chance if ever we had dealings together. Yet I did not think that he would come so near the wall."

"It is God's miracle that you also chanced to be near it," she breathed.

"It is not all chance," he answered. "I have been here more than one night since they began to set the tables under the trees. Torchlight attracts other things besides sharks. It is like watching the red lights of the North, to watch the cook-fires shine on the branches; and when the men sing over their wine, the sound reaches out here so that it is almost the same as though I were among—" He came slowly to self-consciousness, and turned away and gave his attention to sopping with his ragged cloak the blood trickling from his torn limbs.

The sight of wounds brought Gudrid instantly to her capable self. "Tch" she said; and tearing her apron into strips, she put his hands aside and fell to work with skilful swiftness. For a little, nothing was said between them.

Yet it was not of the bleeding flesh that either was thinking in the silence. More than once, Alrek insisted that the work was done and tried to pull away from her and escape; and as her fingers flew, her mind went even faster, seeking some means by which to bind up the bleeding spirit as well. Suddenly, with her eyes on the empty brown hands that were yet so full of power, the way was opened to her.

Looking up from where she knelt beside him, she spoke courageously: "Kinsman, there is little need that I should tell you what you know by yourself,—that although Karlsefne would grant you a pardon in payment for this help, he would not give you his faith, which is what you want."

WITH NO OTHER WEAPON THAN HIS BARE BROWN HANDS.

Though he had not flinched from the touch of her hand on his wounds, the boy winced under her words. "I want neither his faith nor his pardon!" he said between his teeth. "I beg you to let me go."

"Not until you have heard me," she answered. "I have said this to show you that I am not speaking soft lies, but the truth. Now I am going to tell you more truth; the right-minded thing for you to do is to come back to the band and live as one of the men, until some twist of the thread brings your rank back to you."

She worked a while after that without looking up, for she could feel his glance beating down upon her. After a time he said huskily:

"It is of no use . . . I am dishonoured. . . ."

At that she raised her eyes with a hint of scorn. "It is true then that you did slay the Skraelling?"

He looked at her sorrowfully. "I had thought that you would believe in me, kinswoman."

"Why, so I did," she answered, "until I heard you say that you were dishonoured. For if you did not touch the deed, how could it stain you?"

Rising up, she laid her palms upon his breast and made him give her eye for eye. "Did it make your hands helpless because no sword was in them tonight?" she challenged him. "I think I have never seen weapons more powerful; nor was your eye less quick to see my peril, nor your heart less brave to help me,—nay, you were twice brave that you came with empty hands! Will you belie the courage and honour which you know you have, because you lack the red cloth and the bit of steel that are the runes which stand for them? If you will, you are not the Alrek Ingolfsson that I had wished my child would be like."

Looking into his eyes she saw a fire, long quenched, kindle and burn; and her palms on his breast felt the deep breath he drew; nor did he have any words of disproof. Discreet as she was bold, she asked for no words of assent. Leaving him, she went and tried to lift the forepart of the limp body.

"Get this upon your back," she said. "The Champions will become glad at this."

Silently he obeyed, drawing the dangling paws over his shoulder so that the long body hung down his back like a tawny cloak. Slowly he followed after as she turned and led the way toward the gate,—until they were within two spear-lengths of it and a hubbub of voices and laughter came out to them like a puff of wind. Then gradually his pace slackened, and she looked around to find that his face was flooded with painful colour.

She had the impulse to reach out and catch hold of him; but it was the impulse which came to her lips that she acted on, speaking as quietly as she would have spoken to her child had he ventured too near the edge of a cliff: "I do not know whether it is to your mind to enter the camp with me, but it is the truth that I shall hear enough of my foolishness without having you lead me home as well as save me. If I slip through this gate, as I came, will you use the east one, which is also nearer your own booth?"

Then she knew that she had guessed aright, for once more he moved forward, and under his breath he answered: "Yes."

By the time she had gained the centre of the green, she knew also that he had kept his word. Suddenly a joyous uproar went up from the tableful of Vinland Champions, and some were rolled off the benches in the haste of others to get on their feet; and crossing the moonlit space beyond them, she saw a soldierly young figure with a mass of yellow fur swinging from his shoulder—saw him and then lost him in the throng that closed, cheering, about him.

Her firm sweet mouth relaxed happily. "That is the first step toward a good outcome," she said. "If the Fates have any justice in their breasts, they will attend to the rest." And from afar she beamed brightly on the group, even as the moon above was beaming upon her.

Chapter 17

Showing How the Champions Broke a Thread in the Huntsman's Net

Over the boulders between which the narrow trail wound down to the building place on the beach, Thorhall's green eyes stared in surprise. After a three days' scouting trip, he had taken a roundabout way campward in order to get a glimpse of the vessel in whose progress he was interested, but it appeared that here was more change than he had anticipated.

Grown to all its graceful outlines the ship still waited on its rollers, high enough up on the shelving beach to rest immune from the whims of the tide. Around it and in it and under it the band worked as usual, whistling and wrangling amiably. But a pace to the right, where a rock humped through the gravel offered chance for a forge, there was a feature new to the scene,—a brown-haired young smith hammering vigorously at a bar of glowing iron. If he did not whistle as he hammered, yet he worked as steadily as though he had always stood there; and above the hum could be heard Brand's voice, speaking with eager deference:

"Alrek, is it your opinion that a bolt is needed here, or will it be sufficient to tie this plank?"

While Ingolf's son made brief answer between the strokes of his hammer, the Huntsman descended the rest of the trail in scowling cogitation. When the noise of question and answer had subsided, he came out suddenly upon the beach.

"Hail to the chief!" he said.

If the salute was designed to ask a question as well as offer greeting, it served its purpose. The brown-haired smith did not even turn his head; it was still Erlend the Amiable who answered to the title, straightening quickly to give back nod for nod.

"Thorhall! Now I am glad you are back to release us from our promise to let no one know the secret of the south country. Tell Alrek without delay about the treasure-land you have found."

There was delay, however, in the manner in which the Huntsman moved forward, paused to look at whatever addition in the boat interested him, paused to unwind a fetter of seaweed bubbles from his ankle, and finally seated himself on a boulder and studied the smith intently.

"Have you come back for good?" he inquired.

Before Alrek could speak, Gard—working behind him—answered by a jeer: "Some may have cause to think that he has come back for ill."

In the interests of peace Erlend raised his voice: "I beg of you, Gard, to turn fox for a while and go down the beach and dig enough clams to fill your cloak-skirt; so that we shall be fed, when noontime comes, without going back to the camp."

It seemed to the Huntsman that there was something suspicious in the docility with which Gard obeyed, somewhat as though he felt that he was leaving a sentinel behind him. The small eyes continued their study of the smith, as an angler might study a fish while he was considering what spear to employ. After a silence, which no one ventured to break, he spoke bluntly:

"The country south and west of here is inhabited by dwarfs. By that I do not mean merely people who are small-shaped, but the Northern race that is skilled in metal-work. You remember that Tyrfing was forged by such? Now I think you have yourself a sword—I ask you not to blame me! I did not mean to press that wound. But at least it serves to make plain to you whom I mean. In this land, they live in caverns of the gold-bearing mountains of which the south and west country is full. I think I have described to you their homes?"

The band answered even rapturously: "Never shall I forget it!" "No king's palace could—" "I wish Alrek had heard—," "Tell over about that one with the golden roof—" "Yes, good Thorhall!" "Yes!" "Yes!"

It did not appear that Thorhall heard them; as a hawk might watch a coop for the appearance of the chickens, he was watching Alrek's mouth for the first word of doubt.

None came. Slowly, the smith's blows became further between. Presently he rested his hammer on the rock and his elbow on the hammer handle. "That is of the greatest interest," he said thoughtfully. "And it comes to my mind to wonder if it could have been your dwarfs that Rolf Erlingsson saw when he was here with Leif the Lucky? He said those creatures were low as junipers, while Skraellings are most of them of good height—Yet he said also that they were poor and mean-looking! Your dwarfs must be as rich as Hnoss herself." He ended uncertainly.

But the Huntsman leaned back and smote his great knee with rare enthusiasm. "Now your comrades are right in valuing your wit above others!" he said. "Never had the thought come to me before, yet it is twice as likely as not. So cunning are they, that it would be altogether according to their custom to disguise themselves like Skraellings when they had the wish to spy upon strangers. It cannot be said that they have a fondness for strangers. You know that it was a dwarf who caused my wreck at Keel Cape?"

"No, that is a story you have not told us," the band cried eagerly.

He looked at them indulgently. "Now it is not much of a tale. The beginning of it is that I pried too deep into an old long-beard's secrets, so that I had to run for my life. I should be feasting on boar-flesh in Valhalla now, if I had not left the boat with its stem toward the water and the oars in the row-locks; for we were no more than out of sight of land when the dwarf-man reached the shore." He paused to glance around the group. "I suppose you remember how King Skiold blew upon a passing ship so that the boom fell over and killed Eystein where he stood by the steering oar?'"he inquired.

While they nodded impatiently, Alrek spoke in confirmation: "I believe that to be true, because once I met a Finnish sailor who could change the wind by turning his cap."

"You have seen so much of the world," the Huntsman said admiringly, "that it would become a great misfortune if you should lose this chance of seeing more wonders. To go on relating,—the dwarf used the same trick, though a little differently. Instead of blowing, he raised a gale only by flapping his cloak; and the water rose behind us in a sea-wall. I had often wondered what it would be like to be at the spot where a storm begins, and that time I found out. The water rose behind us with a roar, and swept us along past the entrance to the Vinland bay until we struck the Keel bar, and the boat went to pieces and the other three went down and Thor saved me. Hallad felt very unwilling to drown. You remember I had on only one boot when you found me? I can remember feeling something pull at the other so that I thought a shark had me and gave it a strong kick off. Now I know that it was Hallad clutching at it. I suppose it was because he got bitter that I did not help him, that he comes back to haunt me."

"That would be in every respect like Hallad," Brand said scornfully. "He was always wont to expect some one to look out for him. Thorhall, will you not let us see that chain again, that Alrek may get it clear before his mind what great things are in store for us?"

It appeared from his manner that there was nothing Thorhall would not do to oblige them. "Willingly," he answered, and straightway undid the bag around his neck. Dropping their tools, they came and stood around him in so cosy a circle that the Ugly One, far down the beach, took one fist out of the oozy gravel it was raking to shake it at them, and never knew that the other hand had turned up a clam until a jet of water struck him in the face.

If the necklace had sparkled in the gray light of the Wonderstrands, it may be imagined what it did here in the sun. Some of the gems encrusting it were blue as the bay before them, and some were like pearls in which a fire had been kindled, and some were like nothing less than stars. The Huntsman let Alrek reach out and take it for himself, and the young Viking drew a quick breath of pleasure as he felt its weight.

"Now I have seen booty taken from kings' palaces, but never anything to match this," he said. "It was without doubt the luck of our lives that we found you that day on the Wonderstrands. I remember overhearing you say to Faste that the reason you would not bring your news forward in the hall was because you did not want the chiefs to take the power out of your hands. I suppose the reason you share the secret with us is because we can give the help of a ship?"

Erlend looked up in surprise, the necessity of a reason for the

Huntsman's cordiality not having before occurred to him. The Huntsman looked out from under roughened brows, though he kept his words smooth.

"Now you do less than justice to your comrades' valour and accomplishments," he began. But he stopped as he saw one of Alrek's eyes close in good-humoured derision.

"When is it your intention to sail?" the Swordless brought him back to the point.

The Huntsman reached out and took back his chain. "That you must ask your chief," he answered; and spite was so evident in his use of the title, that the Amiable One hastened to answer before he could be asked:

"I think it will take about five days more to finish the outfittings, and then two to stock it with food. If a fair wind blows on it, we can surely sail on the tenth day."

Slowly Alrek lowered the hammer he had raised to return to his work. "It must be that you are forgetting the Skraellings," he said. "Because the hunters have seen nothing of them, proves little; Leif Ericsson's men saw nothing of the dwarfs until they were upon them. It is a sure sign, when a slain man is found lying on his face, that he will be revenged. Any day it may happen that they come; and if we should be away hunting gold while our camp-mates fought for their lives, we should get little fame though we brought back—"

The Huntsman rose to his gigantic height. "Are you the chief?" he snarled.

That was the third time he had pressed the wound; the flame in Alrek's cheeks sent sparks to his eyes as he wheeled.

"No, I am not the chief," he answered squarely, "but I have the right of every free man to make my voice heard in deciding matters, and I can tell you that it is going to be heard though you weave all the spells you know."

Perhaps the Huntsman did try to weave a spell, for he turned at once toward those who had so far obeyed his every move like snake-charmed birds. "What of you?" he hissed. "Will you put off this chance for treasure, to fight for the Lawman who disbelieved your oaths and showed disrespect to your high-seat?"

And the chorus answered him loudly: "No!"

And Brand made himself conspicuous by his fierceness. "Let the Skraellings cut blood-eagles in Karlsefne!"

It is likely that he wished directly after that he had kept still, for instead of praise, it brought him a look of scathing contempt from the Swordless.

"Now you talk like fools," the young Viking said, "to think to revenge private wrongs in wartime. He would be a fine soldier who because he had a grudge against his chief would desert in time of battle and leave his comrades to fight alone. No knife could scrape off this shame."

They quailed so under that, that the Huntsman's green eyes became like the eyes of a Vinland elk at bay. Turning where Erlend stood silent, he struck again:

"You then,—if you have any power who call yourself the chief!"

Erlend laughed uneasily; his handsome face had turned painfully red. "It seems that I was mistaken in thinking that that name belonged to me," he answered.

Crimsoning, Alrek fell from his hill of scorn to the valley of abashment. "Erlend, I meant no—no disrespect toward you." he stammered. "I did not mean to step out of my place—" He was obliged to stop, for Erlend's hand closed over his mouth.

"What are you talking about?" the Amiable One said sternly. "That is in no way what I mean. What you did was to step into the place that belongs to you." He exerted some of his strength to keep his palm where he had put it. "Listen to me! I am unfit to have the rule over anything. Never did it come into my head that leaving would be disloyal. I should have done a nithing thing which the saga-men would never have forgotten. I know of no better happening than that you should come into your own in time to save me." He stretched out his other hand toward the assembled Champions. "You shouted before when I said that I should offer the chiefship back. I shall think your tongues of little value if you keep them between your teeth now!"

The eagerness with which Brand offered the first cheer seemed designed to make up for his blunder of the moment before. He was seconded by a deep roar from Gard, who had just come up with his burden on his back. After that, there was no separating the shouts that came; and they banged their tools against the ship in lieu of swords and shields.

When the racket had subsided, Erlend turned back to the Swordless with a smile that had yet a touch of haughtiness. "I shall take it as an insult to my pride if you ask me to keep what so plainly belongs to you," he said.

After a while Alrek looked up from the trenches his foot was digging in the sand. "I will accept it gladly, if Karlsefne will allow me to," he answered; and there was more cheering and all hands were stretched out to him.

All but two, that is; shifting uneasily from one foot to the other. Brand and Gard the Ugly stood aside nor dared make any advances.

The Swordless himself hesitated when finally he came to them, and his face caught some of their embarrassed colour; but at last he put out his hand. They gripped it eagerly, and there was more cheering.

Under cover of it the Huntsman turned and stalked away; and what had been angry suspicion as he descended the trail, was angry certainty as he stamped up it.

Chapter 18
Concerning a Grim Bargain Between the Lawman and Alrek

"And I will seek out Gudrid, whose counsel is good in everything," Alrek said as he and Erlend rose from the morning meal at the table under the trees, "if so be you give me leave to be late to the work."

"If so be you need leave from me, you have it for anything you do," Erlend answered.

Then the Amiable One and all the Champions not bound to kitchen-posts took their leisurely way through the cool green forest to the waiting ship; and Alrek the Swordless turned in the opposite direction and strolled past the empty tables and groups of trencher-laden thralls toward Karlsefne's booth.

Before the doorstep small Snorri tumbled about in the clover, shouting lustily for his mother to come and play with him; which seemed to Alrek so good a reason for expecting her prompt arrival that he troubled himself to go no further. Stretching his lithe length on the grass, he changed the cries into laughter by butting the crier over on his back each time he opened his mouth; and the manoeuvre was crowned with immediate success. After a very little time, Gudrid appeared in the door, a piece of sewing in her hand, inquiry in her blue eyes.

"Oh! That is why he stopped screaming!" she said with an accent of relief. "So long as he is crying, I know that he is safe. Now you are a lazy-goer, kinsman, to be lying on the grass when everyone else is at work."

Shaking the clovers from his hair, Alrek sat up,—he would have stood up if it were not that the Frowner had crept across his feet. "I wait only to ask your advice, kinswoman, about a way to speak alone with Karlsefne. For two days I have looked in vain for a chance. I want to get his justice."

Coming out of the doorway, Gudrid seated herself on the step, and sat absently stabbing holes in her work with her bronze needle. "Justice is a heavy weapon to challenge unless you are sure that you stand very firm on your legs, kinsman," she said at last.

He answered: "I stand very firm," and the sternness of his voice was in singular contrast to the gentleness of his hand as he stretched it out to steady the Frowner in his upward progress.

Watching them, Gudrid's pucker of anxiety smoothed into a fond smile. "Now certainly I know that you are guiltless," she said. "I have only to see your behaviour toward the child to be sure of that." She did not continue her assurances for Alrek's mouth had curved into amiable derision.

"Why, that proves nothing," he said,

Gudrid's foot stirred the clovers. "I will give you the satisfaction of knowing that Karlsefne has made me the same answer. Sometimes it seems to me that a man's wit is like a bat, which disdains the good daylight to go about in, but must show its skill by finding its way in the dark! I can even guess that this very boldness of yours, which causes me to believe in you, will seem to the Lawman to be but another trick of your outlaw blood. Remember how they say in Greenland that a seal who tries to swim against too strong a current has often to turn back and be caught by the hunters. Kinsman, kinsman"—she put out her hand and pressed his shoulder—"be very sure of your strength!"

"Yes," he said, and bent his head to touch his lips to her fingers.

More than the words, the rare caress told her that his mood was no light one; and she warned no more. Rising, she spoke quietly: "I will do the only thing I can to give you help. Karlsefne is making the round of the meadows where the men are haying. I did not send his noon-meal with him—because I did not think it fitting that he should eat old bread, and the new is not yet out of the oven—but I had the intention to send it out to him by a thrall. Now if you choose you may carry it, and so get him apart for your purpose."

"That will serve well, and I give you thanks," Alrek answered.

Nodding, she went swiftly in to hurry the baking; and Alrek arose and setting the Frowner upon his shoulder paced to and fro in the sunshine that had settled over the camp like a golden spell, subduing the bustle of morning activity to a drowsy drone.

Lulled by the hum and the slow motion, Snorri's yellow head began to nod, swaying and bobbing until it rested heavily upon the brown locks of his bearer. Gudrid received a bundle of sweet warm limpness in return for the basket and skin of ale which she finally brought out.

"It is not unlike gathering up a jellyfish," she laughed as she took him.

But Alrek's smile was faint in response. He had been thinking as he paced, and the gravity of what he was about to do was full upon him.

"I give you thanks," he said a second time, gently, and left her.

Outside, in the great free world beyond the wall, it seemed to him that everything was coaxing for a smile. The reach of woodland into which the grove deepened was alluring with the song of hidden brooks and spicy with the breath of pines and hospitable with berry thickets, black and red and blue as the river to which the wood finally gave way. The elms of the bank flaunted wreathing grape-vines; the rushes at the edge sported dragonflies like living jewels,—flashing in the sunlight, the river itself was one broad smile. Dull anger took possession of him when he found his spirits too heavy to rise in response.

"It may be that I should become a coward if this went on," he murmured. "I was not any too quick about making up my mind."

And when, a little further on, he came to a finger of the stream and saw on one of the mossy stepping-stones a water-snake struggling with a frog which was only half swallowed, he made no move to release the victim.

"Better to die whole than to live crippled," he told himself grimly, and kept on his way.

It seemed a very short way now before he came to the broad sunny valley whose fragrant basin was strewed with ripening hay, which men were tossing amid jests and laughter as became a crop planted without toil and raised without care. Spying him, they shouted greetings of good-humoured banter; and he raised his hand mechanically, as his eyes roved to and fro seeking the blue-clad figure of the Lawman. It formed no part of the groups scattered over the valley, nor was it anywhere alone in the open—Ah, yonder it was in the shade of the spreading willow that rose solitary in the middle of the meadow! A smile twisted Alrek's lips as he moved forward.

"I wonder," he mused, "if it is a bad omen that I find him ready under a tree."

At least his luck was good enough so that he found the Lawman alone, sitting where two rocks made a seat beneath the willow; nor did he turn away when he saw who it was coming toward him through the sunshine. Over the fist upon which his bearded chin was resting, he watched the approach immovably.

When Alrek had come up and saluted him, he answered: "I shall know better how to receive you when I hear your purpose in taking this service on yourself."

"Gudrid allowed me to do this that I might speak alone with you," Alrek made brief explanation.

It seemed that Karlsefne's challenging gaze relaxed a little. "There is the greatest reason why Gudrid should wish to aid you," he said, "and scarcely am I out of your debt. I should be glad to hear that your errand hither is to ask a pardon from my gratefulness."

Sliding the ale-skin to the ground, the boy straightened proudly; but before he could answer, Karlsefne spoke on, unclenching his hand to pass it before his eyes:

"As you came toward me, you looked even as your father looked when he came to the Assembly Plain to hear the judges condemn him for his crimes; and now as then I hate the deeds and love the doer so that the two feelings are like two fires raging within me." Taking away his hand he showed the stern beauty of his face aglow with feeling, as some lofty rock under the touch of a red Northern light. "I beg of you to throw yourself upon my mercy. Defiance has gathered like drift-ice in your breast, shutting out all that would come through to bring you good. Break from it before it shuts you in forever. I beg of you to yield and give me the joy of trusting you again."

Ending, his deep voice held a note of yearning love that made the boy's heart swell strangely in his breast. He had to speak hardly and shortly in order to be able to speak at all.

"Hard is it to know how to answer, for you offer me what I do not need. I came here to get your justice. If I broke your order, I deserve an evil death; if I did not, it is my right to live unshamed. If you know that it is I who slew the Skraelling, I ask you to have me placed against this tree and shot."

As a Northern light fades from a rock and leaves no warmth behind, so the glow faded from the Lawman's face. "Do you like it so well to die?" he asked.

"Sooner would I die than live as I have lived since your doom,"

Alrek answered.

Silence settled heavily upon them. When a great fly boomed out of the sunlit space and hung for a wink of time at the boy's ear, the sound seemed thunder-loud. But at last the Lawman spoke, his voice as hard as clanging iron:

"Not many men would go so far as to deal with me by force and overbearing, but you play the game as well as is to be expected of your father's son. Though I am sure of your guilt, you are right in believing that I am not sure enough to take your life when you lay it in my hand. And since it is proved that I am not sure, I may not punish you at all. It is well played. There are two choices before you,—the one is to let matters stand as they are now, so that your life is safe and the future is yours to redeem your credit in; the other is to get back your honours as you demand, with the condition that if ever this case comes again before my high-seat and so much as a feather's weight more of evidence is given against you, I shall declare your life to be forfeit."

The long safe way is seldom the way of youth; one must have travelled far and fallen often to make that choice. The young Viking answered without hesitation: "I will take my honours and the risk."

Rising, the Lawman made him a chiefs salute. "So be it," he said. "Tonight in the hall, even as I took them from you, I will give them back before all eyes. In this and whatever follows, it shall be as you have chosen." He lifted his hand as the boy would have thanked him.

In obedience to the gesture, the chief of the Champions halted and bowed before him in silence; but his brown head was carried high when he walked away, and his eyes were two radiant suns of hope.

Chapter 19

Relating the Adventure with the Men of the Forest

Like dew on a fresh berry a silver gauze of mist lay over the fresh day, and the birds' answers to the sun were still far-between and sleepy, as Hjalmar Thick-Skull came out of the bayward gate and sauntered down the meadow-slope to the beach. Of late he had given over fishing in the river for fishing in the bay, where a flat island lay like a lily-pad on the water. With his tackle on his shoulder and a song on his lips, he came down where his boat was waiting and sent a careless glance around the horizon. Then the song was changed to a cry, and he went back up the slope in long bounds, deafening the man at the gate as he burst in upon him.

"Skraellings! Around the long point they are coming in shoals!"

Staring, the guards stammered the words after him; but an Icelander who was passing caught them up with a roar and started on a run for Karlsefne's booth. The hounds lying under the trees leaped up and raced beside him, barking; out of every door that he passed uncombed heads were thrust, shouting questions. In the draft of a breathy the news had spread like fire.

Reaching the chief of the Champions where he stood in his doorway, he sheathed the sword that he was polishing with so much pride and took a step toward the gate; then, bethinking himself of a quicker way to verify the report, he turned and made for a great pine-tree standing on a little knoll. With a run and a leap he went up the trunk, and clambered from one great bough to the next as though they were steps, until his head came out through the last layer of needles.

The Thick-Skulled had spoken truly. The bright plain of the bay was specked with dark skin-boats; eastward around the longest of the capes, they were like a dark tide rolling in upon the land. Something seemed to tighten in the Sword-Bearer's throat; and he was about to turn and let himself down swiftly to the bough below, when his eye was caught by a movement up the river bank, the passing of something dark athwart the green of a bush. Drawing his head down under the green roof, he hung by his arms, gazing intently. There was no open anywhere for the Thing to cross, and just that dark streak flitting through the bush-tops told nothing—and yonder was a white streak behind it! And beyond that a dark one! His hands tightened on the branch so that it crackled. Unless motes were dancing before his eyes, the bush was alive with the fleeting wisps, shapeless, soundless, but bearing down upon the camp. His heart seemed to turn over in his body, and he dropped like an ape from limb to limb.

Descending into the camp was like falling from the peacefulness of a masthead into the roar of the ocean. Wrangling and stamping about, the men were struggling into their shirts of ring-mail. Hammering on their shields to get attention, the chiefs were shouting orders. Bearing messages and distributing weapons, thralls rushed back and forth, followed by the yelping of dogs and the screaming of bondwomen from the doorways. It took main force on the part of the Champions' leader to get them aside and make them understand that it was not the enemy before them against whom they were to turn their blades.

"The number of those in the boats is so many times greater than we, that no men can be spared from the front," he concluded swiftly. "To find out what these Things are, and defend the gates against them, will be our share. And it is likely that much depends upon our getting into position without loss of time. Olaf and the Hare, I appoint to be my messengers; and I want to give Olaf a message now, while the Hare goes after my ring-shirt." Drawing the Fair One aside, he spoke forcefully in his ear until he yielded reluctant obedience and darted away in the direction of the pastures.

It may be admitted that reluctance was in most faces when a little later they turned their backs upon the uproar of the camp and stole out into the loneliness of the grove. Over their shield-rims, their eyes rolled apprehensively as their chief spread them into a broad crescent covering both gates, and led them warily forward. When the first high ground gained failed to reveal anything, they jumped at the idea that he had been mistaken in his spying, that the sun had dazzled his eyes, that what he had seen was but a line of low-flying swallows. They were urging it eagerly at the very instant that he was justified.

All at once it was as though every twig in the undergrowth ahead had turned into a bow, and the bow had shot an arrow at them. The rattle on their iron helmets was like the pelting of hail. If their bodies had not been armoured, they would have gone down as grain before a scythe.

Alrek's voice rang out strongly: "Skraellings! Under cover! Make ready for their charge!"

In a flash they had leaped backward, behind trees, bushes, boulders, anything. The sunbeams broke into jagged lightnings as the bright swords sprang from the scabbards.

But no flesh appeared from the thicket beyond. The grove remained empty and silent as a grave. It shattered the stillness startlingly when Njal screamed:

"If they are Skraellings, why do they not come out and show themselves?" Then, pausing for reply, he added another shout: "Those in the boats have landed!"

From the camp behind them swelled a din of Skraelling yells answered by Norse battle-cries, enforced at regular intervals by the hoarse barking of the leaders.

Njal cried shrilly: "*That* is the way in which Skraellings fight! These are trolls! Let us get loose from their net and turn back."

Only Alrek's uplifted spear stayed the rush. "I think you will find my weapon sharp if you do," he warned. "Whether they be men or trolls, we must take heart as we can and hold them from the gates. I urge you all to grip your swords and manfully hold your ground. They can not do you harm while you are under cover."

But it was not their bodies that they were afraid with, but their minds which had raised up spectres. The sunlit space seemed all at once a cloak for shapes of horror. Dreading with every breath that the cloak would be drawn aside, their eyes shrank from what it might reveal as their flesh would not have shrunk from knives. They spoke as with one voice:

"This is jugglery and trickery only! We will go back where men fight against men!"

"You will not," spoke Alrek the Chief between his teeth. But even as he said it, he saw the hopelessness of expecting to hold them quiet, and made his last move. Throwing aside his spear he leaped out in front of them, brandishing his sword. "If you must move—move forward!" he cried. "You are nithings unless you follow my fate!"

Even then it is not certain that they would have obeyed if Brand had not redeemed much by promptly advancing to his chiefs side.

"*I* follow!" he shouted; and Erlend and Gard were only a step behind him.

At that, the rest turned like sheep and came after, dodging from cover to cover, clambering, stumbling, ducking, jumping, lashing their courage with a fury of yelling.

Before the cold stillness had chilled them again, they saw the foe. Rising from behind boulders, slipping around trees, gliding through bushes, came creatures with gaudy-coloured bodies naked as earthworms, and bristling black heads feathered like monstrous birds; so like and yet so hideously unlike the Skraellings, that Gard cried "Forest devils!" and the band turned with one impulse for flight. But behind them, across the ground they believed they had cleared, in the space between them and the gates, stretched another line. Out of their frenzy of fear, sprang a frenzy of hate; and they leaped upon the creatures with drawn swords and the others met them, brandishing stone hatchets.

For a time it was a wild game of dodging, with death as a penalty for awkwardness. Whether they were men or demons, the hatchet-bearers showed a dread of steel which kept them hovering beyond arm's reach whenever they were not darting at an opening. But at last the hungry swords tasted the flesh they craved, and their wielders' shouts of triumph stirred the rest to exulting excitement.

"We will wipe them out like flies!" Alrek cried.

Even as the words left his lips, he made a startling discovery. Laying low the figure in front of him, he glanced over his shoulder to make sure that there was no one behind him; and turned back to find a man standing on the very spot that he had cleared. Striking him down, he whirled to see another hideous shape in the place that—a breath before—he had made empty.

At the same instant, Brand cried wildly: "It seems to me that they must rise from the dead since no matter how many one kills, there is always the same number confronting him."

Into Alrek's throat came the sense of choking which had seized him in the tree-top when he beheld that dark tide rolling in upon the land. Something seemed to mock in his ear: "It will be like killing the flies of the air one by one!" Then blotting out this came the wonder that Brand's voice should seem so far away; and he risked a glance around the grove, and his heart stood still.

In their mad charge, the Champions had broken their line; until now no two fought shoulder to shoulder but each stood alone, his back against a tree or a rock, a circle of hatchet-men around him. Even while their chief looked, three Champions were tempted into making dashes which carried them still wider apart. It would not be long before they would be lost to one another's sight, and the swarms would close in around them—He opened his mouth to send forth a frantic recall.

But the fiend-cunning of the black eyes watching him seemed to read his purpose on his lips. Suddenly the shapes around him raised an unearthly howl, which those on all sides caught up and kept up until the din was like a wall through which no sound could come or go.

Alrek's hands continued to fight from instinct, but his brain became numb. The horror long hovering over him settled lead-like upon him.

"They are trolls!" he told himself; and his strength began to ooze out of him in icy droops.

He did not turn his head when above the din rose a roar even more appalling than the yells. When the creatures around him dropped their weapons to fly frantically this way and that, he remained standing where they had left him, plucking at an arrow which had pierced his arm below his mail. Gazing wonderingly, he saw a huge milk-white bull with mouth afoam and eyes like red flame come snorting out of the thicket, pausing now to paw up the earth before him, now to throw back his horned head with a terrific bellow.

Then, in a flash, his wits came back to him. Memory reminded him that his own lips had bidden Olaf drive the animal from the pasture for their re-enforcement; and sense told him that—even as he had hoped it might happen—the hatchet-bearers had taken the apparition to be the white man's god, come to his people's aid. Leaning back against the tree, he began to shake with laughter which was half weeping.

It seemed to little Olaf the Fair that there was something peculiar about the bearing of all the Champions, when a while later he met them back near the gates. Their greetings came in voices of unsteady shrillness, and their eyes were strangely bright. He said, pouting:

"I do not know whether you mean that the fight went against you or that you got the victory, but I warn you that I shall dislike it if you upbraid me for fetching the bull there so soon. I have got scolded enough by the men in camp. It appears that they spent the first part of the battle in running away from arrows, and they had only just got to work with their swords when I came through with the Bellower and sent the Skraellings flying to their boats. I thought the Icelanders would have thrashed me. I shall not take it well if you also find fault—"

Their shaking high-pitched laughter drowned his voice.

"We will try to excuse you," Alrek said in a drawl that was still rather unsteady; whereat there was another outburst; and they swept clamouring shrilly through the gate.

Inside the wall it looked at the first glance like a trading day, with shining shirted groups scattered everywhere across the green, each man flourishing some kind of weapon while he talked at the top of his great lungs. But at a second glance the resemblance was less, for no fair-time mood was in the mien of Karlsefne and his chiefs where they stood under the council-tree, wiping the paste of sweat and blood from their faces; and here and there men were writhing on the earth while the sharp knives of comrades cut arrow-heads out of their flesh. And suddenly the likeness ceased altogether, as four men came through the bayward gate, each pair carrying between them the body of a dead Icelander. Silence touched each group the four passed; and through the hush, Karlsefne's voice clanged out like a bell, vibrating with wrath:

"I wonder at it that you have control enough left to hold your teeth over your tongues when the dead are borne past! Up to this time you have run mad like wolves that have tasted blood. I suppose the strange thing is not that you have broken the peace-bands at last but that I was able to hold your beast-cravings so long in check. It is all I can find to lessen the gall of my defeat."

So long as he stood before them, fixing them with his eyes like swords, they remained silent; but the booth door had no more than closed behind him than the excitement leaked out again. In a little while it was running as high as ever, as the men boasted of the great feats they had been on the verge of achieving, and vowed exulting vows about what they would do at the next meeting. It was plain indeed that the peace-bands which had held their swords in their scabbards were snapped forever.

Chapter 20
Showing How the Huntsman Bagged His Game

The next day, under a storm-charged sky, the camp lay storm-charged. In the doorways, men stood talking restlessly, with now and again an outburst of sharp wrangling; out on the green, others refreshed their knowledge of spear-throwing; around the tables, still others plied sharpening stones upon axe blades which would never be used for trees. Setting forth with their last load of outfittings for the ship, the Champions shouted a battle-song in the face of the muttering thunder:

And as the foeman's ships drew near
The dreadful din you well might hear;
Savage Berserks roaring mad.
And Champions fierce in wolf-skins clad.
Howling like wolves; and clanking jar
Of many a mail-clad man of war.

"Let us not try to settle in another place until we are off our feet on account of old age," Brand spoke with energy. "Karlsefne says truly that Norsemen are too wolf-like to endure it when they are penned like sheep. Let us live like Fridtjof the Bold, with the ship for our hall and the sky for our roof."

"And strike where we choose," Erlend added. "There is no good reason why we should never make warfare against any but dwarfs. I have heard it said that fine things are to be found in Ireland—"

"And in England—" "And in Rolfs country—" "And the East—" cried a chorus; and each began at once to urge the merits of his particular choice amid an eager clamour that was interrupted only by their arrival at the path which wound down between the boulders.

There, however, the interruption was final. Glancing over the boulders, the first boy shrieked: "What! "the second one: "Where—?" then, all together, they roared: "The ship!" and tumbled one over the other and out upon the beach. Save for the rollers which lay where they had left them, not a vestige was to be seen of *The-Fire-That-Runs-on-the-Waves.*

Some of them cried: "The tide!" while others cried: "Skraellings!" And one detachment went swarming up the trees of the bank to sweep the length and breadth of the bay; and the other, drawing swords, raced along the shore to explore the crescent curves with which it was scalloped. But neither party brought back any news to the third group, that seemed as yet unable to do more than stand staring at the rollers and ejaculating. The clue came from a peevish voice on the bank above them:

"I think you have little reason to boast of your eyesight if it has not yet told you that I am here." Above the rocks a thin face rose, wanly white in the glare of the lightning that was shivering across the sky.

Shrieking: "Hallad!" the band whirled up the beach like wind-driven sand; and their chief had taken several steps to follow them before he pulled himself up and turned around to face the intruder firmly.

"This looks to be an evil happening, if anyone thinks you to be of importance, which I do not. No fault of ours is it that you were drowned. Why do you not stay under the water with the other dead men?"

The colourless lips showed a curl. "Dead men! Do you think that if I had a ghost's power I would allow Thorhall to bind me, and stay up here to be made a gazing-stock—"

"Thorhal!" Alrek repeated; and he came a step nearer, so that Brand and Erlend and the Ugly One, pausing in their flight to look around for him, took courage and came a little way back. "I do not know why it did not come to my mind sooner that the Huntsman had a hand in this matter. Yet he would scarcely be able to do it alone."

"There was little need to. After such a stirring-up as took place yesterday, men might be expected to be ready for any fun. There were no less than twenty of them with him, and their spirits scraped the sky. Had it not happened that their humour was so good, it is likely they would have killed me when they found out that I had followed them here, instead of doing no more than tie me so that I should not give the alarm too soon. They left at daybreak. I managed it to pull one arm free and slide down on the ground and get some sleep, but the thongs are like red-hot irons upon my ankles. Fetch your knife up here as quickly as you can, and free me."

Alrek was taking another step toward him, when the expostulations of his comrades brought him again to a standstill. "If you are not drowned, what is the reason?" he inquired.

The claw-like hands beat the rock fretfully. "One reason is because I never fell into the water. Whether Thorhall told you so or not, I was not with him when he was wrecked on the Cape. Two days before that, he had deserted me in the south country because I was overlong in getting back to the boat after an exploring trip. It had happened twice before that I was rather late, and he pretended to think that this time also it was carelessness. It is the truth that I had hurt my leg and could not get back earlier. It took me three weeks after that to make my way here. By that time he had got home and told everyone that I was dead; and he took it so ill that I should belie him that he would have made it the truth if I had not run away. The time you saw me climbing out of the ice-hole which I had fallen through, was one time when I barely got away from him. After that, however, it was less difficult; for when he saw how you ran from me, he was willing that I should stay alive so long as I remained dead. The reason I have the appearance of a dead man is because I can not, more than others, get fat and colour-full on fish and raw eggs and water." He broke off impatiently: "Is it not clear to you yet, you blocks of peat?"

The Champions looked at one another doubtfully. It sounded reasonable, and yet—

"You have always made it a point that your foster-father, Biorn, should help you out of difficulties. What is the reason that you did not go to him with this one?" Brand demanded.

At least, Hallad's temper was alive; it sparkled in his hollow eye-sockets. "As well go to Biorn's dogs because they have teeth! It seems to me that you have been fooled enough to be able to understand that the glance of Thorhall's sly green eyes has more power in it than Biorn's blundering fist."

Though it is a strange thing, it is true that for the time being they had forgotten the ship. Of one accord they started forward as it came back to them.

"You know how much of the story is true—" "—what he did intend—" "Give us your opinion whither he has gone—"

"I—will—not—tell—you—one—thing—until—you—come—

up—here—and—release—me," Hallad's thin lips bit off his decision.

Alrek set forth his counter-condition. "If you will allow me to prick your skin with my sword so that I see blood come out of your flesh, I will believe that you are not a ghost."

One of the skeleton-like arms was stretched over the rock before he had finished. Drawing his sword, he went forward and scratched a cross upon it; the lines were instantly blurred with blood. Without more ado, he climbed up the bank and around the boulder and cut the bands, and the ghost returned his hand-clasp with most unghostlike pressure,—after which he sank down upon the bank to rub his chafed ankles.

"It was like his spitefulness to tie them so tight," he whimpered. "And besides this, I am starved. If there are any tidings you want to know, you would better be quick about asking, before I take myself where I can get some curds and bread."

From their answer it appeared that they had several things to ask. "Tell us where he is going with our ship—" "Tell us how much truth there was in the dwarf-story—" "No, about his purpose in sharing his secret—"

While one of Hallad's hands continued rubbing his ankles, the other one scratched his head. "Now if he has gabbled about dwarfs, it does not appear to me that he did share his secret. Certainly I did not see any dwarfs, nor hear of any. One day when Thord and I had staid with the boat and he and Swipdag had gone far inland, he came back with a gold chain; and they both said that they had seen Asbrandsson, the Broadwicker's Champion whom Snorri Godi outlawed from Iceland many years ago. Where a story passes through many mouths it is likely to become somewhat chewed, and it may be that they were lying then also; but they told how Asbrandsson related about a settlement which white men from Ireland had made further south. He dwelt among them, he said; but it seemed that they lived too quietly and sang too many priest-songs to please him well, and therefore he would like to come to Vinland if so be that Karlsefne the Lawman would admit a fellow of his bad fame. As a present to get him goodwill, he sent the Lawman a chain by Thorhall; but that Thorhall put it to other uses is easily guessed. It is less easy to know whither he intends taking the ship. It may be that he has gone south; and it may be, as I said before, that the story of White Man's Land is also a lie."

They loosed mouthfuls of angry denunciations. "But why take so much trouble to make up a story—" "What aid was it expected that we should give?" "Why did he not give the message to the Lawman?"

"Now are you so witless that I do not wonder he found pleasure in fooling you," Hallad snapped as he got painfully upon his feet. "How would he have got booty if he had told Karlsefne, who would have forbidden fighting between the settlements? It is likely that he made up the dwarf-story because he thought it unadvisable to trust you with the truth. And the reason he stood in need of you was because it was necessary that he should have some one to fight under him, and until yesterday the men would not listen to him. It is not certain, however, that he would not have taken the ship alone anyway, after Alrek got back to the chieftainship. It appears that the Sword-Bearer's power is greater than the Huntsman liked."

Alrek straightened from the boulder against which he was leaning, and put out his hand as Hallad turned and planted a foot higher up the path.

"There is one question more—about the man who killed the first Skraelling. Do you know who that is?"

Pausing with one foot up and one foot down, Hallad looked at them strangely. "Do you not all know?" he asked at last.

They cried in one triumphant breath: "It was the Huntsman!"

"The Huntsman?" Hallad repeated, and amazement was too plain in his voice to be mistaken. After a minute, he grasped a down-hanging root and pulled himself up to the next step, and would have departed without another word if Alrek had not reached up and clasped him around the ankle.

"What do you mean by that?" the Sword-Bearer asked him. "If it was not Thorhall, who was it? I shall not let you go until you tell me." He gripped the raw ankle harder than he knew; Hallad gave a great gasp of mingled pain and anger.

"I have not as yet said too much, but I think I need not spare you since you challenge me! It was you yourself; my own eyes saw you. It happened that I was hiding behind a wood-pile in the hope that I could slip into one of the booths and get a weapon for myself. I saw you fall, and I saw the Skraelling lean over you and make a grab at your sword; whereupon you leaped up and buried the hatchet in his head, and he toppled over into the hollow—Now there is no need of your looking at me in that manner! I would not have spoken if you had not dared me. I will say nothing about it anywhere else. I—"

But it is not likely that Alrek heard; he stood as though turned to stone, gazing at the speaker out of horror-widened eyes. "You saw . . . me . . . do it?" he breathed.

Looking down upon him, Hallad's face was red and regretful. Although it was plain that no great boldness was in his spirit, it was also clear that his mind was not ill-intentioned. "A great mishap was this that you should ask me," he stammered. "I suppose it was the knock on your head that caused you to forget. But I thought that—Of what use was it to dig it up again! I had the intention to say nothing to any one. It seems most likely to me that the Huntsman put a spell upon you; his eyes are more than equal to it. You need not be so sensitive as to blame. So long as Karlsefne has pardoned you and given you your honours back, your fate does not depend on this "

Through his speech, the voices of Gard and Brand and Erlend broke shrilly: "You flung back his pardon!" "You bought your honours—" "You pledged your life on your guiltlessness."

Out of stiff lips, Alrek confirmed it: "I pledged my life."

Hallad turned, wailing, and ran up the bank and into the forest; and the four comrades were left to face it together.

Chapter 21

In Which Alrek Sword-Bearer Faces Death

Brand lay on the ground, shaking with great sobs; and Gard squatted, half sitting, half kneeling, his huge hand crushing to powder the shells he had picked up without knowing what he did. It spoke much for the lessons the two had learned that neither offered plans of rebellion or suggested escaping through the loophole of a trick. Dully, the Ugly One spoke to Alrek Sword-Bearer, where he stood as though turned to stone.

"Alrek, say that the lie did not make it any worse for you. Let me have that to remember."

Alrek answered without turning his eyes from the sullen water, wrinkled now with raindrops: "It did not make it any worse for me. . . . I did you wrong in believing you guilty."

"Why was this so? If only we could have got away on the ship, it is not likely that you would ever have found it out," Brand sobbed passionately.

"I wish that I might have had one voyage on *The Fire*," Alrek said slowly. "More than anything else I like to stand on a ship when the wind is blowing under her wings, and feel how I am being carried forward into happenings of interest. I thought I had many such voyages before me, and that I should accomplish some things which the saga-men would think worth talking about. And I believed that I should die in a manner to leave honour behind me. Never did I guess in the deepest hiding-place of my mind that I should be put to death for causing the defeat of my chief—" His voice broke in uncontrollable revolt. "I can not believe that I was such a madman! It must be as he says, that the Huntsman laid a spell upon me. I can not believe that I would so lose my sense!"

"It is often said in Greenland that the Huntsman's eyes are capable of turning curses on whomsoever he will," Gard said heavily.

"It was seen by everyone that he felt hatred against you," Brand added in his unsteady voice. "Ever since he saw that you had better sense than others, he has wished you evil."

Lifting his head out of his hands, Erlend spoke bravely: "It does not seem likely to me that Heaven would deal with you so unfairly. It is foolish to hurry ahead of one's luck. I have hope of getting rid of this trouble because of Karlsefne's love for you. Of his own accord he offered you mercy—"

"And I chose justice," the Sword-Bearer reminded him grimly. "Do you not see? I may not even ask for a pardon. It is a jest of the Fates,—a nithing jest!" It may be that his voice would have broken again if a great roar of thunder had not cut him short; the rapping of his fists was sharp upon the boulder at which he was staring down.

But, gradually, the control which seldom slipped far out of his grasp was gathered again into his hands. When once more it was quiet save for the rustle of the rain on the leaves, he spoke steadily: "I recollect how my father used to say that a soldier had a low mind who could not trust the chief he had chosen enough to follow him through some moves which he could not understand. Now it is certain that I can not see why Heaven has the wish to turn this against me, but I am not going to be so poor-spirited as to make a fuss about it. Let us go back now. Waiting will not help if death is fated to me."

It showed again the discipline they had gone through that although Brand's throat was rent anew with sobs and Gard's face became as white as was possible to its swarthiness, neither had any resistance to offer. Rising heavily, they followed their chief up the bank and along the wood-paths which always before they had travelled plan-laden and light-footed with hope.

Because of the rain, the tables under the trees were deserted; what sound of voices there was came from Karlsefne's booth. In wordless understanding the comrades walked toward it; only as they passed the empty booth of the Champions, Alrek spoke:

"It is likely that the band is loitering somewhere in the woods to talk about the fate of the ship. I am glad it happened so, unless they come back just as I am being fetched out. I give it into your hands, Erlend, to see that they do not behave foolishly."

Out of his tear-stained face, Erlend's honest blue eyes met his chief's fairly. "I will see that you have your way," he promised.

Alrek, walking in the middle, stretched out his arms and put one around Erlend's neck and one across the shoulders of Brand'; and so they came across the rain-beaten green in silence. At the threshold, they paused to grasp one another's hands strongly and long; then the Sword-Bearer pushed wide the half-open door and they went in.

In the dignity of his high-seat Karlsefne sat, holding council with his chiefs. Snorri of Iceland occupied the seat of honour opposite him; and on his left was Gudrid, and on his right the burly and big-hearted Biorn Gudbrandsson, his hand still patting the shoulder of his foster-son who sat on the footstool before him, munching bread as though he would never leave off. That the excitement of Hallad's return had subsided, however, was evident since it was of something altogether different that the Lawman was speaking as the Champions entered.

"You need not get afraid that I undervalue your power of fighting," he was saying to the triple rank of sullen faces that lined the walls. "That one Northman is more than equal to one Skraelling—provided he can get within arm's reach of him—I do not deny. It would be a strange thing if Northmen could not fight, after the practise they have had! What I want to get into your heads is that you will never face them one to one, nor one to five, nor yet one to ten; but that they will always come in herds and shoals and swarms, as when the Lord sends a plague of creatures on a country. For I think it is as a plague they have come upon us. Here the All-Father had spread a Heaven-like land, and stored it with food and property for all. Here He brought us in peace to take as free gifts whatsoever we would. It might have been a never-emptied treasure-house for all our race, a peace-land for Northmen of all time. The trouble that has come into it is of our own bringing, brought in our blood as vermin are brought in ships. The hand of the Lord is against us; it is my advice that we bow before His wrath. Natures such as ours have no right to softer things than Greenland cold and Iceland rock. It is my ruling that when the spring comes we shall go back over the ocean."

Like a mighty bell tolling for a death, his voice echoed through the hall. For a time they seemed awed against their will; and here and there a man made the cross-sign. But presently the heavy voice of Hjalmar Thick-Skull was heard saying to his neighbour:

"A Viking voyage, comrade,—that is what it means! A Viking voyage from Norway before the grass comes up again!"

Quickly those around him caught up the words: "Viking voyages,—that is true!" "Hail to the Lawman!" "Ho for Norway!" "For England and the Danes!" "Ho for warrior-life again!" "Hail!" "Hail!" "Hail!" Their swelling cheers vied with the thunder pealing overhead.

To Alrek Ingolfsson, waiting with blood-marked lips held between his teeth, further delay was unbearable. Suddenly he made a step forward where Karlsefne's gaze would fall upon him from the high-seat. As he had expected, the Lawman spoke with frozen courtesy:

"The Chief of the Champions has a right to his place in the council. I give him greeting and ask him to come forward and take the place that belongs to him."

The Chief of the Champions went forward, but he did not take his place upon the bench. Standing before the footstool of the high-seat he spoke briefly:

"I thank you for your greeting, but I came to claim no right, but to render the pledge I made. It has happened that Hallad saw me kill the Skraelling, in that time which I lost out of my mind." He could not bring himself to meet Karlsefne's eyes when he had finished, but turned away and laid a hand on Gard's shoulder and hid his face on his arm.

Above the hubbub that rose, two voices made themselves heard, Gudrid's crying distressfully: "I do not believe it!" and Hallad's wailing: "Why do you betray yourself?" Then the Lawman spoke in a tone that silenced them both:

"Let Hallad tell what he has seen."

It is but justice to Hallad to say that he would have refused if he had dared; and not daring, he mingled his recital with pleas for mercy. But the terrible evidence had to come out at last.

When the tale was finished and the teller had sunk down in tears upon Biorn's footstool, Alrek lifted a face that seemed pale because such black misery was in his brown eyes.

"I ask you only to believe that when I said I was innocent, I did not know that I was guilty."

After a while the Lawman bent his head. "I believe that," he granted. But he granted no more; and his closed mouth was like a line graven on stone.

It was as though the wind had brought a breath from a glacier through the warm summer day. No man's heart but felt the chill; and gradually the whispers, even the motions, ceased and the room was as still as a Greenland winter.

Slowly the Lawman rose and stood before his high-seat, an awefull figure as the light fell coldly on the chiselled beauty of his face and the iron of his hair and his beard.

"I believe that you did not know your guilt," he said, "but I believe also that you acted out your true nature when you did the slaying. What Hallad says about the Huntsman's spell-power is child's talk. No spell was on your father when he committed such crimes, and none was on you when you attacked the Skraelling on the Cape of the Crosses. I think now what I have thought always,—that you struck this blow in the Berserk madness which is like poison in your blood; even as you struck on the Cape, even as you would strike again though the welfare of a thousand men should hang on your peacefulness. The cause of a hundred you have already defeated because I pardoned you once; I dare not risk sparing you again. You offered me your life. I take it. There is a gallows ready where a pine-tree stands by the Skraelling's mound. It is my command that Lodin and Asgrim and the men beside them, put you into fetters and take you forth and hang you there."

Gudrid fell back in a half-swoon, and through the hall swelled a murmur like the rush of a rising wave. But the Lawman stretched forth his hand, the flash of his eyes like the gleam of ice in the moonlight; and the wave fell, sputtering and hissing, until it had smoothed out into silence.

Alrek Ingolfsson spoke only once, when they had finished pinioning his arms. "Like a sheep-killing dog!" he said under his breath; and his head sank beneath its weight of shame, and he did not raise it again but went away without looking into anyone's face.

With the opening of the door came in the noise of rushing wind; then the door closed upon it, and throughout the length and breadth of the hall there was no sound save for the half-sobbing breaths of Gudrid struggling back from her swoon, and no motion until all at once the Lawman sank into his high-seat and covered his face with his mantle.

It is a strange thing that at the moment Karlsefne's eyes were covered, the veil fell from Gudrid's. Lighting on Hallad, her glance rested there dully for a while; then all at once it sharpened to more than ordinary keenness. Rising from her seat, she levelled one slender arm at the cowering figure.

"I think you did the slaying yourself!" she breathed.

At Hallad's recoil and Biorn's bewildered query, the Lawman looked up questioningly; and Gudrid put her other hand upon his shoulder and shook him in her passion of eagerness.

"Will you allow your kinsman to die because of your slowness? Promise life to this coward and he will confess guilt. I see it in his face."

But the Lawman had no need to speak, for this sudden focusing of all eyes upon Hallad lay bare his secret like a bolt from the skies, and struck him down at Gudrid's feet.

"It was the Huntsman who made me!" he screamed, and grovelled shrieking it over and over. Gradually, his foster-father gathered from the broken words that the Huntsman had made it the one condition of his remaining alive and coming back to camp after his own departure, that he should break up the peace by a man-slaying; and he had used the stone hatchet, which he had stolen from Alrek's unconscious body, because that chanced to be his only weapon when a moment later he came unexpectedly upon the Skraelling.

But only Biorn, his foster-father, stayed to hear more. At the first cry, Karlsefne had crossed the booth in three strides and vanished through the door, and Gudrid had followed him, and the three Champions. And now the maids and the throng of men turned from Hallad and streamed out into the clearing air and across the green toward the Champions' booth, beyond which a knot of people stood under a pine-tree from whose outreaching bough dangled a grape-vine noose.

The loop was empty, for Alrek Sword-Bearer stood below, freed of his bonds, his head bent over Gudrid's hands; and Karlsefne was speaking with a quiver in his deep voice:

"I will make this up to you a hundredfold. My smiths shall build you another ship and a finer one, and you shall furnish it from my stores and have the rule over it and take it where you choose. My own son shall have no larger share in my property and my honour and my love."

Alrek lifted his brown eyes, glowing golden like the sunshine filtering through the rain-washed air; through lips not yet steady, he answered: "The debt will be more than paid."

Suddenly Karlsefne laid a hand upon his shoulder and spoke so that all around could hear:

"I will call no voyage unlucky which has brought me to know a man with so high a mind and so brave a heart. I look on this as a proof that good intentions will get the victory over evil in the most unexpected way; and I will take it as an omen that the good which I have tried to get out of this land for my countrymen will come to them yet in some way which I can not now see. We will go back neither bitterly nor despairingly, but giving thanks for the good we have received and cherishing hope for the future. Now, it is my offer and will that every one in hearing shall come tonight to the best feast I can make, in honour of the Chief of the Vinland Champions and his men."

It is a good thing that he intended to stop there for not another word could be heard, such jubilating and weapon-clatter went up; and the Champions took their chief upon their shoulders and bore him back in triumph, followed by a cheering train.

Epilogue

These are the rest of the sayings about this expedition.

All the ships came safely to Greenland except the vessel of Biorn Gudbrandsson, which was driven out into the ocean that stretches between Greenland and Iceland and there came into a worm-filled sea. By the time Biorn had discovered their danger, the ship was worm-eaten beneath them; and it was seen that the only way was to go down into their long-boat which was coated with seal tar. Since the boat was too small to hold more than half of them, they cast lots for the places; and it fell to Biorn and half of the men to go down in safety, while the other half remained with the sinking vessel. No one thought of making any fuss about this save the boy who had come with Biorn from Iceland. When he saw the others go down into the boat, he began to whimper:

"Do you intend, Biorn, to leave me here?"

Biorn glanced up at him absently. "So it seems," he answered.

The boy began to sob. "You did not promise my father that you would part from me like this, when I left Iceland with you," he said. "You promised that we should always share the same fate."

Biorn made the men a sign that they were not yet to cast the boat loose. Big-hearted kindliness was in his voice as always.

"So be it," he answered. "It shall not remain this way, since you are so eager for life. Do you come down here and I will go up on the ship."

It may be imagined that the young Icelander lost little time obeying. When he had come down, the chief went back upon the vessel; and the two parties separated. In time, the men of the longboat came to Dublin in Ireland, where they told this story; but it is believed by most people that Biorn and those with him went down in the sea of worms, for they were never heard of again.

It is but little more than this which is known about the fate of the Huntsman and his followers. One time, traders came back to Greenland with the tale that Thorhall had been shipwrecked in Ireland, and that his men had been made thralls of and grievously misused, and that he had met his death there. No one ever got other tidings than these.

Better luck went with Thorfinn Karlsefne and Gudrid and those in their following, for the summer after they had landed in Greenland they went home to Iceland, and lived there in great splendour and happiness; and many famous men and high-minded women have descended from them.

Best luck of all, the foretelling of Karlsefne has come true; and despite delays and hindrances, his countrymen have found a peace-land and a never-emptied treasure-house not only in Vinland the Good but in the whole of the new-world country which those who are alive today call America the Free.

Randvar the Songsmith

Yet onward still to ear and eye
The baffling marvel calls;
I fain would look before I die
On Norumbega's walls.
—John Greenleaf Whittier

CHAPTER 1

A man's foes are those of his own house
—Northern saying.

In the old world over the ocean the storm of the Norman Conquest was raging, but no rumble of it reached across the water to the new world and that oasis in the wilderness which men call now the lost city of Norumbega, but which was known in those days as the town of Starkad Jarl. There in the primeval forest the breath of October was a silver elixir in the air, and the morning breeze carried only the notes of hunting-horns. When half a dozen young Norsemen came galloping down a tree-arched aisle, their talk dealt with no greater matter than the latest freak of their *jarl's* freakish son.

"It is seen from the hoofmarks that he has not turned aside. We need not wait long to over take—"

"Suppose he should not want to turn back—"

"Heard I never of a *jarl's* hunt that began by hunting the *jarl's* son!"

"He was quiet in riding out of the town with us; what caused him to spur ahead?"

"Only that he had a whim to be alone, as he is apt."

"I remember how he broke away once last spring."

"It may be that this fall he has done it once too often. Starkad is wroth."

So the talk ran on until the tall leader drew rein, signalling to those behind him to check their pace.

"Slowly!" he said. "Yonder is his horse tethered. It would ill become us to ride upon Starkad's son as though we were charging a boar."

"Even though we shall be as ill-received as if we were," the youngest of the horsemen added with a laugh of some uneasiness.

The leader smiled tolerantly. He wore on his long body fine clothes of scarlet leather, and on his thin lips the semblance of a perpetual smile. "Everything grows big in your eyes," he observed. "There! I think I see gray cloth among those green bushes. It were best to ride on until we come where he may see that there are too many of us to withstand; then one of us can dismount and approach him with the message."

The youngest of the riders laughed again, this time somewhat sarcastically. "No one is better fitted to take that task on him than yourself, Olaf Thorgrim's son. For what else did you spend your fosterhood in France but to get smooth manners to use in rough places?"

"Yes, yes! By all means, Olaf is the man!" the others chorused, a hint of malice in their promptness.

If Thorgrim's French-reared son read the sign, it made no difference in the confidence of his bearing. He answered that if it was their wish he would certainly undertake the errand, and immediately swung from his saddle as gaining the green bushes, they came into view of the wearer of the gray kirtle.

Prone on the earth's broad bosom the young noble had thrown himself and lay with his head pillowed on his folded arms, a figure of utter abandon. Only at the clink of spur and bridle-chain did he turn upon his side and fling back a mass of blood-red hair from a face of startling pallor. What look came into it when he beheld the horsemen, they were not near enough to tell. By the time Olaf stood before him, his teeth were showing a snarl.

"Well, dog, you have tracked your quarry," he said. "No wonder your trainers set store by you! What is the rest of your master's bidding?"

Olaf laughed lightly. "Certainly, *jarl's* son, you should be a scald; you speak so glibly in figures. Starkad sends you orders to turn back and take your place again in the following."

Starkad's son drew himself slowly into a sitting posture. Then of a sudden his body was convulsed with laughter,—laughter mocking as the mirth of a devil.

"Who am I that I should stand in the way of the *jarl's* will?" he gasped between his paroxysms, and shaking with them rose to his feet.

But when he had come where the youngest of the riders was holding his horse in waiting, either the young man's ill-concealed uneasiness, or some reminder growing out of it, caused his mood to change. With his foot in the stirrup he lingered, sobering until his face betrayed even the pinching hand of dread. Vaulting into his saddle, he spoke to his attendant without looking at him.

"I see they have turned my hound Sam into the pack, though the wound on his foot is still unhealed. Will you, Gunnar, do one thing for me? Separate him from the rest and bring him to me in a strong leash."

"In this as in everything you have only to speak to have your will," Gunnar gave the prescribed answer absently. It was not until he felt the foot of a friend behind him that he awoke to the mockery of the phrase, and glanced up appalled.

But the exasperation lightning at him did not strike. Amid silence, breathless, storm-charged, the *jarl's* son took the reins from him, wheeled his horse and rode back up the leafy path and out of sight.

In a moment Olaf was spurring after Starkad's son, but the remainder of the escort appeared to be in no great haste to follow. First they waited while Gunnar examined the buckle of his girth; then they turned to scrutinise two figures just emerging into the open from a brush-hidden trail a few paces on their right.

Two young stags browsing the scarlet berries under the pines would scarcely have looked more natural to the scene, for one was a savage of that new-world race which the early Norse explorers called Skraellings, with hair as black as freshly turned leaf-mould, and a shining naked body of the hue of an oak-leaf in November; and the other, in the deer-skin garb of a forester, with uncovered locks reflecting the sun, was a descendant of the Vikings themselves and showed untamed blood in his handsome face as he raised it to look ahead at the horsemen.

The red man the courtiers passed over indifferently, but on the white one they were beginning favourable comment when the call of a distant horn cut them short. Wheeling hastily, they gave their horses spur and rein, and passed up the shaded alley like a whirl of frost-tinted maple-leaves.

Upon them, the young forester made but one remark. He and his companion had halted as at a parting of the ways, and his hands were busy detaching a deer's-horn cup from his belt.

"I would travel a day's journey to see a horse run like that," he said. "Often I dream of feeling one between my knees, and waken because my enjoyment is too real for a vision."

The young savage's throat gave out a sound of comprehending, and his friend did not wait for a longer response. He had filled the horn from a flask of porcupine-skin that hung around his neck; now he raised it aloft.

"To you, comrade! May your arrows and your swallow's always go the right way. *Skoal!*" he toasted, then refilled the cup and handed it to the other, who answered in the same Northern tongue, though haltingly.

"To my brother! May he drink much of his enemies blood—as much as his friends have drunk of his wine. *Skoal!*"

It was not seen that the Northman made any grimace. While his mouth showed no blood-thirstiness, its hard line bespoke one used to grim ways. He said carelessly:

"My foster-mother has the gift of double sight, but even she has never seen that I have enemies. How came that notion into your head, brother?"

After the manner of his kind, the Skraelling was deliberate in answering, letting the purple juice trickle slowly down his throat; but he finished at last, and nodded in the direction of the departed courtmen.

"There went some of the young men who follow the head of my brother's people. They are more bright than white fire-bugs with the gifts they get for their friendship. My brother is also young—a warrior—the son of a warrior—yet he lives apart in the forest, with a handful of women and old men—gets himself nothing. It must be that he has enemies among his people."

The young forester shrugged his broad shoulders. "No gifts would I buy at the price Starkad Jarl asks, comrade. My little foster-brother Eric is page to his daughter; I know the lot of those who follow him. When he gives the sign they go to roost, whether they are sleepy or not. When his priest rings a bell they say their prayers, even though it break in at a time when cursing would come more easily to them. It is not allowed them to enjoy any sports that he sets his face against; and they drink no lower in the cup than he gives them leave. May illness eat me if I would ever tame myself to run with such a pack! That a man like my father should have been willing to lie quiet in a woman's net is something I shall never be able to comprehend. I understand him better when I see how he built the tower with the lower part left open so that the wind could blow on him all the year round and help him to forget that he was under a roof."

Once more the Skraelling's deliberate speech was delayed, this time by a baying of deep-voiced hounds rumbling up out of the distance like thunder. Following it, the pack streamed past—stragglers bursting from the brush behind them to skirt them with extended noses or jostle between them, leaving froth-flecks on their sides—and hard after the hounds rode the hunting party, led by a band of green-clad pages winding gilded horns. With the leisureliness of one whose pride forbids a display of curiosity, the Skraelling set his eagle face again over his shoulder; and his companion, who had started to remark upon the scene, gave up with a shrug the attempt to make himself heard against the blaring.

The din passed at last, and on its heels came a colourful train—stately old priests and chieftains gravely discussing the hunts of their youth, high born maidens with shining uncovered locks, and matrons whose lace veils floated cloudily from their moonlike faces, stocky young thralls bent under hampers and wine-skins, and towering leather-clad guardsmen bearing bright spears on their shoulders. With the hoofbeat of the prancing horses deadened by the matted leaves, they went by as lightly as shapes in a vision, each for an instant illumined as he passed where a shaft of sunlight fell through a rift in the arching tree-tops.

As the first pair of the noble maidens reached it, sitting gracefully erect in their saddles like gilded chairs, the forester motioned towards them.

"The one with her face turned away is the *jarl's* daughter, Brynhild the Proud. It is said that she is worth looking at, though it has never happened to me to do so."

If the Skraelling looked at her, that was all the notice he vouchsafed. It was not until the last maiden had gone by that he was stirred to interest.

"That is the great *sachem* that the sun now shines on?" he asked.

"That is Starkad Jarl," the Northman confirmed; and even as he said it, the old man with the jaw, like iron and the beard like steel had passed on into the shade, and the light was playing on the comely group that followed, revealing foppish secrets of gay embroidery and golden buckle.

"Here are the battle-twigs we saw a while ago," the young forester added. "I wish I knew if any of them is Helvin, the *jarl's* son."

The Skraelling answered but one word. "Blood!" he said; and while the young men remained in sight his eyes rested on one in garments of gray, whose bowed head was hooded by hair of the very shade of clotted blood.

Looking after the young courtmen, the forester seemed to lose all who followed. When leaves had blotted out the last guard's broad brown back, and the music of the horns had dwindled to a silver speck in the gray silence, he spoke musingly:

"Take Helvin, now, if you wish to judge what metal comes of Starkad's forging. It is said that he was born with the wanderlust upon him, so that his every breath is a panting to take ship and travel over the sea-king's road wheresoever the wolf of the sail might choose to drive him. But because the sons that came before him are dead, and the only other heir is a maiden, his sister, it is not allowed him to risk his life. It may be they will find out that they have cherished the scabbard and rusted the blade,—they say that the fire cased in his flesh has given him an unlucky disposition."

The savage's black eyes gave forth a sympathetic flash, though his training in repression kept the feeling out of his voice. He said calmly:

"A day will come when it will be over. The old man cannot live forever. Already he has passed so far beyond the timber-line that nothing grows on his scalp."

The Northman shook his head. "Starkad's death will bring Helvin no nearer what lies at his heart; he is oath-bound to take the rule after his father,—so full of fear are they lest quarrels over the inheritance gnaw at the root of the *jarldom*. But I will say that I think his rule will prove to be a good thing for the town, which is now in danger of becoming more lifeless than a bone-heap. From all I have heard of his dislike of making a show of himself and his love of free ways, I have good hopes of him. It has often been in my mind to take service under him when he shall get the leadership. For Starkad I have no respect what ever. It is told that when he was young he was called Starkad the Berserker, and had the most hand in every Viking voyage and man-slaying; but now that the sap has dried in him, and he has put on Olaf the Saint's religion, he expects all men to live like monks."

The Skraelling gazed reflectively in the direction of the vanished cavalcade.

"Truth to say, the young braves of my race do not feel much love for the white man," he said, presently. "He comes among us as one who comes among animals—driving them out to possess himself of their feeding-ground—dealing with them only when he wants profit out of their hides. The gray-heads give us counsel to live in peace with the settlers of Norumbega. On the four trading-days of the year when they let us into their walls, they trade us useful things for our furs. But those of us whose teeth are still firm in our jaws do not like it to be led in as white men's cows are led in to be milked, then turned out to pasture, the bars put up behind them."

Straightening, he stood a bronze image of wounded pride. The young forester, as he bent to fasten one of his *moccasin*-strings, looked up at him understandingly. The softening feature of the Northman's face was his eyes, deep blue as an evening sky, under level brows, broad and dark. When the thong was tied, he put out a hand and rested it on his companion's bare shoulder.

"Judge not, brother, all of the white race from the behaviour of one overbearing old man. It seems to me as if your people and my people should dwell together like sons of one father. Our hands are equally open to a friend, and no less hard-clinched against a foe; and you do not surpass us much in freedom and fearing nothing. When it has befallen the other white men to see the wonder of your woodcraft as I have seen it, and to be sheltered and fed by your hospitality as I have been, there will be much awanting if they do not hold you as high in honour as I do."

Unbending gravely, the born heir of the forest laid his hand upon the breast of the forest's adopted son.

"I know good of you; I will try to believe good of your people," he said. "Come back with me now, brother. The lodge of the *sachem*, my father, is open to you. Always open to you."

A second time the Northman shook his head. "That cannot be, comrade, for I came up here to learn a trap secret from an old huntsman, and having got it, I must hasten back and put it to use before I forget it. Do you on your side bear in mind, when next you paddle your bark-boat near the island, that the tower will offer heartier welcome to none than to you."

His hand fell from the bronze shoulder to the bronze palm, and with a strong clasp the two men parted,—the red man to melt into the russet shades beside them, the forester to go forward in the wake of the hunting party.

Had it blazed its path with axes, the cavalcade would scarcely have left a plainer track. Wherever foot and hoof had failed to print themselves on the path of leathery leaves, there was always the clew of a bruised lichen or a fern with a broken spine. Swinging along easily, mile after mile, the forester devoted his superfluous breath to humming scraps of melody and his alert eye to reading the fantastic runes. Here a bleeding tangle of wild grape-vine stretched out plundered hands. Yonder a long golden hair, floating like fairy gossamer from a low-growing limb, showed how the forest had exacted *weregeld*. Still farther on, a patch of flattened moss and ploughed-up earth told sly tales of a horseman brought low. When he came at last to the place where his road branched westward from theirs, he yielded the runepage with regret.

That he might overtake any of the company did not occur to him. His attention was centred in his song, gradually becoming articulate and rising melodiously from under his breath. It broke a word in two when he caught the hoarse snarl of a hound in the thicket ahead.

As well as though he could see through the intervening leaves he knew the hideous landmark that lay before him,—a pond which the Skraellings called by a word meaning "the black pool," be cause some sinister combination of soil and shadow gave its water the appearance of being dully thickly black. Tradition added that rather than enter it, a fleeing stag would let his pursuer kill him on the brink. If any hunted thing had been brought to bay there now, the finish might be worth seeing. Quickening his step, the young Northman leaped the stony channel of a dead brook and swept aside the screening boughs.

Set amid frost-blasted bushes and leafless barkless tree-skeletons, the Black Pool met his gaze; but it was no four-footed creature that fought for life at the black water's edge. Above the brush rose the gray-clad shoulders of the young courtman with the blood-coloured hair. Rearing as tall as he, one of the great hunting-dogs had sprung upon him; while one hand strove to draw his dagger, the other was struggling to hold foaming jaws from his throat.

To see his peril was to will to aid him; and with the forester, to will was to act. But even as the impulse thrilled him, a strange sensation blotted it out. With his first forward motion, he was seized by a sudden whirling madness as though he had stepped within the ring of a whirlpool and was being sucked into a black abyss of horror.

It lasted but an instant. Battling against it, his fingers clutched instinctively at his knife-hilt, missed it and closed instead upon the blade, and the smart of cut flesh brought him to himself.

But in the time that he hesitated, the courtman's hand had freed his weapon and plunged it into the straining throat; there was a death howl, the hiss of spurting blood, and the danger was over. The great body relaxed, stiffened, sank heavily out of sight between the bushes, and the young man stood wiping his blood-bathed face upon his sleeve.

Bewilderment and shame claimed the forester. He with a lion's strength in the girth of his chest and in his long sinewy limbs—he whose coolness had cheated Death a hundred times—*he* to falter when a man was in jeopardy of life before him! It was beyond belief.

He saw without caring that the courtman seemed all at once to become aware of another presence, and turned and espied him. He heard without heeding a peremptory order to approach. All that he was conscious of was a desire to get away and fight it out with himself. Raising his hand in apology, he stepped backward, pushed between two tall bushes, and let the wiry brush spring to like doors behind him.

As he drew clear of the branches a silvered arrow sped above them, so well aimed that it severed a lock of his hair. He caught his breath with a short laugh.

"I forgot that high-born men do not take it well to be disregarded," he muttered as he plunged into the undergrowth.

What would he have said if the shaft could have whispered as it whistled past that—back under the frost-blasted bushes—Starkad Jarl lay murdered, and that he of the guilty blood-coloured hair believed the forester had witnessed his deed!

Chapter 2

No tree falls at the first stroke
     —Northern saying.

"One touch of a certain three-cornered leaf," the forester reasoned as he moved along the winding trail, "is able to make a man's flesh change colour and swell over his eyes like a wild hog's fat. More power lies in the earth than simpletons think of. What would be wonderful about it if such water should breed a vapour befogging to the wits? Not the wits of all men, perhaps—it was seen that the courtman had his about him—but those of all who have not Sigmund's strength against poison." Reasoning relapsed into mortification. "It goes hard to be taught that I am one of the weaklings. Troll take the Pool!" For a while his track over the soft leaf-mould showed that his heels ground deeply.

Presently he made an effort to crowd the incident out of his thoughts by taking up the broken thread of his song, and reeling it off with a dogged energy that sent the words far through the silent forest and set its echo-heart athrob. They were brave words, telling the brave old tale of the wooing of Fridtjof the Bold; perhaps they would have charmed away his ill-humour if they had not been cut short.

Parting like gold-embroidered tapestries, two yellow-leaved bushes a little way ahead disclosed another courtman from the hunting train, a young man magnificent in scarlet leather clothes of distinctly un-Norse make. After a critical survey of the figure in deerskin, he lifted the forefinger of one gloved hand,—a gesture that had upon the forester the effect which the scarlet dress would have had upon a bull.

"Fellow," he said blandly, "I have to tell you that your voice has had the good luck to please a noble maiden's ears. Follow me that she may gratify her curiosity."

Akin to the motion of his finger was a perpetual slight smile moulding his thin lips. The forester took note of that also, and felt antagonism become a deep satisfying force within him. Coming slowly to a halt, he picked his answer with drawling de liberation.

"Fellow, if you had not the good luck to be foreign to the forest, I would make you unpleasing to a noble maiden's eyes. As it is, I have to say that to see me following you would be more apt to provoke curiosity than to gratify it,—and you may take that as best suits you!"

The stranger took it with the utmost quietness, observing as though to himself that it was surprising there should still be places where a churl thought he had the right to choose when he was commanded; but while he was saying it he was stepping from the bushes. Now he drew his sword from its jewelled sheath.

The gleam which the steel sent through the glade was reflected in the forester's face. He made cordial haste to pluck forth his hunting-knife.

Glancing from that short blade to his own long one, the courtman hesitated an instant; then he laughed softly at himself.

"It is no lie about Norse habits that they stick to one like iron in frosty weather!" he murmured. "Almost I was in danger of treating the matter as a combat between equals."

Having escaped that danger, he wasted no more time on preliminaries, but delivered his first thrust. If his opponent had stood upon ceremony, he would have been disabled by a pierced right arm.

Luckily it. was the school of emergency that had given the forester his training. Though a smothered word betokened surprise, his instant leap backward carried him lightly out of range, and yet not so far out of reach but that his knife was able to strike up the other's point and take advantage of the opening to land a stroke upon the tasselled breast. A buckle turned the blade away, but the profanity of the contact could not be denied. The courtman lowered his weapon for the purpose of removing his gold-stitched gloves.

"I see now that I shall have to let off more of your hot blood than I thought," he remarked as he tucked the gloves under his belt. "Since you *will* have it—"

Driving suddenly past the other's guard, he drove his sword into the deerskin shoulder, would have driven it through, indeed, if the bite of the knife into his wrist had not momentarily relaxed his grasp.

The forester recovered his balance coolly.

"It will then be a fair bargain if I let off some of your breath," he returned, and straightway asserted the one advantage he had foreseen to offset the difference in blade-lengths by leading his adversary a round of gnarled roots and hidden hollows and tangles of creeping things.

As a trout knows the rapids, his feet knew the snares; but to the stranger it was like walking in fetters. What with the distraction of watching his footing and the difficulty of aiming, two out of every three thrusts went astray; while for every lunge that went home he got a wound in return. Twice his foot twisted on a hidden stone and he measured his length on the ground, plastering pine-needles and earth to every bloodstain. Twice he tripped over a root and fell headlong and almost into the arms of his jeering opponent. That the combat was between equals, there could now be no question.

That there could be any doubt of his ultimate victory, however, did not appear to enter into the courtman's reckoning. After each fall he merely became a little more quietly determined, came on with a little more glitter in his ice-blue eyes. His unshaken assurance exasperated the forester at last; when he saw a chance to end it, he seized the opportunity promptly.

At the next lunge, instead of springing aside he took advantage of a hollow behind him to duck suddenly, so that the blade hissed like an out-leaping flame above his head. Then, before the other could recover, he sprang upon him. Seizing his sword-wrist in an iron grip, he forced it aside, tore his own right arm free from the clutching fingers, and raised it to strike.

His arm rose,—but it did not fall. In the very instant of aiming, a cloak flew between him and his mark, enveloping him head and shoulders, smothering him head and face. Muscular hands followed the cloak, pinioning his elbows and dragging him backward. Through the folds he caught a babble of exclamations; above them a girl's anxious voice calling, "Is he wounded?" and a man's rough tones answering dryly, "Only enough to spot his clothes, *jarl's* daughter."

Jarl's daughter! The forester had left off struggling—he understood that it would be foolishness in that grasp—now his wrath gave place to disgust. This was a pretty trick of the Fates, who had already snatched the fruit of victory from between his teeth, to follow it up by delivering him over to the upbraidings of an hysterical girl! Sullenly he gazed before him when at last they plucked off the cloak.

The first thing he saw was his little foster-brother in his gay page's livery, just picking up the courtman's plumed cap; but the sight did not improve his temper for he found that the boy avoided his glance of greeting. His brows drawing together, his gaze moved on over the picture.

It was a maiden's following, certainly. The rugged men-at-arms surrounding him were far out numbered by the slim pages who made a green hedge around the wounded favourite. Bright against the dark background, groups of maids and matrons rustled and fluttered. Only one figure in the scene had composure, a girl standing a few paces ahead of the others, erect and motionless as a stone column against tossing trees. It was her stillness that drew the forester's attention to her curiously; then, looking, he forgot curiosity, for got his recognition of her for the *jarl's* daughter, felt only the thrill of her beauty.

Long of limb, long of throat, she was nobly tall, her eyes but little below the level of his own. The habit fitting close the flowing curves of her body trailed heavily behind her, and a velvet mantle dragged from jewelled clasps; but her broad sloping shoulders bore their weight as lightly as her proudly poised head held up its great braids, hanging far down the purple folds like cables of red gold. No power had the sight of bared blades and struggling men to deepen or pale the exquisite colour of her face, or shake the pride of her beautiful mouth. In their high spirit, her clear gray eyes were Valkyria's eyes. Gazing at her, his heart leaped in his breast; he understood, for the first time, why a sea-wolf of a Viking might lie quiet in the net of a woman.

For the first time, also, he knew envy of his foe. Brushing aside the pages, the courtman advanced now, the long end of his mantle drawn up gracefully over his shoulder to hide the stains of his tunic. It was maddening to see how fit he looked to bend before Brynhild the Proud and set to his lips the hand she gave him.

"I should be glad to know, madam, that I am pardoned for thus marring your pleasure with alarm," he said. "Scarcely can I be easy in my mind until I hear that."

To see such favour as hers squandered on such as he was worse than maddening. She answered most kindly:

"No man should have a better right to mar my pleasure than you who have so often made it. And it was bearing my message that became a misfortune to you! Will you receive my necklace for *weregeld*?" Reminded by the law-term, she glanced for the first time towards the prisoner, her white lids drooping coldly. "Let Visbur lay bonds on the fellow and take him where the lawmen can deal with him."

It was not the tightening grip of the men that wrung words from the forester's silence; it was the pang of standing ill with her that caused him to speak earnestly.

"One thing I wish, *jarl's* daughter, and that is that you yourself would hear how little I am to blame."

Again she looked at him, this time squarely.

"You will have no cause to complain of the law men's justice," she said.

"Then will they judge me innocent, and how shall it be made up to me that I have endured the disgrace of bonds, and been a gazing-stock for your followers? Be as fair in your actions as you are fair in your face, noble one."

The guards around gasped, but she did not belie her Valkyria eyes. As steel answers steel with a spark they answered the demand, even while her proud mouth resented his boldness in every curve. After a moment she turned back where a tree had fallen across the glade, and seated herself upon the mossy trunk.

"Will you lay it upon Norse custom and not upon me, my friend Olaf, if I think it necessary to grant the forester's request?" she asked. "And will you support me further by feigning that this is a law-place and telling me here what he did that you disliked?"

"Is it true that Norse custom is so childish?" Olaf queried, with rising shoulders. Then as she continued to look at him entreatingly, he yielded, smiling, to come forward with playful ceremony and take up his stand before her.

While he was bowing, however, one of the guards—a burly ruddy-faced fellow—entered into the conversation, after the off-hand manner of Northern retainers. Hemming loudly, he held up the horn-handled knife which he had taken from the forester's unresisting hold.

"This can be told about the youth, *jarl's* daughter," he said, "that he is no better than a crazy Berserker. Behold with what a cheese-cutter he met the flail of Thorgrim's son!"

"And not alone met, but also mastered the flail!" a second guard chuckled; while a third, their grizzled old leader, vented a gruff laugh and openly patted his prisoner on the back.

"I will hang you if Starkad's daughter decides that way," he declared, "but you may hang me if I do not tell afterwards that you were a young hawk!" Whereupon a rumble of acquiescence came from every point where a brass helmet gleamed amid the russet leaves.

At any other time the forester might have shown appreciation of their friendliness, but just now it was the favour of the purple-robed judge upon which his heart was set. The silver-trunked birches behind her were not more impassive than her finely chiselled face, as she ignored all but the man she had addressed.

When quiet was entirely restored, Olaf spoke lightly: "Most gentle law-giver, if it is through Norse eyes that we must look, I have to tell you that the churl is in no way to blame. That he should show rudeness is a result to be expected from the barbarity in the land. That I who am French-bred should have a wish to civilize him was no less to be expected. As has been pointed out, he had no more than a hunting-knife; while my feet are more used to paved roads than to fox-trails. It made a merry game, altogether too merry to fall to the ground here. But for Norse law, fairest law-woman, there is no handle to take hold of. Turn him loose, and forget that so unworthy a happening ever quickened your fragrant breath." He ended with another bow, his last words almost lost amid the applauding murmurs of the women and the pages.

With an unconscious gesture of relief, the *Jarl's* daughter rose quickly.

"Now as always, your broad-mindedness puts all other Norsemen to shame," she said. "For taking it in this way and making my task easy, I thank you much." A second time she extended her hand to him, while over her shoulder she spoke coldly to the prisoner: "I give you peace, woodsman. Go your way."

"Come behind the bushes and tell us more news about this fight," the burly man-at-arms muttered in the forester's ear as he gave him back his hunting-knife.

Pretending to hustle him along, they accompanied him eagerly, the gentlewomen making a great show of getting out of his path as out of the way of a bear unchained. But after he had made a dozen paces, the forester stopped, shook them off and turned back to Brynhild the Proud.

"This I will beg of you, *jarl's* daughter," he said, "that you will tell me why you wanted to see me."

The guards gave him admonishing nudges. The prettiest of the veil-bound matrons uttered a little scream of derisive laughter. The *jarl's* daughter turned haughtily.

Of her alone he seemed to be conscious as he advanced. "You admit that I am not blame worthy, yet I see that I have your dislike. Is it because I appear to you no better than a savage? I beg you to believe that I am not one. I beg you to believe that if I had known it was you who wanted me, I would have been as glad in coming to you as the lark in rising to the sun."

Her gaze moving up and down between his moccasins and his mane of sun-burnished hair, she studied him wonderingly; but she was bred too high to flout him. She said, at last, with an inclination of her head:

"I owe you thanks for goodwill. I will also confess that I was made curious by the Song of Fridtjof you were singing. You are the forester—are you not—whom men call the Songsmith? I have heard my brother tell of hearing you sing once, as he happened to be passing a hunter's cabin. I wished to ask why you sang words about Fridtjof that my father's minstrels do not sing."

"That, and more, I will tell you," he answered. "The end of the song, I made out of my own imaginings. In the unsettled places where I live, one hears only those verses which the old people brought over the ocean under the hatches of memory. I got a habit of finishing out such fragments in the way I thought likeliest to be right. From that my nickname sprang. My foster-father, who had worked at a forge in his youth, said that all the *skalds* he had met with were like traders, who do no more than pass on what other men have made; but that a singer who melts scraps together and hammers them out in new shapes is a song-smith."

The figure appealed to the guardsmen, drawing forth laughter and compliment; but that to the Songsmith was nothing beside the fact that in the expression of their mistress curiosity had deepened to interest.

"Why, that is no small thing to do!" she said. "Times out of number, when I have been listening to my father's *skald*, I have wished that he could make an ending which would be new even if it were untrue, so that there might be something to keep awake for."

Calmly oblivious to maidens frowns and matrons' murmurs, she let herself sink again upon the tree-trunk, and made him a sign to come nearer.

"I want to know why you have not brought such an accomplishment to market?" she inquired. "Where is your home?"

"It is not so easy to tell that, *jarl's* daughter, since it is unlikely that you have ever heard of Freya's Tower. But it stands south of here, on an island which a bridge links to this—"

For the first time, one of the court-maidens drew near,—a slender spray of a girl, whose face was a pink bud peeping from a wood of brown hair.

"*I* have heard of it!" she cried, eagerly. "The *skalds* are not so bold as to sing songs about it; but no maiden but knows how the Swedish Viking Rolf stole King Hildebrand's daughter out of her father's court in Norway, and brought her to these shores and built her a bower and—"

Her impulse would have carried her still further if the *jarl's* daughter had not laid a light hand on her arm.

"I also know of the place," Brynhild said. "Is it there you live? A band of Rolf's comrades still live there, I have been told—Yet are you too young to have place among them! Will you tell me your name and kin?"

As he started to reply, the Songsmith's glance fell upon the handsome little page who had refused to recognise him, and who had now taken advantage of the delay to approach Olaf the French and set about removing the debris of dead leaves from his gold fringes. The forester's dark eyes gave out a glint of mischief.

"Willingly—and more than that—*jarl's* daughter," he answered. "I will have one of your own train name me to you, so that you may know it is well done." Stepping aside, he touched the boy on the shoulder. "Eric, look up here and tell your mistress my name and kin."

In a panic the youngster whirled, denial trembling on his tongue. Then he met the unswerving gaze from under the level brows; his eyes fell and his colour rose. Seemingly without his consent, his lips formed the words:

"Randvar is his name; and he is the son of Rolf and Freya, King Hildebrand's daughter."

Brynhild rose from her seat. "The son of King Hildebrand's daughter!" she repeated, and all her gentlewomen breathed it after her.

But it was Rolf's name that the guardsmen echoed, closing in upon Rolf's son to shake his hand and his shoulder.

"Rolf the Viking! A well-known name have you!"

"Now he was my shipmate for five years!"

"My father harried England with him—"

"A better warrior never fed the ravens!"

"Small wonder his son measured a knife against—"

"I take credit upon myself that I was the first to clap you on the shoulder!"

But between the brass helmets Rolf's son caught a glimpse of the *jarl's* daughter, and made the discovery that in turning his low rank into a high one he had but turned the cheek of his offence. She said, when she could make herself heard:

"There seems to me to be two sides to this matter. For a churl to bear such a bold look beneath his brows would be bad enough, but I find it far worse that a man of high birth should form himself after the manner of savages. Have you no regard for your king's blood?" Again her glance took stock of his deerskin husk and his untrimmed hair.

That she could not also take stock of the brand of temper with which the king and the Viking had bequested him, was shown by the fact that, even more than her words, her look was a challenge. In the fillip of a finger perversity possessed him, and moved him to answer:

"If my king's blood cannot show itself through a layer of deerskin, daughter of *jarls*, I hold it for a spring that is run dry."

A wrinkle of displeasure marred the satin smoothness of her forehead. "That speech would make your fortune with my brother. Pray keep such word-flourishes for him. I would show you honour if I might. This empty forest life is unbecoming a man of your birth. You are welcome to join my following and make new song-endings in my household, if you like."

His voice was more indifferent than formality prescribed, his bow less deep.

"With all thankfulness, I should not like it," he answered.

Her frown was more than a wrinkle as she asked him, "Why not?"

"I do not lack reasons. One is that I think my life more full than yours, that is laid out in straight lines like an old woman's herb-garden and weeded of all excitement. Another is that I do not think a man adds any honour to himself by following a woman."

Again she was the only quiet figure amid a hubbub, the women crying out, the guards them selves growling remonstrance. She stood queen-fully quiet, though her face blazed.

"Even churls are apt to behave with respect towards me," she said, and the contempt in her voice was keen enough to draw blood in his cheeks. He answered in kind.

"I behave with respect when I give you the truth. Are lies more to your mind?"

The tumult passed into the more alarming accompaniment of silence. The flash of her steel-gray eyes was as though they had drawn swords. From weapon-play Rolf's son had never turned back; he faced her readily, his look giving back whatever it received.

So they fronted each other until there was kindled in Brynhild's face a kind of fury, the rage of a Valkyria upon encountering her match. Just in time, the words on her lips were checked. Like a pebble into a pool, a page's voice fell upon the pause.

"Ingolf comes seeking you, *jarl's* daughter."

The spell was shattered. In less time than it took the Songsmith to shift his weight, Brynhild had shifted her expression, recalled to her wonted world. Women and pages started up like a covey of impatient birds. With his blandest smile, Olaf stepped forward and claimed his own.

"In all likelihood, madam, the messenger brings word that your noble father is ready to take his meal, and seeks you at the spot where he left you. Will you allow me so much happiness?" Baring his head, he extended his hand.

She laid hers upon it immediately, motioning Eric to take up the grape-purple train. All at once she seemed to the forester to have withdrawn herself an immeasurable distance beyond his ken. Across the space her voice came to him coldly.

"I would have shown you friendliness, Freya's son, but it may be that this way is better. The truth grows in me that you would hardly know how to behave in a court. It is likely you have chosen your life wisely. I wish you good luck in it, and bid you farewell."

She bent her head; her women dropped him awestruck courtesies. Under cover of a salute, Olaf's hard blue eyes held him long enough to remind him that their quarrel was by no means at an end. Then, leaning on the courtman's arm, the *jarl's* daughter turned and left, nor looked back, though Rolf's son watched as long as he could catch any gleam of her bright hair.

When the band had crossed the glade and gained the trees, they met the helmeted figure; and following the instant of meeting, it seemed to the forester that the breeze brought him a sound of shrieks. But whatever their cause, it did not delay the departure. Soon the many-coloured troop had become blended with the many-coloured leaves, and forest solitude closed again around him.

CHAPTER 3

Nose is next of kin to eyes
   —Northern saying.

With signs of the day's ruffling influence still visible at his mouth-corners, Randvar, Rolf's son, put aside the cables of wild grapevine that drooped curtain-like over the end of the home-trail, and paused to look before him. "Poor and mean must this have seemed in my mother's sight," he mused.

A few steps ahead the path broadened into an open grassy space, in whose middle rose a low round tower, touched by the last rays of the setting sun. Built of gray stones held together by gray mortar, it stood out coldly amid the green and garnet and golden maples that walled it round; and among branching trees and wreathing vines its outline was as stark as the outline of an Iceland rock. No spire sprouted from its flat top; no balconies rounded out beneath the windows of its upper story, and its lower part was no more than eight gray pillars standing in a circle. On one of them now a tangle of fish-nets was hanging; against another leaned a frame on which a wild-cat skin had been stretched to dry, and before a third stood a herring-keg and a barrel of wild-grape wine. Between the pillars, eight wide archways gave plain view into the round ground-room, in whose centre a fire was burning under a kettle. A flaxen-haired girl moved back and forth before the fire, and under one of the arches a tall, muscular woman stood looking out and wiping her heated face upon her homespun apron.

Understanding that her watch was for him, Randvar raised his hand in greeting; but his gaze remained on the small deep-set window high up on the tower's seaward side, where he had often seen his mother's face looking out over the green wastes of trees and the blue wastes of water that stretched between her and the home she had left.

It seemed to him now that he could see her again, flower-fair and crowned with hair like winter's pale sunshine. The contrast between her delicacy and the rough setting came home to him with new force. In the bubbling caldron of his mind, awe came uppermost.

"It was a wondrous thing, my mother's love," he murmured as he moved slowly forward.

The greeting of the woman in the archway brought him back to the present. She was a weather-beaten woman, almost as severe in out line as the tower itself, and with but little more colour; yet proof remained that she had once been as freshly blooming as her daughter, and her work-roughened hand had a gentle touch as she laid it on his arm. She spoke quickly, regarding him with keen eyes.

"There is a new stain on your kirtle, foster-son, and a cut in the middle of it. What have you been doing to yourself?" As she talked, she was unfastening a buckle, and now laid bare his blood-soaked shirt.

He looked down at it with surprised recognition. "Did the courtman do all that? I had altogether forgotten it."

"Courtman! Have you seen someone from the *jarl's* town?" The girl caught him up and left her broth-stirring eagerly, but her mother motioned her away.

"Go up and get one of his linen shirts out of my chest, and fetch down the ointment," she ordered her; then to her foster-son: "Bring in the water-pail and pull off those things and sit down here. Some day your carelessness will bring it to pass that you bleed to death, and it will not be a brave end, but a foolish one."

"None the less is it pleasant to realize what state the French One's fine clothes must be in," Randvar chuckled, as he allowed himself to be pushed down on a bench by the fire.

The girl, returning headlong down the ladder-like stairs, repeated her entreaty for news; so while his foster-mother washed his wound, and his foster-sister rolled bandages for him, he related his adventure.

They listened without interruption until he came to the appearance of Brynhild and her following, when both stayed their hands to question him eagerly.

"Was Eric with her?"

"How did he look?"

"What did he say?"

"Did he send us a message?"

The first warm colour came into the cheeks of Erna, the woman; her eyes shone hungrily.

Regarding her, her foster-son began deliberately to parry. "What did he say? Snowfrid, you are a simpleton! Do you suppose that folks gabble like wild turkeys while a noblewoman and her frippery are standing around? As for his looks, I can tell you that a red-headed woodpecker would get bashful beside him, all in green cloth from top to toe, with his hair cut like the *jarl's*. I did not wonder at all that the maiden wanted him for a page only from seeing him pick up her necklace in the road."

The thin lips of Eric's mother relaxed unconsciously into a smile, as her hands took up the last bandage; but Eric's sister gave her flaxen braids a toss.

"I think he would not have been hindered from asking about us if he had wished," she said. "It is my belief that the young one is puffed up with pride. Three times has the trading-ship on which he went up to see the wonders of the Town been back without bringing him for so much as a visit. It is my belief that he was ashamed to speak to Rand—" She was startled into swallowing the rest of the word by the sharpness with which Erna turned upon her.

"I know that he was not," his mother said, sternly. "That his wits get dizzy from living with high people may well be. I was foolish myself about court ways when I came to be bowermaid to King Hildebrand's daughter; but that he should ever fall off so much as to be ungrateful is not likely. I know that he remembered what is due to Freya's son, and greeted him with respect."

Randvar's face was hidden by the shirt he was drawing on, but from its linen depths he chuckled.

"Never fear but what he greeted me! And named me to his mistress besides, else might she have thought me some shaggy beast."

"There!" said Erna; and Snowfrid, somewhat abashed, turned her attention to dishing up the evening meal of venison broth and bread.

After the meal was under way, however, it occurred to her to ask concerning the appearance of Brynhild the Proud.

The power which the mere mention of that name had to upset his peace of mind amazed Randvar, even while he curtly denied any recollection of her whatever. It was a relief when at last eating was over, and Snowfrid had gone off to carry a jug of broth to the cabinful of old men, who were all that was left of Rolf's lusty crew. Erna took up her knitting, then, and retired into her wonted silence and to her wonted seat on the other side of the fire; and he was free to stretch himself upon the floor of cedar boughs, and yield unreservedly to the strange turmoil of his thoughts.

Gazing out where the moon was steering between white cloud-reefs towards the open blue, he spoke dreamily: "Foster-mother, you knew the turns of Freya's mind as a forester knows his home-trail—tell me how she took this life here."

Without lessening the click of her needles, Erna glanced over at him. "I suppose you were made curious by seeing for the first time what kind of things a high-born maiden is accustomed to. It is the truth, however, that Freya took it well. Out of everything she made a jest. She used to look at the leaf-walls around the tower, and say that no queen had such an elf-woven tapestry, or changed her hangings so often. She was always smiling."

"Her lips were always smiling," Randvar said doubtfully, "but her eyes? It may be that I do not remember aright, since I was but a child in age when she died, yet it seems to me now that her eyes were always sorrowful."

To that, Freya's bowerwoman made no answer. The pause lasted so long unbroken by anything save the rattling of her wooden needles and the chirping of the crickets under the stone hearth that presently her foster-son threw a twig at her.

"Wake up, foster-mother! Are you going to have a weird spell, that you drowse and do not hear me?"

"Do your words need an answer, foster-son?" Erna returned. "As well as I, you should know that Freya's nature was not such that she could be altogether happy in a life that sprang from the death of her kin."

"I had forgotten that," Randvar admitted.

She looked at him again across the fire. "This is where you show Rolf's breed. I think he never even guessed it. Yet always the memory that he was the slayer of her father lay between them like a blade that no tenderness could sheathe. She loved him in spite of it, but I speak no more than the truth when I say that it was the effort of doing so which wore her out before half her life was lived."

Supporting himself on his hand, Rolf's son sat up and gazed at her earnestly. "The strange wonder is that she could feel any love towards him! Until today, what I could not get through my head was how my father could gentle himself to so weak a thing as a woman; but now I regard it as the greatest wonder that so proud and fine and wonderful a thing as a high-born maiden should give herself to a rough-minded brawling—"

"You need not take it upon yourself to speak in that manner of Rolf," Erna interrupted him with some sternness. "All the fineness that was possible to his nature he gave her. For Freya, he who had never handled aught but a sword, toiled and sweat like a thrall to build this tower; and afterwards he made his drinking-bouts as mild as a woman's, lest she be touched with fear. And when she died, he slew himself from grief, as not many men have done before him. It is true that your mind is higher than his, through having her blood in your veins; but enough of his rough temper is in you, and his heedlessness about clothes and polite ways, to make any girl but a forest-bred wench like Snowfrid turn her eyes from you as from a bear."

Wincing, Randvar dropped again to his elbow, averted his crimsoning face from the firelight. It came as a welcome diversion that at that moment Snowfrid's voice was heard out in the darkness.

But Snowfrid's half-frightened giggle, as she answered the questions of someone coming after her, was a surprise. It was not after that fashion that she conversed with Lame Farsek or his half-dozen decrepit old mates. Her mother and her foster-brother bestirred themselves to look out.

Erna's surprise was not lessened to see her daughter emerge from the bush-shadows followed by a strapping fellow in the brass helmet and leather clothes of the *jarl's* guard; and Randvar's astonishment increased as he recognized in the visitor the guardsman who had first spoken up for him in his adventure with Olaf and the *jarl's* daughter. While Erna rose hastily, smoothing down her apron, he leaped to his feet with a thumping heart. If by any possibility Brynhild should have sent him a message!

Even more than in the morning, the man-at-arms looked the soul of bluff good-fellowship as Snowfrid led him up to them, naming him as Bolverk of the *jarl's* guard, and explaining stammeringly that she had found him beating about in a berry-tangle in search of the path. He added a wink for her to his jovial recognition of the Songsmith, vowed that if the soldiers of the *Jarl's* Town had but dreamed to what that path led, it would have been beaten broad enough to need no hunting for. Snowfrid relapsed into a blushing examination of her braids which struck her foster-brother as particularly ill-timed and foolish. He said with impatient politeness:

"It is to be regretted that the path failed your need, Guardsman Bolverk, for it must needs be urgent to bring you here at this hour."

The guardsman made an effort to pull his round face to a solemn length. "Certainly it is no light errand that keeps me abroad, though my being here springs from a whim of Helvin, *jarl's* son—I should say, Helvin Jarl, for Starkad, his father, is dead. Saints grant him as much rest as he will accept of!"

After the manner of people hearing news, all three cried the word after him, "Dead!" Then Erna murmured, "Thus the old leaves drop off, one by one!" And Snowfrid cried impulsively: "Now will the young man take some comfort?" And Randvar smote his knee.

"No longer ago than this morning was I talking about Helvin, and how his father's death would but free him from one trap to spring another on him."

Bolverk's ruddy face relaxed into its wonted curves. "So you all know what manner of man he was? Then I need not pretend to shed tears for him, though I should think it sinful to wish any but an enemy such a death."

Even while they drew near together, the women questioned him with their eyes. Randvar put it into words.

"In what manner did he come to his death? I saw him ride past to the hunt,—I suppose it was caused by a fall from his horse?"

The guardsman shook his head ponderously. "No such quiet end for Starkad the Berserker. One of the hunting-dogs sprang on him and tore his throat to pieces. Ingolf brought the tidings just after we parted from you. The place where it happened was on the brink of as hideous a pond as a bad dream ever painted. I went and looked at it afterwards. I give you my word that the water was as black as—"

"The Black Pool!" cried Erna and Snowfrid together. Randvar had become as motionless as the bench on which his foot was resting.

Bolverk nodded. "Naught else should it be called; any dead branch sticking out of it gets the look of a bleached bone. You may imagine what a sight it was to come upon,—Starkad sprawling on the brink, and Helvin leaning against a tree, more white than a halter-corpse, except—"

"Helvin!" This time the echo came from Randvar.

Drawing a step nearer, Bolverk lowered his voice.

"I will not be so mean as to draw the cup back after you have had one swallow. Only I ask you to forget who brought the tidings hither. The hound was Kelvin's. He had taken it out of the pack and kept it with him because of a wound in its foot, and it is thought that it did not attack the *jarl* without cause.

"Father and son had many words about something before they set forth this morning. When Helvin dashed ahead by himself, the *jarl* sent men after him to fetch him back. And when at last they came to the point where the party broke up, and the women went aside to the waiting-place and each man struck out for himself, Starkad forced Helvin to ride apart with him, though it was seen by everyone that the young man had the greatest dread of accompanying him. What passed between them Helvin does not tell, and no one dares ask, but it is guessed that Starkad worked himself into a Berserk rage and fell upon him—"

"Odin!" gasped Erna, and at the same time crossed herself.

"And that the dog broke loose to protect its master. And many believe that the taste of blood maddened it so that it went so far as to attack Helvin when he dragged it off the Jarl, for the claws had torn the silver lace on his sleeves, and one of the proofs that he must have been grappling with it when he slew it is that his kirtle is all one gore of blood—What do you say?"

But Randvar would not repeat the curse that had been wrung from him; and Bolverk, encountering Snowfrid's horrified gaze, became diverted by the amiable desire to recall her blushing smile.

"And that," he went on, "is the beginning of the reason why this bright-haired maiden of victory found me battling with thorns and led me to Valhalla. When a move was made to go back to the town, Helvin seemed to come crazy out of his black silence. He vowed that he would have one night of freedom before the rule came on him, and forbade any to follow, and broke from us into the forest—It is likely you know, also, that he has dreaded the rule more than most men dread Hel! But old Mord, who was the first of Starkad's advice-givers, counselled us to follow at a distance, that we might be within call in case danger threatened him from Skraellings or other wild animals. In the moonlight we kept him in sight almost to the head of your Island, but there it happened that we lost him. The rest declared that he had turned aside, and I declared that he had not; so I set out alone, and finding so plain a path, kept on out of adventuresomeness. It is possible that I shall have to stand some banter, and yet I cannot find it in my heart to be sorry about my blunder." Again he winked at Snowfrid over the huge fist caressing his yellow moustache, then drew himself up with a prodigious sigh. "My one regret is that I must now return to my duty. Will you not guide me back as far as the cabin, my fair one? I cannot seem to remember the way at all between here and there."

Snowfrid's eyes answered him delightedly, but her lips waited bashfully for her mother. She ran no risk in doing so, however, for under Erna's apparent sternness there lay as much Norse simplicity as Norse kindness.

She said, "Go, child, of course," and poured Bolverk so excellent a stirrup-cup, and shook his hand so warmly at parting, that he went away without even observing that the master of the tower had bidden him no farewell, but still stood with his foot on the bench and his eyes on the fire.

Erna looked at him curiously when she had resumed her seat and her knitting. At last she spoke:

"Hard tidings are these and great to hear; yet I cannot see, foster-son, that they touch us so nearly as you appear to feel."

"You will see when I tell you what spell some troll laid upon me," he retorted. Straightening, he went and threw himself down in his favourite place upon the fragrant mat, and began to pour out wrathfully the story of his adventure at the Black Pool.

"There you have it all before you," he wound up. "I was made to behave in an unfavourable manner before the man with whom, above all others, I would wish to stand well. I thought, first, it was some poison from the pool that beset me; but since it worked no harm to anyone else, I know it was a curse turned on me alone—Hel take the luck! Hel take it, I say!"

When she had let her suspended breath go from her in a yawn, murmuring, "That was a strange happening—a strange happening," she answered gravely: "You throw blame undeservedly. It is your guardian spirit that has given you power to feel it better than others when an evil deed is in the air. I have often heard of people who had such a gift—"

He flung up his arms to snap the fingers sharply. "Take my share of such white-livered gifts! Power? I call that a weakness which makes me a stick in the hands of something stronger than I! If I knew what part of me it had root in, it should not last long."

"You will bring punishment upon yourself for your ungratefulness," she said, but said it without force, seeming to wander among her thoughts. His scorn held the field.

"I should be glad to hear what I am to be grateful for! Nothing could make Helvin believe now that I am any better than a coward. It shows what a cur he took me for that his first impulse was to send an arrow after me. I am as much outlawed from his following as though a lawman had laid a ban upon me."

She had no answer to that, or else the heat of the fire was making her drowsy. Leaning forward, she sat blinking at it, her arms folded on her knees.

Breaking up twigs with one hand to jerk them into the flames with the other, he went on piling up causes for bitterness, though he no longer spoke them aloud,—they came from too near his heart for that.

"I should have helped him, if I had acted out my own nature, and he would have done me honor in return. I should have left this emptiness of beasts and trees to measure myself against men. It would go hard with me if I could not prove my self more than that grinning French-broken ape. She showed him favour; she would have shown me more.... She might... in time... she might even.... More unlikely things happened to my father!"

Chapter 4

Where I see the ears, I expect the wolf
      —Northern saying.

Neither of them paid any attention to Snowfrid on her return, and the girl on her side seemed to find her thoughts quite as interesting as conversation. After a few minutes, she said that she was going to bed, and lighted a splinter at the embers. The firelight, as she bent, showed her bashful mouth to be smiling with the memory of kisses. She seemed to be walking in a blissful dream as she went lightly up the stairs.

What aroused Randvar, finally, was the consciousness that his foster-mother was moving with unnatural deliberation. Sitting up to look at her, he found that her gaze had become fixed upon the space beyond the fire, and she was lifting her arm from her knee to stretch it out in that direction.

"Look at that wolf yonder," she said. "A wolf?" He rose to his feet, bent to pick up a brand. Then as his gaze followed her finger, he dropped the wood impatiently. "It is the fire dazzling you. There is no wolf there."

Yawning, Erna lifted both her arms to stretch them above her head. "I forgot that I was seeing with the eyes of my mind, instead of with the eyes of my body," she said. "It stood yonder, where the moonlight ends and the firelight begins. There was a goldlike glow to its fur, and its eyes were as bright embers. It must have been the Other Shape of Kelvin Jarl."

The voice in which he repeated the name was in such contrast to her monotone that it startled himself; he went on with stern restraint: "Do you intend to tell me that Helvin Jarl's wanderings will lead him here, where I shall have to face him and explain what ailed me today?"

She would not curtail the yawn that was stretching her jaws, but she nodded.

Randvar made no attempt to hide his impulse, snatching his coat down from the antler-rack for instant flight.

"It is a good thing that you can do the honours without me," he said. "I shall spend the night with the birds in Fenrir's Jaws."

But Erna's mouth was again practicable for talking, and she was using it drowsily. "Yes, I know for certain that he will come by here. And I am altogether too sleepy to remember anything about manners. I will lose no time in getting out of your way." Rubbing her eyes with one hand, she gathered up her knitting with the other, as oblivious to his position as though she had never understood it.

It came back to her foster-son, then, that mental numbness follows as well as precedes the use of double sight. There was nothing to do but throw the cloak upon the floor and himself into a sulk, while she moved through the routine of her nightly tasks, making sure that Snowfrid had covered the jar of venison broth, letting down against the fresh night-wind two or three of the bearskin curtains with which the arches were provided.

"If I should ever get so dulled by wine as she by this," he fumed inwardly, "I should smart for it while her tongue could wag; yet how much better is she than drunk?"

When she had climbed stiffly up the stairs, and the light of her torch-splinter had been swallowed by the upper darkness, his resentment overflowed his lips.

"Again I declare my belief that weird powers are an accursed hindrance. What avail is it to warn a man of coming evil if no way is shown him to ward it off?" He emphasised his words by a kick at the great log just before him.

The sudden flare of flames and flight of sparks and jarring of charred parts asunder seemed to afford him some relief; while regarding them, he bethought him of a loop-hole.

"After all, I do not know how we make it out that the visitor must be Helvin! A wolf is the animal-spirit that runs before many a valiant man. Nine chances to one, it will be no more than the French Olaf in search of him."

The possibility made his alarm seem senseless. Snapping his fingers at the world beyond the bright ring, he gave the log a second kick, this time of friendly correction.

"Comes the Devil himself, he must have no fault to find with the hospitality of Freya's Tower," he said, and set to work to replenish the fire.

Tearing the great saplings free from the pile and breaking them resoundingly under his heel, he worked too vigorously for a while to leave any space for brooding, and he had no opportunity to take it up again when the task was finished. Even as he rose from laying on the last bough and turned again to the outer dusk, he saw the grapevine thrust aside from the head of the path—saw a man appear in the opening and stand there—a peculiarly proportioned man whose breadth of shoulder and length of arm suggested that he had been formed for towering tallness, and that it was blasting mischance which had stopped him at medium height.

Randvar's panic took the form of obstinate unbelief. Even when the apparition quitted its hold on the vine and came slowly towards him over the grass, he doggedly refused to believe that the Fates would be so contrary.

But on the spot where the moonlight ended and the firelight began, the visitor came to a stand still; the red glow meeting him eagerly illumined him from head to foot. There was no mistaking the gray garments, blood-drenched and torn; there was no mistaking the mass of blood-red hair; and looking at the haggard face in the sinister frame, the Songsmith's own figure came back to him, "fire cased in flesh." In the ash-gray eyes, live embers were glowing. Suddenly something else came to Randvar,—a consciousness that murderous hatred was looking at him out of those eyes.

Scorn he had been prepared for, but this—this amazed him. It was instinct that acted to stiffen him alertly, as he made salute, saying, "I give you welcome, Helvin Jarl."

Whatever his temper, Starkad's son had a *jarl's* dignity of bearing. He answered grimly:

"I hold that welcome for true which is told by the face as well as by the tongue. I think you did not expect to see me so soon?"

That seemed so easy to answer that Randvar had said "No," before he recollected the truth, when he amended it with "Yes," and stopped short in angry confusion. His embarrassment was not lessened by the inevitable next question:

"Why did you run away when I called to you?"

He said desperately, at last: "*Jarl*, I do not know how to put it into words. You can believe that I went mad."

He had braced himself to meet jeering laughter, to endure it without strangling the jeerer. It took him a breath's space to realize that Kelvin's mind was no longer on him. The arm by which he had been steadying himself against the pillar had doubled under him like a broken reed; now he swung forward against the stone, and would have pitched into the fire if Randvar had not leaped the flames and caught him.

When he had lowered him upon a bench with his back against a support, the next move was naturally to fill a horn at the wine-cask and bring it to him. Remembering only his old feeling towards the *jarl's* son, Rolf's son performed the service with swift goodwill. He was recalled to their present relations by Kelvin's lifting a hand in refusal of his hospitality.

It obliged him to fall back a step and hesitate, balancing the rejected cup, but it emboldened him presently to protest.

"*Jarl*, it does not seem to me that this matter is going according to good sense. That I have done nothing to earn friendship, I own; but I deny that I have done aught to call for ill-will. If you think me a milksop, I cannot come to words with you about that; but it is the truth that I would have been eager in joining you."

Leaning back with closed eyes, Kelvin's face was yet drawn awry by mocking laughter.

"Eager!" he murmured. "Eager!" Then, "It may be that if I had not come here tonight, your eagerness would have urged you to seek me out in the town?"

"Surely not. I did not say that I had the wish to be thrown out of your hall."

"More likely would you have been carried out," Helvin answered dryly.

Despite his resentment, Randvar had a feeling of admiration for a man who dared say such a thing to him,—a man whose exhausted body would have been a rag in the forester's hands. He said, as he turned and threw the untasted wine into the fire:

"If you have set your heart on hating me, have it your own way. It must be because your temper has been tried today. I will only say that I am sorry, for I have always felt a liking towards you."

Though his head continued to lean heavily against the pillar, the *jarl's* eyes opened to flash at him. "Excepting once today and once last season, when you sang in a hunter's cabin, I do not know that I have ever seen you."

"I mean that I have been so told about you Randvar was beginning, but was checked as much by his own sense of intrusion as by a flame from the smouldering eyes.

The young *jarl* went on haughtily: "It had come to my mind, before, that my affairs must be a juicy mouthful for gabblers to chew over the fire; but I did not know that the things they said were the kind to attract friends to me, and there will be much awanting before I believe it."

Randvar gave up then; shrugging, he said only: "Believe whatever you like about it; yet I wish I had a chance to prove my goodwill."

Again he expected the jeering laughter, and again he missed his foretelling. A long time Starkad's son sat staring out at the darkness, strange expressions playing over his white face like flickerings of his inner fire; then, at last, his thoughts formed themselves into slow-spoken words:

"Never could it happen that my look encountered you without recalling how I saw you this morning,—yet what else is to be done? To hold enmity against a man who offers me goodwill—This, at least, you have never heard of me, Songsmith, that I am low-minded! Only one way is open to me." He stretched out his hand for the horn. "I will accept it from you now," he said, and drained gratefully the second draught his host brought him, the rich juice imparting some of its own warm life to his ghastly face. He drew himself erect as he gave back the cup. "There shall be peace between us, only I make it a condition that you shall enter my following."

Once or twice before the conversation had taken turns unexpected to Randvar, but nothing to compare with this.

"You make that a *condition!*" he repeated.

Kelvin's finely marked brows drew nearer together. "You should not take it ill, if you have as much mind to serve me as you said a while ago. You shall have the honourable post of my song-maker,—my father's *skald* is years overdue in Valhalla."

To imagine such an offer in his daydreams had seemed to the Songsmith as natural as eating; but hearing it now in his waking ears, he wondered if he were not asleep. He said, "I give you thanks," but so dazedly that like lightning playing over a distant peak, a flash of that devil-mockery flickered over Helvin's face.

"What now! Does your brisk friendship get weak in the knees when it comes to trusting yourself in my power?"

Flushing, Rolf's son swallowed a boast and answered only: "Why should I be afraid, *jarl?* You have given me your word that this happening shall not weigh against me."

Again it struck him as odd the way Helvin leaned forward and scrutinised him, long and in credulously.

"I did not mean because of this matter," he said, at last. "I meant because you might feel some doubts about the turn of temper I have." The strange mockery of the smile in which his lips drew away from his white teeth, as he said that, was made stranger still by the awful intentness of his eyes.

So much strangeness began to tell upon Randvar's stock of patience. He said bluntly:

"*Jarl*, if the truth must be told, I have no doubts whatever about your temper, for I have seen plainly that you have a very bad one. But neither have I been used to lamblike men. Willingly will I strike a bargain on these terms, if I have the choice."

After they were out, the words struck him as being a trifle unceremonious; he did not wonder much that Starkad's son should sit staring like one dumfounded. But that scorn should gradually grow up in his face!

"Behold, I believe you!" the young *jarl* said with biting slowness. "I believe you have the Devil's boldness to match against my Devil's nature,—and at the back of that, the ambition of Lucifer! Now, it is told that the closeness of a court breeds rottenness; but what shall be said of such foulness as this, out in the forest's untainted air? When such as I go before, a worse is not to be looked for behind; and this man knows it; and still is he willing to sell his manhood for my miserable gifts!"

It was not only his voice and his words that bit, but his look as well. Rolf's son winced under the smart, and spoke between his teeth.

"Such wrong you do me, Helvin, *jarl's* son, that it will be hard work for you to atone for it. If I had been willing to sell my manhood for gifts, would I not have put on your father's yoke? That I want to become your man is because I expect that you will make following you an honour. The evil I know of you I think no more your fault than I think it blame to an oak that a poison vine is thrown around its branches. Now, as things stand, I believe you will shake it off, and the oak strength in your breast will send your mind up oak-high and oak-broad to be a strong pillar to other men."

He had got his temper back by the time he finished. From under his level brows, his eyes looked steadfast as sunlight into the face of his lord. As the sun draws a tree upward, so the young *jarl* was drawn upright by the look.

"All my life," he breathed, "have I believed that of myself, but never did I think to find an other who would believe it—who could believe it! Does not some troll mock me?"

The Songsmith answered: "I think you know that I speak the truth."

Looking into his eyes, it seemed that Helvin did know it. It seemed that he was opening his lips to say so, when into the stillness was dropped a sound like the distant clink of spur against stone. In the beat of a pulse, his face had become distorted by that hatred which springs from fear. He dropped back upon the bench, his words slipping out disjointedly.

"Let us see who has dared to follow me—who has dared! Mind this—that you make it appear as if I lingered to hear you sing. Go yonder to your harp, if that be a harp!"

Though of home-make and rude shape, it was a harp that hung on the pillar above the bed of fox-skins. Laying it on his breast, the Songsmith played as he was bidden,—random chords that fell absently from the ends of his fingers. Standing there in the shelter of the bearskin that had been drawn across the arch, he could not longer see the head of the path; but he knew when the pursuer emerged from the bushes by Helvin's smothered cry:

"Olaf!"

Gripping the edge of the seat, the *jarl* leaned there gazing out with distended eyes. "He is the likeliest man to find it out and follow. . . . Since the day of my birth he has hounded me. . . . He followed me into the world by an hour, but I think he will go out of it before me." . . . His voice died away in murmur,—ceased at last so that between the harp-chords could be heard the soft rustle of footsteps through grass. Soon after that, the imposing form of Olaf the French came into the range of the Songsmith's vision.

Not to Randvar either had it occurred that Olaf could be seeking any but the *jarl*. It amazed him, also, that at sight of the gray-clad figure leaning on the bench Thorgrim's son showed unmistakable surprise.

"Lord!" he said. Then, with the suavest gesture in his stock of

French graces: "Lord, I would give much if I had not this appearance of having so little regard for your orders as to come prying upon your grief. Believe me—"

"My grief!" Helvin repeated. "My—" A quiver of terrible laughter undermined his voice and it fell; then, in the drawing of a breath it rose defiantly. "Since this matter has been spoken of, let me make it plain to you that you may make it plain to others, and tongue need never be laid to it again. *I have no grief.* Nor to save anyone's feelings will I make pretence of any. Let no man urge it on me, if his ears would go unscathed!"

Olaf made no attempt to urge it, certainly. As in toleration of some noble whim, he smiled blandly and bowed acquiescence. After a moment the *jarl* resumed curtly:

"If it was not to seek me that you came hither, what may it be that you want?"

That it might be to finish their interrupted duel had already occurred to Randvar; but if he imagined that Olaf would have any difficulty in presenting their quarrel in a light favourable to himself, his estimate fell short. The French One answered without hesitation:

"It so happens that I am in this neighbourhood, *jarl*, because your men have made a night-camp near the head of the island. And I am come to the tower to fulfil a task I have set myself, which is to avenge on this fellow his insolence towards your sister."

"My sister!" the young noble repeated, sitting erect.

"In this wise will I answer you, lord, as is the very truth. This morning the gold-adorned maid enchanced upon him in the forest; and after the fashion of damsels with things that are new to them, she showed interest in his jingling accomplishments. Word followed word until, on discovering that there was gentle blood in him, she had gone so far as to honour him with an invitation to join her following. You would say that if he had one good strain in him he would have shown thankfulness for her favour. Instead of that, however, he answered her even with ill-temper, jeered at the life she offered him, ended the talk by in forming her that he did not think her service good enough for him. If you think I am making it out worse than it is, I shall not blame you,—only ask him to deny it."

It is strange how different one's own sentiments can seem when echoed by another's mouth, and after time has allayed the irritation from which they sprang. The song-maker had enough gentle blood to dye his face at the recollection of his quarrel with the beautiful

Brynhild; nor could he meet the glance the *jarl* bent on him, but stood grinding the cedar twigs under his heel and wishing that they were some portion of the French One's comely body.

But Helvin Jarl spoke tranquilly. With the passing of his belief that Olaf was in pursuit of him, fierceness like a storm wind had passed from his bearing and left him *jarlfully* poised.

"That is to be said of his fault, *beausire*, that it needs mending; but hardly are you the man to do it. This one thing is enough to hinder it, that you are known to be the most jealous of all my sister's suitors. Think only how spiteful tongues might slander you, and say that instead of resenting rudeness you were in truth avenging it on the Songsmith that Starkad's daughter showed him such great kindness! Better that you hand it over to me, *beausire*, since, besides being her brother, I am also answerable for this man. For I may as well take this time to make it known that the Songsmith has consented to enter my household, and make for me the songs which, even before I strayed here tonight, I found pleasure in. What needs be said, I will say, *beausire*, and overtake you shortly."

Rising, he made a gesture of dismissal which, if it lacked French grace, had at least Norse decision. Before it Thorgrim's bland son was forced to bow, and, bowing, to back out of the circle of the firelight. When he had become a dark shape in the moonshine, the *jarl* turned to where his new follower was waiting in keen discomfort.

"Do not imagine," he said, "that I am going to pretend to be surprised that you lost your temper with my sister. So has her haughtiness grown, that what I wonder at is that some man is not driven to slay her. Only for your own sake do I remind you as so often I have been reminded—that good manners are like a coat of mail in that every breach of them opens a hole for the thrust of your enemies."

Of reproof it was the mildest. In his self-dissatisfaction, the songmaker was even moved to outdo it, and muttered with another kick at the log in front of him:

"You say less than you might if you wanted to push the matter. It is seen that your sister thinks me no better than a boor."

"I should be two-faced to say more," Helvin returned, "for to me the happening is even of service. Now, when I no longer have before me the honesty of your face to make me believe in you, it will stand me in some stead to be able to tell myself that I know you spoke the truth about scorning court ways and preferring my service over that of another, as has not been the case before. Do not take it ill that I need proof. This happens to me for the first time that I trust anyone. Yet I wish it were possible for you to fare back with me tonight."

Remembering the crops that must be talked over with Erna, the traps that must be explained to the old Vikings, the young master of the tower hesitated; but the instant the *jarl* read his difficulty, he ended it courteously.

"I see, however, that you have needful business to arrange. Take two days to attend to it, and join me on the third day at sunset. Only assure me that you will not fail me on that day."

Rather an appeal than a command did it become in the gentleness of his voice, the friendliness of the hand he stretched out. Taking the hand in both of his, the Songsmith answered from the sincerity of his heart:

"May my luck fail me if I fail you either in this or in greater things! For all it is worth you have my loyalty, I take oath on it."

Returning the pressure of the Songsmith's warm clasp, the *jarl's* gaze held him long and strangely.

"I believe you," he said. "For whatever it is worth, I swear you my friendship—for whatever it is worth!"

On that they parted.

CHAPTER 5

His hands are clean who warns another
                                            —Northern saying.

"Wait a moment," Erna commanded, quickening her descent of the stairs. Wrapped in his cloak of russet homespun, Randvar had just come in from his morning swim, and was hastening where his heap of clothing waited by the fire. He quieted the chattering of his teeth to look at her inquiringly.

Two days and three nights had passed since the strain of using her double sight had numbed her wits; once more she was her capable keen-eyed self. Yet there was a quiver of unusual emotion in her stern face as she came up and laid her hand upon his arm.

"I want to find out whether you are in danger of sinking by swords," she said with her customary terseness, and her grasp tightened determinedly as he started to move away.

"I have declared, foster-mother, that I will endure no more magic though my life lies on it!"

"What magic is it that my palms, like those of many another witch-craft-knowing woman, have the power to feel where steel is going to pierce a vital part, and to strengthen that part? I tell you to let me have my will. I dreamed last night that I saw a wounded eagle, which may well be your Other Shape."

"Foster-mother, I tell you that any more of this spell-work is going to put me into a bad temper; and it is my wish to behave well towards you the last morning we are together." Involuntarily, his voice softened.

Though usually she disdained them, she was not without a knowledge of woman's weapons. She assumed them rather than lose her point.

"Maybe so, but you behave all the other way to set your self-will against my peace of mind. Do you think I could bear Eric's absence if I had not the assurance of my hands that his body is sound?"

Wondering whether she had also tested the soundness of Eric's head tempted the Songsmith to a chuckle. The discovery that half the fierce brightness of her eyes was due to tears finished his disarming. Half sighing, half growling, he let his cloak slip off his shoulders.

"When did I ever get my will against you,—after I got out of swaddling-bands? I ask, however, that you do not keep me feeling foolish here longer than is necessary."

Probably it was the same to her as though he were still in swaddling-bands, when once she had closed her eyes that all her forces might be concentrated in her sense of touch. The palms she pressed upon his firm cool flesh—polished satin-smooth by the water, glistening satin-fair in the firelight—moved as tenderly as though the sinewy frame were still the soft child-body that she had tended in its helplessness. Each time his glance fell upon her worn face with its mouth hard-set in anxiety for him, he swallowed his impatience one time more; and when the waxing light made delay no longer possible, his efforts to free himself were begun with all gentleness.

"Foster-mother, be good enough to remember that I cannot start later than sunrise, if I am to reach there by sunset."

She clutched him with one hand, while the other pressed hard upon his left side.

"I thought I felt a place—stand still!—over your heart. It would be a death wound, indeed. *There!* Cold! A spot as cold as Hel's mouth!" She opened eyes dilated with excitement in a face that had become ashen pale.

An involuntary shiver passed over him, cooling his impatience. He watched thoughtfully while she began to knead his flesh with her warm and tingling finger-balls. After a time he said:

"It cannot be gainsaid that this is a better place to give a thrust than to take one. I admit that I expect to meet some unexpected things in the path I am entering. Not a little overgrowth hides it. Although I cannot tell why, much that the *jarl* said that night came to me as a surprise. I suppose that the strangeness of his temper is the explanation of it.... Yet there is one thing that I can find no answer to,—why should he act as if it were important to him to have an unknown man like me in his following?"

Instead of answering, she began to rub at what she considered a vulnerable place in his discretion. "Never make the mistake of belittling yourself like that, and least of all where strangers can hear you. The result might be that they would take you at your word and believe you to be a man of no mark."

He stirred impatiently. "Brisk enough am I, and many shall give place to me; but this I know not,—why it should matter to the *Jarl* of New Norway where I spend my days."

Neither did she know, when she came to think it over. She soon gave up the attempt to fall back upon what she did know.

"It will be all the same in the end. I have done all I can in protecting your vitals. Safe into the fray you will go; safe out of the fray you will come,—if you do not let your flesh get cut so that you bleed to death. Stand still that I may see if I have brought back the life-warmth. ... Yes ... yes, the cold is entirely gone." When she had pulled herself up stiffly by his arm, she released him. "Scant time will you have to jump into your clothes. The sun is not far away when the top of that chestnut-tree stands out so boldly."

"That is true!" he assented, and cleared at a bound the distance between himself and his clothing.

For a while there were no other sounds to be heard save the simmering of the kettle and the song of Snowfrid overhead, sweet as the lilt of a meadow-lark in a field of golden grain.

As he rose from swallowing his last mouthful of broth, the girl came clattering down the stairs, waving over her head a great sword whose hilt was of iron inlaid with silver, and whose sheath was made from a rattlesnake-skin.

"I knew that though you should forget to say farewell to me, you would remember to wait for this," she said. "I took it upstairs last night and polished it a long time after you were all asleep. Does it not look well?"

"I did not remember it," Randvar admitted, "so little used am I to anything more than a hunting-knife." Taking it from her as she unsheathed it, he felt its edges critically, and feigned to test them on one of her yellow braids. "The hilt cleaves to my hand like the palm of a friend. I shall feel more self-respecting to go among strangers with my father's sword at my side. Perhaps some of his good-fortune will come from it to me." His brown face reddened, and he turned it away suddenly to watch the girl's nimble fingers fastening at his hip the sword-belt which she had drawn across his shoulder.

But Snowfrid jumped up with her usual liveliness, crying, "If your luck is most good, it may even happen that the *jarl* will make you a guardsman like Bolverk," and he bestirred himself to tease her as usual.

"Pooh! If he cannot do any more for me than that, I shall come home again!"

The emphasis with which her hands planted themselves upon her hips boded ill for him, but Erna came between them to make sure that the strap which held his harp to his back was also secure. When that had been seen to, there was no further excuse for lingering.

Stretching out his arms to his foster-mother, he said: "Live as well as you can, and do not worry about Eric or me. Your luck will take care of me, and I will take care of him."

She clasped him around the neck, and kissed him with passionate fierceness.

"If you owe me anything, pay it to Eric," she whispered in his ear, and then turned away and began violently to stir the soup.

At that, Snowfrid took a hand from her hip to draw the back of the wrist across her eyes, and signified that she was going to see him off by slipping out ahead into the gray light.

Though the darkness had melted from the air, there lingered in it yet that chill of unreality which makes earth and trees and even rocks seem but phantoms of themselves. As they crossed the grass, Randvar said, "It has the look of a dead world that is waiting for the sun to bring it to life," and the girl shivered assent and drew closer to him.

At the entrance to the path she stopped, and he turned for a parting look at the dwelling that his father's gentled strength had built and his mother's courageous love had hallowed. In the grayness it loomed as remote and unreal as all the rest, the firelight that showed wanly through the archways only adding to its shadowy strangeness.

"It seems to me that life is only just beginning for me, too," he said slowly as he gazed.

"You ought not to feel so," the girl cried reproachfully. "You ought to feel that you are going away from your father and mother."

He shook his head. "I feel instead that I am coming closer to them. It was my father's lot before me to leave his home and go forth to try what the gods would grant him." As standing on the same spot he had lifted his hand in greeting to Erna, so now he raised it in farewell to the home scene. "It was a good dream while it lasted, but I am glad to be awake at last."

Snowfrid burst into tears on his shoulder. "It is a wicked thing that men must grow up and go away!"

Times there were when she would have been shaken off with severity; even now he put her from him hastily, though he bent and kissed her, bantering.

"What foolishness is here! If a guardsman had not grown up and gone away from his home, where would your fun have come in?"

Rain clouds were, not so thick in her blue eyes but that sun shone through at that. Tiptoeing to reach his ear, she whispered, "Remind him of me, sometimes!" Then hiding her face, she fled back to the tower; and he set forth laughing.

A silvery haze veiled all but the path just before his feet, so that he appeared to be ever advancing from mystery to mystery. He would have been less than a song-maker if it had not seemed to him a symbol of the unknown life into which he was entering, if he had not given himself un reservedly to musing on his hopes and fears. His feet travelled the trails by instinct that day, and by instinct forded the streams and threaded the marshes; his mind was travelling the roads of the *jarl's* town, fording the deeps of Brynhild's pride, threading the maze of Kelvin's temper.

Burning its way through the grayness, the sun came out. Like a ball of fire, it rolled up the eastern slope of the heavens. Like a ball of fire, it rolled down the sky's western side. Still he walked in a dream, conscious only of the light of his visions. It was not until the hills showed like nicks in the fire-ball's rim, and he had reached the last knoll rising between him and the sight of the *jarl's* town, that he was recalled to the present.

Half-way to the crest loomed a mass of cinder-hued rusty-veined rock. Rounding this brought him suddenly upon Eric the Page, squatted on his heels beside a patch of the wintergreen berries which the youth of New Norway valued next to honey. In the process of adjusting his attention to this abrupt demand, the Songsmith stood gazing at him; but the youngster scrambled up with an involuntary "Odin!" which was as much a prayer as an exclamation. When, presently, Randvar put out a hand and lifted him by his embroidered collar, he began to talk much more like a small boy caught robbing a trap than the haughty page of a *jarl's* daughter.

"Now, foster-brother! I have not done anything. I did your bidding with her. I have not done anything, foster-brother."

"Plain enough you have it before your mind what I ought to do," Randvar said with his short laugh. Then he gave him a slight shake and let him go. "Have it even as you have chosen. It may be that I shall not find it harder to forget you than you found it to forget me." While his one hand quitted the gay collar, his other took toll from the berry-laden cap, and he passed on.

That he should not be allowed to forget, however, he was able to guess. It was no surprise when the boy's voice sounded again at his elbow, in the wheedling tone that was as familiar as the gleam of his curly head.

"Foster-brother, what is the need of taking it in that way, either? I could explain it with a mouthful of words if you would listen."

As the Songsmith could not deny some curiosity to hear the explanation, he allowed his pace to slacken. Eric read the sign quickly.

"You need not think it was lack of friendliness. As well as you, I know that because I have been able to get honour and fine manners for myself is the more reason why I ought to protect and help lesser men, and I have the intention to do so. But the truth is that in these clothes you look so like a dead tree that has got out of a moss-bed and walked in from the forest, that I became too embarrassed at the thought of anyone's remembering that I used to be like you to be able to think of aught else. It was not until afterwards that it crossed my mind that you might feel hurt, and I got ashamed of myself."

Of a sudden, Randvar began to laugh and pulled the boy up to him and hugged him; and then of a sudden he frowned and held him off at arm's-length.

"I suppose," he said, "that is also the explanation why you have not been home to see your kinswomen since the *jarl's* sister picked you out for her page three seasons ago,—not because you do not have love towards them, but because you dislike to be put in mind of the poor way in which you used to live?"

Eric did not answer immediately, but walked a while making embarrassed snatches at the flaming *sumacs* they were passing.

"I have so little time," he muttered at last.

The Songsmith looked down at him severely. "Whether your dignity takes it well or not," he said, "I am going to tell you that I think you in a worse way than the man in the werewolf story. Every ninth night it happened to him to change his man's shape for a wolf's body, but never did he lose his man's nature. Even when his appetite forced him to prey upon cattle, his man's eyes looked out of the wolf's sockets in loathing. You have shed your forest ways for these mincing court manners, but you have changed your manful nature also, that used to have honesty in it, and love of kin. I foresee that as time goes on there will be a harder nut to crack than this which we two have just had a hand in."

Enough honesty remained in the boy so that he showed himself abashed. Again his voice cajoled, when it came after a long interval of silent plodding.

"I *have* got love towards my kin. I was going to send good gifts to them the next time a trading-ship went that way. I will send some back by you now, if you are willing to take them. I suppose you fared hither to see Starkad set adrift?"

"To see *what?*" Randvar repeated, losing sternness in surprise.

A change of subject appeared to be much to Eric's taste. He launched forth eagerly:

"They are going to set him adrift on the river, of course. Is it possible that you have not heard of it? Saint Olaf was disposed of in that way, because after the battle his foes would for no sake allow him to be buried on Norwegian ground. His friends put his body on a boat and sent it out to sea; and so bound was old Starkad to follow him in everything, he gave orders long ago that this should be his end also. It will happen as soon as the sun sets, and it will be a great sight to see. I came over here myself to look at it, since Brynhild has little need of pages while she sits mourning in her bower."

Randvar made no answer, for they came just then to the top of the ridge and saw below them the broad river, uncoiled through the land like a Midgard serpent of glittering gold, and saw beyond it the spreading grain-fields and vine-clad slopes of the *jarl's* town, its light streaks of stone walls winding between dark tree-trunks, its clusters of brown roofs blotting the gay autumn foliage, its clouds of gray smoke drifting across the bright face of the sky.

Around every group of roofs circled broad acres of farm-land and pasture-land, for the settlement was no straggling line of cabins, no huddle of tented booths, but a typical Norse town almost as prosperous as Nidaros itself. From the *jarl's* domain, the scores upon scores of great estates radiated like spokes from a hub, separated from it and from one another by stretches of wood and grassy common, and bound together by tree-arched lanes and broad white roads, and by the shining highway of the river with its stone wharves and anchored ships.

Truly it was a wonderful sight to come upon in the midst of the new-world wilderness. The two on the ridge lingered to gaze at it, and Randvar's air-castles paled beside the deeper interest of reality.

He said thoughtfully: "It is a testing-place of men's mettle. They alone will get fame here of whom it can be said that they are well-tempered. . . . Only by many accomplished men coming to a spot at one time, with all their wealth on their backs, could such a stronghold be built inside the space of two-score years. Do you know, young one, how many people make up the town?"

"While I cannot say for certain," Eric answered, "I think I have heard it reckoned that there are two thousand, counting in women and thralls; for it is said that everyone brought all his kin and his property with him. That was not a little to take out of Norway at one time. Starkad was wont to say that if Saint Olaf's foes did get a great gain over him in the battle in which they slew him, yet was it some loss to them when so many of his following preferred rather to go into exile than to bear the new rule—"

Randvar's uplifted hand checked him. "Hush! I heard a horn," he said, and they held their breath in listening.

For the first time they noticed that the sounds of the day had waned with its light, which was now almost gone, no more of the sun's fiery ball remaining than would have served for a signal-light on the hill-top. Already the eastern side of the trees was sombre with shadow; and the lazy splash of the river seemed to fill the world until, faint and sweet, the funeral music was brought to them by the breeze. Growing moment strongly with the emerging of the train of sable-garbed horsemen from the little wood through which the road ran, the dirge throbbed solemnly in their ears.

Upon Eric the Page it seemed to be borne in suddenly that he was in charge of a grand spectacle with which to amaze and delight his forest-bred companion. He assumed the responsibility willingly.

"Now am I well pleased," he said, "that you are going to get so good a chance to see something of court ways. That is the black bearskin that they are carrying the corpse on. Those men riding beside it are the priests. The tall haughty one is the bishop. The name given him is Magnus Fire-and-Sword, because he has the custom of burning and slaying all who do not believe as he does. The clumsy one coming last men call the Shepherd Priest, because it was his lot to herd sheep on a Swedish dairy-farm before it came into his head to be a holy man. The leather-clad fellows who ride after him with bags at their saddle-bows are guards bearing the treasures that are to go with Starkad,—his armour and his weapons and his jewelled ornaments, even the gold circlet he wore on his head. The new *jarl* would have it so; he would not keep so much as a—That is he—Helvin, Starkad's son—with the red hair—riding a black horse—do you see?"

Randvar nodded absently; since first the black horse came into view, his eyes had been fixed upon its rider.

"He bears himself as stark as the dead man," he muttered, then finding that he was speaking aloud, shook himself back to attention.

Wading waist-deep into the water, the eight bearers of the litter had placed their burden upon the black-draped boat waiting on the darkening waves. Now the contents of the treasure-bags were handed to them, piece by piece, and they built with it a glittering bulwark around the moundlike form. Then the oldest of the advice-givers, an old man gnarled and bald as an ancient oak, came stiffly down the bank with a lighted torch in his hand, and laid the flame against the rope of plaited straw that held the boat to the shore.

Leaping out hungrily, the yellow tongues licked up the morsel and reached out for the food that lay beyond, while the loosened boat swung gently from the land. With the rush of wind, the fire rose crackling and hissing, and gradually the sun set light was lost in the new glare that filled the river valley. Rising as it rose, and quivering like it, rose the voice of the dead *jarl's skald*, chanting his death-song.

In the red glare the boat slipped seaward. As it drifted past them, the man and the boy on the knoll could see every fire-lit jewel sparkling and flashing in a ring of splendour around the form under the black pall. Then it drifted farther, and once more the sunset glory became visible around it. By-and-by it was no more than a star in the gathering dusk; and the old *skald's* voice strained thin and high in the effort to send his song after the departing voyager—cracked and broke, and there was silence on both sides of the river.

On the side opposite the town it was Eric who broke the pause, rousing himself with a yawn and a stretch.

"I declare this to be the best entertainment Starkad ever gave me," he remarked. "But one cannot be always enjoying himself. I suppose you will pass the night at the hostelry before going back?" He brushed a leaf from his tunic with Olaf's own elegance of gesture, then made use of Olaf's own oath as he glimpsed his companion's face. "By Saint Michael! you look as solemn as though you were going to be buried yourself."

Straightening from the cramped attitude of the watcher, the Songsmith shook off the mood that had held him and became quietly purposeful. He said briefly:

"I go neither back to the tower nor forward to the hostelry, but to join the *jarl's* following. Does it lie within your knowledge whether it is the custom to go directly to him? Or should I speak first to one of those around him?"

Whether or not the knowledge lay in Eric, his mouth was blocked by amazement; only horror could leak through.

"Go to Helvin Jarl in those clothes! He would order his dogs set on you! You look more like a stag than a man."

It is likely that he went on at some length, but Randvar gave him no further attention. Making his way down the hill and across the bridge, he came into the crowd just beginning to disperse. His final decision was to submit the question of etiquette to Bolverk, whose burly figure had come into sight in the throng; but before he could reach the guardsman, his glance encountered Kelvin's.

Rigidly erect rode the young *jarl* in his sable mourning clothes, his face an ivory mask to hide what lay beneath it; but into his eyes there leaped now such a look as a man gnawed by torturing fear might give the man who brought him relief. What the look meant, the Songsmith did not ask himself; he knew only that response to it rose in him as rises a river in flood-time. Like a wooden bridge before a freshet, etiquette was swept out of his thoughts.

Pushing between the courtmen, he made his way to the *jarl*. Without speaking, Helvin put out a hand and gripped the deerskin shoulder, and so rode holding to it as Rolf's son walked beside him.

Chapter 6

Ill luck is the end of ill redes
    —Northern saying.

It was three weeks later. A group of old fur-traders stood in the porch of the *jarl's* feasting-hall, answering in chorus the remark of one of their number:

"A favourite so soon? Time is not allowed to go to seed when a young man gets the rule!"

"Ah, the good old days of peace and order!"

"More than ever, now, the doubt works in me whether it is Kelvin's good training or his bad temper that will be uppermost."

"It is not to be looked for that he will get tame counsel from his new friend," returned the man who had spoken first. "My son, who brought the tidings home last week, says that already the forester has fought with Olaf, Thorgrim's son, and so won his way to great love with the young courtmen, who are all jealous of Olaf's favour with Starkad's daughter."

The chorus interrupted him, growling in their beards.

"Though he came off with honour from the young men, still it is not settled that he will fare in the same way with us!"

"No man has brought back such accomplishments as Olaf the French—"

"It is plain in everything that little good will come from this sea-rover's son—"

"I am getting curious to see him."

"You will not have to wait long—"

"As soon as this pine-mast of a hunter gets out of the road—"

That was not very soon for a great throng was ahead of the hunter, and no hurrying or struggling competition marked their progress, since the course of a river between its banks is not more fixed than was the place of each. Dropping out or pushing on, they settled leisurely into orderly rows upon the long benches against the wainscot—advice-givers and courtmen and guards along the southern wall, priests and lawmen and land-owners along the northern, the eastern cross-bench for women guests, the western for the women of the court, such small-fry as armourers and harpers and tumblers filling the draughty corners by the doors. The time came at last, however, when the hunter's tow head brushed under the lintel; and pushing after him, the traders came into the cheer of the heir's inheritance feast.

Gone was the darkness and coldness and silence of mourning that for three Norse weeks had brooded over the mighty pillared hall. Once more, the light of fragrant juniper torches played upon pictured tapestry and garlanded column. Once more, the round gilded shields hanging above the benches were turned into so many suns by the ruddy glow of fires leaping on the stone hearths down the middle of the long nave. At the white-spread tables that formed an oblong around the fires, the gorgeous feasting dresses of the court-folk made streaks of rainbow colour through the brightness.

Running his eye up the line of the southern wall, the trader who had spoken last said over his shoulder: "Yonder he is, on Kelvin's left, as was to be expected."

He might have done better to say, "on the left of the high-seat," whose towering carven posts marked plainly its place midway the length of the hall, for the heir was in no way conspicuous in the line of his guests as he sat on the footstool of the ruler's seat, awaiting the ceremony which should elevate him to its empty cushions. But the traders found the spot at once where the new face looked out over the scene, and they studied it critically as they moved forward.

What they saw was a superbly proportioned young fellow of four-and-twenty, rising as erectly tall beside the guardsmen as a pine-tree beside oaks. Level as pine branches was the line of his thick dark brows, and no gold but the sun's glowing burnish was on the mass of hair that shadowed his sun-ripened face. Of the might of the primeval wastes and of the wilderness's virile beauty, he was expressive. One of the old men spoke for them all when he said:

"Since Helvin, Starkad's son, has been likened to a captive eagle, it would not be amiss to call this fellow an eagle of the forest that has come to perch beside him because of a kinship between their natures. The Fates alone can tell what will come of such a partnership!" Doubt was heavy in the wagging of their heads as they turned away to follow the overseer of guests to the seats appointed them.

Following after them went the eyes of Randvar the Songsmith. Though their words had not carried across the fire, their scrutiny had, so that gradually his mouth took on a satirical twist. Presently he spoke to the heir on the footstool—spoke without having been spoken to—to the indignation of the old counsellors on the right of the high-seat.

"Lord, when I see how your people stare at me as at a black Jotun, I realize it is not a dream that I am in your court. Other times it seems to me as if I must be lying on the cedar branches by the tower fire and imagining what I should wish to happen."

To the added displeasure of the old chieftains, Helvin justified the familiarity by returning it. He had been sitting with his chin on his hand, a figure of weary splendour in his furred and jewelled dress of state; now he straightened and resting his elbow on the seat-cushion, entered into conversation with the son of the sea-rover,—it was fortunate that the old men could not also hear his frank remarks.

"Your luck is great, Songsmith, that you can get interest out of this. Just before you spoke, I was thinking that though I were blindfolded, I should still be able to describe every tapestry on the walls, put every man, woman, and thrall in place, count up every dish and goblet and knife on the table. At times, when I sat where you sit now, I used to amuse myself by rearranging the people in my imagination, beginning by putting yonder fat-chopped buffoon in the proud priest's place. I can tell you that it came the nearest to making sport of anything I have had in this hall."

The song-maker's smile came readily as he glanced across at the high-seat of the northern wall, which had been held during Starkad's time by that warrior-bishop of Saint Olaf who was known as Magnus Fire-and-Sword, but which now awaited in emptiness the pleasure of the new ruler.

"It will be rearranging them in earnest this time, *jarl*. Lord, is it possible that you do not feel the excitement in the air as every person here draws breath with hope or fear of your rule? The force of their eyes upon you is like the beat of waves upon the shore."

As brand from brand, the face of the *jarl's* son kindled; but before he was ready to reply, the Song-smith's glance had flown past him and lighted on the eastern door.

Through the broad portal was advancing a train of court-women, walking far apart because of the trailing length of their silken robes, stately matrons with towering head-dresses, and white-armed maidens whose bright tresses fell free from golden bands, and moving before them—the jewel for whom all their splendour was but a setting— Brynhild the Proud, bending now her queenly head to the greeting of some old warrior, now yielding a smile to some young courtman's eager salute.

It was the first glimpse Randvar had had of her since that day in the forest, so rigidly had mourning custom secluded her in her bower. As a man who has lived long on a memory, he drank thirstily of the wine of her beauty, felt it course hotly through his veins. He was still leaning forward when he felt the *jarl's* gaze upon him, and knew that his face had betrayed him. In confusion he dropped his eyes.

Helvin said dryly: "It is seen that you did not reject my sister's favor because you did not find her good to look upon, Songsmith."

Randvar overcame enough of his embarrassment to mutter that no one could find her otherwise.

The *jarl's* son shook his head as he watched his sister advance. "Here you may see how much man differs from man. To Olaf, Thorgrim's son, yonder, she looks like the goddess Sif after the dwarfs wove her hair of red gold, as no doubt he is telling her now with his smile. To me"— he turned wearily as her approach made rising incumbent— "to me she looks only like a rune standing for a life I hate." Rising, he faced her with cold civility.

Splendid in her feasting dress of shining gold colour, she came towards them, bent in a deep courtesy before the high-seat, mocked the lowliness of the salutation by the loftiness to which she rose.

"Brother," she said, "will you grant me a boon which I would beg of you?"

He answered: "Grant it I would before it were asked if I were not desirous to hear how you would beg; but what is it you wish?"

Her white lids drooped haughtily. "It is known far and wide, brother, how you hate formalities, so it is not to be expected that you will hold to them now that you can do what you like about everything. What I want is your leave to retire with my women as soon as the amusements begin. I dislike brawling freedom."

Curling like the petals of a rose, her beautiful lips curved disdainfully. Kelvin's smoke-gray eyes showed a spark as they rested on her.

"It is well that my face is not set against what you ask, kinswoman," he said, "for your way of entreating would be unlikely to move a man to much gentleness. This I grant you willingly, that you may leave as soon as any brawling begins."

She thanked him in the formal phrase, and mocking him again with the bend of courtly submission, made as though she would have passed on. Then, seemingly for the first time, she saw the deerskin-clad figure leaning on the arm of the high-seat, and paused to look him up and down in displeasure.

"Greeting, Randvar, Rolf's son, and welcome to you!" she said. "Yet I think, after all, you would have done better to take service with me, if my brother's generosity towards you is to be measured by the clothes you wear."

Deep in the cave of his breast, Randvar felt his temper stir like a sleeping bear; but craving a smile from her starry eyes, he made an attempt at conciliation.

"I had thought you would guess, gold-bright maiden, that it is the *jarl's* forbearance which lets me be slow in shedding my bark."

The tilt of her chin showed how little his deprecation had helped him.

"An economical virtue is the *jarl's* forbearance," she said, "and Freya's son is more than expectedly dull at learning what beseems him."

The bear awoke then with a snarl. Randvar gasped afterwards at remembering what he would have answered if Helvin had not taken the word, laying a hand on his shoulder.

"Do not grudge me one plain man, my kinswoman, while you have so many gay ones at your beck. It is at my desire he has kept on the wood land garb; that seeing how different the outside of him is from all around me, I may ever be reminded how much of new interest I have found inside him."

Too courtly was she bred to dispute a ruler's whim; to that she gave prompt if haughty ac quiescence.

"In this as in everything, it must be done as you wish, brother, only I take it upon me to urge you to show us the inside of him as soon as you can," she made answer. Then she passed on; and her women went rustling by, moving to laughter as to music.

Randvar's bitter reflections were interrupted by the pressure of Kelvin's hand upon his shoulder.

"If I had not taken the word out of your mouth, my friend," the *jarl* said in his ear, "your hot head would have got you into further difficulties; but I like you none the worse for that. I liked it less when I thought that after the manner of all other men, you were going to fall on your knees to her only because she is beautiful of face. It would have been the first matter in which our minds did not match as blade matches sheath. So long as you have manfulness enough to resent her pride, I forgive it to you that her fairness has bewitched your eyes."

Again embarrassment left the song-maker speech less. Under the *jarl's* hand he stood so constrainedly that the old men who were watching imagined him to be cast down by some rebuke, and experienced a sense of satisfaction. And their relief was no greater than his when the duties of the heir's station put an end to further confidences.

Bearing the baton of state, two pages advanced and took their place before the *jarl's* son. While one received his sword from him with many flourishes, the other delivered to him the gilded wand. Stretching it forth, a bar of light, he gave the signal for the feasting to begin.

Like white-robed statues called to life, the thralls waiting at the doors moved forward with their burdens of gilded flagons and silver chargers. Through the fragrance of the juniper torches and the pine-tips of the floor-covering rose the savour of roasted meats and the spicy aroma of mead and wine. To the hum of blended voices was added the clink of silver-rimmed horns. The oftener the resounding salute rang out, the louder the hum arose, the merrier the laughter that burst forth where groups of young men were scattered among the old ones like poppies among wheat.

No higher note of noisy revelry was left to strike when at last the moment came for the old advice-giver, Mord, to lead the heir up into his father's seat and put in his hands the sacred horn that he might make his inheritance-vow. From high mirth they passed to deep feeling, as each man rose holding his shining horn above his head. Excitement shook some of the young hands so that their wine was spilled—excitement and exultation at the spectacle of a young ruler in the high-seat!—and to some of the old eyes tears came unconsciously, so that they seemed to look through a mist at the figure of their old leader's son.

Noble in splendour was Helvin Jarl as the firelight caught the golden embroideries and jewelled clasps of his sweeping robes; and noble in purpose was his pale finely cut face under the mass of blood-red hair when he raised the great horn and spoke so that all could hear him.

"I drink the toast to the old gods and to the new," he said, "and to those who have gone before me; but the vow I make is no vow that I shall be great. What I promise is that I shall make no other man small. I take oath that under my rule every man shall live a free life in all such matters as concern himself, nor shall any be forced into ways against which his mind rebels. I take Heaven and all of you as witnesses!" Putting the horn to his lips, he drank.

Mechanically, the ranks of standing men imitated the motion, their eyes continuing to stare at him over their cup rims. But before the draught was down, the call of free blood to free blood had been heard. From young courtmen and young guardsmen went up ringing cheers. It counted for little that some of the lawmen murmured, and Magnus Fire-and-Sword spoke to his neighbour from under a frown.

Only the *jarl* noticed that, and noticing, smiled mockingly. When the tumult had sunk once more he spoke, the smile dwindling to a droop of his mouth-corner.

"The first thing that I must try my hand on is the filling of the other high-seat with the man I hold highest in honour. That would be to take a great deal on my hands if custom did not say that he must be a holy man, which makes the choice easy."

He paused to clear his throat with a swallow of wine, and perhaps to note how the arrogant face of Magnus was losing some of its displeasure. Then he went on, his voice so cool and keen that it bit like a blade:

"As for you, priests, I know only one of you for whom I have any honour at all. I have heard many talk of the mercy of Christ, whose hands had cut blood-eagles in other men only for being unable to believe as they did. I have heard not a few talk of Christ's humbleness whose tempers were so overbearing that men would have risen up and slain them if they had not held up their holy names for shields. I have seen many Odin-men who put on the Christ-faith like a kirtle, but I have seen only one who made it a part of his nature and showed it forth in his acts. He is the Swede whom men call the Shepherd Priest. It is my offer and will that he shall come forward and take the place opposite me."

At the eastern end of the room, in the lowliest seat by the door, a man rose hastily—an ungainly old man in rusty robes—and lifted a hand in protest; and in the same instant the stately velvet-draped form of Magnus became wrathfully erect before his place.

"This—this is sacrilege!" he thundered. "I call all Christian men to resist this mockery—this—"

"Sacrilege?" The young *jarl's* voice pierced like a spear, scornbarbed. "This I have often said, that it was a sacrilege that you should give rein to a devil's nature in the name of Christ! That I honour the cause by honouring the man who stands most truly for it—be he king-born or thrall-born—that is honesty. Had you any love of your faith amid your self-love, you would see it."

If the rage-purpled face of the Fire-and-Sword had not been the face of a bishop, they might have thought it the face of a Berserker. The names which he called his godson were the names that fighting-men use when their tempers pressed hardest for relief. Upon the openest-minded of the old counsellors was forced slowly a doubt whether there really was much holiness about him; and the young men broke loose and drowned his voice in hisses.

But Helvin Jarl rose in his high-seat, his glance like the outleaping of flame.

"I am all that which you call me, and more," he said, "and it is because I am—because I need only to bring forward the straits I have fallen in to prove what kind of harvests spring from your sowing—that I vow you shall never sow again while my rule is in New Norway. In the spring, ships shall take you back whence you came; meanwhile, come you no more before my face, hypocrite that you are to your marrow!"

Starkad's own inexorableness in the gesture, he levelled his baton at the door; then before the aghast silence could give rise to any sign, he turned where the Shepherd Priest waited and spoke to him respectfully and yet sternly.

"You whose sincereness has won my honour, bear in mind that cowardice no less than arrogance is love of self. If your faith is indeed first with you, remember that I offer you a chance to do great work for it, and forget any lesser thing."

With the ceasing of his voice there was again silence, but the Shepherd Priest made no attempt to use it for his protests. After a time he lifted his bent head, and his rugged face was as a mean lantern through which a light is shining. Amid breathless stillness, the velvet-clad form of Magnus stalked out of the western door, and the ungainly form in rusty black walked slowly to the northern high-seat, walking uncertainly like a man in the dark, holding to his crucifix as to a guiding hand.

Again the *jarl* forestalled an outburst, speaking once more with the graciousness of a noble heir on his inheritance-night.

"One thing more I wish to tell you, then I will no longer hinder you from your amusements. It has to do with the Skraellings. Always it has seemed to me that much good might come of having them for partners in this business of settling the new lands, and now I have heard that of them which makes me want them also for friends. So have I sent a message to their lord which asks him to meet me ten days hence at some middle point between our abodes, and over a feast talk about how we can get good from each other. That is the end of my speaking."

It was the beginning of uproar. All at once the half-dozen old traders, who had entered the hall in such doubting humour, rose to their feet, swung their horns above their heads and cried as with one voice:

"I drink to Kelvin Jarl!"

Then: "Young blood for gainfulness !"

"New ways for new—"

"Down with old boundaries—"
Spread out! Spread out!"
"Luck to the new rule!"

The new step being approved by such undoubted authorities, the other old men joined for the first time in the applause; while the young men were brought to the point of handling their cups like gavels, and one whose wine did not sit well upon his wits clambered upon the seat and began to use shields from the wall for cymbals. Even to the women's cross-bench it sped. Eagerly Yrsa the Lovely spoke to her young mistress by whom she sat.

"*Jarl's* sister, do you call to mind how fair and fine we thought that bead-embroidery we saw last trading-day? Now we can get a Skraelling woman to teach us how to do it,—if so be there are women among them," she added doubtfully.

It seemed that Brynhild spoke because she had been addressed rather than because she heeded what was said to her. Fingering her jewelled necklace, she continued frowning at the fire.

"Never saw I aught to equal it," she said. "That Magnus should behave so boorishly—And yet that we should have a thrall-born bishop—And yet it seems to me that Helvin behaved well—It must be that the earth is coming loose from its moorings!"

From her place farther down the line, the pretty matron who had laughed at the forester bent for ward urgently. "*Jarl's* sister, is it your will that we should take our leave now? The amusements are beginning. Yonder deerskin fellow has just beckoned to the harp-bearer. She motioned with her lace-crowned head. Brynhild's gaze, however, did not follow the motion, but remained upon her, gathering displeasure.

"Deerskin fellow!" she repeated. "Is it in that manner, Sigrid, that you speak of Freya's son? However he forgets it himself, it behoves you to remember that he has king's blood in him." Arranging her gold-coloured draperies about her and settling to formal attention, she finished severely: "Had he no blood at all, a song-maker has the right to courteous treatment. I expect that you will, all of you, leave off chattering and give him the attention due a man of accomplishments." When she had seen her orders carried out, she fixed her eyes calmly upon the spot where Randvar stood beside the towering gilded harp of the court-*skald*.

The Songsmith's heart leaped and tried to strangle him as he met her gaze, yet it was not long that his hands swept aimlessly across the strings. In him had awakened a desire to interpret to these folk of

Norse blood the lives of the forest men, whose creed was so like theirs in strong simplicity.

Soon he struck a chord and sang with a voice as untaught as a bird's, and as full of unconscious ecstasy, the story of the Skraelling chief who gave his life to save his followers from the wrath of their offended god.

Singing, he forgot that he sang among strangers. Listening, they forgot that he told a stranger's story; as at the deeds of a brother, their minds quickened with understanding. A stillness gathered over the room that lasted even after the song was ended, and was broken only when cries for more rose from every direction.

But it was not their applause that was the crown of his success. It was turning to find little Eric standing beside him—bewildered and ruffled—holding out an arm-ring of golden filigree, saying as one repeating a lesson:

"Starkad's daughter bids you cover some of the deerskin with this."

Chapter 7

The tongue is the bane of the head
—Northern saying.

It was a fantastic scene, the wilds of a forest river-bank turned into a guest-house for court-folk. Athwart the living green of the pines, camp-fires sent their spirals of blue smoke, and groups of thralls made white rings around the blaze as they roasted the game and heated the wine with which pages skimmed to and fro. Down by the sparkling water, knots of old chieftains and young courtmen divided their time between eating and gazing across the stream at the Skraellings encampment of the opposite shore.

Back among the trees, where the drifted leaves had been heaped into cushions of russet and gold, groups of gentlewomen chatted as merrily amid the great stillness as though they were among the whirring wheels of their own bower. Still farther up the brown slope and deeper in the grove, Helvin Jarl, in his splendid riding dress of gold-embroidered green, sat upon a heap of bowlders over which red wolf-skins had been thrown, his song-maker lounging beside him, wild-locked and wild-garbed as a creature of the wood, except for the harp at his back.

Randvar had finished eating and was staring contentedly at nothing. Over the forest lay the hush of that strange season which falls like a breathless pause in the brisk round of the autumn. Dropped suddenly motionless were the winds that had been lashing the trees like mighty flails; and as a conjuror changes knives to roses, so had the keen cold of the morning been changed to balmy warmth by the red noon sun. A fancy came to him that the golden haze veiling the end of every tree-aisle was the visible shape of a dream in the air.

"It feels like noon-spell in harvest-time," he said aloud. "I think the earth has worked so hard that it has fallen asleep and dreams now of the summer."

"Say the same thing later on when the day is at an end," Helvin answered. "To me it feels like a devil's fit of repentance. After his spite has been for weeks like a rasp in the air, and his fury has torn all within reach, he tires of his rage for a day or two—holds his peace and puts on a watery smile."

Even while the song-making part of Randvar smiled approval of the figure, his woodsman's alertness detected something odd about the voice in which the words were uttered. Sideways he sent a glance at his lord.

It seemed to him that there was also something odd about Kelvin's expression; but he had no chance to scrutinize it for on the instant it was gone, while the *jarl* caught his look and challenged it.

"Why do you stare as if you saw a hedge-rider?"

"Lord, your voice sounded as though it came hard for you to breathe," Randvar answered after a moment.

Kelvin's words leaped out like tigers from a cage. "Why should it not? in this smothering stillness where even the trees are holding their breath to listen for something. Oh, for the plains! the plains! where the wind blows, and a man can see all around him, and not so much as a ghost can creep on him unawares! It is a trap, this forest of yours; and every rank of trees is a wall to shut one tighter in with his thoughts. Had I an axe ready to my hand, and the might in my arm—"

Even as it seemed that his body would be wrung by a violent gesture, he caught himself; and his voice slackened to a mocking drawl.

"What a good thing it is that I have three wise-minded old ravens to make sport for me! Hither they wing their way now to give me final advice in this treaty-making. Odin be thanked, it will not be long before we are on the move! Yonder my kinswoman's hand sends a summons to you, Songsmith. Go, sting Olaf's jealousy again. The entertainment I have in torturing him, teaches me for the first time why Starkad had delight in bear-baiting."

In words now as well as voice, he was strange to his song-maker. Randvar mused on it as he descended the slope; again the feeling that he was wakening from a dream came over him.

"Seldom have I experienced such strange things in my sleep as I have done since that day at the Black Pool," he murmured; then as his wandering gaze fell upon the group before him, he finished contentedly: "But if it be a dream, it must be said that it is a good one."

Surrounded by her band of comely women, with the elegant Olaf outstretched before her, the *jarl's* sister sat enthroned on the slope at the foot of an ancient oak. The masses of bronze foliage still clinging around the base of the mighty limbs, spread like a canopy above her. The huge trunk was as a background for her rounded form in its kirtle of wine-red, gold-embroidered; against the black bark, her hair was as a spot of golden fire. The song-maker saw neither Yrsa's pretty smile of welcome nor the shrug of Thorgrim's son when their mistress greeted him graciously.

"Make me a song in tune with the forest, Song-smith," she requested. "Olaf's French ballads that chime so well with my bower sound in this place like the tinkling of bells, though I would not seem thankless in saying so."

Olaf rose and acknowledged playfully the apologetic gesture she made him.

"Be in no fear of hurting my feelings, madam, by preferring his songs over mine," he said. "I have amusement in trifling with the singing-craft, as becomes a high-born man; but to do such work seriously is the portion of churls."

She took back the conciliating hand to fold it on the other in her lap, and spoke a trifle haughtily. "In France, it may be so, *beausire*. Among Norse men, *skaldship* has always been held in honour. If the truth must be told, I am in best tune with Norse ways."

"Then will I take away the discordant note of my presence," he said, and smiled at her quizzically as he turned. But he was not so unscathed that his eyes could pass the Songsmith as they encountered him; there, with his will or without it, they froze. "Unless," he added, "the forester has the wish to make some reply to me."

Time was when the forester would have replied with the tongue of his snake-skin scabbard, but he was not dull in learning new ways. Almost his smile was a match for Olaf's as he answered:

"To what end should I do that, courtman? It is not for the contented moon to bark at the jealous dog."

It was not only Thorgrim's son who drew breath quickly, then; every maiden of the group caught hers with a little scream. The *jarl's* sister rose swiftly, standing erect as a red lily.

"This thing comes ill to pass that you forget me as well as yourselves," she said.

After a moment, Olaf lowered his glittering eyes and finished his withdrawal; when Brynhild sank again to her place among the mossy roots, and settled herself as one preparing for a treat.

"Sing, I pray you," she said to the Songsmith.

For him, Olaf ceased to exist. Unslinging his rude harp, he leaned easily against a tree before her and sang her a Skraelling love-song, a song made of murmuring brook-sounds, of the calls of mating birds, of the wild note of the blast in the tree-tops, a song that tuned well with the hush and the haze of the autumn forest. In a silken tangle of interlocked arms, the women made a rapt circle around him; and the *jarl's* sister was drawn forward on her moss-cushion. She freed a long breath when the last note had died away among the leafless branches above them.

"It seems to me," she said slowly, "that the work which interpreters do between men of different tongues is the work that song-makers do between people of different ranks. When I hear you sing, creatures who have seemed to me no more than beasts become human like myself. If there were enough singers to interpret people to one another, perhaps there would be no strife in the world."

Pleasure so deepened the colour in the Songsmith's face that he was glad to shake his long hair over it by bowing low; he was saved the necessity of answering for after a little Brynhild spoke again, sinking back in her seat to regard him thoughtfully.

"The first time that ever it happened to me to hear your voice was also in the forest, as you sang the Song of Fridtjof the way you would have liked it to happen. Ever since then I have wondered what kind of ending you gave to it. It seems to me that this would be a good time to sing it, if you are willing that we should get further good from your gift of song."

"The *best* time!" cried Yrsa, clapping her hands; while urgent murmurs came from all the rest, from Sigrid, the haughtiest of the matrons, down to the shyest of the maids.

Once Randvar would have struck up without further consideration; now he fingered the harp-strings hesitatingly before he answered.

"*Jarl's* sister, we have not quarrelled for two weeks, and I confess that the friendliness has been worth much to me. I beg you not to urge me to do that which will set us against each other again."

Her eyebrows went down with displeasure, then up in wonder.

"I do not know what you mean," she said.

"The ending I have made would offend your pride, noble one; and then your scorn would tread on the heel of my temper. When plenty of paths open before us, why choose one that we know leads to bad walking?"

Why, indeed? Unless because she was a woman? Her gray Valkyria eyes lighted as at a challenge, for all that she remained leaning against her tree.

"You make a mistake, Songsmith," she told him, "to think that I would be offended with you for doing a thing which I asked you to do. Give me a chance, I pray, to show that I am not so with out sense."

Randvar drew his harp up higher upon his breast, then lowered it until it rested upon the ground.

"My singing-mood has passed," he said shortly, "but I will tell you the ending, since you will have your way. My story branches from your *skald's* song where Fridtjof comes to ask Ingeborg of her brother Helge. Your song has it that when Helge refuses to make the match, because Fridtjof has no more than a freeman's rank while Ingeborg is king-born, she takes it quietly and marries the old King Ring and sees no more of the man she loves, until Ring gets so old as to be tired of living and gives her to the young man, with his crown and the other things he is through with. Bah!" The Songsmith warmed in spite of himself, flung back his sun-burnished mane with the fierce grace of a stallion. "A man of spirit, your Fridtjof! Mine would have laughed in her face. My Fridtjof takes her in the teeth of Helge's refusal; and she comes to him willingly, as befits a woman of brave kin; and he wrests Ring's kingdom from him in battle. That is the way I end it."

"That is the best way!" cried two little pages who had come up with cups of hot spiced wine, and their shrill enthusiasm changed the women's breathless listening into laughter.

The *jarl's* sister laughed too, turning aside to beckon her favourite, Eric, to bring her own particular cup.

"Have thanks for the telling, Songsmith," she said, and swung the horn lightly aloft in the graceful gesture of drinking to him. "Would it be to your mind now to tell us some tale of forest adventure?"

No word of comment! It was in accordance with her promise not to be offended, but Randvar discovered of a sudden that he would rather she had quarrelled with him. He did not answer her question, but busied himself drinking the wine that was offered him. When he had given the cup back, he said abruptly:

"It is to my mind to see first how this matter stands. Maybe you believe that because she was king-born, Ingeborg would marry Ring even though she had love towards Fridtjof?"

"I do not believe that she would have had love towards Fridtjof," Brynhild answered calmly.

He felt himself growing angry as he asked her why not.

Her shapely shoulders rose. "For one thing, his manners would not be at all after her taste. He would think it big and manful to be careless about his clothes and his hair and such matters, and she would think it disgusting."

A moment Rolf's son was dumb, marvelling that a word-arrow could sting so; then, as blood to a wound, his temper surged into his face, till Eric thought it an imposing thing to step in front of his mistress. Immediately after, he was picking himself out of a briar-patch, a dozen steps away; and Randvar faced the *jarl's* sister, his voice deep with ire.

"Have you the intention to tell me," he demanded, "that it is a woman's turn of mind to care only about the cut of a man's garments or the length of his hair? That a great love could not lay hold of her as a hurricane lays hold of an oak and shake down all little matters like acorns?" He folded his arms tightly across his breast as he waited for her answer, conscious that if she should shrug her shoulders at him again he would be tempted to shake her.

But she yawned instead.

"I dare say it might befall a bondmaid to get carried out of herself," she assented. "Rulers daughters learn to rule themselves, and noble women take everything coldly."

He unfolded his arms, then, and began to laugh. "Coldly! It were good had I a shield to show you yourself in as you say that, Starkad's daughter! Through every fibre of your beauty, from the light in your eyes to the ruddy gold of your hair, runs the colour of flame. The red of your lips is the fiery blood of the North that no ice can cool; and every motion of your slim hand kindles fire in the breasts of the men who look on you. *Jarl's* sister, when that fire shall break out against your rule, it will blaze as much higher than a bond maid's passion as your spirit is stronger than hers. Coldly!" He laughed again, as he stepped back to swing his harp over his shoulder.

It seemed that his laughter pressed her pride hard; she rose suddenly, her hand crushing a mottled eagle-feather she had picked up; but she did not quite lose the composure she had pledged. After a moment she tossed the feather aside, smiling haughtily.

"Behold how you are so bent on a quarrel that you try to make one all by yourself," she said. "Let us talk about something else. I wish you would tell me whether it is because the Skraellings cannot say the word Norway that they call the town by that queer name of Norumbega—But, listen! Is it as it seems, that I hear my kinsman calling you?"

Randvar hoped that she did, realizing that his humour made a change of scene advisable. He welcomed the sound of his name shouted peremptorily from the group around the bowlders. A muttered word and a hasty bow, and he was in retreat, trampling savagely every creeping green thing he encountered.

The temper of the group into which he came matched well his own. The three old counsellors were growling like three dogs over a bone; and like Randvar the Songsmith a bone picked almost bare of endurance, the *jarl* held his rigid place among them. He turned sharply as the song-maker approached, and Randvar was startled to see how in that short time the fleeting expression had become fixed upon him. Fierceness unmistakable it showed now. In the struggle to hold it under, he had bitten his lips bloody.

"Songsmith," he said, "you know best why you gave me the counsel to fare across the river with but few men, and trust myself unarmed in the Skraelling camp. If any power lies at your tongue-roots, make the reason clear to these Mimir-heads. I have tried until my tongue foams like a goaded horse, but it seems that I do not speak their language."

Sigvat Smooth-Speech made him a gesture that was half deprecating, half paternal. "There is nothing new in that, lord, that to the ears of age the fancies of youth sound like a forgotten language. To talk of trusting a wild man that he may trust you—*jarl*, the Fenrir-wolf will be let loose before good will come of that!"

"To talk of trusting wild beasts because they have the shape of men!" snorted the adviser who stood beside Sigvat.

And Mord the Grim frowned at the son of Rolf, as he stroked the grizzled beard that clung to his chin like foliage to an oak's lower branches after its poll is bare.

"*Jarl*, it will never answer our end that you should give yourself into the guidance of a raw woodsman. That the youth is skilled in wood craft, no one gainsays,—let him rule your hunting, then. Since he has the singing-gift, hand over your entertainments to him. But when it comes to a matter in which one may so act that men's lives hang on it—lord, leave that to us!"

"Leave that to us!" the others echoed.

Helvin made no reply. He had flung himself back upon the wolf-skins and was gazing far away into the haze, his blood-streaked lip held between his white teeth. It was left for Randvar to answer.

Long enough to conquer the itch to bandy words with them, the forester stood pushing about a stalk of orange-splotched fungus with his *moccasined* foot. Then he spoke curtly:

"To this I will reply that because you are raw in knowledge of the Skraellings, you could not follow the track of my reasoning. But like enough you will believe that I am not guessing if I prove how sure of it I am. On what I have said, I will lay down my life. Say, then, that the *jarl* shall leave me bound in your hands to suffer death for any harm that befalls him."

The stillness seemed to deepen around them as the three old chiefs drew nearer to him. It was Mord who broke the silence.

"That you would bear yourself boldly was to be looked for, but it will not stand to your good if your dream-spinning has made you over-trustful. Though there be no guile behind it, and your mistake be the most excusable that man was ever tricked into, you should not come off with your life."

"I shall make no mistake," Randvar answered.

Again the stillness settled, as the Grim One's eyes probed from their beetling ambush. But he moved at last with a curt gesture.

"So be it," he assented, and laid a light hand on the young *jarl's* knee. "Lord, all is in readiness."

As though the touch were fire, Helvin started up. "Too long have we waited as it is! Songsmith, I forgot to listen to your pleading, but it must have been all-powerful. Thorbiorn, be good enough to call those whom I have chosen to ac company me,—I have warned you openly that no old men shall have part there. Such suspicion as cries from your wrinkles would breed murder in a lamb's heart! Call Bolverk and five guards men, and Gunnar and—" He broke off at the spectacle of Randvar delivering his sword into the keeping of Mord. "What is the meaning of this?"

When Mord had told him in a few words, he burst out angrily. "That shall not be! He is my friend. The risk is mine. How is any peace-talk to be made with out him? Who else can speak enough of the Skraelling tongue?"

"It is no less your people's risk," the old counsellor made him stern reminder; and Randvar reassured him briefly:

"Lord, when I learned the Skraelling tongue of the *sachem's* son, as I told you, he learned Norse of me in return."

It would seem that all objections had been met, but Helvin did not yield with his usual reasonableness. Instead, he stood scowling at the tree beside him, his hands picking and tearing at a gray lichen plastered on the bark. Finally, while they waited perplexed around him, he turned his head and looked at the Songsmith.

Meeting the look, Randvar stiffened and spoke amazedly: "Lord, what have I done?"

In words, Helvin made him no answer; but for the space of a heartbeat murder glared from his murky eyes. Then, flinging a sign towards the waiting escort, he strode down to the point where the horses waited at the fording-place, hailed eagerly by the idling groups.

Mord's tap on the song-maker's shoulder reminded him of his share in the bargain. Going aside with the three old men to the prison-chamber they had selected, he submitted his body to be bound to a tree with ropes of walrus-hide.

A wall of evergreens hid the water from his view, but he could follow the progress of the peace party only by interpreting the outbursts of the throng. A farewell of cheers marked the *jarl's* departure from this bank; a babble of comment showed when his dark-skinned hosts had received him on the other. Then a waning of interest betokened that he had passed beyond the spectators range of vision as the Skraelling ranks closed about him to conduct him to the council-fire.

With the suspension of the amusement, the crowd on the shore broke up and came strolling back; sound dwindled to the buzz of the gossips, the occasional shouts of the dice-throwers. Out of the lull there came again to the Songsmith the feeling that he was wakening from a dream, and this time the sensation remained with him.

Slowly, amid the chaos of his mind, thought took shape like this: "When a man is asleep, a hundred strange tokens are of no account; but too many of them in waking life should be taken heed of. I cannot see wherein I have done aught to deserve anger. . . . Once before

183

has he been wroth without enough cause,—the night he came to the tower. . . . Surely I must have been dreaming these five weeks to have so seldom thought of the strange things which took place that night! . . . Now I begin to understand why he harped upon his temper when he offered me to join his following. Offered? Commanded! Here is a riddle that is not solved yet! Why should he force the *skaldship* on me as though it were the penalty for some crime against him, instead of an honour for which every mouth is watering? Unless, indeed, he feels that his fretfulness makes it more a peril than a pleasure. . . . Certainly to follow a chief who for no cause whatever shifts from a friendly mood to a murderous one—Now that is not possible! I have ever found him the highest-minded man. Some hidden reason must lie under this. It must be that I have stumbled into some misdeed without knowing it. But what? . . . What?"

Slowly his thoughts lost shape, resolved into chaos again. He stood staring down abstractedly at the billowing leaves.

CHAPTER 8

Courage is better than sword-strength
 —Northern saying.

Once, as time dragged by, the song-maker had a vague impression that Olaf was looking at him over a bush; but he was too absorbed to care I whether it was so or not. He did not come out of his meditations until the dark hemlock tapestry before him was put aside by a white hand and between the gloomy branches there appeared the bright figure of the *jarl's* sister, the trailing riches of her gown upgathered on her arm as she strolled forth to explore the recesses of the new guest-house.

At sight of him bound to a pine and staked in by three stark old chiefs looking like three shell-barked hickories in their sombre robes, she came to a stand-still, stood with shining head aloft as one who has caught the note of a distant battle-horn. At sight of her, the blood rose in a hot wave to the roots of his hair, and he muttered a prayer to the nearest of his keepers.

"Be kind enough to tell her that I have no man's blame for anything,—that I put on these bonds of my own free will."

It chanced that the man appealed to was Mord the Grim; the old counsellor justified the nickname by the look he bent on Rolf's son.

"Are you forward in this direction, also?" he inquired. "Starkad's daughter will not think that news so much worth having."

Brynhild drew a step nearer and answered for herself: "I should think it a sad story if I did *not* want news about a brave man's fate. To come from a circle of merrymakers into a group of such menace— Though it were no more than a thrall that was bound here, I should wish to know what this betided him! I beg you to tell me as quick as you can."

Like a nurse who would scare away an inquisitive child, Mord made his voice ominous. "You guess well that we are not in play, young maiden. The fellow has given himself as a hostage for the Skraellings good faith. If he has made any false step in truthfulness or judgment—" A motion towards the sword at his side completed the meaning. "I warn you that you will get sorry sport here. Be pleased to return to your playmates."

With peremptoriness thinly disguised as courtesy, he stepped forward and swung back the branches that she might pass out of the prison-chamber. From the other side of the hemlock wall came like an invitation the rippling laughter of the gossips, the shouts of the dice-throwers. For an instant it was as though she stood on the threshold between two worlds.

It did not take her more than an instant to choose between them. Even disdainfully, she put aside Mord and the merrymakers.

"Do you think me fit only to watch throws for light stakes? I prefer to watch your game with the Fates," she said, and joined the sinister group under the pine.

In his bound wrists, Randvar's pulses leaped; but the three advice-givers raised a chorus of protest, of entreaty, of command. What would have resulted is doubtful if there had not come suddenly from the river-bank sounds that struck them dumb,—an outburst of voices rising high above the hum of the slope, a clangour of weapons, a piercing cry:

"The *jarl* is attacked!"

In the wink-long hush that followed the outbreak there was discernible a distant noise of savage whoops and yells.

Forgetting his helplessness, the Songsmith tried to leap forward, so that the thongs that held him strained and creaked; and at the same instant the three old chiefs turned upon him such faces that Brynhild stepped in front of him as though their knotted hands on their hilts had already drawn their weapons.

"Make sure of it, first!" she demanded. "It may be no more than one of their hideous dances of entertainment. It is said that they sound as bad as battles."

Disputing, their voices rose shrilly; but Randvar relaxed in his bonds, and bent his head to wipe off on his shoulder the cold drops that had sprung to his upper lip.

"You have a cool wit, *jarl's* sister!" he breathed. "That is the only thing it can be." He spoke curtly to his keepers: "Why do you spend your force on me? There will be time enough for that hereafter. I advise you to see to it that your own people do not imperil Helvin by breaking the peace without cause."

It seemed that that danger had already occurred to the old chieftains, as well it might with such uproar of voice and weapon coming from the river-bank. Before Randvar ceased speaking, Thorbiorn and Sigvat had plunged through the hemlocks into the seething caldron below. Now, cursing and brandishing his weapon, Mord flung himself after them, his voice distinguishable above the tumult until the din gradually sank and he occupied the air alone.

Far removed from the turmoil of the bank seemed the stillness of the hemlock nook where Rolf's son stood worshipping Starkad's daughter. Much as he had claimed to know of the spirit under her pride, he gathered wonder with gazing at her now. As Northern skies by Northern Lights, so were her gray eyes fired; and measured constraint had melted like ice from her motions. Swallow-swift, she had slipped through the branches and come back again, bearing in her white fingers a glowing brand from one of the deserted campfires.

He looked at her somewhat blankly, then, asking in wonder: "Are you going to light my funeral pyre?"

"I am going to set you free," she answered, "so that you may have more chances for life than Mord's mercy will grant you if it should prove that the Skraellings are not dancing."

Her silken robes sweeping the leaves, she knelt down before him. Almost she had the fire laid to the ankle-thongs before he could speak.

"No, no! What is coming to me, I must abide here, as I have sworn."

In her upturned face, Valkyria's honour fought with woman's pity. Yet though she took the brand away, she did not rise; the woman in her pleaded as before a lawman.

"Death is too hard an atonement for a mistake. Forfeit your post, your hopes of fame, but not your life. I admit that you must pay some fine,—but not your life!" Again she stretched forth the burning wood,

She knelt down before him. The woman in her pleaded as before a Lawman desperately, this time, as one who dreads interference.

Strong as a hand, his voice overtook her. "No. I should get the greatest shame."

The purpose failed in her face before her arm yielded; but at last she rose and cast the brand from her, and stood with hands pressed hard upon her breast.

He had seen in his visions that she would be true to a friend, but he saw now for the first time that she could suffer for one. His love fed on her distress, even while he hastened to reassure her.

"Let it not worry you a jot, sunbright maiden. No likelihood at all is there that I shall come to harm. As I know the temper of my sword, I know the trustworthiness of the men I am leaning on."

She took her hands from her bosom to wring them. "How can you be certain of that? Your mind is shapen altogether like a dream-spinner's, that believes good of everyone—of savages whom others hold no better than beasts—of Helvin, whom everyone else thinks—Ah!" A sudden thought seemed to arrest her. "Now is that likely? That Helvin would be so foolish as to let them dance when he knows what lies upon it for you? As easily believe that he wishes your death! I must find out what is happening now." Heedless of her trailing skirts, she was gone over stubble and stone, her step more light and free than the tread of Odin's shield-maidens in the high halls of his chosen, as she climbed farther up the hill to a ledge of rock which had pushed through the soil and risen in a watch-tower.

When he could no longer catch any gleam of her glowing robes, the song-maker stood with his head leaning back against the tree as if his hope would mount to the sky. He wandered among singing stars until his attention was gradually drawn earthward by a stealthy crackling of the brush on his left.

Between the interlacing twigs, he made out presently a patch of such blue fabric as Thorgrim's son's cloak was fashioned of; but it did not seem reasonable to him that the French One should have strayed so far from the scene of excitement. He could not understand it until Olaf glided into the open and moved towards him, an unsheathed knife glittering against his blue sleeve.

No impulse to call for help came to Randvar—that instinct his life of solitude had blunted—but he put forth all his strength against his bonds, swelling out his chest, hardening the sinews of his limbs, until the thongs that withstood him were as iron sawing the flesh. When he found that they would not yield, he became as motionless as the tree behind him; his mouth twisted sardonically as he wondered in what way Erna's proving of his heart against steel was going to serve him now.

As their eyes held each other it is unlikely that either man realised that any but his foe was in the world. Upon their tense nerves it vibrated like a blow when the voice of the *jarl's* sister rang out behind them:

"Stand!"

The surprise of it seemed to paralyse Olaf so that for an instant he did stand, remaining poised in the air. Then the curve of his parted lips lost all resemblance to a smile.

"Bright Brynhild, this hand shall show you Helvin avenged!" he said, and cleared the remaining space at a stride, his arm uplifted.

In the draught of a breath she was before him, her slim hands locked about his wrist in the effort to pull it down.

"I bid you stop! Helvin is safe! Do you hear me?"

Perhaps his mind really did not hear her. With each word, his eyes froze faster to the Songsmith. Without so much as glancing at her, he put up his sinewy left hand and pried loose her grasp. The bound man cried out to her to give way and leave them,—so little even he knew her Valkyria spirit.

Thunder-strong it gathered in her, lightning-swift it struck. Swooping on the sword which Olaf's move left exposed at his side, she tore it free. With its upward sweep, she struck the knife from his hold. With its downward stroke she levelled at his breast. He leaped back just in time to save his life, if the rigidness of her arm told the truth.

"Do you think I am as poor-spirited as you are dastardly?" she said.

At a bound his mind was brought back to her, then; and once back, it would have been a dull mind not to see that his suit was in even greater danger than his body. In a trice he had doffed passion, donned reproach.

"Brynhild! Is it really as it seems, that because my loyalty runs away with my manners, you speak so to me?"

"I know not why you will talk of manners," she retorted, "when what your passion ran away with was your honour, that ought to have taught even a thrall better than to fall upon a fettered man."

"A thrall?" He spread out his hands in indignant protest. "Little shall a thrall know of a high-born man's wrath over the slaying of his chief! Am I not, before all else, a free Norseman? Only this morning, maiden, did you upbraid me because my French rearing had underlaid my Norse temper! Now, behold, when my Northern blood breaks out in its native wildness you stab me with eyes, words!—oh, use the sword! The steel would be more kind."

Gracefully he sank on his knee before her, making as though he would bare his breast for the stroke. Perhaps a maid of France would have shrunk or swooned. Perhaps it took him by surprise that she stood with unshaken hand, studying him as one studies an unfamiliar object.

"I do not know that I have the wish to be kind to you," she said slowly. "I do not know how I feel towards you, for you are not the man I thought I knew. Perhaps you should not have blame, since you believed Helvin slain, yet—"

Her voice quickened as a chorus sounding through the trees heralded the old counsellors return. She shifted the sword with an imperious gesture.

"Rise up! It will happen to you to be seen in that foolish position! I cannot tell whether I shall ever have liking towards you again or not. Rise up, and go away from me until I find out."

He had risen while she was speaking, but whether he would obey her last command was for an instant uncertain. Turning from her, his eyes rested again on the Songsmith; his empty hands began to open and shut at his sides. Only the grim voice of Mord, falling on the pause, seemed to catch and hold him. Even as he gave way step by step, his vulture eyes clung to the song-maker until the bushes rose like walls between them.

While the branches that closed behind Olaf were still aquiver, the hemlock boughs opened upon Mord and his associates. Filing in stiffly, they sat them down heavily upon bowlder and hummock.

"A man of my years," Mord panted, "does not take it lightly to have his heart turned over in him because some red apes choose to hop around in mock warfare. Get what enjoyment you can out of it, Rolf's son, that so far your savages have not belied you. When their foolishness was over, the *jarl* let so much news out as to send a messenger over to tell us that he was safe and getting all the favours he asked for,—after we had spent that much time in doubt and endangered as many lives as there are bodies among us! May Hel take fools and leave knaves, if she have not room for both! *Jarl's* sister, even you seem to have lost your wits, to go about flourishing a sword, with cheeks as red to look at as your kirtle. I thought you made it your boast to take things coldly."

Coldly! For the first time Randvar recalled their dispute of the morning, looked at the fire-breathing Valkyria, and smiled in spite of himself.

At the same breath, she darted him a glance that was half startled and half menacing. The flaming of her colour was not more marked than the stiffening of her spine as she caught his expression.

He sobered in haste. "*Jarl's* sister, no faintest intention had I of making mockery!"

She deigned him no answer whatever. With awful precision she planted the sword in the earth beside her, with awful deliberation gathered up her silken skirts, without a backward glance swept from the prison-chamber. Twice he called after her without avail,—so disastrous may a victory be!

Like a fog, sullen rage settled upon him then. When the old chiefs asked him what Starkad's daughter was doing with the sword, he clipped his answer as close as might be:

"Olaf Thorgrim's son, lent it to her to cut his luck-thread with."

When they questioned him about her displeasure, he conceded no more than an ungracious movement of his shoulders. Old Mord was impelled at last to scowl at him over the cloak-end with which he was mopping his face.

"Olaf the French," he observed, "was fostered in a land where they have the good custom of teaching manners as well as courage. Sure am I that such a training would have bettered you, Rolf's son, more than you think. I have, however, a good hope that even as autumn thunder ripens the grain, this tempest may have ripened your green judgment; so that hereafter you will be less quick to sneer at the caution of old men, and more slow to stake your all on any belief. Though the Skraellings keep faith with you, remember this—that you came near losing your life through your lord's folly, who accepted such entertainment without any regard to the effect it might have upon your state. If you had offended him so that he had the wish to murder you, he could not have gone about it better."

Mopping his face, he continued to speak at intervals in praise of discretion; but Rolf's son lost what followed by reason of the ringing of that one sentence in his ears—"If you had offended him so that he had the wish to murder you, he could not have gone about it better." . . . It seemed that Helvin had thought himself offended . . . that murder had looked out of his eyes. . . .

His head falling forward upon his breast, Randvar stood as one listening to an evil voice within him.

Chapter 9

Gift always looks to recompense
                        —Northern saying.

Through the dusk, the Skraelling fires across the river made no more showing than a cluster of glow worms on a log; but—true to the saying that *"Famine-pinched stomachs are the greatest gluttons"*—the Norse fire-builders had heaped wood on blaze until their forest guest-house revelled in a brightness as of noonday.

The peace-party had been back for the space of three candle-burnings, long enough for the first tumult of greeting to have subsided, and yet not so long but that the aroma of the new interest still flavoured the air. In complacent beard-stroking groups, the old chiefs stood about the bank, congratulating one another upon the advantages which the alliance would secure to the fur-traffic and the trade in *massur*-wood. Trying on shell necklaces and quill-embroidered shoes, Brynhild's women were turning the leaf-carpeted slope into a bower. In the hemlock nook which had been the prison-chamber, two guardsmen were giving an imitation of an Indian war-dance which sent the pages rolling on the earth in convulsions of merriment; and near by, another gathering watched with breathless interest while Gunnar the Merry experimented with the trophy which he had brought back,—a strange smoke-producing implement made up of a long reed, a big stone thimble, and a pinch of strangely smelling leaves.

Of none of these groups, however, was the *jarl* or his song-maker a part. Still farther up the rising ground, on the very edge of the shadow-breeding wood, a mighty pine had toppled over and lay head downward, its huge clod of roots and soil upturned like a dead giant's feet. There, skulking wolf-like in the shade, Helvin leaned against the writhen mass, bending and tearing the tough fibres with his restless hands; while along the huge trunk below him, as a panther along a bough, the deerskin-clad figure of Rolf's son lay stretched out.

Now and again, from the fireside groups came up snatches of song or a merry outburst of voices. But none of it moved the *jarl* to speech, and for once the Songsmith chose to remain under cover of custom and wait until he was addressed.

Now and again, a largess of dead leaves caused a grateful dancing of the flames that stretched the circle of ruddy light even to the timber's edge. Gazing upward, Randvar had a fleeting glimpse of the brooding white face on which that strange, evil expression had deepened to a stain. But always before he had a chance to study it, the light failed.

Convinced at last that he fronted the unknown, he waited tense as a bowstring, alert as an arrow. Almost he shot from his place when low laughter burst from Starkad's son,—laughter so devil-like that a wave of coldness started at his neck and rippled down to his heels.

"You think yourself a sly fox as you lie there watching me!" Helvin said, "but you need not take so much trouble. I have got over the wish to kill you."

It seemed to Randvar as if the rippling wave must have frozen, so rigid did he become.

"Is it even so, then, that you tried to betray me?" he asked slowly.

"I hope you did not look for anything better from me," Helvin returned, and laughed again.

So unbearable was the low sound that Randvar sat up sharply, and spoke with anger: "I did though! I expected that even if your wrath rose like a sea-wall against me, you would vent it in some honourable way."

"You know better now," Helvin answered grimly.

"That is certain," Randvar assented with equal curtness; and for a space there was silence between them, save for the sound of Kelvin's hands tearing the root-fibres.

In the low choked voice of one holding under a fearful force, Helvin broke out at last. "I never saw a greater blockhead! and I treated you better than you deserved. It mattered not that you were quick to mark the change in my manner,—still you could not guess that from the time the trees closed around me, I saw nothing but the old troll's twisted face in every shadow, heard nothing but his cursed ghost gibbering vengeance in my ear! Never did I so need that you should closely stand by me with your fearless mind; and what did you do, instead, but bungle it so that I had to leave you behind! I can tell you that death was likelier than life as you stood then. I wonder I did not become the fiend you saw at the pool."

"The fiend I saw at the pool!" Randvar repeated, and the impulse to face standing whatever might lie before him made him start to rise to his feet. But at the first motion, Kelvin's hand fell upon his shoulder with the weight of a lion's paw and crushed him back upon his seat.

"Now are you hot-headed," he snarled, "and there is rashness in your actions, and that is foolish in a cool-witted man like you. It is not enough that you have made the bargain to go through torment with me; you have got to go quietly. Quietly! do you understand that or not? *Ah!* You are not going to be so great a fool as to struggle. Bear in mind what it means to thwart me!"

But it was not the gripping hand that Randvar was struggling against, though the fingers had sunk into his flesh like iron hooks. It was against that awful dizzy madness that had come again upon him at the touch of Starkad's son. In the same flash of time he knew two things—that his "gift" was making him aware of a terrible presence, and that he resented that gift with every fibre of his forest-bred body. Doubly racked, he battled for the space of a heart-beat, then reached instinctively for the sharp medicine of his blade.

Even as his flesh tasted it and his disorder passed, the fire leaped redly, revealing the blazing eyes of rage above him, disclosing his horror-twisted mouth to the *jarl*. With a stifled cry, Starkad's son quitted his hold.

"Why do you look at me like that? Oh God, do the marks show on me? I thought I should escape—escape—"

His voice lost the semblance of a voice, became an inarticulate wail; and to it was added the sound of rending cloth as he started up in his lair. In frantic haste he strove to disentangle his cloak and draw it up over his breast and around him in a hood; but he only tangled it harder and pulled the folds awry and lost the end from between his numb fingers. Giving up the attempt, finally, he cast it over his head and flung himself down upon the earth, moaning a single word over and over like a wounded bird of one note.

More like was it to a sound of bird or beast than to human speech. Every nerve strained in the endeavour to comprehend, every sense baffled, the song-maker stood staring down at him. At last he bent, speaking desperately:

"Either you are dumb or I am deaf! Make me a sign."

Plunging and reeling, the black shape reared itself from the ground; though even in the shadow it would not uncover its face. From the cloak-folds came forth a shaking hand, which fell on the Songsmith's arm and groped its way to his shoulder. Brushing his cheek, it left the skin wet, though its touch was the touch of fire. From his shoulder, it passed over to the harp at his back and put all its force into smiting the strings into one discordant cry, before it fell back into the cloak-folds, and the cloaked form fell prone upon the earth.

Randvar understood then that he was to sing; and before he was erect, the harp was off his back. Like the voice of a night-bird pouring out its soul to the listening forest, his voice rang from the shadow.

Down on the firelit slope, the merry groups, ceased their sports and gave him joyous hearing; and the echoes in the hills across the splashing river awoke and answered him sleepily; but of what he sang he had no consciousness, nor ever afterwards could recall it. Like a dead thing lay the mound at his feet; and as flies around the dead, his thoughts buzzed around its secret.

Slowly understanding came. . . . The troll-temper of the father had descended upon the son . . . Denied the vent of battle-fury, it had taken some uglier shape, some monstrous shape that galled the *jarl's* pride to own! . . . It had possessed him that day at the pool, and he believed that the forester had seen its degrading marks. . . . Its marks! Shrinking, Randvar's memory groped among the myriad tales he had heard of men accursed . . . yelping teeth-gnashing Berserkers with frothing distorted mouths . . . souls doomed to raven in brutes bodies . . . wits to sleep in the bestial forms of swinish cinder-biters. . . .

Like a strain falling from Valhalla to the World of the Dead, the voice of Yrsa the Lovely fell presently on his ear, calling out a merry goodnight as she went away with the rustling train of women to the booths that had been erected for them. A moment his gaze wandered to follow out of sight the head of fiery gold that moved before them, but still he sang on.

Above the trees, presently, Night raised her silver bow and shot bright arrows through the leafless branches. Watching the shafts strike and melt into pools of moonshine at his feet, his eyes lost their alertness; his song grew dreamy, slackened and sank low as the note of a dreaming bird. But still he kept on.

Breathing the melody rather than singing it, he saw unheeding how the bright beams reached to the cloak-wrapped form and groped like hands along it; he was slow in realizing that one of the pale spots in the shadow was not moonlight, but a wan face upturned. His song ended in a gasp, when the truth did come home to him. Sometime he stood motionless before he dared speak and ask:

"Lord, how is it with you?"

The answer came out of the shadow, "It is well with me," but no minor chord ever made the song-maker's heart swell in his breast as did the voice in which the words were spoken. It became nothing to him what mask the tortured face might be wearing. Kneeling beside the prostrate body, he raised it up until the mass of blood-red hair rested even on his shoulder.

As a drowned man rises out of the deeps, so the *jarl* seemed to rise out of the shadow into the moonlight. And as the face of one who has known the agony of buffeting waves, so was his face blanched and drawn; but no other mark was upon him. Only infinite weariness was on the finely cut mouth; in the sea-gray eyes, only in finite sadness. The swelling of the song-maker's heart became a sharp pain in his throat.

But the *jarl* said gently: "Once when I had fallen into such a strait as this, I would not accept your help. See now how I lean on you! There will ever be most help in you when there is most need of it. My true friend, for this—this!—what shall requite you?" He put up his hand; and because Randvar could not speak, he wrung it in silence.

Then gradually Helvin's strength came back to him, so that he put out his other hand and taking hold of a branch, drew himself to his feet, and stood supported half by the tree, half by the shoulder of the Songsmith.

"Soon are my powers renewed in me," he said. "Even as David did for Saul, you cast the devil out; and before he had gone his length— God! the length he goes! Can you raise before your mind what my state was that day, when I turned Randvar the Songsmith and espied a man watching me from the bushes? When my arrow missed him, and I knew that my secret was loose in the world? Ah! I do not want to remember that! Wine! Give me wine!"

Randvar's hand unfastened the flask from his neck without the knowledge of his wits, that were like thunder in his ears, roaring explanation of all that had puzzled him. Out of the tumult, he spoke earnestly:

"*Jarl*, I am five weeks too slow in telling you that a great mistake has been made. It is the truth that horror drove me mad that day, but not horror of you,—never of *you!* Listen! Even as I stepped from the bushes and saw the pool and saw you—"

On the Songsmith's lips, Kelvin's hand fell lightly. Wincing, he had turned away.

"Let not that be put into words which in thought alone is more than I can bear!" he said. "Besides, to what end is it? I know that it was not from me that you shrank, but from the devil that uses my body; and for any hatred you feel towards that, or harm you do it—if ever you come together, which God avert!—you need have no remorse. Though all your power were bent upon it, you could never hate it—

abhor—"

A shuddering fit shook him, so that words be came but bubbles of sound bursting idly on his lips. When he spoke again, his voice was very low.

"Bitter is it to speak of! For love's sake, spare me the need. I know now that—even with that vision before your eyes—your song-maker's spirit was able to separate me from the Thing which Fate has linked me to. Had not myself experienced it, I would not have believed any man brave enough to make that separation. Times there are when *I* cannot make it; when I loathe myself as Satan never loathed himself, else would his heart change and the world be sinless! I call your help no more than it is when I tell you that I should die of self-horror if I could not look at you and say, I am not beyond the pale, for here is a man who gives me friendship and honour even while knowing the worst of me!"! His voice, which had sunk to an unsteady breath, was smothered out as he pressed his face against the rough bark of the tree.

The Songsmith did not use the opportunity, however, to finish the explanation he had begun. Instead, he stood staring down at the sleeping camp and weighing the possibility of seeming to have this knowledge, foreseeing the blind maze he should enter on, the sword he should hang over his life, the horror to which he should bind himself.

It was Helvin who ended the pause, as he had made it. Turning, he laid both hands on Randvar's shoulders, and as he spoke, looked lovingly into his face.

"Good is your singing and your service, but your friendship is worth still more! Such it is, that no reward can match it,—the joy of giving must be its own reward. Only can I tell you what it has meant to me that never hoped to know the support of a friend. When my dreams were brightest, I dreamed only of getting goodwill by hiding the truth. What makeshift would that have been! What peace is this! Greater loss to me than to you would it have been if you had lost your life today. My friend, I do not ask that this may be forgiven me, for that would be to own that it was I who sought to work you harm, and that fiend was not I. Yet this I will say, that I should think it the best gift I ever got if you could tell me with a whole heart that this has not caused any breach to rise in our friendship."

After a little, the Songsmith raised his bowed head and met the gray eyes steadily.

"My love is great, lord, towards many men," he said, "but towards none so much as you. Till my death-day, I will hold to my faithfulness to you."

Chapter 10

It must be worse before it gets better
                    —Northern saying.

His ruddy face thrice ruddy with cold, Bolverk, the guardsman, came stamping into the great trading-booth, kicked the door shut upon the ice-bound out-of-doors and let go a shivering breath of appreciation at the sight of the fur-littered weapon-hung room, down whose middle fires were leaping, and along whose wall-benches shaggy-maned hunters and sleek-locked Skraellings sat consuming hot drink in the intervals of bargaining.

"Hail, friends!" he greeted the company. "Now does the bread of life seem to be buttered on both sides! Here are you on the inside, as snug as fleas on a goat; and outside, I just met a young one merry because his breath froze in such clouds that he had only to stick a knob-ended root between his lips to have the appearance of smoking like a Skraelling."

The double row of faces that had turned towards him answered variously by grins or jests or grunts, but the trader's headman looked up from the heap of beaver skins that thralls were sorting before him to wave a cordial hand.

"Now this day seems to have been set for the return of long-absent people! Welcome to you, Bolverk the Bold! Not so much as a hair have I seen of you for three months and more."

"That is easily true," the guardsman assented, "for since Treaty Day I have camped as far south as Freya's Tower. And I have worn out my shoes there, as you may see. How long would it be before you could look me up another pair? From the appearance of your benches, I should not say that the lack of my custom had caused suffering to you."

"Nay, it is your company that we have suffered for," the trader's man answered, as became a trader's man. "But I need not keep you waiting if you will give to Eldir, here, one of your old shoes for a sample."

He beckoned a bondsman to attend on the guard, while with his head he signed another thrall to bring forward the smoking ale; and Bolverk succumbed contentedly into a seat.

"Mind this, that you get me a pair that is easy across the toes," he admonished the slave kneeling before him. Then he stretched out his hand to take the offering of the one standing beside him, and questioned lazily as he sipped: "Who are the rest of the long-absent people who have arrived?"

"Some score of them you may see before you; and in that end room yonder, among the gold things, is Olaf, Thorgrim's son,—the most open-handed man! Since Treaty Day, for some reason, he has turned his back on the court and dwelt at the house of Mord the Grim, and only—"

Bolverk left off sipping to interrupt joyfully: "Now I wonder if it is going to happen that there is a fight? As I turned in here, I looked down a lane and saw Randvar the Songsmith headed in this direction."

The row of hunters straightened, some of them rolling on their tongues the word "fight"; some raising their horns with shouts of "The Songsmith!" but the trader's man shook his head above the furs to which he had turned back.

"They cannot lock horns. The lawmen have bound them to peace, on pain of outlawry to the one who breaks it. On the way home from the treaty-making, it befell that the Songsmith flew at Olaf, and would have given him a swift death if men had not come between them. They do not dare to do aught else than be good. It is unlikely, moreover, that the Songsmith has the slightest intention of coming hither. So long as he has that deerskin-husk and that battered sword, no use has he for a trading-booth."

Disapproval was in the headman's gesture as he kicked aside the fur heap he had finished examining. But Bolverk shook his helmed head in disapproval of him.

"It is your traders thrift that talks now, comrade, not your Norse spirit," he said. "Some bad habits the Fates allot every man at his birth; and he should be considered lucky who uses up his allowance of them on clothes, and keeps his mind high and his courage without stain, as Randvar, Rolf's son, has done."

"Yes, yes!" chorused the fur-clad hunters, banging the benches with their fists. And the youngest of them brought his drink-drenched body upright with a jerk, and tried to look severely through sleepy eyes.

"Whosoever says aught slighting of Rolf's son gives offence to me," he made announcement. "I l-ove him because he wears clothes like mine. I l-l-ove him because he is poor. I l-l-l—"

"Poor!" The trader's man laughed impatiently. "Good Bend-the-Bow, are you too drunk to understand that I am talking about the *jarl's* favourite, whose shabby belt-pouch is fuller of gold than your head of wits,—even when you are sober and they are all at home? If he were still a ringless forester, who would stir tongue about his habits? It is because he has gold to spend but is too careless to do it, that he has my blame; and I would lay my purse on it that this is a part of the cause why he has lost credit with the *jarl's* sister, as gossips say he has. Yet you need not think that I undervalue what is in side his shell. Far and wide, it is known that he brought this treaty to pass which is going to send such ship-loads to Norway in the spring as never left port before. For that, all traders lift their horns to him; and I should dislike to have it come to his ears that I—"

"Then hold your peace for here he comes!" the guardsman interrupted, and stood up with a genial bellow to pitch at the opening door one of the shoes which a thrall had just handed him.

It was a rash act since the newcomer might just as easily have been the *jarl* as the *jarl's* song-maker—the trading-house standing at the junction of many paths—but it came to no bad end for the doorway actually did frame the tall sinewy form of Randvar, Rolf's son, his harp occupying a cloak's place at his back. At sight of him, even the Skraellings changed from bronze images into men with cordial eyes; while the hunters swung up their horns with a burst of cheers. Barely they gave him time to hand over his broken harp to the trader's man before they forced him into the place they had made for him, plied him with drink, with toasts, with questions and banter. Bolverk was obliged to limp over in one shoe to get a seat beside him, and get his attention for the confidences with which he was bursting.

They seemed to be of a nature more absorbing to the teller than to the listener for even while he gave one ear to them, Randvar left the other open to the hunter's chaff, and broke out restlessly, now and again, to gibe back or to answer in their own tongue some inquiries from his Skraelling friends. But he did not fail to make the required promise to go down to the wedding-feast in the spring, and aroused himself with proper enthusiasm when the lover came at last to an exulting climax.

"There! If you can anywhere see a better look out than that, I shall say your eyesight is keener than Erna's."

"Nothing but the sun's can equal it in brightness! I call upon every man who hears my voice to drink to your luck at my expense," the Songsmith answered promptly, and drew a handful of silver rings from his shabby pouch.

If cup-wishes count, never was bride more richly dowered than Snowfrid of Freya's Tower. When it was over, the beaming Bolverk slapped his prospective foster-kinsman affectionately upon the back.

"Nowhere have I found a better comrade than you! To talk one's affairs over with you is a good help. Now let me show as much friendship and hear how matters have fared with you, these three months. I can see one thing that you have not done, and that is to get fat."

An old trapper clad in bear's fur uttered a bear-like grunt.

"Huh! See the gainfulness of having young eyes! As soon as the boy came into the room, I saw that there were lines between his eyebrows like a wagon's ruts,—and not an empty wagon, either! Better take to the forest again, Rolf's son, if it weighs so heavily upon your spirit to be a *jarl's* favourite."

"Better come back to the forest than bear any harness!" the young hunter who sat next to the Songsmith cried scornfully; and a chorus rose after him:

"Never did I think you would stand it, who hate rules as a bear hates a chain!"

"You are a fool to stay in it—"

"Sooner should the Troll take me than I should follow a man who behaved overbearingly, as one of Starkad's breed must needs—"

"It is not possible that you can be contented in his servic—"

"Come back—"

"What is the jest?"

"What is the cause of your grinning?"

The song-maker's smile ended in his short laugh.

"You," he answered. "It crossed my mind to fancy myself listening to a pack of wild wolves yelping at a tame one, who had found love for a man and followed him home and broken himself to house-ways. But I will give you a better answer than that to your foolishness."

He leaned forward where all could see him, the fire showing his thin face to be unmistakably earnest.

"For what you said about Kelvin's behaviour towards me, I will tell you the first half of a saying the courtmen have made, which is altogether truthful, and which is this: If the *jarl's* song-maker should want the *jarl's* crown for a dog-collar, he would have to do no more than ask for it. And now, for what you said about my liking his service,

I will give you the rest of the saying, which is even more true than what went before: And if it should happen to the *jarl* to want the Songsmith's head for a hand-ball, he would have to do no more than ask for that. Is it clear to you now or not?"

The hunters had no opportunity to answer. While they were still adjusting their minds to the amazing conviction that their one-time comrade had meant what he said, the door was flung open with a flourish. In all his bravery of embroidered cloak and silver-spurred riding-boots, Eric the Page appeared and proclaimed in his young treble:

"Way for the *jarl's* sister!"

It was the first time the woodsmen had seen this woodland sprig in his splendour. To assail him with familiar greetings and ironical comment be came instantly their sole object in life, carried on under their breath even after the *jarl's* sister had entered, and they had scrambled to their feet in rough homage. Randvar was able to step unobserved behind a smoke-blackened pillar and gaze with what bitterness he would upon the face that his pride had come to curse by day while his love starved for it in his dreams.

"I would give all I own in the world had I not known how to smile!" his heart cried out in sudden sharp wretchedness. Then he cursed himself for a fool, cursed her vanity for a curse worse than Kelvin's, and wore the rut deeper between his heavy brows with scowling at her as she passed.

Of rich purple, fur-edged, was the mantle that hung from her fine shoulders; and purple was the velvet hood that lay like an evening cloud upon the sunset glory of her hair; but it needed not the royal colouring to betoken the loftiness of her temper. Even more than its wonted haughtiness was in the carriage of her head as she moved up the long room and passed into the inner chamber, which was the shrine of the jewelled ornaments and gold things.

Bolverk shut one eye expressively, when the fox-skin curtain had fallen behind her and her page.

"Every man to his taste!" he said. "Yet I for one feel no envy of Olaf Thorgrim's son, that he is kissing her fingers at this moment. Give me Snowfrid with the kissable mouth!" He was reaching for his horn to seal the sentiment when Randvar's hand closed on his arm.

"Is Olaf, Thorgrim's son, in there?" the Songsmith asked in his ear.

The man-at-arms regarded him admonishingly. "Why, I think they say he is. But they say also that the one of you two who begins a fight will get outlawed."

Randvar made no answer; his gaze had gone back to the door-curtain. If the French One should remain there after she entered, it would be a sign that his disfavour was at an end, that she had taken him back into her friendship—He broke off to watch with suspended breath.

Dashing the fox-skins aside, Mord the Grim stamped through the door; and after him Olaf backed into the room, bowing ceremoniously before the presence he was leaving. If further proof were needed that the greeting of the *jarl's* sister had not been cordial, that proof was furnished as he turned on the threshold and espied his rival watching him. Seizing his sword-hilt, regardless of Mord's shrill expostulations, he strode towards the Songsmith.

They seemed for once to have changed places for Randvar made no more motion to attack than to evade, only stood smiling at him in unconcealed malicious enjoyment. When Thorgrim's son was within a pace of him, he took off his fur cap and swept him a salute mockingly elaborate, then folded his arms upon his breast in the formal sign of peace.

White on purple showed the veins of Olaf's fore head, as he came to a standstill before the exasperating figure. Perhaps even at the price of banishment he would have purchased revenge, if his friends had not saved him from the rash bargain. To the utter disgust of the bystanders, three of the traders men seized upon him now and with respectful words but peremptory hands, dragged him past temptation and out of the door.

Raising a chorus of disappointment, the loungers closed again around the laughing Songsmith, scolding him, some of them, for not preferring banishment to a life of such restraint; others chaffing him for his decline in spirit; while the Skraellings be came almost urgent in their desire to understand why two men should start to fight each other and stop before either was killed.

Lingering to buckle his many mantles, old Mord watched the group. When at last he was muffled for his ride, he halted on his way out to look at the jesting song-maker from under an arch of bristling brows.

"Since I see what a man you are to get friends behind you," he said, "my wonder grows less at the boldness you showed at the treaty-making. Soon, instead of the favourite of the *jarl*, you will be calling yourself the favourite of New Norway."

Over the ring of tow manes surrounding him, Randvar gave back his look carelessly, wondering what new fuel his fiery prejudice had chanced upon. He found out when Mord had reached the door and, opening it, flung this parting shot over his shoulder.

"A most beloved man you appear to be,—I bid you only beware how you carry it too far. The sagas do not lack instances of king-born men whose bane came out of their boldness. It would be unlucky if someone should whisper to the *jarl* that you are ambitious to get more popularity than he has."

The Songsmith doffed his merry mood at that, his eyes narrowing dangerously. Then they widened in dismay as darting past Mord to the threshold, they encountered the gray-clad form of the *jarl* himself, silhouetted against the white glare of the sunlit snow.

In the pause that followed, Starkad's son appeared to be the only one at ease. Inclining his head in acknowledgment of the advice-giver's salute and the hunters uncertain murmur, he came slowly forward, drawing off his furred gloves.

"That is rightly said," he assented, "that if such a whisper should come to my ears it would be very unlucky. The prophecy is wrong only in hinting that it is for the song-maker that the bad luck would come in." He answered with a reproachful look Randvar's look of relief.

What Mord answered could not be heard for the cheers that the hunters let forth for Helvin Jarl. Only the slamming of the door behind the advice-giver made a faint jar.

The *jarl* thanked them graciously when the racket was over, then addressed himself to his friend:

"So long was your harp-string in mending that it pleased me to come on here and look for an arrow-ornament to take the place of the one I lost. Let us betake ourselves now to the search. It is likely to be in the inner chamber among the gold things." Laying a hand upon Randvar's shoulder, he moved him forward, speaking carelessly of this or that weapon on the wall.

But only so long as they were within ear-shot of the groups on the benches did the Songsmith yield to the pressure. Fire-colour had flamed in his face. By main force he came at last to a stand-still, and spoke without looking at his companion:

"I think, lord, that I will not go in with you. I am not used to so much heat—and the smell of the furs—I will await you under the oak. I find that—I am not well. By your leave!"

But the tightening of his lord's hand upon his shoulder showed that he did not have his leave.

"Not well? What nonsense is here! It was on my tongue to say that not since Treaty Day have I seen you wear such a merry face. For more than two months have you moped like a captive hawk, with sullen temper and feathers adroop, but now—Why, it was the first thing I marked when I looked through the door and saw you bantering with your hunter friends! Comrade, swear to me that your mind-sickness is not homesickness. If I should think that the fetters of my service were eating into your brave heart—"

"I swear I have no homesickness."

"God is to be thanked for that! Take oath also that I would have no power to straighten the threads if you should tell me what the snarl is."

The song-maker flung back his hair restlessly from his face of fierce unhappiness. "*Jarl*, it stings my pride that I have not been able to hide from you the soreness of my mind. Let it pass for the spring sap working in me. I take oath that no man alive can give me aught I want. Be pleased, lord, since it is your will!" As with one hand he put the matter aside, with the other he put aside the fox-skin curtain. After a moment, Helvin yielded and entered.

It was plainly indifferent to the *jarl* that Brynhild the Proud should chance to be coming from the iron-bound chests, preceded by a walking heap of rainbow silks. He returned her reverence with a courtly greeting, then turned and made a kindly motion towards the figure drawn up rigid as a spear-shaft in the shadow of the doorway.

"We have seen little of you, my kinswoman, since you made the winter weather an excuse for staying away from our feasts," he added, "yet do not lose us your remembrance. Will you not give a greeting to my song-maker here? It is not unlikely that he has felt the lack of your presence as much as you have missed his songs."

Perforce, the Songsmith plucked the cap from his head and advanced. Perforce, her gaze was turned upon him.

"Oh, is it your song-maker?" she said indifferently. "I thought one of the woodsmen had followed you in to get some hunting-gear." Deliberately she looked him up and down, her gray eyes more forbidding than a gray ice-waste under Northern skies. With a shrug she turned from him at last.

"If you please, brother, I think I would rather not greet him," she said. "Better that we should look on it as though he were a woodsman after all, who might mistake my condescension and become forward."

Curtseying as low as her manner was high, she swept past the *jarl* and through the door, beyond which the silk-laden page was awaiting her.

Chapter 11

A wise man's guess is a prophecy
—Northern saying.

Out in the long trading-hall there was a confusion of shuffling feet, as the company rose to show respect to the *jarl's* kinswoman; but over the inner chamber such silence reigned that the rows of rich garments hanging around the walls took on the semblance of listening figures. Rooted where his sister had left him, the *jarl* stood gazing incredulously at his friend, and the song-maker's head was bowed over the cap he was tearing in strips.

Helvin said at last: "Songsmith, you took oath that no man could give you aught,—is it as it would seem, that what you desire is a woman's help?"

The Songsmith made no other answer than a movement of his bent shoulders, but that was answer enough. Starkad's son said disgustedly:

"This is how it is, then,—you have sulked and chafed for lack of my sister's favour, even though you have my friendship and every honour that friendship can devise. There is more shame in your falling before her than of all men else. I wonder not that you were ashamed to own it to me. To confess that after all your boasted wildness you had put on her yoke as tamely as any mincing courtman among them! Tamely? Cravenly! How does this hang together, that you have a man's pride yet like any whipped hound give love in return for abuse!"

"*Trolls*, lord!" the song-maker gasped, flinging his cap on the floor.

Helvin made a change from scorn to sternness. Placing his foot upon an iron-bound chest, he set his elbow on his knee in an attitude of exhortation.

"Curse and stamp as much as suits you,—I should do no friend's part if I did not deal severely with you. You go not hence until I have given you such a bitter dose as shall cure your mind of that sickness while life lasts in you. So take breath to swallow—"

Randvar let breath go, instead, in desperate protest. "It needs not, lord! I am cured. Could you give me anything to equal her look in bitterness? I am cured from this day forth. Give me leave to go."

But the *jarl's* outstretched arm made a bar across the path to the door.

"Too sudden is your recovery; it suggests that of a child who sees the medicine-bowl coming his way. It has come to this, that I shall be convinced only when we have talked the matter out at length and—What! wincing already? Is that a sign of sound flesh? Face about, there! You may make up your mind to one of two things: either to answer my questions and so disgust yourself with your folly, or else to listen while I drag your weakness forth into such bright light as—"

"I will answer," Randvar said between his teeth, and set them hard.

"Begin then by telling me what I think I know already, that she had no reason for believing her dignity trod upon."

"Who shall say what looks like reason to a woman? If you must know, she had this much cause that on Treaty Day we disputed together about a matter and in an evil hour it happened that I was proved to be right, and when I saw it, I smiled,—no more than a twitching back of the lips, lord! In the same breath I asked her to excuse it! But she left me without a word, refused me admittance when I went to her hall, flouted me when I accosted her—slighted—scorned—Only the Devil who made them knows why women do anything!" He gave the cap a vicious kick as he started to pace the floor.

But Helvin added severely: "And only the Lord who made men knows why they hanker after such creatures! Behold how your own mouth has convicted you of the greatest folly!"

That was all, perhaps, that the song-maker was able to behold, even though his gaze halted here and there upon garments and weapons as he moved restlessly to and fro. At last he cried out for mercy.

"I will confess myself the greatest fool alive if it will save me from your tongue! I know now what I have always suspected, that King Helge in the song wasted his time in avenging it on Fridtjof that he loved the boneless Ingeborg. That love alone was punishment enough—Like one struck by a new thought, he stopped before the *jarl*.

"It occurs to me, lord," he said, "that you are not carrying out your share of that song! Here am I, a man of no more than free birth—since no one gets his rank from his mother—who have dared to love a ruler's daughter. Why do you not rage against it, as is to be expected? I swear an oath that I would rather endure your wrath for my boldness than continue this talk about my weakness."

"That choice is less hero-like than it sounds, my friend," Helvin answered gravely. "You do yourself wrong if you do not know that since Time's morning a man whom Odin has led into the high-seat of *skaldship* has been held the equal of any blood. And you do me wrong to think that I should forget the nobleness of your mind, whatever your rank. Is it not even because I love you as the very eyes in my head that I cannot bear to see you bend your neck to a pride-crazed woman?"

He took his foot down from the coffer to face the song-maker fairly.

"Oh my comrade, what shall I do to ease you?" he said. "Will you that I should grapple with you and pluck out the barb, though your heart-roots come with it? Or are there any kindly ser vices I might do to heal the flesh and let the thing remain imbedded and forgotten? Do you prescribe now for my love,—I swear no dose shall be too bitter. Though that course be not so good, I would still go to her myself on your behalf, were there hope that she had a heart in her bosom to answer when one knocked."

"It is not that she has not a heart, lord. It is that I am not high enough to reach the bolt upon its door," Randvar answered sadly. He wrung the hand that had clasped his, then threw himself down upon the chest and buried his face in his palms. His words came disjointedly.

"Think only what her love would be like, who is so steadfast in her friendship! Had you seen her that day of the Treaty when she came upon me in my bonds!—Why do I rail at her pride, when I would not have her bright head held one jot lower? When Mord turned upon me, I had her as my shield—Lord, when Olaf came against me with his knife, she closed with him! Her slim fingers twined vinelike around the great bole of his wrist. And one of her long braids flew out as she whirled and brushed like a bird's wing across my lips! Likely it is the last time they will ever feel it." He got up suddenly and resumed his walking, too deep in wretchedness to heed the quiver of mocking laughter to which Helvin was stirred.

"Think only what her love of her brother must be like, who was so cool-witted while she thought he was being slaughtered!" Starkad's son murmured.

As swiftly as the mood came, so swiftly it passed. Stepping forward, he began to move beside his friend, speaking indulgently:

"Be of good cheer, comrade,—I foresee now that you shall even kiss her lips if you will."

Randvar came to himself with a start, and stopped short in anger. "Lord, there are some remedies that even you may not try upon me. If this is done to deride—" His manner changed as he met the gentleness of the gray eyes. "Bear with me! I know you mean me only good. But I cannot see your cheer."

"It is not to the man down in the thick of the fight, but to the man up in the crow's-nest, that it is given to see which way the battle is going. You see only the fury of your foe. I see that she is putting that fury forward to hide the weakness that lies behind it."

Again the song-maker checked his pacing, but this time to ask wonderingly: "Lord, what mean you?"

"My meaning is that she has found out that her breast holds love for you."

"*Love!*"

"What else, my friend, would make Brynhild the Cold forget her estate and show openly—to Mord—to Olaf—to whomsoever chose to look—the store she set by your safety?"

So lightning-bright grew the radiance in Randvar's face that it could last only lightning-long, then flickered and died in gloom.

"Lord, how dare I believe that? It might have been no more than friendliness, or woman's pity."

Through the mass of dark hair from which he had plucked off his jewelled cap, the *jarl* ran his white hands, throwing back his head with a movement of impatience.

"Why is it that it comes so much easier to believe in Hel than in Valhalla? Is it because the earth-clods we are made of weigh us down when we try to mount? If I cannot prove her love to you through her gentleness, then will I prove it through her hardness. No ball leaps up high that has not gone down hard,—had she stooped no lower than pity, she had never risen so high as hate. Now I can make a guess that the most surprised person to whom Brynhild betrayed her love was Brynhild herself! One thing I hope,—that it was not this moment which a bantering fate took to make you smile?"

"What other time should it have been, lord? It was not until the excitement was over that I called to mind how she had boasted that nothing could shake her coldness. When I saw her—sword in hand—eyes ablaze—Odin himself would have drawn back his lips!"

"Then would Odin himself have gone behind the clouds for a while," Helvin said; and one of his rare smiles, faint as a glimmer of arctic sun shine, touched the curves of his mouth. "Think of the firebrand it hurled into her pride, when she thought that this love which she herself had just discovered had been betrayed to you, and that you were triumphing—"

The Songsmith cried out the word "Triumphing!" with such bitterness in his voice that, to hide a smile, the *jarl* turned away and feigned to be absorbed in a kirtle on the wall, nor looked around again until Randvar appealed to him. Dropped heavily upon the chest, the Songsmith sat frowning desperately at the floor.

"If you, lord, would but do one thing which is easy to you?" he said. "Furnish me with some errand that will bring me into her presence, even against her will. I mean so to act that it will be made evident to her that she misjudged in fearing I should become forward."

Again the *jarl* set his foot upon the coffer and his elbow on his knee, but the look he bent on his friend now had a hint of amiable amusement.

"True it is that much lies on that! You might feign sickness and be taken into the guest-chamber off the women's hall, where it is the custom for sick men to—But the ill-luck might befall you that unless you seemed balancing on the grave-edge, she would leave you to her women. Better would it be to make up some errand concerning the dress of state which she and her maids are covering with needlework for my wear—Yet that is not certain, either, for I have some fear that she might hear your message and then dismiss you before you could get out your conciliating words."

Some diffidence had come into the Songsmith's manner, as if he foresaw chaff for what he was about to say. Yet now he said it:

"One plan came to me, lord, by which I could show without words that I had a desire to please her. You heard how she spoke of woodsmen ?. . . More than once has she upbraided me for wearing clothes unbefitting the son of Freya, the king-born. For myself, I prefer to be the son of Rolf the Viking, but for her sake—to show that I will do all in my power to deserve the honour she does me—I would go so far as to change—"

He broke off in embarrassment, for even as he had feared, the *jarl's* whimsical amusement in creased. Laying hold of the shoulder before him, Helvin shook it banteringly.

"Let us hope it will not be with you as the priest's story says it was with Samson and Delilah! And I will forbear reminding you that in casting off your forest garb you cast off my livery, and confess that I no longer stand first in your allegiance—Nay, I said that I would forbear reminding you of that, so never stir your tongue to protest. Now that I see that you have not thrown your dice for a worthless stake, I begin to find interest in the game. Call the trader in to set forth his goods. You shall go to her at once, while her heart is still at war with her temper for having ill-treated you. There is no good striving against me! I say you shall. Call Asgrim—Nay, if you will not, I will do it myself—Ah, that is better! Since I have staked my reputation as a foretelling man, I am going to see that the game is played properly."

CHAPTER 12

The mind rules one-half of the victory
　　　　　　　　　　—Northern saying.

"Jarl, it is not fitting that you should even seem to attend on me! Let me accompany you to your hall as be comes me, and afterwards go my way alone—"

"And rob me of a chance to see the horses come up to the post in a race I have wagered on?" the *jarl* interrupted. "Out upon your idea of fitness! I am not sure that I shall not even go upon that slope behind the women's house and watch you through a broken window I know of. Would it not give you a sense of being supported to feel my eyes upon you?" He walked on as one serenely unaware that his companion had stopped short in dismay.

He did not go so far as to carry out his threat, however. When—by snow-banked roads and snow-buried lanes, dim in the early gloaming—they had come to the courtyard and the looming pile of the women's house, Helvin halted in the shadow of a tree.

"I think I will go no farther," he said. "If it happen as I expect, they will not close the doors after you immediately, as after one whose welcome is certain. I shall be able to see some of the sport from here, before the banging of them in my face tells me that my foretelling has come true."

"It is for you to decide," Randvar made use of the proper phrase. And he had made a stride forward when—like the jerk of a cord suddenly stretched—an impulse turned him back.

"Lord," he said, almost with fierceness, "tell me that you were jesting when you accused me of forsaking my allegiance to you. Say that you do not hold me for a deserter, or my foot shall wither before ever it makes a move to leave you!"

Out of the shadow in which he stood, Helvin's voice sounded presently like a harp strain with one minor chord.

"We must take this, comrade, as it is. It was a jest,—and it was the truth. You could no more hold back than I could stay you, and I would not keep you if I could. All that man can give to man, you have given me,—I ask not woman's share besides. Go, and good go with you for your love!"

Down in the shadow, their hands met and clasped; then the song-maker turned and once more went forward towards the dark mass. After some delay the broad doors opened before him, and—as had been foretold—did not close after him.

Through the ruddy gap, the *jarl's* gaze followed his song-maker into a fire-bright hall whose wall-benches were aflower with women in kirtles of deep red and dull yellow and corn-flower blue. Like green beads from a broken necklace, pages were scattered over the floor playing a game of ball; and dodging between them and stumbling over them, swarthy thrall-men were bringing in tables for the evening meal. A fancy came to amuse the *jarl* that it was like the arrival of a war-arrow in a peace-camp when his messenger stepped into the ring of the firelight. From chess-board and bead-stringing and gossip, the women turned with smothered exclamations; while the purple-robed girl in the high-seat sat like one stricken motion less, her hand still holding out the silk ball she was winding from the skein which a page held apart before her.

Splendid in raiment now was the son of Freya, the king-born. As sun-burnished waves shone his newly trimmed hair, and his garments were all of velvet banded with fine sable, and sable lined the cloak that fell from his mighty shoulders. Regarding him, another fancy brought a smile to the *jarl*.

"He put on fine clothes as a man puts on armour, and like a flight of arrows are the glances shot against him. I would lay down my life on it that he would sooner go against arrows."

If that were so, still no one could tell from the song-maker's bearing whether desperation or confidence ruled in his mind. Passing between the fires, he came before the footstool of Brynhild the Proud. When he had made salute, he stood waiting in the attitude of courtly submission, one hand on his hilt and one on his breast, an attitude that took on new meaning because proud strength spoke from every line of his virile face and his sinewy body.

Motionless, she sat gazing at him, whether in speechless displeasure or speechless amazement, no one could tell from her expression. Signing the petrified page to withdraw out of ear-shot, she said at last:

"This behaviour seems to me so bold that I have never seen any act so bold as this. What is your errand with me?"

"I will speak it aloud and not mutter about it," he answered. "I have two. The first, which I care the most about, is to reconcile myself to you. The other is a message from the *jarl*, which I hold as a shield against an unfavourable reception."

She drew back to the extreme limit of her high-seat, her face set like a cameo against the dark wood. The best she could do was to observe presently, with haughtiness:

"To me it would seem more becoming to carry out your lord's business first."

"Becoming it might be, but more imprudent than to lay aside a shield in unequal combat."

"Unequal?" She managed to curl her flower-like lips. "Hear a wonder! On Treaty Day, you claimed the victory over me."

"Said I that I got the victory over you? Here now I do confess that you have me at your pleasure. If you bid me leave you, I can do nothing against it. If you refuse me your friendship, no power is strong enough to get it for me; though no man on earth will lack joy more than I, if that must be."

One swift look she sent round to make sure that no one else could hear the low-voiced words, then sat tapping the chair arm with her jewelled fingers, her bosom rising and falling like a white billow under the lace of her kerchief. Out of the stormy deeps, passionate words rose at last.

"I do not wish that you should value me like that, any more than I want to feel the way you make me feel. Do you not know that your offence against me was heavier even than Olaf's? He pushed my hands away, and recked little what I said; but you—though you stood with bound hands—you laid hold of my mind and moulded it to your will! You made of me—of *me*—a screaming shield-maiden, ready to slay my childhood's friend! And then you stood there and laughed in your triumph!"

He said slowly: "True enough I laughed—for one breath's space— and that passed for an offence; but for three months you have made me the soberest man in the New Lands. Is not that atonement?"

A glance she flashed to challenge his sincerity, but her eyes could not withstand his eyes steady wooing. She spoke without looking at him:

"If that were all! But you have done more. There is that which survives even that madness. Some door you have opened in my mind through which all my peace and pride have gone. Things I have never wanted before, now look good to me; and all I have seems as nothing, and the heavens reel around me, and I do not know one day what I am going to want the next. You have made me a thrall-woman in my own eyes, in proving to me that the passions that shake such base creatures can also shake me—that I can fear like them—hate like them sin like them love like them! Only if this be love, I tell you this,—that I will never yield to it! *I will not love you!*"

Her gaze was meeting his now with all a Valkyria's weapon-play. It was he who lowered his eyes, lest their fire offend her.

"Why you should love me, I know no reason at all," he said. "I hope for it only as a priest hopes for a miracle. This alone I know,—that I love you, so that to waken in the morning and look forward to the hope of speaking with you is to sit in a Greenland winter and look forward to the summer. Will you not grant me the boon I beg because to you it means so little, and to me it means so much?"

"I will not say that it meant little to hear your songs and your adventures," she answered presently, with courtesy. Soon after that, in the gloaming of her eyes a light flickered starlike. "Any more than I can deny that Freya's son can be a courtman when he chooses," she added. Then her mouth became as grave as it was gracious. "It may be that if you will give me your promise never to talk to me about—miracles—"

"So shall it be that I will take banishment from you as from a lawman, if once I break the agreement!"

After a moment she rose with queenful composure, stretching out her hand to the group around the entrance.

"Why do you allow the doors to remain open?" she called. "Our guest will not leave until he has partaken of our hospitality."

With a crash, the great doors swung to, startling the *jarl* where he stood in the darkness of the courtyard. At first he smiled whimsically, and made a gesture of drinking to his companion within. Then, as he turned to go back alone, the smile faded. The face he lifted to the stars seemed to be asking a bitter question of the planet that had stood over his birth.

Chapter 13

Mix hops with honey when thou mead wilt brew
                                                    —Northern saying.

Stirring before the great awakening, the southern slopes had thrown off their coverings of snow, and bared their brown bosoms to the fresh wind. The pools of the muddy road gave back unclouded blue, and blithe as the call of the robins in the sunny meadows were the voices of the young courtmen who had met at a crossing of the ways. Winter maintained its hold only on the face of Mord the Grim, as looking back from the crest of the hill he was riding over, he saw that the centre of the group was the *jarl's* tall song-maker.

Some of the young nobles had set forth to shoot ducks from the broken ice of the river, and were unfolding their plans to the forester's sympathetic ear. Some were seeking ground for a horse-race, when the sod should be firm enough, and were demanding of the favourite that he use his influence with the *jarl* to have a feast given in honour of the sport. And others, who knew that Rolf's son was now on his way home to the tower to take part in the wedding-feast of his foster-sister, were chaffing him about the effect his fine clothes of buff leather would have upon such Skraellings as he might encounter. The chatter came to an end only when the hoofbeat of two horses was heard on a road near by; and one youth surmised that it must be the bridegroom and the priest, whom Randvar was waiting to join; and another stepped out to look around the curve, vowing that if Bolverk's dress was too fine it should be subdued by a rain of mud. The youth stepped back, however, with a shrug.

"Only Brynhild's pet page; and behind him, Olaf the French. Tighten the peace-bands on your sword, Songsmith!"

A third gave Randvar's ribs a nudge with his elbow.

"No better than wasted breath is that warning!" he laughed. "As though the Songsmith had any cause now to be jealous of Olaf, Thorgrim's son!" So the laughter and chaff went up boisterously.

The Songsmith who had stood quietly listening, save for an occasional word of comment or banter, became yet more silent, and gave his entire attention to remedying a mistake in the lacing of one of his high Cordovan boots.

On his bent head, half the hail of jests continued to fall; and the other half flew on to meet the boy just turning into the road, fresh as a sprouting grass blade in his green livery.

"Lucky Bolverk, to be allying himself with such splendour!"

"Picture the cub doing the honours from the high-seat!"

"Are you going to give the bride away, young one?"

"Oh, why give your sister to an everyday body like a guardsman, Eric?"

"Nobody less than the *jarl* himself—"

"Ay, the *jarl*, by all means! Has it not been proved that *jarl's* sisters take well to forest-bred men?" Again a shout of laughter went up, and the song-maker gravely addressed himself to the relacing of his other boot.

Because Randvar remained stooping, the page on his arrival did not notice him; disdainfully he answered the merry group before which he had drawn rein.

"No intention have I to break through the brush to any wedding-feast. My errand hither is to tell the Songsmith that my mind has changed about going,—only I shall tell him that it is because Brynhild cannot spare me. He is to meet Bolverk here and go with him; but they must get along without me. It is to be seen that he left the tower too late to outgrow his fondness for moose-hump! Much better would you save your banter for his backwoods ways."

Like the impudent red-breasted bird now strutting on a stone wall across the road, Eric thrust out his chest with an air. Laughing and nudging, the young courtmen made a semicircle around him.

"Oh, a well-bred man is what you are, that is clear as day!"

"Small wonder you have no admiration for that lout of a song-maker!"

Tell us what you think of the showy clothes he has begun to—"

Yes, give us your opinion of his habits!" they chorused.

Still like the bright-eyed bird on the wall, Eric cocked his handsome little head knowingly; but even as they waited in laughing expectation, Olaf the French came cantering around the bend, and Eric's censure gave way to eulogy as he turned and recognised the newcomer.

"I will tell you a man I have got admiration for, and that is the one who comes riding hither! When I have my growth, I shall be as near like him as possible; and I am going to France with him when ever he goes back,—am I not, Olaf?"

"So it shall be," Thorgrim's son assented benignly, as he returned with inimitable grace the rather careless greetings of the group.

Importance swelled in Eric's chest until it burst out of his lips as ecstatically as the red-breasted bird's song.

"That will be the finest part of my life! I shall wipe this little town of cabins off my mind as completely as I have wiped off that old tower,—and that is as much gone from remembrance as though it had never been. Do you know, masters, it looks to me sometimes as though I could never have been born there? What seems likeliest is that some great chief of Norumbega had one child too many, so that he gave it to thralls to carry into the forest; and then Erna came along and found it and called it hers, so much nobler is my nature than my moth—" He left the word unfinished as his rapt gaze came down for the first time to the Songsmith, where he had risen and stood beside Gunnar the Merry. "By that I do not mean that she is not a worthy woman," he added hastily.

His foster-brother answered not a word. Stepping to the head of Eric's horse, he said briefly:

"Get down."

It did not appear that the page liked the tone overmuch, but neither did he seem willing to trifle with it. He made a parade of stretching in his saddle.

"You need not say it as though I meant to keep on," he retorted. "I have been waiting until you came, as everyone here knows, to get down and talk to you." Slowly he dismounted, taking great pains to keep his bright spurs out of the puddles.

"Give me now that chain off your neck, as a gift for your sister."

The page muttered something about meaning to give her a better gift, when he should have had time to visit the trading-booth; but his foster-brother's hand remained before him, immovable as a stone cup. He dropped the chain into it at last, and watched ruefully the stowing away of the trinket in the pouch of buff leather. Then the owner of the pouch made another demand:

"Now give me a message to go with it. Say, 'I send therewith my hearty greeting.'"

At that, Eric so far forgot his finery as to stamp and spatter it with mud. But after a second look from under the heavy brows, he said the words, rebelling only when the circle of grinning courtmen sent up a roar of laughter at the contrast between the sentiment and the tone in which it was uttered.

"In meddling in private affairs you show bad manners," he told them, and sent Rolf's son a glance that was half sulky, half coaxing. "Nor do I think you have any right to scold me after I have made atonement."

Far from scolding, his foster-brother turned to one of the courtmen who had come from a horse-fight and borrowed his riding-rod of twisted leather.

"You have made atonement for slighting Snowfrid," he said, "but for the way you behaved about Erna, you cannot redeem yourself from stripes. Pluck off your kirtle and stand forth."

"Foster-brother! If you will listen while I explain—"

"Already you have talked enough. Stand forth."

"Foster-brother—"

"In a word, you will take it or run."

"That is a good hint, young one," laughed Gunnar the Merry. "Pick up your heels." Then he laughed again at the glare that Eric turned on him.

"Will you keep your nose out of this?" the small Viking demanded. "If you think I am afraid to bear a flogging—!"

The end of the sentence was that his gay tunic lay on the ground and he stood forth in his shirt of fine linen, his arms locked upon his sturdy chest. From that attitude he did not flinch when the lashes fell, though they were neither light nor few. When it was over, the young men gave him good-humoured applause.

Gratification pulled at his mouth-corners as he looked at them out of the corner of his eye; but enough vanity had been taken out of him so that when his gaze passed on to his stern foster-kinsman, he showed only as a shamefaced little boy, now humbly desirous of being restored to favour.

"If you think it will give my kinswomen a great deal of pleasure, I will go to the feast with you," he offered, when he was clothed again and lingered shaping mud-balls with the toe of his boot.

"If I have my way, you will not be allowed to go back until it will give you so much pleasure that you cannot stay away," the Songsmith returned severely, rejecting utterly the blandishments of the rosy coaxing face. The culprit gave up the attempt, after a while. Climbing into his saddle he rode back up the highway—his sleeve in suspicious proximity to his eyes—and vanished into a brush-walled lane.

Watching the dejected withdrawal seemed to suggest to Olaf the French a welcome thought. He moved his horse a step forward, and broke in upon the scattered chatter.

"Surely," he said, "if you, Rolf's son, choose to attack a young friend of mine, and I choose to avenge the boy on you, that should be sufficient to excuse me in challenging you?"

Over his shoulder, Randvar looked at him with his short laugh,— he had stepped aside to whistle back his horse from the meadow in which it had strayed to browse.

"Surely! If you, Thorgrim's son, believe that you could get that excuse accepted,—in case you were alive to offer it!" he consented.

But three of the young courtmen spoke in the same breath: "Far from it, Olaf! Unless you were the boy's master."

Rolf's son said nothing, only stood waiting with his bridle in his hand.

But gradually Olaf settled back in his saddle, and sat thoughtfully stroking his short moustaches. "Ill might it be, then, since I lack a lawful claim. I should kill you, and then if I could not save myself from outlawry, I should get no good from your death."

"This I take the ring-oath on, that I would do my best to keep you from being put in that unsatisfying position," Randvar retorted.

It seemed to Gunnar the Merry that the conversation had gone as far as was advisable; and he said so, good-naturedly, several others seconding him. And while they debated, their cause drew strength from another source.

Standing farthest out in the road, where he could see around the curve, a youth named Aslak called out that the bridegroom and the priest were coming at last. With that announcement, all seriousness was put to rout; it was not even noticed that on a sudden impulse, Thorgrim's son wheeled and galloped back up the highway and disappeared into the lane whose bush-whiskered mouth had already swallowed up the crestfallen page.

Around the bend bowled the wedding party, the gorgeous bridegroom explaining at the top of his lungs how mistakes in the coming home of his marriage clothes had detained him. At sight of him, such cheers and chaff arose that he shouted himself hoarse with trying to repay a quarter of it, gave it up finally and set spurs to his horse and fled, followed by the ruddy-cheeked priest, cursing genially at the unwonted jolting of his fat sides. After them galloped the laughing song-maker, dividing his gibes between the group behind and the pair before.

What could have suited his wild blood better than to wander through the wonder-world of awakening forest? What could taste sweeter than a wedding-feast to a man who was watching his own hope grow with every day of spring shine and spring storm?

Chapter 14

More than all winter can one spring day yield
　　　　　　　　　　　　　　　—Northern saying.

The third month of spring was come upon the year when the Songsmith rode back through the forest from his visit at Freya's Tower; and the spirit of spring was come upon him, so that his blood worked in his veins like sap in a tree.

Sometimes the billowy clouds above him parted over tender blue, and let through bursts of radiant sunshine that tiled his path with gold and golden-lighted the dim aisle stretching out before him. Sometimes they drew together in a lowering mass of gray, and let fall snow-flakes to lie daisy-like upon the patches of springing green. Sometimes it was bright streaks of rain that fell, meeting his cheek like so many soft mouths, changing with the returning sun into laughing eyes winking from every leaf. Whatever came, he took as joyously as the teeming earth.

The thrill that the earth must have known when it looked up at the first rainbow, the Songsmith knew when he came at last to the cross-roads and, through a bushy lattice, glimpsed bright-coloured mantles and divined that Brynhild had ridden out to meet him.

Feigning that she had checked her horse only to give her pages more time to search the sodden thickets for flowers, she was lingering between the budding walls of the lane, herself very like a spring flower in her wrappings of leaf-green. When the horseman appeared at the head of the lane, her first impulse was plainly to wheel and ride away from him; her second, to draw her queenfulself erect and flash such lightnings from her eyes gray sky as should strike dead any presumptuous thought.

But he had no need to tame his joy for it had mounted to that height where it was changed into a delicious terror. Almost was it beyond his power to salute her, to answer becomingly the merry welcome of her women. When at last he had reached her side and dismounted to receive her greeting, the touch of her white hand lighting bird-like on his brown one made his fingers tremble so that she could not fail to mark it.

A moment it seemed as though the blissful panic would even fall on her, so speechless she sat before him, the wild-rose colour blowing in her cheeks. But even at the first hint of a surprised pause in the women's chatter, she recovered herself, and spoke with gracious composure.

"The weeks have seemed long without your songs, my friend. They say my brother has begun to suffer in his temper through missing you and them. Tell us if you gained enough pleasure by the visit to make up his loss; and tell us about the bride, and how her mother likes her strapping new son."

She said "us," but after a little space of polite pretence it became doubtful how much interest her maidens had in the telling. As if enamoured of the song-maker's sleek black horse, they gathered around it to caress its arching neck while they listened. From that, they drew off to the side of the path to pluck up young grass spears for its refreshment; then still farther off to the hedge of lilac bushes, gemmed with long green buds. The time came at last when all who had not slipped through the hedge had vanished around it, into the road, whence the murmur of their voices came back sweetly, blending softly with the tinkle of a brook flowing somewhere through the thicket.

It did not appear that their mistress knew whether they stayed or went, save that she seemed to feel more freedom now in allowing her eyes to follow their inclination to droop and rest on the trailing sprays of fragrant buds with which the pages had filled her lap. Her lover neither knew nor cared. He rambled on without even knowing what he was saying,-more than that it was something which held her listening while his eyes drank their fill of her exquisite face. He would have stood there gazing at her in silence, when he had finished telling of the feast, if she had not roused herself hastily to end the pause.

"It has the sound of a song come true," she said. "I wish I had better tidings to give in return than this which you will think bad, that your little foster-brother has deserted my service for Olaf's, Thorgrim's son."

"For Olaf's!" he repeated in surprise. "What possessed the cub?"

"It surprised me also," she assented, "for since he came to me, we have never been apart either in word or deed. Yet Olaf looks grand in his eyes, and lavishes on him a great store of gifts and privileges. I am afraid he will get spoiled by it."

His straight brows joining, the Songsmith gazed before him reflectively.

"I wonder if it would have been better had I taken him with me?" he mused. "Yet would it have been to Erna a lasting sorrow to see the change in him. . . . And it would have made him set greater store by himself to see their mean clothes. . . ." His musing branched unconsciously. "It is a poor place, the tower, yet I would not trade it for the *jarl's* house to be born in."

"Tell me how it appeared to you now?" she asked him, smiling. "The tower that let the wind blow in all the year around! Did it stir your wild blood so that it became a hardship for you to come back to walls?"

It seemed that she saw the danger of such a question as soon as she had given it voice, for she half put out her hand to snatch it back. But he read the meaning of the gesture and obeyed it.

"It was no hardship to come back, *jarl's* sister.... Yet the place had never seemed to me so fair. When I came home to it, that day after it had happened to me to meet you in the forest, I saw only its bareness and its poverty. Now it was as a song, every stone a word to tell of my father's love. I never knew a greater love among all men upon earth. Night after night, while the others slept, I walked before the gray pile and read its runes. Great bowlders are there that must have challenged his strength to wrest from their beds in the earth, which yet he wrestled with rejoicingly, since even so ingloriously he was conquering something for his beloved one. The fragments over the archways Could you but see, *jarl's* sister, the patient labour of their fitting! Never monk toiled more devoutly with his brush! Night after night, it was as though Rolf walked beside me pouring out his mind, so could I enter into his joy that knew his love returned. Knowing that, what was it to fight Hildebrand and twenty-forty—horsemen! Here I, his son, may not even end where he began. I—"

He broke off because her hand had risen to for bid him, and stood awhile with head bent and turned aside, his breath coming fast. But she did not call her women as he had feared; he had time to master himself and begin again.

"The stones Rolf placed were the words of the song; the memory of my mother was the music. When I said the Tower was poverty stricken, I was blind. More rich than an altar-shrine I think it, now that I know what a woman's love may mean. *Jarl's* sister, you could not even dream such visions as my memory gave me to see in the moonlight there! ...Visions of my king-born mother watering linen on the grass before the tower ... bringing drink to Rolf as he rested from his labour ... standing waiting to bear back the cup when he should have finished, the leaf-shadows playing on the soft masses of her hair.... Waiting before him, Freya, the king-born! As I live, it looks to me now as if it must have been a dream! Here, I cannot myself believe it."

"I can," the *jarl's* sister said dreamily, then started awake as she saw passion flame up in his face past any checking. As a straw, it burned away the barrier she sought to raise.

"Brynhild! If you had aught to give me, it cannot be that you would hold it back! I will await your pleasure. I will wrestle with the roughness in me even as Rolf wrestled with the bowlders, till I have made my mind a place more worthy of your dwelling. But even as Freya cheered with her love the man who loved her, give me some token that in time your pride will yield! Some sign!"

"What would you?" she murmured. "My hands—"

He seized them both, crushed them against his lips. But he stayed not at the arm's-length she would have kept him. Holding her hands, he leaned nearer; and the mystic might of spring throbbing in his veins purpled his eyes and held her like a spell.

"Your mouth!" he prayed. "Olaf—Gunnar—fifty others—have had your hands. Your mouth!"

He knew not that he drew her towards him; doubtless she knew not that she yielded. Only, each knew that her lips were there before his, and he had gathered their perfect flower.

Chapter 15

Bare is back without brother behind it
　　　　　　　　—Northern saying.

The waning light falling into the *jarl's* bedchamber from its one small window under the eaves disclosed dimly the figures of the priest and the counsellor and the courtman, as they waited in the middle of the floor, but showed little more than the mass of the high curtained bed that stood under the window against the wall. The old advice-giver, declaiming before it, had the feeling that he was talking into space, even while he knew that somewhere in the gloom beneath the hangings the young ruler must lounge listening to him.

"Whether you take it well or not, you shall not keep on in a false step for want of my foresight. Long ago I told you that the son of Freya, the king-born, was trying to get friends behind him. Now I tell you that he has got them. Courtmen tag at his heels. Traders and guardsmen clink horns at the sound of his name; while the saying runs that hunters show fight if they think that so much as his cloak-hem has been trod on. In a year more, he will have wormed his way into the high-seat. I foretell it."

Mord's voice rose to a wrathful climax; and the gesture of his knotted hands, when it looked as though the silence of the bed was going to continue unmoved, suggested that he would like to use them on the sullen shoulders.

But the *jarl's* voice sounded presently in measured accents: "Has it come to your ears that men are speaking against my rule?"

Slightly appeased, Mord's hands relaxed to smooth his beard. "I do not mean that, Starkad's son. You mistake me if you think I mean that the fellow has yet power enough to get you disliked. Well spoken of over all the land is your rule. Only—"

Measured and relentless as the boom of surf, the *jarl's* voice sounded through his. "When it happens that they do find fault, come and tell me of it; and I will listen patiently. Only about aught which belongs to my life as a free man—"

A moment it seemed as though his control weakened, as if measure might be lost in fury; but he recovered himself and beat it out slowly to the end.

"Witness, priest! and Olaf as well! I know how well-beloved the Songsmith is; and I know also how little loved I am. Plain as you, I see how proud my sister is; nor do I forget that she is my heir. Yet I have given leave to the son of Freya, the king-born, to woo and wed her and join his power to her ambition. Judge from that how I trust him, and take other counsel than to slander him to my ears again."

Deeper than ever seemed the stillness when he had ceased. All that stirred it was the grating of iron hinges, as Mord jerked open the door which led from the alcove-chamber out into the great living-room of the bodyguard.

The action let in a rush of ruddy firelight that illumined the counsellor's bent figure from head to foot, made a leap at the silver rosary of the black-robed priest behind him, a snatch at the shining lute in the hand of Olaf the French, and came to a halt only at the edge of the curtained bed. Gradually, amid tumbled cushions and blankets of fur, Kelvin's brooding recumbent figure became visible. Frowning at it, Mord paused.

"So, I suppose, it must be; but never yet have I thought your behaviour more untoward. I think now that it would have been good counsel if Starkad had given you a voice in things here, so that you might have found out the danger in it."

As one expecting an explosion, the priest involuntarily shrank into himself; but what came instead was a sly chuckle.

"It has crossed my thoughts also that Starkad might have managed some things better," Kelvin's voice drawled. "I wonder how it looks to the old troll himself now."

The advice-giver turned on the threshold to say with sternness: "Young lord, is it in that manner you speak of the honoured dead?"

For all answer, there came from the bed a peal of mocking laughter.

Like one who dares trust himself no longer, Mord made a swift stride through the door and away; and the Shepherd Priest spoke soothingly:

"Most dear lord!"

It could be seen that the *jarl* lowered one of the fists propping his chin and turned and looked at him. He said presently, with ominous slowness:

"Are you going to take the text now, priest, and edify me with exhortations about honouring the dead? If so, pray begin by explaining why a man should be honoured only because he changes from serving the Devil on earth to serving him in"

The priest lifted a gentle hand. Brawny shepherd's hand though it was, it had no lack of dignity.

"My lord and son, turn not your good gift of speech to your own ill. I would in no way vex you. That you were sorely tried under Starkad's rule was before all eyes. How should I who have not felt the burden chide you that your back is weary? Only I would beseech of you that fairness towards him which we show to you, when in your less worthy turns of mind we still remember how noble is your nature. Old sayings have it that men are wolves and bears in their Other Shapes,—it is but a turn of the cloak to hold with the Christ-faith that the blackest-hearted man has a better self within him. Believe of your father that he had a gentler spirit somewhere hid, that his life bound him as yours binds you. Believe, and pardon."

From resting on his elbow, Starkad's son started passionately upright.

"Pardon,—and give up my hate that is as meat to my teeth! Priest, are you Northern born and know not that such satisfaction comes from hating a foe as makes the joy of loving a friend look like pale moonshine by red fire? My foe was what he was—doubly my foe in that he owed me help—and blow shall go for blow between us. Pardon that I may be pardoned? Rather than forgive him one jot of his punishment would I share his torture and count it gain! Rather would I burn by his side until that spirit which cannot be subdued by Norway's rocks or Greenland's snow-wastes or Iceland's belching mountains has burned out of both of us, and left no more than two dead cinders! Nor will I bear rebuke!"

"Nay, how should I do aught else than sorrow for you who choose for yourself so hard a way?" the old priest said sadly. "Methinks my heart would break over you if I did not know that even at the goal of that road, at the end of that torture, One will stand waiting for you beside whose love mine is but a taper to a star. His mercy be upon you and save you from yourself!"

As a star through the night, shone his soul through his swarthy face; but Starkad's son averted his eyes that he might not see it.

"Everything bides its time. When I feel desire for that goal, it may be that I shall believe in it. You are an honest man,—do what you can among my people. For my malady, your medicine is too mild."

With a hand raised in dismissal, he met the hand raised in benediction and flung himself back on his cushions, speaking curtly to Olaf Thorgrim's son.

"Do you sing, until I decide whether your jingling or my humour makes the worst discord in my ears."

As a man wakened out of deep abstraction, the courtman came to himself with a start. Though he sought to cover it with his graceful bow, and set his shapely fingers instantly to their task on the lute-strings, his customary tactfulness was lacking. In the middle of the first verse of his ballad, the *jarl's* hand—that had come out into the firelight and begun to pick and tear at the gold-embroidered flowers of the bed-hangings—flew up irritably.

"What the devil! Have you nothing but tinkling love-tunes in stock? Do they rear their men in the women's house in France? Some song of might—fire—you milksop!"

Murmuring apologies, Olaf tried plainly to re gain his wonted poise; but before he had got out so much as the first couplet of the battle-song he had struck into, the hand had leaped from the embroidery, snatched his instrument from his hold and dashed it against the opposite wall.

"Fool! I have warned you that battle-songs are my love-songs," Kelvin's voice rose in thunder. "To sing them to me when I am doomed to in action is to heat the fever in my veins to madness! Oh, where in the Troll's name is the Songsmith? The three weeks leave I gave him was up when the candle of the sun marked noon today; and here the sun is burned out, and he has not come. What can he mean by it?"

Olaf laughed, neither mirthfully nor yet perfunctorily, but with the frank discordance of his mind.

"Lord, who shall take it on him to say what anyone means at this court? If it were in France, now, I could interpret your relations well enough; but here—here you go not by any rules I know. I give up the riddle." With a gesture of less than usual grace and more than usual feeling, he went over to pick up his lute.

But Helvin spoke with unusual softness from the darkness of the bed-curtains: "How would you interpret our relations if you were in France, *beausire?*"

"Nay, noble one, it has no meaning here," Thorgrim's son answered almost impatiently, "here where no house reaches underground, and women count for naught. There, men would say that the fellow had some secret of yours in his power and you took insolence from him because you feared to resent it."

That he was aiming a shaft is unlikely for he did not look up to see if the shot told, but went on examining the broken strings, his mouth working like that of a man who is trying also to mend a rift in his damaged composure. It was not until the stillness behind the curtains had lasted so long as to become ominous that he started as though struck by a possibility, lowered the lute slowly, and slowly turned his gaze towards the recumbent figure.

Even the restless hand had been drawn in from the light now; crouching as for a spring, Starkad's son loomed in the dimness. Like vultures hovering over their prey, Olaf's eyes settled on him, tearing their way in as though they would reach the inmost places of his heart.

So they faced each other until they were startled by an outburst of jovial voices in the guard-room without, shouting the name of Rolf's son with words of noisy welcome.

Straightening, then, Olaf made a salute of studied mockery.

"Lord," he said, "I will give place to your—confidant."

The *jarl* stretched out an arm grown strangely unsteady, and spoke in a voice become strangely breathless. "Wait! You think that I am afraid to make him smart for an offence? Wait a little."

Surprise took some of the assurance from Olaf's bearing, as he resumed his place at the bed-foot; then, in expectant malice, he folded his arms and leaned against the carven post to watch through the open door the song-maker's buoyant approach.

Delayed by the questions rained on him, by the hands thrust out to clasp his, Randvar was long in making his passage through the hall; but the alcove doorway framed him at last, a vision of light and of life as the fire-glow touched his burnished hair and the new happiness in him rang in his voice of greeting.

The *jarl's* grim tone sounded doubly grim by contrast. "However wroth I was before, now I am half as wroth again. What befits you, lazy-goer, is humblest explanation .

Accustoming his light-filled eyes to the gloom, the Songsmith had lingered on the threshold; now as he was about to advance he stopped once more, attuning his harmony-filled ears to this discord.

"Lord!" he said in amazement. "Lord, what should I explain?" then, incredulously, "This can not be because I am a half-day late! No stress was laid upon the time—no need of haste" He broke off as his clearer vision separated Olaf's blue-and-gold figure from the blue-and-gold curtains. "You here! Now is it likely that any lying tale of yours could have worked this —Yet it is not possible, lord, that you would have listened to him! That—"

Again he broke off; but this time with a smothered cry as, turning, he beheld the face that Helvin thrust into the light. Gnawed and blood-streaked lips, it showed; while bright as the ruddy light in the dusky room flickered devil-fire in the murky eyes. They turned to keep watch of Thorgrim's son, even while the tongue belonging to them ad dressed the song-maker.

"Is it not possible, boor that you are, that you could have leaned too heavily on my favour? Olaf says justly that one would think I feared you had some secret knowledge of me, so forbearing have I been. What! because out of my service I spare you three weeks time—ill spare it—must you take a half-day more? Without a word—a sign—and then defend your fault with noisy voice and rampant head? Let me see you tame it. Speak me humbly if you would not push my temper to the uttermost."

And yet Rolf's son did not throttle him,—only stood looking at him with head lowered and thrust forward like a bull moose at bay. The hand Olaf had laid on his hilt, in the hope of being called upon to defend his lord, fell paralysed. He doubted the ears that brought him Randvar's low answer:

"Lord, I entreat you to hold down your anger. Remember that we are not alone, and—"

"Call you that humbleness which would command me where and before whom I shall rebuke you?" Starkad's son snarled. "Now do you stand so stubborn as to think that I will hold back from punishing you? Bend lower—low as your knee!"

Again Olaf made a hopeful move towards his sword. Again his arm fell benumbed. Rigidly as a man of iron, Rolf's son had knelt, his sinewy, brown hands gripping each other behind his back.

Who was the stillest for a while it would have been hard to say the Songsmith or the gaping courtman or the young ruler, who stood wiping great drops from his forehead while his devil-like eyes watched Olaf from under his palm.

"Are your French courtmen better broken?" he sneered at last.

Out of his trance Olaf came slowly. Drawing his shapely form erect, he laughed mellowly in his enjoyment.

"*Jarl*, I make you a hundred compliments! The proudest king in France had not dared say one-half as much to his meanest lackey. I make you a thousand apologies for my stupidity! I see now that what makes the forester a comfort to you is not his boldness but his meekness. I give you ten thousand thanks for the merry lesson you have taught me!"

Bowing almost at the song-maker's side, he laughed almost in the song-maker's ear, and laughing bowed himself gracefully out of the room.

Swiftly as well as gracefully it must have been, for while the sound of the soft mirth was still in the air, the *jarl* rushed forward with the snarl of a wolf robbed of its bone, yet Randvar had time to leap ahead of him. On Olaf's heels, the song-maker shut the door with a thunderous crash, and set his back against it.

Chapter 16

He that guesseth, often goes wrong
       —Northern saying.

In the sudden darkness that shut down upon them, the Songsmith felt Helvin's body dash against his, heard Helvin's hiss at his ear:

"Let me after him, do you hear?"

"Let you betray your state to all men? Lord, I have saved your secret—"

"I will kill him only for coming so near to guessing it!"

"Has all sense left you?"

"Off, or he will reach the hall-door before I can catch him! Would you turn my wrath upon yourself?"

"Keep your wrath within bounds, lord, as I kept mine. Do you suppose that after stripping off my pride to wrap it about your cursed secret, I shall allow your folly to undo—"

"Allow? Mother of Heaven! do you know what you are defying?"

"Do you forget that I am not the rabbit-hearted thing I feigned to be—"

"Out of the way!"

"No—"

Short as the word was, it was cut in two by the slam of the great doors at the guardroom's farther end. One breath Randvar let out in relief, then drew in one in dread and braced himself for the grapple.

But nothing came.

No use to strain his eyes, for darkness was now so thick upon them that it carried a sense of smothering with it. He strained his woodsman's ear, trained to catch the lightest bending of a twig beneath a fox's foot, but not so much as the sound of a faintly drawn breath rewarded him. Delicately as a butterfly uses its feelers, he put out a ringer, then, and found that the spot where Helvin had stood was empty. More silent than the stealthiest wind that tries to creep unnoted through the forest, he had withdrawn to some quarter of the darkness.

From his head to his feet, shuddering shook the song-maker as his mind strove to follow that withdrawal to its goal, to picture him who stood hidden there. The temptation to let in the fire light to show what thing he faced was so torture-strong that he took his hands off the door-panels on which they were spread out and locked them before him, and gave himself the relief of speaking Kelvin's name in a low voice, entreating, soothing.

No answer came. A windless cavern in the marrow of the earth's bones had not been stiller. From the living-room without came the rattle of knife and trencher, as the evening meal wore on; the clink of horns with the arrival of drinking-time; by-and-by, snatches of maudlin song. Even the shuffling patter of the thralls the Songsmith caught through the oaken panels, but in the room where he kept vigil, only the thundering echo of his heart throbbing in his ears.

Perhaps its pealing was enough to blunt his hearing. Though he detected no rustle of approach, his cheek was touched of a sudden by a fiery breath, which like a poisonous vapour brought with it dizzy horror. The torture of two hands falling stealthily upon his shoulders—tightening swift to the grip of claws—recalled him for an instant to himself; then again his brain whirled, as a bushy thing that he knew for the mass of Kelvin's blood-red hair was pressed against his face. Back from it he strained with all his might, fought it off with all the power of his toughened sinews; but with a strength beyond the strength of man, the hands drew him slowly steadily downward.

Suddenly, to his mounting madness, it was no longer Helvin with whom he struggled. It was some being from another world, some nameless Thing against which his gorge rose up in loathing hate. Twice he gasped out warning, then loosened his grasp on the bushy hair, wrenched out his sword and stabbed downward.

With the sinking of blade in flesh, a sharp unhuman scream rang out; the clutch on his shoulders loosened. Even before he could tear off the dragging weight and hurl it from him, it had fallen heavily, shaking the timbered floor.

Like an echo came cries from the guard-room without, thunder of feet, clangour of weapons. Randvar was sent staggering across the room as the door behind him was burst open by a dozen brawny shoulders. On the threshold appeared Visbur, the grizzled old leader; behind him, two-score excited faces.

On the threshold they paused, staring at the sight the inrushing firelight revealed,—Helvin Jarl lying in a pool of blood; beyond him the figure of his song-maker, bristling-haired, a bloody sword in his hand. Half wrathful, half incredulous, their voices rose:

"Rolf's son a traitor!"

But no thought had the Songsmith for them. On the face upturned from the blood pool his gaze was riveted. It was Kelvin's face, unmarred, unchanged; in the gray eyes only unutterable anguish; anguish unutterable on the finely cut mouth that was trying vainly to form and send forth words. It was Helvin, his friend, that his madness had laid low. With a hoarse cry, he flung the weapon from him, and turned and buried his head in the bed-curtains.

As from a distance, he heard the scuffling of feet staggering under a heavy burden, and felt the jar of the bed as they lowered their load upon it; but he came back to consciousness only when stern hands laid hold of him and drew him from his shelter. He realised, then, the consequences of his deed as he met the awful reproach of the looks bent on him and saw the barrier of crossed spears that had been set before him.

Visbur said: "Chief, there is no need for us to wait for lawmen. Say only whether he is to be shot or hanged."

Pushing off those who were trying to cut away his robe and find his wound, the *jarl* dragged himself up by the bed-draperies, turning a ghastly face upon the room.

"Free him," his lips made out to shape.

After a bewildered pause, the old warrior said slowly: "I suppose what you are trying to order is, Slay him, not understanding that I said it should be done before the clots on his blade were dry. All I ask, chief, is in what manner he is to suffer death?"

With as much force as his half-swoon left him, the *jarl* shook his head, repeating the words so that there was no mistaking them: "Free him—and let him to me."

But even as the Songsmith turned, speaking his friend's name unsteadily, Visbur made his men a sign; and the spear-wall remained.

"Hold him and take him forth," the leader commanded. "Starkad's son has gone astray out of his wits. I will answer for the act when he is sane again."

"You will answer—with your life," the *jarl* said between gasping breaths. "While I live—I shall have my way. And my luck is not so good that I am dying. It is no more than a flesh-wound. I swooned from—from my rage. Let him to me."

This time he stretched out a shaking hand, and the spears fell. In a moment the Songsmith was kneeling beside the bed, the arm that had so nearly mastered him lying around his neck.

"Tell them—enough. Enough to clear yourself," Helvin murmured.

Around the circle of hard old faces that until now had met his glance so cordially, Rolf's son sent a beseeching look, then dropped his eyes in despair.

"*Jarl*, I could never say so much as to make them believe me; before them I stand proved a traitor who has turned blade against his lord. And how shall I speak against the truth of that judgment? I am every man's dastard. Lord, I would as lief go out with them." His voice broke, and he did not seek to mend it.

But Helvin spoke as curtly as his faintness allowed, "Raise me up," and when that was done, "Bring me wine." From the beaker, he lifted a face pitched to determination.

"Let all listen to my words, that I need not speak twice. He bore from me more than any of you would have borne. He lost his temper only when I drove him to frenzy. He struck only to save his life."

"To save his life, chief? And you with bare hands!" old Visbur said slowly.

Of a sudden, sick shuddering seized upon the *jarl*, so that his head drooped and sank. But even as they started towards him, he raised it—raised himself with the force of his passion.

"Now damnation take such loyalty!" he cried.

"I have told you that he is not guilty as you think,—I will lower myself to no more explaining. He goes free because I will it. And if any man reports this happening outside, so that even in people's thoughts my friend be held up to reproach, that man shall be outlawed, and have my wrath besides. Bear that in mind—and leave me now to him—whose support I have always found best."

Upon the song-maker's shoulder he fell, spent; and the guard who went last from the room heard his moan:

"My friend, my friend, this is that one thing that could tear us asunder! It will be your life or mine."

The man had passed out of hearing when Randvar answered slowly: "If that be true, lord, then mine is the life that will end. I know now which would be the easier to bear."

Chapter 17

Cold are the counsels of women
                    —Northern saying.

Blinded by the change from the hall's unbroken shade to the courtyard's untempered light, Randvar lingered on the threshold. As upon helpless prey, the unsparing sunshine of the spring morning fastened on him and pointed out that his leather tunic had been dragged open at the throat and his sleeves torn out at the shoulders, that his face was haggard and his eyes blood shot. The thralls, hurrying to and from the buildings with fresh water and clean straw, laughed indulgently as they glanced at him, and murmured one to another: "Behold a man who drank deep last night!"

No more than if he had been wine-deadened was he conscious of their comments or their presence. He had drunk of misery as of a heady liquor, and like a drunkard's thirst for water was his longing for the presence of the woman he loved. Seeking her—conscious only of his need of her—he made his way across the glaring stretch of the courtyard, through the dim length of the women's hall, to the shrine of her alcove bower.

Before he reached it, its open door gave him view of tapestried walls in whose dusky east a mirror of silver-gilt hung like a rising sun, of white-robed tirewomen moving now and again across it, of the girl who stood before it while they finished dressing her, her exquisite head agleam against the dark hangings like a jewel in its casket. His sense of beauty stirred through his heaviness, and quickened song-makers fancies in his mind.

"The web of her hair glows as the dragon's treasure glowed in the gloom of his den. . . . As a pearl from a setting of red gold shines her face from her tresses. . . . As rare as a jewel is Brynhild the Proud . . . as unbending . . . as untender . . ."

Into his longing crept something akin to wistfulness. He stood gazing at her in silence as encountering his eyes in the mirror she raised her head with a motion of surprise. He wondered why she did not turn when he advanced, but remained regarding his reflection and spoke as to the man in the bright oval.

"Has Freya's son lost sight of my dignity, as well as of his own, that he comes in disorder into my presence?"

"Disorder?" he repeated, looking for the first time at his reflection.

An instant he stood abashed before it, so did it jar upon the stately harmony; then the grim scene that had brought him to that condition came back and dwarfed everything else. With a gesture of passionate scorn, he turned from the mirror.

"*Jarl's* sister, if ever it happen to you to reach the sap of the Tree of Life, such things as clothes will seem less important than cobwebs blowing from its branches!" he said, and whirling on his heel, he turned and stood in the door, staring away with unseeing eyes.

Yrsa the Lovely, fastening a velvet pouch to her mistress's girdle of filigree, let it fall with a soft thud; but that was all the sound there was in the room until the *jarl's* sister began to speak coldly to the other maids:

"I want to wear the silver neck-chain—No, not that one the one to match this girdle. Yes, that. And, Nanna, I wish you would bring me the kerchiefs,—all that have a silver fringe." As light footsteps answered her, and the rustle of silk, she gave other low-voiced orders.

Gradually, the calm routine brought the Songsmith back into touch with the world about him. Staring away over the whirring wheels, he told himself that it must look to her as though he had come unsobered from a night's carousal,—that it was even better she should think so than guess the true reason for his dulled wits. Girding up his patience for this new trial, he turned back wearily.

"It is fair and right, *jarl's* sister, that I should have blame for showing you aught but the bright side of my manners, which are tarnished enough at best. I will take my leave now, and come back only when the wine-clouds have cleared from my mind." He was crossing the threshold when her outstretched hand stayed him.

"I would rather you would remain, if you have nothing against it," she said, then spoke over her shoulder to the kneeling tirewomen, who were making the arrangement of her train an excuse for lingering. "Maidens, you have done enough work on those folds. Go out now to your spinning,—excepting only Yrsa. Foster-sister, do you take your quill embroidery to that stool under the window, yonder."

When she had seen them obey her, she turned back to her lover a face whose expression he could not understand.

"I will begin by saying outright that you need not try to hide the truth under the pretence that it is wine instead of trouble which ails you. I should know better than that even if Thorgrim's son had not taken pains to let me hear how you were likely to pass the night."

In his mind he repeated the name of Thorgrim's son, at first wonderingly, then vengefully; but aloud he said nothing, only continued to look at her in haggard suspense.

A moment her high pride wavered, her beautiful mouth seeming to struggle against tenderness. Coming up to him, she touched her fingers lightly to his rent sleeves, his torn collar, the furrow between his dark brows.

"It is seen that Helvin went even further, after Olaf left! Do you think that his being my brother holds me back from hating him?"

Two emotions the song-maker suddenly knew,—relief that the whole truth was still unknown to her, and a desire to delay those caressing fingers. Capturing them, he held them against his cheek while he asked her what had been said to make her think the *jarl* was behaving badly towards him.

At that, her mouth surrendered to indignation.

"Enough was said—and more! I liked it well to have Olaf fetch such news,—Olaf, whom I cast off in your favour! And he brought it around so artfully that I could not stop him until it was out. He said that because you had lingered that little while in the lane, Helvin dared to upbraid you, to threaten you— Now, I will not put it into words! He said that the *jarl* spoke to you as a man dare not speak to his thrall, lest the slave turn,—and that you did not turn!" She plucked her hands from his hold, drew herself away from him. "He said that you took it submissively—that when he came away, you were on your knees!"

No longer was she pearl-pale, but crimson with the blood of her scourged pride. An instant her passion reacted on him, so that his face reflected her flush. He muttered that Thorgrim's son went heavily into debt for a creature that had only one life with which to pay. Then the emotion passed, too slight really to stir his heaviness.

"Yes, I submitted to him,—" he said, "as a well man puts up with the fretfulness of a sick one. Would you have a whole man contend against a cripple? For that is what Helvin is when he speaks temper-trying words, a man crippled in his mind. What difference does it make? since you must know that cowardice could have nothing to do with my behaviour. I can think of much pleasanter things to speak of."

Again a certain wistfulness came into his eyes, and he drew nearer to her.

"Let me feel that I have a peace land in your heart, though all other ports are war-bound. If I were in a death-swoon, the sound of your voice would trickle into my ears like cordial and spread healing through me. Give me of its balm now of your smile your love."

Another step he made towards her,—then stopped short. For it was not as a minister of healing she faced him, but as a Valkyria of battle, armoured in pride. Like spears she threw her words at him.

"As soon would I that you were a coward as a churl! Churl's blood—Rolf's blood—that must be what it is! Freya's stock would have struck the words from his lips though he were thrice a jarl. Now better be a coward than a clod, too base to know it when you are insulted."

This time the colour that rose to his face remained there, a darkling shade. From under lowering lids he stood looking at her.

"If you would not have me show churl's blood by losing temper with you," he said presently, "I ask you to stop talking about this happening. So soon as Helvin got himself in hand again, he made atonement; and that is an end to the matter. What lies on you, who say you love me, is to have faith in my manfulness. And I ask you, more over, to remember that you are fretting a churl who has already been galled to the quick."

She greeted the warning as a Valkyria might greet a sign that her opponent is aroused. In her governed voice was the thrill of a trumpet.

"Lose your temper, then, as fast as you may,—and so find your pride! Halfway, I think it is good-nature that makes you bend to him; and halfway, gratefulness for the favours you have taken from him; though you have long known what my wish is, that you should never look to anyone else than to me when you stand in need of anything."

Her satin-shod foot stirred with an angry impulse. "A fine atonement that is given in secret, while he chose that time when you were under the eyes of your enemy to put shame upon you! Can you not understand, Rolf's son, that you drag me down in your disgrace, since I have done you the honour to promise to wed you? If you have no pride for yourself—for Freya's name—make some for me, that it be not told around that the man I hold highest in honour is a man Starkad's son uses like a thrall!"

The Songsmith opened his compressed lips wide enough to let a question through: "Is this a sample of the honour you hold me in?"

"It is the kindest treatment you will ever receive from me until you have wiped out this stain," she told him.

Then because he did not reply to her, but folding his arms across his breast, turned as though to leave her, she blazed out at him:

"The end of this shall be that you take your choice of two things! Either you go to him and renounce his service, or else you go from me and renounce the hope that I shall ever call you husband."

He answered her then, his arms outflung like stones from a volcano's crest, though his voice only deepened.

"May my tongue wither if ever I ask to call myself your thrall! A bad bargain would that be to throw off a man's rule to be commanded by a woman! Not though she be as fair as you, and I love her as I love you! I have sworn an oath to Helvin Jarl to stand by him as by a brother, and never shall you egg me on to break it. If your lover's love is not enough, and you must have his freedom also, seek out a lesser man for your favour; for as God lives, my pride that you have scorned—be it king-born or churl-born—will never stoop to your rule!"

With the last word, the door closed behind him.

Chapter 18

But a short while is hand fain of blow
                                    —*Northern saying.*

Over field and fallow, through wood and meadow, up hill and down, on—on—on—the song-maker strode, no goal before him, only driving revolt I within him.

Whenever road or lane made a turn towards the east, the glaring May sunshine struck him in the face. Fending it off with his bended arm, he conceived a hatred of its stare, of the garish blue sky it fell from, of the bustling sounds it called forth. On all sides they rose in a strident chorus, chattering birds in the hedges, screaming cocks in the barnyards, racketing children on every green, shrill-laughing women washing clothes at every pond,—even the shouts of distant ploughmen were added by the breeze.

In fitful gusts the warm dry wind went with him like some romping oaf, now rushing ahead down the road to beat up the dust with clumsy glee, now lying in wait around some corner to pounce upon him with snorts of mirth and buffet him and wind his hair across his face. Struggling with it, his fury rose as against some boorish jester. He shouted in its teeth:

"If you had but a body that hands could lay hold of—!"

The craving for combat—like fire it was fanned in him by the dry gusts. He drew breath sharply when following a narrow wood-trail brought him suddenly into the highway and face to face with Gunnar and half a dozen of the young courtmen. If they would but jostle him in their careless mood—so much as kick up the dust about him—give him any excuse whatsoever—His mouth watered at the thought of what would follow! Disappointment increased his rage when after one look at him—they toned their familiar hails down to punctilious salutes, and picked their way around him as around a fire.

His head set low, he was standing looking after them, when another wayfarer came cantering around the bend behind him and almost rode him down. He had seized the horse by its bridle and forced it back upon its haunches before he realized that the befringed and befeathered rider in blue-and-silver was no other than his small foster-brother.

Releasing the bronze chain, he stepped aside with a smothered oath.

"You elf!" he said. "Erna's luck will not last you long if you draw on it often in this way. Take yourself on."

Undeniably, the elf's first impulse was towards obedience. He had drawn in his chin and let his horse carry him by, before he remembered his new dignity and pulled rein alike on steed and inclination. Like one adjusting new garments, he thrust out his chest and stiffened his spine as he turned.

"I must ask you not to call me by familiar names as though we were still on good terms," he said. "I find that it concerns my honour, while I am page to the noble Olaf, to stand up for my rights with point and edge."

The Songsmith's impulse towards laughter was strong enough to send a note beyond his unmirthful lips. Then, as the splendid personage began solemnly to clamber to the ground, he shook himself irritably.

"Eric, you are not wont to be a fool—with me—and this is a bad time to begin. Stay in your saddle and ride along."

Either Eric's flowery phrases felt the blight of contempt, or else no more of them had taken root under his curly hair. In silence he came on, his rosy mouth screwed up to the point of his resolve, and planted himself before his foster-brother.

"You have got to do one of two things—either make atonement for the blows I received at your hand, or else cross swords with me," he issued his ultimatum, with a circling sweep of his arm towards the longer of the two silver-ornamented sheaths that were a part of his new attire.

Again the song-maker wavered between laughter and irritation, looking down at the manful swagger in which the small legs were spread apart.

"Be good enough to say what use you could be put to after I had crossed swords with you?" he inquired.

The boy pushed back his curls eagerly.

"I told Olaf that I believed you would not be slow in understanding honourable ways!" he cried. "It is not my meaning that we should really fight each other. Only that you shall draw your weapon and let me make some thrusts at you, and then you can make some passes at me—easy ones—and after that I will declare myself satisfied and—"

"So that is the kind of stuff your new master is filling your head with," his foster-brother's voice crossed his. "If I were not afraid of losing my temper with you, I would use the flat of my blade on your back in a way that would not increase your dignity, but rather—" Of a sudden, what patience he had deserted him; he flung out his arms in a gesture before which the small warrior scuttled involuntarily. "Trolls, am I to be plagued by a gnat when I am in the mood to attack giants? Keep away from me if you would not run the risk as to how it turns out."

Pressing his fingers to his ears to shut out an other burst of French-made eloquence, he strode on, and stopped only to save himself from stumbling over the youngster, who had again thrown himself in the way, dancing gnatlike.

"You have got to fight me," he was shrieking. "I shall lose my credit with Olaf unless you do. I will cut your kirtle with my knife,—do you hear? I will cut off one of your buttons."

Whether or not Rolf's son heard the threats or the grating of the steel against the gold, he felt the sharp jerk at his sleeve, and exasperation rose in him. Before he well knew what he was about, he had reached out and seized the boy by a leg and an arm and swung him high in the air. Only that he realised what a toy the body was to his strength saved him from dashing it head foremost against the stones of the road-side wall, and recalled him to himself so that he tumbled it lightly on the grass instead.

"Well that it was no worse! Do you want to be killed that you try me so?" he cried under his breath, and turned to flee temptation before the blue-and-silver heap could right itself.

Turning, he found himself within a dozen paces of Olaf Thorgrim's son, who had followed his page round the curve and sat in his saddle awaiting the boy's fate with keen interest.

Not soon enough could Olaf hide the disappointment that had convulsed him on seeing Eric dropped unscathed. The Songsmith caught the expression and read it and understood at last the snare that had been set for him. Scorn brought his rage to that point of white heat where his voice sounded curiously still.

"You—dastard!" he said. "So that is what you were plotting, that I should be fretted into slaying the young one, and furnish you with the excuse of avenging him. That is why you beguiled him into your service—poisoned his mind against me—set him on me when you suspected that my temper would be raw."

No answer came from Olaf's parted curving lips; only he leaped expectant from his horse and stood looking at his enemy, the glitter of his eyes heightened to a white glare. As metal bars under white heat, Randvar's prudence lost shape and ran. In the relief from its restraint, he vented his short laugh, plucking the cap from his head with a fantastic flourish before he tossed it aside.

"Behold, how much needless trouble you took!" he cried. "Here have I walked the roads all morning only in the hope of meeting you, caring never a whit whether you gave me a new excuse or not! At any price would the joy of slaying you be a bargain. Shall I make it plain that I challenge?"

As a bolt from a bow shot his fist from his shoulder, landing fair and square on the smiling mouth he hated. At sight of its marred line, its starting blood, he laughed again and drew back and unsheathed his sword.

Olaf's curse cut the short laugh shorter, as his brand flashed forth. The next sound was curter still, the jarring clash of steel on steel.

Far as sound could carry, it bore the news that mortal enemies had met. Catching no more than a faint echo, Gunnar and his mates far down the road—whirled, crying, "The Songsmith!" and, "Thorgrim's son!" and then, as with one voice, "Randvar is not his match!" and after that came loping back, their eyes agleam. Sweeter than harp-music, it filled the ears of the men wielding the swords.

Fierce is the thirst for water, but fiercer still the thirst for life. Parching his veins, it spread through Rolf's son. Now it seemed appeased as he felt the parting of flesh under his blade, saw red water rise in the well he had digged. Now he knew the fiery pang of Olaf's point entering his own flesh, and the thirst consumed him anew. *Kill! kill! kill!* it roared in his ears above the clashing.

Olaf's greater skill against his charmed body—it was a fair game. To leave his heart unguarded that Thorgrim's son might lunge at the opening and in the act of lunging leave himself exposed—that was the way to play it; and he played with all his might, drove home each thrust with laughter.

Round the road-bend Gunnar came panting, followed by Aslak, and behind him, the others. At the ghastly glimpse they caught, through swirl-dust-clouds, of the song-maker laughing like a madman while blood oozed through every slit in his slashed garments, they uttered cries of dismay; but he paid them back with jests shouted hoarsely above the clatter. How could they know what wild joy it was, unhampered as the sweeping fury of a storm! He would have wished never to end it, had he not feared betrayal by that oozing blood. If his strength were to fail before his vengeance was complete—!

To the friends watching him, it was a welcome relief when laughter left his face, and it set instead in the stony lines of one rallying all his forces. Gripping his sword in both hands, he abandoned all pretence of defending himself, bent all his might on beating down Olaf's guard. Twice, they saw the French One's blade reach him and open crimson gaps; but he seemed not to feel it. Step by step, he drove his enemy backward until he had him at bay against a tree—until it wanted but one thrust to pin him there—

Why he did not give that thrust, the onlookers knew first, who saw Eric spring forward with a shrill cry and strike his foster-brother on the breast, plunging into his heart a knife he held. Then their wrath was lost in wonder that the Songsmith did not fall, only staggered back against the low stone wall and leaned there, passing his hand before his eyes as a man trying to clear mist from his vision.

"Eric! It was never you?" he said.

But even as he said it, his glance fell to the reddened blade in the boy's hand; while Olaf jeered him over the heads of those who were holding him back, telling him that the fight was finished:

"You need not to stare at him. It is even as you see; he has betrayed you."

No more effort the Songsmith made to maintain his weakening hold upon his sword. Slipping, swaying, staggering, he sank, nor struggled against it. If friends had not been there to care for him, his life had surely passed out through his wounds open gates.

Chapter 19

By bending most, the truest sword is known
　　　　　　　　　　　　　—Northern saying.

Across the courtyard came the *jarl's* sister and her following of white-armed maids and graceful pages, and the evening breeze went before her like a herald. With sleepy sighs, the budding fruit-trees dreaming in the starlight bestirred themselves to offer tribute of fragrant bloom, made the earth fair for her treading, made the air sweet for her breathing. Floating down upon her bosom, the roseate petals blended with it as flower with flower. Drifting down upon her hair, they lay like unmelting flakes amid its golden fire. So wondrous lovely was she thus crowned that Yrsa walking beside her had an impulse of admiring affection, and slipped a caressing hand into hers.

Immediately after she would have withdrawn it, making excuses for her boldness, but that Brynhild's gray eyes came down to her as serene as the starlit sky. Gathering up the timid fingers with her own firm supple ones, she drew her foster-sister's arm around her; and so they moved on together to the women's house that awaited with open doors their return from evening service. Gaining the light that came through the dusk to meet them like a golden welcome, the *jarl's* sister paused to look back and raise a warning finger.

"Keep in mind our guest," she cautioned.

Soft as the rippling chat and laughter had been, it smoothed out now to waveless quiet. With only the swish of trailing silk, the rustle of feet through grass, they went up the bright path to the door.

On the threshold they were met by the stately old stewardess, who was mother to Yrsa and the foster-mother of Brynhild the Proud. Cheerily the *jarl's* sister accosted her:

"If he has changed by so much as the set of an eyelash, good Thorgerda, I expect you to tell me without delay," she said. Then she took her hand from Yrsa's, took a swift step forward, as from the lace lappings of the head-dress the old face looked towards her somewhat soberly. "It is not possible that you are going to tell me that his heart-wound is serious after all! That the saints would let it be so, when I have been daily to their altars praising them for the miracle by which they saved him!"

"By no means," Thorgerda answered hastily. "Just after you left, I looked at it again; and it has knit together as by a miracle during the sleep which has held him so strangely. But as I was putting the bandages back, he came out of his sleep."

"Ah!" Brynhild said softly, and put an uncertain finger to her lips. "What was his mood?" she asked at last.

"I wish I were altogether sure, foster-daughter. If I tell the truth of him, I must say that there is a squareness to his mouth which I—But you shall hear—But, first, be pleased to come in and take your seat. It is not fitting—"

"I will not take time to put one foot over the threshold until I hear what lies so near my happiness," the *jarl's* sister interrupted her. Her foster-mother began without preamble.

"Thus it was, then. The first thing I knew, he had put up his eyelids like a man putting off blankets, and was gazing at the embroideries on the bed-curtains. Then he saw me, where I stood near the head, and asked me slowly what place he was in. I said it was the room in the women's house whither it was the *jarl's* custom to send sick courtmen to be taken care of, I thought it unadvisable to be hasty in speaking your name. And then—"

The *jarl's* sister crossed the threshold to get nearer to her. "And then?"

"For a while his expression told me nothing. He lay so long staring ahead of him that I thought he was falling asleep again, and turned to leave. He has more strength than you would think likely in a man so drained of blood. A rustle made me turn back to find that he had pulled himself up and was looking about for his clothes."

A sound that was half a laugh and half a sob came from Brynhild's round throat. "His clothes! Those slashed and slitted—blood-sponges! Yet what said he when he saw what garments we had prepared?"

"Nothing, foster-daughter. As yet, stained and tattered leather and gold-embroidered fabric are all one to him. I pointed out where they hung, and did not even tell him that they were useless to him. As I had expected, he was not long in finding it out. With his first motion to rise, he fell back on his pillows, nor even argued with me when I proved to him how foolish he was to attempt to move. Yet if I know anything about the set of a man's mouth, he will not do our bidding long, the old dame ended somewhat unexpectedly.

The *jarl's* sister made Yrsa a sign to help her off with the lace scarf that lay around her shoulders, like a mist about a rose.

"I will go to him," was all she said.

If Thorgerda had any thought of dissuading her, it was abandoned upon a second glance. She spoke only a word of admonishment as Starkad's daughter turned towards the foot of the hall.

"So it shall be, then. Still it is good counsel to tread softly. It may be that he is sleeping. I advised him to do so when I left."

The girl nodded her bright head impatiently, then shook it at the thralls who sprang forward from the benches at her approach. Hushing with her hands the rustling of her skirts, she hastened down the hall to the western guest-chamber, and gently pushed open the door.

The song-maker was not sleeping. Instead, he had risen and dressed himself in the garments of grape-purple,—as the sheen on ungathered grapes the precious embroideries were sparkling with every move he made in the flickering torch-light. Under one of the fragrant juniper wall-candles, he stood buckling the last buckle of the tunic. From the task he did not look up as the hinges creaked, but seemed to take for granted that it was Thorgerda returned.

"I beg that you will come in and close the door behind you before you make any fuss," he said.

She came in and closed the door behind her, without making any fuss; and he went on, his eyes still aiding his fingers.

"While it is altogether unlikely that the *jarl's* sister would raise any objections to my departure, yet because Helvin sent me here it might be that she would think it her duty to make some protests; so I beg of you that you will not say anything to her about my going."

Again from the fountain of Brynhild's white throat welled up a sound that was half of laughter, half of weeping.

"I will promise you that," she answered.

He looked up, then; and from bloodless white, his face went blood-red. After a moment, he made her the most ceremonious salutation at his command.

"I ask you to understand that I mistook you for your stewardess," he said. "She was with me but a short while ago, when I came back to my wits. It may be you know that I have been out of them these days, or I would have gone before."

To grope along the walls for the weapon that was missing from his belt, he turned away. She had a strange feeling that his mind was so far from her as scarcely to realize that she was there. She offered the feeble commonplaces she might have offered a stranger.

"Why should you leave? It is the custom for *jarl's* men to be taken care of here."

From his eyes that were like dark caves in the side of a snow-mountain came forth a flash as he glanced round at her. "That you have a poor opinion of me I know, but I did not know you thought me capable of making Kelvin's order an excuse for quartering myself upon you."

Feeling with his hands where the sword leaned in a corner, he brought it forth, and stood gazing at the highly polished blade. Once more she had the sensation of being forgotten.

"It is cleaner than it was the last time I saw it," he said, "but I liked it better then. What is Olaf's fate?"

She answered mechanically: "It is told that he still keeps his bed at Mord's house."

"Is that true?" he asked wonderingly, and a smile that had no connection with her widened his nostrils. When he had laboriously buckled on the sword, he came unsteadily towards her. "All the thanks that are due to your women I pay,—or at least I pay all I have. If you will allow me to pass now, I will take the task off their hands."

Some of her sense of strangeness was lost, then, in alarm. But even before she could tell him of his weakness, he was forced to catch at a chair's high back to save himself from falling.

"And bid one of your servants give me his shoulder across the court-yard," he murmured.

"I will bid two of them take you by force and put you back in bed where you belong," she said indignantly, and turned to throw open the door.

Though he remained leaning heavily on the chair, he spoke slowly:

"If you do—I swear to you—that I will struggle against them—until every wound on me starts open."

She took her hand from the door, but only to make of her rounded arms a bar across it, defying him:

"You would not struggle against me."

Holding to the chair-back he stood looking at her, at first in surprise, then with weary patience.

"I should have remembered," he said, "that it would be a part of your high breeding not to let me feel that I had been a burden on your hospitality."

Of one colour were her-cheeks and her rose-red kirtle, as she shaped her unskilled lips to pleading. "It was not Helvin who ordered them to bring you here. It was I who asked it.... I shared the care of you with my women ... and found it ... no burden."

Lowered for the first time was the lofty banner of her head. His gaze rested on it wistfully even while he continued his slow progress towards the door.

"My wounds have made you wondrous kind," he said. "I have heard it told that such crimson mouths, for all that they are tongueless, are full of eloquence for women. But you see that they are healing fast. It would not last much longer anyway. Let me go while I can."

Pain sharpened his voice, yet his hand was in every way gentle when he put aside the living bar that dared not tempt his weakness by overmuch resistance.

Almost in fear she looked up at him. "Randvar! Has it happened that this has slain your love for me?"

He touched with his lips the wrist he had taken. "I wish it had done so; then I should dare to stay and sun myself, and take it easily when, tomorrow or the day after, the skies change and you storm me forth with hard words—"

"Never, my loved one! Never again!" April-faced, she leaned towards him. "It will always be good weather for you now. Always! You a song-maker, and doubt the summer because of a storm or two!"

"It must be because I am a song-maker that I have had faith in so many things," he answered. "It is mercy I am asking of you, Brynhild. You have so much for my body,—have a little for my mind, that since first I saw you has been a leaf in the wind of your moods. Let me go while I can, before your fairness knits the net once more around me."

As gently as might be, he gathered her other wrist into his clasp, and holding the two in one hand, laid the other on the door. She dared not struggle with him. But one way was left her. Light as the apple-blossoms float down, she drifted to her knees.

"My friend, you prayed me once to let you stay because to you it meant so much and to me—you thought—it meant so little. I beg the boon back from you. Stay, because it will be easy to you who are so generous in giving, and to me it would be so hard to give you up."

As he had done that day in the road, he passed his hands before his eyes to clear them.

"This and my blood on Eric's blade—are the two last sights that ever I thought to see," he murmured. "Yet since that one was true, it may be that this other is." Looking down at her, a faint smile touched his mouth. "What dream-mockery to see you so,—you who twist me between your fingers like any willow out of the forest! But your work will seem better to you if you have your way in this. Until your mind changes, then!"

Releasing her, he sat down on the stool beside the door, his elbows on his knees, his head on his hands. From kneeling, she sank into a sitting posture on the rush-strewn floor beside him, glad perhaps to hide her face against his sleeve. It was he who kept their footing against the swaying shimmering dream-river that seemed to rise about them, and forded it at last to the shore of reality.

"Yet what right have I to a place in your hall, who have made myself an outlaw?"

Stifling a sigh, she walked on land again.

"It is unlikely that you will be banished. In the teeth of all the lawmen, Helvin has refused it. And while it may not turn out to your honour with the advice-givers, I think the *jarl* will push it through by boldness. Today, he rode out himself to seek counsel from Flokki of Iceland, who is the greatest man for bending the law to his wishes. I might be tempted to reproach you for doing this joy to your foe, my friend, if I did not guess that I have some blame for your temper."

Perhaps she wanted to lure him into taking her part against herself, but he did not even see the bait. Through the hands still supporting his head, he spoke absently.

"You had not the most share in the matter, *jarl's* sister. For the hardships he dragged me under with Helvin, I should have followed up Olaf; and on top of that, there was the trap he baited with Eric. Eric! Who would have believed a false heart grew in the boy!"

Looking up through his hands, she saw how bitter his mouth had become. Of a sudden she rose and pressed her lips to it, as one who would draw poison from a wound.

"The little viper! Never think of him!" she breathed.

Whether it changed his look she did not see, for even more quickly she dropped back and hid her eyes upon his arm. Only she knew that he sat a long time looking down at her.

"At least you cannot take the memory of that from me. Give you thanks for that!" he said at last, and for an instant she felt the touch of his lips upon her hair. But he ventured no further caress. When he spoke again, she knew that his gaze had gone back to the rush-strewn floor.

"What I should do is to be grateful that I was hindered from killing the boy. To have had that news come to Erna's ears—" She felt the muscles harden in his arm with the clinching of his fist. Then he went on somewhat anxiously: "Yet she would like his deed little better. I hope there is no likelihood of her hearing of it. It seems that he has not fled to the forest, since you say he was before the lawmen. I suppose Olaf has taken him under his safeguard?"

She shook her head without raising it. "You do not know Thorgrim's son, if you think he troubles himself about a tool after it has served his purpose. In the first place, he prevented the boy from running away that he might send him as a witness before the lawmen. Then, when that had been accomplished, he resigned him willingly to Kelvin's demand. Nothing has been done to him as yet, for it was not until today that the herb-woman would say how it was like to go with your life—so has your heart-wound puzzled everyone—but tomorrow they are to take him out and hew off his hand—" She broke off in a gasp, as the Songsmith's fingers crushed her arm unknowingly.

"Ill will it be, then! Do they forget that he is but a child?"

The eyes which she lifted to his were Valkyria's eyes, that would look without flinching on the torture of a friend's foe.

"Now you argue like the goddess Frigg when, because it was young, she allowed the mistletoe-bush to become the shaft which killed Balder the Beautiful. If you had got your death from the boy, Helvin would have had him slain, and it would have been rightly done!"

The song-maker's broad shoulders shrugged as once more he leaned forward upon his knees.

"Though it may sound less well to your ears, *jarl's* sister," he said dryly, "the true reason why Helvin is set against the boy is because the young one was the hindrance in the way of my killing Olaf. Is it also out of love towards me that Eric's friends have failed to help him? Or is it another reason that no one dares to go against the *Jarl's* pleasure?"

"It might be that and yet be no shame to their manhood," she answered suddenly, and put back the clustering masses of her hair to look at him with earnestness. "An unheard-of thing is his temper becoming, Randvar! The evening after the duel, he rode out to Mord's house and went in where Olaf lay and stood for the space of two candle-burnings staring down at him, without speaking, only tearing his mantle between his teeth. And yesterday when he was here, he put to me the most unexpected question. He asked me if ever I saw our father in my sleep, or in dark corners. And when I said, 'By no means,' he laughed—cold trickled over me at the sound!—and muttered that Starkad showed favouritism in giving all the visits to him. Heard you ever anything to equal that in strangeness?"

"Never," the song-maker assented. But he said no more, nor moved so much as his bent shoulders. After a glance up at him, she began studying his face from the ambush of her hair, and sank so deep in musing that she started when he spoke.

"Where have they caged the cub?"

"In that storehouse loft, which has been thought bad enough to be a prison since a guard killed another one there by pushing him through the floor-hole so that he drowned in the beer-vat below." She came further out of her study to slip her hand into his, where it hung between his knees. "Laugh if you will, my friend, still I shall hold it for true that no one has freed the little snake because no man will lift a finger for one who has injured you. Only bolts keep the door—no guard stands watch there—any could have helped him if, they had a mind."

He did laugh, shortly and suddenly; then pressing her hand, he released it and stood up.

"By this time, the *jarl* will have returned from Flokki's; and I will go to him." As she rose swiftly, he lifted one of her silken braids and laid it lightly across her lips. "Noble maiden, I am a wild hawk that has been caged over-long. Let me stretch my wings, and I shall come back all the more gladly,—if so be your kind mood lasts until tomorrow."

Above the shining bar of her hair, her colour flamed so brightly that she was fain to extinguish it upon his breast. Her words came to him faintly:

"Will you believe, when I tell you that I have made this plan,—that tomorrow shall be our wedding-day?"

He stood a long time looking down at her, then said slowly: "If—after this—you fail me, I shall lose the wish to live."

"If ever I fail you again, I give you leave to die," she answered.

Then she let him take from her mouth a kiss of farewell; she clasped behind her the hands that wished to hold him back, and let him go forth into the starlit night.

Chapter 20

Need proves a friend
   —Northern saying.

Steep as the way to Heaven seemed the steps of the prison loft as Randvar dragged himself up them; yet he dared not pause on the unsheltered Handing, but goaded his nerveless fingers on to their task of drawing the bolts. Whining, the rusty bars yielded, and he staggered into the musty gloom. Closing the door behind him, he leaned against it to recover his breath.

Across every corner of the huge one-windowed room, the spider Night had woven dense shadows. Like a small blue fly in the meshes of a black web, Eric was curled upon the straw-littered floor,—a forlorn and crumpled fly with limp legs and gaudy wings adroop. To stare at the opening door, he started up; but recognising the Songsmith in the wink of time that the tall form was silhouetted against the starlight, he tipped over again, hiding his face upon the straw as though he would burrow into it, while his voice rose in a muffled wail:

"Oh, foster-brother, do not be angry with me! Do not be angry with me!"

"Come here—and give me your shoulder—to that bench yonder," Randvar commanded between breaths.

When it had been twice repeated, the boy obeyed shrinkingly. As soon as he felt the weight lighten on his shoulder, he would have drawn back into the darkness again if the hand had not slipped down his arm to his wrist and held him. He curved his other arm before his face, then, and began to wail anew.

"I beseech you not to scold me! I have had all the blame that I can stand!"

"I am not going to scold you," the song-maker said wearily. His head had fallen back heavily against the wall behind him, and his eyes were shut. "It has happened to older people than you to think that the man who gives them hard words is their foe and the man who smiles on them is their friend. If you have not found out yet that you behaved badly, no good is to be had from talking about it."

The boy burrowed further into the bend of his arm.

"I *hate* Olaf," he sobbed.

"It is likely that you do now, since he has stopped making much of you," the Songsmith returned sternly, "still it should be remembered for a while longer that you thought enough of him once to try to take my life for his sake."

Wriggling, the culprit tried hard to pull away. "Now you are scolding me, though you said you would not. You know I did not mean to stab you."

His foster-brother shook the arm he held. "Never lie to me, Eric!"

"I am not lying to you," Eric lifted up his voice and wept. "Never did I lie to you in my life,—not even though I had meddled with your skin-boat and you were trimming a willow switch as you asked me about it. If you had any sense, you would guess that it had gone out of my mind that I was holding a knife. I thought I was striking you with my fist,—and for that you cannot throw blame on me for you have told me yourself that a man must be loyal to the lord he has chosen, and Olaf says the Devil gets all pages who do not fight for their masters. I thought that if I attacked you, you would turn on me, and he would get a chance to recover himself and—"

The Songsmith brought him nearer by the wrist he held, and drew down with his other hand the arm shielding the woebegone face.

"Say that over again, Eric, while I look in your eyes."

They were swollen eyes, and now resentful and now beseeching, but clear as blue lakes to show what lay under them. Before the explanation was half repeated, his foster-brother showed that he accepted it by drawing him into a close embrace and holding him so. Feeling the encircling arm change from a shackle to a caress, the boy subsided on the broad shoulder and wept there unrestrainedly.

"Tell them that you do not blame me, so they will not look at me the way they did. You can not imagine how they behaved! When I met some of my best friends out of Brynhild's house, not a maiden of them would speak to me. And old Visbur said that the forest bred traitors like acorns, and that they ought to hang like acorns on the trees; and his eyes—you could not bring before your mind how his eyes looked!"

"I wish I could not!" the song-maker muttered, and shook himself as though he were a baited bear and his memories sharp-toothed hounds. But the boy pressed harder against him.

"You must not go until you promise me your help. The guards will act in any way you say,—tell them to let me go back to the tower. If you knew how much I want to see my mother and Snowfrid!—and Lame Forsek and the others—who look at me as if they thought well of me. I cannot bear to be looked at the other way. My heart will break if I have to see one of these hateful court-people again. Until I get to be a man, when I shall come back and kill Olaf and— Foster-brother, you are not going to refuse me?"

He abandoned vengeance to press his face coaxingly against the Songsmith's, and try to forestall the answer he read there.

"I *beg* it of you! You wanted me to go back to see Erna,—and now I will do everything she asks of me. Foster-brother, listen! I will not once forget to chop the wood or fetch the water. I—Listen! If I do, she can tell you and you can—"

"What I am trying to say," the Songsmith made himself heard at last, "is that my words would have no weight at all with the guards. Even the *jarl's* favour I dare not lean on this time—Stand still! I am not saying it to frighten you, only to show you that carefulness is necessary. The worst part of your bad fortune is past, for I have already planned it that you are to slip away tonight. Yonder is the door with the bolts drawn, and beyond the court lies an open road to the forest. Some starlight is in the courtyard, but there are also many trees; and you have learned Skraelling tricks of skulking. The night has only just passed its noon, so you are unlikely to see anyone,—but a beggar snoring on the steps of the women's house. You can avoid the sentinels at the gates by getting over the wall where the *jarl's* stable shadows it. After you are once in the road, you know what to do as well as I. Luck go with you!"

Before the last word was out, the boy had reached the door; but the impulse was not quite strong enough to carry him through it. Digging his boot-toe into the straw, he hesitated, squirming in evident anguish of mind.

"Are you going to stay here and be their prisoner instead of me?" he faltered.

A light that was not starlight made the Songsmith's white face bright as he turned it towards him. "You show in this that you have a good heart, little comrade; but you need not trouble yourself. I do not intend that anyone shall know that I have been here. As soon as you have had time to get clear of the courtyard, I shall go back and lie down under a tree, and pretend that I have been swooning there all night."

Again the boy laid a hand on the door; then again he turned,— and this time he came all the way back and threw his arms about his foster-brother's neck in a strangling hug. From somewhere under the curly mop came the broken whisper:

"Say that you think as much of me as ever."

Tousling the yellow head in the old familiar caress, his foster-brother gave him the desired assurance and tried to disengage himself; but Eric clung burrlike.

"Never did I love Olaf one-half as well as you,—may the Giant take me if I did! When are you coming back to the tower? Olaf says that the *jarl* behaves so badly towards you that one of you will surely kill the other, if you do not run away."

"If I were not unwilling to pay compliments to Olaf, I should say that truth came out of his mouth," the song-maker muttered; then he put the boy from him firmly. "Do you want to linger so long that the thralls will be waking up and coming out to catch you?"

Eric made one dash at his foster-brother's cheek, flattening his face against it, and was gone through the narrowest opening of the door.

Like the patter of spring rain, the tap of his feet on the steps came back to the Songsmith. Smiling faintly he followed him with his fancy, pictured him holding himself down to creep across the court, then letting himself out as he reached the sheltered lane, snuffing in freedom until he broke and ran—ran—ran like a homeward-turned horse.

"It will be some time before *I* shall be able to run," he reflected ruefully, and began to realise how exhausted he was now that excitement like a prop had fallen from under him. He shook his knees irritably.

"Troll take a man's legs, that will go back upon him at such a time as this!" he muttered. "If I do not look out, I shall founder here. . . . He has had time now to gain the lane. . . . I wish I knew if the room is really darkening, as it seems, or if it is only a trick of my eyes!" He tried in vain with groping hands to sweep the shadows from before him, then to shake off the heaviness settling on him.

"A grim jest that would be, to be caught within three strides of an unbarred door!" he told himself with an impulse of anger. Again he shook off the heaviness, desperately; summoning all his strength, he rose to his feet.

One step he made, and part of another; then his knees sank under him as under a crushing weight; his body sank until his head rested on the floor,—then it seemed that the floor began to sink! After that, he let the Fates have their way.

Chapter 21
What must be is sure to happen
—Northern saying.

Coming back to his senses, the Songsmith lay awhile adjusting his memory.... Once, he had fallen asleep on bloody grass and wakened amid the silken fragrance of the women's house.... Here was another change.... Cobwebbed rafters and bare walls and heavy air as close as the grave. He snuffed up a resentful breath of it—then forgot to exhale in the suddenly added consciousness that someone was gazing at him. Turning his head, his eyes met gray eyes staring at him from a jungle of blood-coloured hair. On the bench to which the song-maker had been helped the night before, Helvin Jarl was now sitting, his elbows on his knees, his hands dropped between to hold the sword with which he was stirring and prodding the straw of the floor. He laid the flat of the blade against Randvar's breast as the Songsmith started up, forcing him gently back.

"Lie still. No one is looking to see whether we go through with the foolish rules which some simpleton has laid down. I have sent the guards below." He took the blade away as he felt the song-maker yield to its pressure, sheathing it as he went on: "Their state was laughable, between not knowing whether they should get my wrath because they had not at once carried you out of here, or because they had not at once slain you. See how they have tried to trim both sides of their sail to the wind, by making you comfortable and at the same time holding you prisoner."

He nodded floorward, and Randvar noticed for the first time that a charger of food and drink stood within reach of his hand, that a cushion had been put under his head and a cloak spread over him. At another time he might have smiled. Now his gaze came back with unrelieved gravity to the *jarl's* face that in some way was strange to him.

"Which kind of behaviour is most to your mind, lord?" he asked.

Clasping his hands behind his head, Helvin leaned back against the wall and returned his look sombrely.

"I am only just getting to know surely, comrade. When they

brought me word this morning that you had set free the brat who stepped between Olaf and death, there was a spell when my fingers itched for your throat. You can see that I came to you straight out of the hands of my shoe-boy." He lifted one of his legs to show that the silk bands which should have been wound around it were still hanging. "If the sight of your peaceful sleep had not fallen coolingly upon my hot humour, there is a likelihood that . . . that ..." Though his eyes remained upon the song-maker, they set in a vacant stare. "You would be lying there like an empty wine-skin . . . and I should be raving beside you, trying to put back the wine I had spilled . . . seeing it creep away towards the cracks . . . feeling it slip slimy through my fingers. . . . Ah!"

The hand that had gone out groping before him he dashed against his eyes as though to break the spell that bound them, springing to his feet with a wild cry.

"Why do I torture myself with what is not true? I have not slain you. You are alive, for all that you have the colour of a dead man. Speak to me! Drive away this madness!"

White as the dead the song-maker was, as much from increasing alarm as from the weakness of his blood-drained body; yet he managed to lift himself to his knees and then to his feet, to stand steadying himself against the wall. Only his voice failed to obey his summons, so that he was glad to have the pause filled by the thundering tread of a man hurrying up the steps. In the doorway appeared a guard, his spear gripped in his hand.

"Jarl, was it for help you cried out?" he demanded.

A moment Starkad's son held his breath, as though the nethermost deeps of his mind must be dredged for adequate words,—then all words seemed to prove inadequate. Snatching a wine-flagon from the tray, he hurled it at the intruder's head. The force with which it crashed against the door frame suggested what it would have done to the mark that it missed.

How the guardsman took his leave, Randvar did not see. Dropping down upon the bench, he burst into high-keyed laughter.

"Help—against—*me!*" he gasped, and leaned there laughing until Kelvin's hand fell upon his shoulder and shook him with friendly severity.

"Stop! That is the end of such laughter that weeping follows it. Stop! Drink this."

The pressure of a cup against his lip compelled obedience, and the draught brought some of his strength back to him; but the *jarl's* remained the dominating spirit.

"More of that is needed, and food in your stomach. I will be your dish-bearer for a change," he said, and himself dropped down cross-legged on the straw beside the charger that he might pass up its contents.

Patient as the hand of a woman, his hand that had sped the missile ministered now to his friend. Now and again, over crust or bone, Randvar met in the gray eyes a brooding tenderness that tightened the muscles around his heart.

It was a relief when Kelvin's mind began to turn away to musing, drawing him over upon his elbow to lie staring into the empty cup he held, like a wizard reading fortunes in the wine-dregs. Dreamy as the note of droning bees, his voice sounded when presently he began to muse aloud.

"I only wish I could have found some excuse to give drink to Olaf .... Every moment I stood by him, I was wondering if there was not some way.... It would not have been necessary to kill him. One drop of the right herb-juice would be enough to addle his wits until he could pass for mad. Whatever he betrayed, I should have only to shrug my shoulders and tap my head. Conceive of his rage! It would have been sport for a king!"

As a dog over a sweet bone, he put out the tip of his tongue and noiselessly licked his lips. Wincing, Randvar spoke hastily:

"*Jarl*, this is an unprofitable mood! Recall it to your mind that Olaf knows nothing to betray."

From the folds of strange craftiness that had been drawing over them, Kelvin's eyes looked up dazedly. Then—slowly—the gaze that he met steadied the flickering torch of his reason.

"Why, that is true," he admitted. "I forgot that he had not yet found the carrion which his vulture-scent warned him of.... Still in the Fates hands is that happening.... Only I can see it coming ... slipping through their bony fingers...." In a mutter his voice died away. Stretched at full length he lay in brooding reverie, so sombre a figure that the cup of dregs took on new suggestiveness.

The song-maker began to speak quietly, gazing out through the open door where the rosy snow of blossoming crab-trees was banked against the blue sky, and sun like golden wine steeped all the noonday world.

"It befell me once to see a place far-west of here where the earth had shaken and rent a rock in twain, and out of the chasm had leaped a brook of sweet water. So I think this happening with Eric must have shaken me; for like a well of water, a song rose in my mind while I slept,—a song that never had place there before."

In the black morass of his musing the *jarl* turned, lured by the will-o-the-wisp curiosity.

"Never have I heard of a song coming in that manner," he said. "Even you have always hammered them out before. Has it risen as far as your lips so that any of it could brim over into words?"

Though he continued to gaze out at the blowing trees, the song-maker bent all his energies upon his story-weaving.

"Little of it has yet got so high as that. But it will be a song about the good which is in a man even though his actions appear to be evil. . . . Perhaps I shall say that he had Thor's wrath for turning to the Christ-faith; and the Thunderer cursed him so that he had no other choice than to do three nithing deeds, even though his mind was noble. . . . He will have a friend—perhaps it will be a maiden who is brave enough to believe in his honourable mind in spite of the unworthiness of his actions. ... I do not know yet what those crimes will be . . . except that the first must be that he slays a kinsman"

"Are—you—mad?" Starkad's son said slowly.

With a start, Randvar turned. That the *jarl* had risen gradually from his place on the straw he had realized, but he had taken it for interest. Now for the first time he looked at him. Looking, he sprang to his feet.

"What ails you?"

"Are you mad?"—Helvin repeated his slow question—"that you dare to make my life into a song and tell it to my face?"

"*Your* life!" the Songsmith breathed. Then, even angrily, he swept the suspicion aside with his arm. "Lord, this is an unbecoming jest! You must know that such a song would be true of any man in the world."

Futile as the dash of waves against a rock, the words fell down unheeded. Unmoved as a rock, Helvin stood gazing at him.

"Has your swooning so dulled your wits that you really cannot see that to sing that song in anyone's hearing would be to tell him that you saw me murder my father?"

It was too late to check the words, though Randvar's arm had shot out in the attempt. Then he stood with his head gripped in his hands, like a man into whose mind a terrible truth is eating. As though he had forgotten he was not alone, he started when Kelvin's hand fell upon his breast and pressed him back upon the bench.

A strange softness had come into the voice of Starkad's son,—a softness from which the ear recoiled as the hand recoils from the softness of decayed fruit.

"Now I see by your dismay at finding how near you had come to betraying me that it was neither madness nor treachery that prompted you, but the awful knowledge working in you as the awful guilt has worked in me. Of no avail to remind myself that he brought it on his own head—that I tried to keep away from him when I felt it coming but he forced me aside with him, goaded me until I could no more keep hold of myself than my shaking hands could keep hold of the leash—It may well be forgiven you that you shudder! I might have known that soon or late the horror must work out of you. Yet am I glad that I trusted you as long as was possible. Bear that in mind about me, even though it must come here to an end."

With quick light step he went and shut the door. The sound of its closing fell ominously on the song-maker's ears, even as a sense of smothering fell on him with the passing of the glimpse of sky. He asked slowly:

"Is it my death-warning that you give me?"

Still with gentleness, Starkad's son shook his head. "Only what my safety has need of I take,—your liberty. I will give you the comforts and amusements you may choose yourself—"

"Amusements!" Rough scorn was in the gesture with which the Songsmith sprang up. "Why do you talk thus, or what do you think of me? Do you forget that I am bred to no lower roof than the tent of the sun? Better might you cage an eagle and bid him be content with a branch where before he had ranged the forest! But I belie you in thinking it! Your sane self could never deal so wrongfully with me,—and you must be sane! You must be sane! No marks of the curse are on you. If you are whole-minded, listen to me! For this song, I take the Cross-oath that it shall never pass my lips—even in solitude. Nay, I will dash it out of my memory! By your love, believe me!"

To take his hand and press and stroke it, the *jarl* came all the way from the door.

"Do I not believe you?" he said caressingly. "On your good intentions I would lay down my life. It is luck that I dare not trust so much to. Did I not for a dozen years hide my curse so that not even my own kin dreamed it was there, only to have it burst out like smouldering fire at last? So would your uttermost effort be set at naught with such a secret pressing for outlet—"

Almost with repulsion, Randvar freed himself from the fondling hands, and pushed the other away that he might front him squarely.

"Jarl, as God hears me, I would sooner that you should rage! It is not sound, this softness! Face me like a man—or a devil—or anything but this! Listen, and I will lay the truth before you so that no room shall be left for doubt to stand between us. If it rouse you to anger, so much the better! Lord, I never knew your secret,—only I let you think so because in no other way would you believe in my love. Of that hard happening at the pool, I saw no more than your struggle with the hound. That you loosed him on Starkad, I become aware for the first time—"

He broke off because it was plain that Helvin was no longer listening. He stood gazing at his song-maker, his eyes retreating deeper and deeper between crafty folds.

He said as to himself: "Love of life! How strong it must be in a mightful man like you! . . . Doubly strong since you have the love of the maiden that is dear to you. . . . It is not strange that it should be strong enough to make you lie to me—"

"Jarl!" the Songsmith broke in fiercely,—but stopped, conscious that his voice could not carry across the chasm that had opened between them. Only he could see across it the expression with which Helvin was regarding him; and more awful than the slyness of his half-shut eyes was the gaze in which they were widening, the rapt gaze of one who sees beyond the veil.

"Behold, what weird powers are allotted to me!" he said under his breath. "As through a keyhole, I can see through this lie into the hall of What Is To Come. The next time fear pricked you, you would lie again. . . . And then to keep off fear, you would begin to act lies. . . . And after that it would seem so natural that you would be thinking lies . . . lies . . . lies . . . till, like a worm-riddled boat, only your fair shape would be left. You who were the most unlying and bravest-hearted of men! Rather than you shall come to that pass, I will slay you in your prime." From the tangled mass of blood-coloured hair, his wide eyes turned slowly to the song-maker, fired with crazy purpose.

Then at last Randvar understood that the torch of his friend's reason—so often flickering, so often burned low—had been extinguished forever. To shut out the sight of the ghastly ruin it left, he hurled himself against the wall and flattened his face against the rough boards. Unreal as the mouthing of a vision, the caressing voice came to him.

"Does your heart speak so heavily about dying? Try if you cannot bring your mind to the mountain-top on which my mind stands. Then shall you see that what looks to be a storm-sky is but a cloud over one valley, while sun hallows all the rest. I kill you when life holds much for you, yet see this! I keep you from sin. I save your memory fair for those who love you. Above all, I preserve our friendship from the first tremble of dissolution. A nobler tree than our friendship never sprang from man-clay. Would you rather see it withered and decayed than laid low in all its glory by one axe-stroke?"

As from a man on the rack, a cry was wrung from the song-maker: "Oh, Powers of Might, must it indeed end so?"

Yet softer grew the voice of Starkad's son, till it was hushed to the unearthly stillness of a forest-deep.

"Alas, how has the love of woman clouded your eyes, that were once so clear to see the truth! Yet think not I blame the weakness of your flesh. So shrinking is my own that, plain as I see the goodness of the deed, I could not do it as we stand. It is the working of fate that when my Other Shape possesses me, I know no qualms. Until I come in that guise, then! Yet before we part, press my hand once more in love. Friends clasp when they separate for a day,—shall souls sunder forever and say no farewell?"

It was a strange embrace; for in the eyes of Starkad's son, the doomed man was as one dead; and to the mind of the song-maker, his friend had ceased to live. Like the sound of a clod upon a coffin-lid was the sound of the door closing for the last time between them.

Chapter 22

Those live long who are slain by words alone
                                                —Northern saying.

In a black tide night had risen, submerging the farther windowless end of the great loft, blotting out the sides and corners of this end. Like a raft of light afloat upon a sea of darkness was the bright square which the moon let fall from the window under the eaves; and now and again, like a shipwrecked mariner, the song-maker rose out of the engulfing blackness and stood in the light, reviving himself with the sight of the infinite windswept sky. Deeper and deeper into his spirit cut the thongs of the trap that had caught him. Ranging his prison up and down—up and down—his step was the ceaseless hurried tread of a caged tiger. Higher and higher rose the frenzy of impulse to hurl himself against the walls and batter them with hands and feet and head till they or he gave way.

It bent him at last to a thing he scorned, drove him against his will to the door, wrung from him a hoarse appeal.

"Visbur! I cannot meet death like a fox in his earth! Let me fight my way out against your sword. It will come to the same in the end!"

At first it was only the clang of a spear on the landing outside that answered, so slow was the old guard's voice of irony.

"Why do you talk of dying, Rolf's son? Surely you heard the *jarl* say that you are only held here to appease the lawmen who want your punishment for challenging Olaf."

Upon the cross-bar of the door, Randvar's hand clinched. He had forgotten that the *jarl* would cloak his purpose in that excuse. After a moment Visbur spoke again, this time with biting contempt:

"You need not think, however, that I put more belief than you do in that reason. A witless thing would Kelvin's justice be, to forgive you two attacks upon his life and then imprison you only for challenging your foe or loosing a worthless cub. Likely he is afraid to take open vengeance because so many people are fooled by you as to stand your friends; and therefore—even to me—he makes this poor excuse, and adds an order that no others of his household shall even know that you are here, but believe that it is still Eric that I hold prisoner. He might make himself easy that no guardsman who saw you as you stood over your chief's wounded body, with a bloody sword in your grip, would lift a finger to save you from torture."

The song-maker's voice sounded strange to himself as it came out of the darkness in which he stood: "Only grant me to die a man's death! You can say that you looked in to see how it went with me, and I tried to force my way out, and you slew me. Only that, as you were Rolf's friend!"

The force with which Visbur's spear came down upon the landing made up for the low key in which he was obliged to pitch his voice.

"Do you know how I could find it in my heart to behave because I was Rolf's friend? Because you have stained an honourable name with traitor's deeds, I could see you hanged like a dog. Never make so bold as to speak my name again." Suddenly his feet went thundering down the steps, and his spear could be heard striking against the side of the house as he took up a new post below.

As suddenly, Randvar moved away from the door; and with his coming into the moonlight it could be seen that he held his sword naked in his hand. When he had stood awhile looking down at it, he set its point against his heart; and then he stood for another space with musing eyes fixed on the gleaming blade.

To slay one's self, to run away from the fight—how could that be aught but the act of a coward? And yet to die in a fit of mad terror—with shaking limbs and blanched cheeks and reason overthrown—was that a death for a brave man? Muscle by muscle, his grip on his sword tightened; and then muscle by muscle it relaxed; and he stood arguing it over and over.

Deaf to all but that inner strife, he heard neither voices at the foot of the steps nor the tread of feet ascending. The sound which he had been dreading came at last and even that he did not know. Like the rattling of the casement in some wandering breeze it befell at first, and then slowly it revealed itself for the fumbling of unsteady fingers upon a bolt. Only when a river of moonlight streamed across the floor at his feet did he start awake and turn his head.

On the threshold, dark against the silver night, stood the man who had drawn the bolts. A hood concealed his face, but massive shoulders showed under his cloak; and over one of them could be seen the mailed form of Visbur drawn up in respectful salute. Though it was but a flash of time before the door had closed behind the muffled figure, merging its dark drapery into the darkness of the wall, the song-maker felt no doubt of the visitor's identity. Indeed, almost the only thing he felt—amid the sudden stiffening of his muscles and chilling of his blood—was wild relief that for once his wits stood firm. Pitched to utter recklessness, he flung his sword from him as at sight of the bare blade a smothered cry came from the other's wrappings.

"Have no fear that that was meant for you!" he said, and his strained voice vibrated as with discordant laughter. "Easier were it to be slain by you than to bear the burden of being your slayer. Have your will with—"

Like over-strained wire his voice snapped, and he did not gather up the ends. Only in passing through that strip of shadow, the man had become another man; and it was the Shepherd Priest who stood revealed in the moonlight.

"I bring you life and not death, my son," he said gently. "Nor was it in my head that Helvin meant to push the matter so far, even though his sister told me that it had stirred his unreasoning wrath against you that you set the boy free. God is to be twice thanked that I can at once save my lord a crime and you a wrong! Yet no long space is given me to do it in."

Moving on up the room, he bent and swept the straw away from the middle of the floor. Across the long cracks of the boarding showed dimly the lines of the wooden hatch that had been set in the hole through which—in the days when the prison-loft had been a store-chamber—the huge vat below had been refilled each brewing season. Easily as one pries the head out of a barrel, he pried up the clumsy door and laid it back from the opening.

Like a half-hanged man whose body has been cut down in time but whose emotions have gone on out of the world of the living, the Songsmith remained gazing at him.

"Even if it had happened to me to remember that place," he said slowly, "I should have been so sure that it was fastened on the underside that I would not have thought it worthwhile to try it."

"It was fastened by bolts on every corner until I drew them," the Shepherd Priest answered.

Dusting his hands upon his cloak in an unconscious habit from his youth, he came back to the moonlight and began to give further directions for the carrying out of the plan he had made, his quiet tones as well-fitted to seem the voice of a priest preparing a sinner for death as the voice of a man guiding a brother man to life.

"For much talking I have now no time, but everything lies on your understanding this much. Listen then, my son! So soon as the door closes upon me, let yourself down through the opening,—I will keep the guard in talk to cover any noise you may make. The door at the back you will find ajar, and an oak's shadow screens the entrance from without. That oak clump, and the shadow of the wall, will make it easy for you to reach the western gate, where a man stands guard whose love for you has got in his eyes so that he will not be able to see you as you pass. When you reach the lane outside— But it will turn out that I reach that before you do, since my road need not be so roundabout—"

Upon his speech fell the sound of Visbur's great fist on the door. He broke off to lay hands upon the song-maker's shoulders and press him down upon his knees. It was a benediction that he was saying over the prisoner when the door opened and the brass-bound head was thrust in. Its owner said gruffly:

"Good-luck go with your prayers, since for love of my soul I let you up to him! But I love my body also, father; and the risk to that gets greater the longer you stay."

"I was even now coming," the priest answered, turning; and Visbur lost no time in fastening up behind him.

As one trying to rouse himself out of a stupor, Randvar arose and stood shaking back his hair and opening and shutting his hands. As one in a dream, he heard the old man's unsteady steps following the guard's rapid descent, heard the gentle voice pleading with the gruff one. Then of a sudden his wandering glance fell upon the black gap in the floor—the loop-hole in what had seemed a dead wall. Like the leap of flame through smoke leapt his blood through his dullness, parching his throat, roaring in his ears. Now it was to restrain frantic eagerness that he crushed his lip between his teeth as he swung himself swiftly through the opening.

A fur-bale that had been placed at the bottom of the now empty vat received him without noise. Drawing himself up to the top of the wall which the vat's side made, he balanced there until on the darkness shrouding him he had found the thread of silver light. Using hands, then, in place of eyes, he climbed out and groped his way between bales and boxes and barrels to the door that had been set ajar, drew it open and stepped through it into the moonlight, and then stepped aside into the shadow of a giant oak that grew there.

Lifting the damp hair on his forehead, the night wind met him freshly. As to meet the lips of a woman, he lifted his burning face and spread wide his arms. For that long a space, his heart sang a song of wild exulting.

For that long—but for no longer. Around the great bole of the oak, looming dark beyond a silver sea, he glimpsed the silent mass of Brynhild's bower. Brynhild! And this should have been their wedding-day!

His hands tearing at his collar to relieve the swelling agony of his throat, he had taken a dozen blind steps towards the silent pile before his senses came back to him, before he thought to ask himself what good would come of it even should he succeed in making his way to her. She armoured in pride, and he an outlawed man! Like a sail which the breeze has deserted, his head sank; he stood becalmed.

When he looked up again, the lines of his white face had hardened as iron settling in a mould.

"Once in his lifetime it is well for a man to tell himself the truth," he said. "To lose me will strike as near her heart as though she had lost a jewel from her ring—no nearer. Once she might look for it, once frown over the loss, once speak regretfully of it,—and that is soon over! The memory of my arms around her, the fire of her lips on mine, the dream of possessing her—what more could I hope for? For the dreamer, a dream-bride! It is well-befitting!"

A smile curled his lips that was new and ill to see, as he looked his last upon the shrine of her he loved. Then he turned and walked on rapidly over the tree-guarded path that led eventually to the shadow of the wall and the western gate.

From a distance he glimpsed again the gray-cloaked beggar, outstretched as if in slumber; but he saw no other living thing until he saw the black-robed priest move across the bright court and pass out of the gate ahead, the sentinel making him reverent salute. Even though it had been foretold him, it deepened his sense of belonging no more to the living world that when he himself reached the exit the man remained gazing fixedly at the sky, and he dared neither greet nor touch him as he passed.

The gate gained and left behind, his instructions were exhausted; and he would have halted to plan further but that out in the radiant lane he found the Shepherd Priest awaiting him, his heavy shock of hair turned into a silver glory around his swarthy face. Moving down the dewy path beside him, the old man began at once to speak:

"One thing I think needful to say, my son; and that is that I should not be less afraid of taking this second step than of taking the first one, if God had not given me to see most plainly what His will is. I want you to know that one week ago He moved the *jarl's* heart to speak and call me as witness that he had solemnly consented in your espousal of his sister."

Randvar could not have replied if he would. His gaze had gone ahead to a blossoming crab-tree that leaned over the low stone wall and canopied half the lane. Masses of snowy bloom were its branches, and snowed over with petals was the earth beneath it, but that white shape moving before it—was that only another branch blowing in the soft night wind? Coming to meet them, it looked like a girl in a thrall's robe of white wool; but the queenful poise of the head—the glint of red-gold hair as the light fell upon it—He put out a hand and gripped the old priest's shoulder.

"Tell me how much this means?" he demanded.

She answered for herself, the girl in the bond-maid skirtle, as she stopped before them; and in voice as well as face she was Brynhild, the *jarl's* sister.

"I should have thought there was more risk of a man's forgetting anything than his wedding-day," she said with lips that smiled through trembling.

Even then he dared not believe it, but stood gazing from her to the pair of saddled horses tethered in the shelter of a spreading tree. Drawing yet nearer, she held out her hands, her gray eyes meeting his as steadfast as the gray North star.

"It means," she said, "that even as Freya followed Rolf, your wife follows you into banishment—Love, what is it?"

For he had flung himself on his knees before her and was kissing the hem of her coarse robe.

Chapter 23

Once must every man die
 —Northern saying.

It was a radiant earth that kindled into colour with the coming of the light. Dipping from a hill-top into a little valley abrim with the yellow of hickory buds and the new green of maples and the red-and-pink of budding oak leaves, the girl on the roan horse spoke dreamily: "Once you told me that trees put on their brightest hues in the autumn as warriors go bravest clad to battle. Now it seems to me as if the spring world had put on its showiest garments to welcome you and me to a new life."

"May that become a true omen!" the man who rode behind her responded absently.

To turn and scan from under his hand the country they had passed over, he had drawn rein upon the crest. On the gray anxiety of his face confidence dawned as slowly as rosy day upon gray night.

Smiling, the girl looked around at him. "What are you doing back there where I cannot see you, my friend? Since daybreak have you made me go first, even when the path was broad enough for two. What masterfulness is that for a man but six hours wed!"

"It must be looked for that a man would be tempted to make the trial of mastering you," he answered as lightly as he could. "What I am doing back here is to watch the haughtiness of your head making derision of your thrall-garb."

"I think thorns are making derision of the fine wedding clothes I sewed for you," she laughed. "It was quite another place that I expected you would wear them in. Yet it pleases me also that you should go fine while I go plain, for in the realm of the forest are you not lord and I the most lowly of followers? Saw you ever a raw man newly come to the bodyguard that bent his neck better to orders?"

A note of laughter was silvering her voice, but passionate earnestness was in his as he spurred abreast of her and leaned over to murmur at her ear:

"Never did woman so stoop to man since the Valkyria came down to Sigurd! How ill do I deserve such love who doubted that love!"

The smile with which she had welcomed him deepened into laughter as tender as the murmur of the brook flowing beside them. "My dear one, if you but knew how warm it lies at my heart—my victory over your doubt! For the first time, I feel myself worthy of your love."

She pressed her face to his, and so they rode a while, cheek to cheek. His arm tightened around her with feeling how she drooped against him in the weariness she was too proud to own. He said under his breath:

"I would give all I hope to possess in the world to spare you this. My one fear is that you will come to repent the choice you have made."

She said without lifting her drooping lids: "Freya came to Rolf over the bodies of slaughtered kin, yet she did not repent it; and between you and me there is no shadow."

He was thankful then that her eyes were closed. Before she could open them and catch the dread which he felt drawing at his mouth, he had made the narrowing of the trail an excuse to draw away and rein back to his post in the rear.

Narrowing to a thread between leaf-walls, the trail wound through a copse of thorn-trees in blossom. The blending of her kirtle with their woolly branches seemed to give Brynhild's thoughts a new turn. Over her shoulder, she opened conversation again:

"It would not be difficult for me to hide among these trees. For another reason I am pleased with myself for thinking of this disguise. Without it, I should never have been able to pass out of the hall unmarked. For two days now there has been a gray-cloaked beggar hanging around the doorstep,—a fellow too ill-natured to speak even to the women who gave him food, but so prying of eye that I have felt his gaze from under his hat-brim every time I went out or in. Why, even you could not pass last night without arousing his curiosity! He was staring out of the western gate after you, as you and the good father came up the lane towards me—"

"Staring after me?" Curt as man's to man was the Songsmith's voice. "And you have not told me of it before!"

She started at the change of tone. Then she said gently:

"I forgot him in—in the other things we spoke of when we met, my friend. And it did not seem in any wise important to me. A wandering beggar could not know you for a prisoner escaped."

He did not tell her that a suspicion had risen in him that the beggar was not a beggar. He did not tell her anything for a space, but rode staring fixedly between his horse's ears. Her question was twice repeated before it reached him:

"What harm could spring from it, Randvar?"

He said, slowly, then: "You saw the fellow more than I, though I have seen him twice. Did it ever cross your mind that he might be Olaf Thorgrim's son, lying in wait for me when I should come healed out of your bower?"

She cried out in mingled amazement and assent: "Olaf! Then he carried his news straight to the *jarl*! Before we had crossed the first hill, guards were spurring after us!"

The whiteness of her face, as she peered back between the flowery branches, brought him out of his musing. Pressing forward, he took the hand she had involuntarily put out.

"Never will Helvin Jarl send guards after me, that I have reason to know for certain. Have faith in my assurance, and no fear."

To get his eyes away from hers, he bent over her hand and touched it with his lips. Whether or not she read his secret dread that Helvin himself would be the pursuer, he could not tell. She made no other answer than to give back his hand-clasp firmly, then turned and urged her tired horse forward.

Falling on the velvet sod, the hoofs brought forth no sound. With the ceasing of their voices, silence like a great sea closed about them. When ever it was rippled by the splash of wind in the tops of the pines or by the soft trill of a bird, the song-maker knew a sense of relief. Nerve and sinew, he was strained forward towards the moment when they should have won through this scented and smothering stillness to some elevation from which he could look back over their track.

So gradually the slope arose that he might not have known when they reached the crest if he had not seen the bright head before him beginning to descend, sunlike. His nails sinking into the leather of his saddle from the force with which he gripped it, he turned and looked back.

Nothing to be seen amid the white drifts of the thorn-trees. Nothing among the furry gray willows bordering the brook. His eye leaped on down to the bottom of the hollow, carpeted with the white flowers of wild berry vines, and leaping, lost a moving dark shape even as they caught it, a moving slinking shape. It might have been a skulking wolf,—and it might have been a man!

The girl riding ahead heard his voice just behind her, speaking with chill quietness:

"As soon as ever you come to that black-budded bush, turn to the left. I remember that a trail begins there. It does not matter where it leads to. It is not a beaten track; hood your head and bend low, if twigs catch at you."

If she wondered why he did not go first to break the road, she did not say so. "Yes," she answered as quietly as he had spoken, and obeyed him as she answered.

Even before the leaves closed on her bravely carried head, his eyes had lost her through the mist that gathered in them. "For her sake!" his heart cried out a prayer to the old gods and the new. Then he had plunged into the thicket behind her, his hand clinched in agony upon his empty sheath. Riding with one ear set over his shoulder, he still kept on telling himself that it was impossible that it should be a man; that no man without the scent of a beast could have followed their trail, even if human limbs could be strong enough to overtake them.

Because his attention was held so fast by what lay behind them, he gave no heed to the sinister road they were flying over, to its blasted bushes and the bone-white trench of a dead brook that cut again and again across it. He leaped in his saddle at a sharp cry from Brynhild before him.

"Randvar! What place are we coming to?"

So like a bolt it fell upon him that he had pushed into the open after her, and checked his horse beside hers, before he himself realized to what goal the unused trail led. Even then it was not he who put it into words, but she, with her distended eyes upon the pond of murky water in the ring of gray tree-skeletons.

"The Black Pool! Where my father got his death! It is an omen!"

He spoke no word either of denial or of comfort. Throwing himself from his horse, he snatched her from her saddle, half carried, half dragged her to where a pile of bowlders rose like a cairn amid the dead trees. Upon the earth behind it, he pushed her down.

"Hide there!" he told her hoarsely. "Whatever happens, hide there,—and *keep your face covered!* He comes now whom I would die sooner than that you should see."

The warning came too late. While he was still speaking, he heard the horses behind him snort and run, saw her eyes flash past him. With a shrill cry, she staggered from her knees to her feet and stood as one frozen there, one rigid arm thrust out in pointing. As an echo to her cry came from the blasted bushes of the trail a note of low laughter, deepening suddenly to a throaty gurgle that was of neither man nor beast.

To that whirlpool of horror, the Songsmith's mind was drawn in. Reeling with its madness, he plunged forward, bruising his fists on the trees in the effort to rouse himself out of it, dashing his hands against his eyes to break the spell of that blind dizziness. As through rents in a veil of blindness, he saw Starkad's son creeping towards them, saw wolf eyes glaring above a frothing mouth. With a final despairing effort, he brought his fist down where the jagged stump of a branch stuck out before him; and pain broke the spell. The strength of desperation on him, he leaped forward and closed with the rearing form.

But even as they grappled, the curse-ridden man sought to free himself, loosing a sudden cry that was half a pealing laugh and half the bark of a wolf. Hurling the song-maker from him upon the earth, he was gone on a bound to some dearer prey beyond.

Struggling to his elbow, Randvar stared after him. Among the trees beside the black water had come in sight a horseman wearing the gray cloak of a beggar but the livid face of Olaf the French,—livid, sweating, from the haste with which he was spurring towerward by the only path he knew. Now creeping, now bounding, the madman had reached him. Springing upon him with outflung claw-barbed hands, he had dragged him fighting from his saddle and flung him upon the ground. Snarling, he dropped upon him and buried his teeth in the upturned throat. An instant of gurgling gasping noises, and he was up and gone into the forest, sounding his terrible cry; and Olaf lay dead even as Starkad Jarl had died, from the fangs of the demon wolf that was the Other Shape of Starkad's son.

Chapter 24

He is happy who gets himself fame while living
                              —Northern saying.

It was two Norse weeks after the death of Olaf, and it was nearly two-score miles south of the Black Pool. Filtering through the dark forest, a long ray of sun lay on Freya's Tower and revealed it as a sanctuary embattled. Here, from the lengthening shadows, the bright beam picked out a circle of shaggy deerskin-clad foresters hammering arrow-heads at a forge made of bowlders. There, in touching the earth, the slanting ray touched another brawny group squatted at knife-sharpening. Yonder, the light streaming golden down a tree-aisle broke over a deerskin-garbed sentinel pacing to and fro. Now the murmur of blended heavy voices and heavier laughter swelled like the noise of the breakers,—until someone's exuberance betrayed him into a burst of over-facetious song, when he was silenced by nudges and missiles and thumbs pointing Tower-ward. Now the lull that followed was broken by scattered hails and chaff, as a Skraelling burdened with a double string of glistening fish came like a shadow up the path of sunshine.

Making his way gravely between the jovial groups, the red man gravely evaded the jesting hands stretched out towards his treasure, and stalked on to the tower. At the foot of one of the gray columns, he lowered the silvery mass to the earth and stood awaiting a chance for speech with his white brother's new wife.

In the dim ground-room there was the flutter of a blue robe—the glint of red-gold hair—and she had appeared in one of the rude archways. Against its gray gloom, the glowing beauty of her face was like a fire; while the stark pillars were a foil for her body's soft and flowing curves. Without speaking, the savage stood gazing at her,—even as every woodsman within eyeshot had stopped short in speech or work to gaze. It was she who spoke, composedly, giving him thanks for his gift, then went and poured him a horn of wild-grape wine and brought it to him.

Even while his mouth busied itself with the drink, his eyes stared at her over the silver rim. But as he gave the horn back, he spoke in broken Norse:

"Say to the white chief that the men of the stone-axe race have set up their houses around him. Say to him that they turn their weapons whither he points. Say to him that they will bring him the white *sachem's* red scalp whenever he gives the sign."

The hand of the white *sachem's* sister made a convulsive movement that lost her the horn, but her brave gray eyes continued to meet his steadily.

"I will tell him," she answered. "His heart will be thankful towards his friends."

Though his face remained set in her direction, the Skraelling turned the rest of him and moved away as he had come, until his dusky shape was lost in the dusky wood.

Gazing after him with unseeing eyes, she stayed a moment in the archway, while—mute and motionless as so many bowlders—the foresters stayed gazing furtively at her. Then a curly-headed boy in a page's ragged dress of blue came out of the tower and broke in upon her thoughts, as he bent to pick up the forgotten cup.

"How clumsy in their manners such creatures must look to you, *jarl's* sister, it is easy for me to understand, for in former days they went against my taste also. But when your experience of life has been as broad as mine has, sooner will you choose their ugly worth than the fair falseness of the town-people. I say it, though I am hard to please!"

A note of unsteady laughter shook the long breath with which the *jarl's* sister straightened; but her arm lay lightly around the boy's neck as they went back indoors, and he expanded under the caress as a bantam that is about to crow.

"It is my wish that you should always lean upon me! I told my mother this noon—when she asked me to fetch you the fowl and the loaf—that it was in my mind to visit you as often as I could find time. And I told her that I meant always to wear these fine clothes so that you should feel at home with me, and not feel that I had grown savage and terrible like the others around you. And perhaps it will also help you to lose it out of your thoughts for a while that you are poor, with no one to wait on you."

Though she laughed again, the sound was more soft than a caress.

"Poor?" she repeated. "Listen, little Viking! Once I was poor, when I thought there was no more to the world than the few hedged roads I knew, and my life was but an empty round that others marked out for me, and I had nothing but ring-bought gifts to give my friends. But now! Now when each hour some wondrous path undreamed of is opened to me—Now that my life is a fabric I weave myself till from the roots of my hair to the soles of my feet I thrill with the joy of the work—Now that my breast is so full of love that ofttimes it aches with the burden and yearns for a worldful of folk to lavish it upon—"

Her ecstasy mounted higher than her words could follow. While it soared, she stood silent. When, because it was of earth, it sank again earth ward, she spoke under her breath:

"Only shall I be poor, Eric, if the Fates take from me the man who has wrought this change in my nature. If it happen to him to meet with—with my kin—someday—and the same overtake him that overtook Olaf—"

Her hand gripped the boy's shoulder so that he would have cried out if he had not guessed from the whitening of her lips how much harder Dread was clutching at her heart. Gritting his teeth, he supported her manfully.

"There is no man like Randvar in all the new lands," he panted, "and I would fight for none as I would fight for him."

Loosening their hold, the fingers rose and swept his cheek fondly, and the *jarl's* sister moved away and bent over the smouldering fire to stir it. Though she did not turn again, her voice came to him with its wonted gracious composure.

"Have thanks for your friendship, little friend! And give my thanks to your mother for her good gifts; and tell her that if she does not come oftener to visit me I shall take it as a sign that because she has gone to live in Snowfrid's booth, she feels that I have crowded her out of her home. Will you bear that in mind?"

For the fourth time since he had begun to think of tearing himself away, Eric picked up his feathered blue cap.

"Naught shall be forgotten, *jarl's* sister," he reassured her. "And now I fear that I must in truth take leave of you. With Bolverk so often away on hunts, I find that the wants of Snowfrid and my mother put not a little care on my shoulders; and my intention is that they shall never lack for anything now that I have come home to take care of them. *Jarl's* sister, I bid you farewell until tomorrow."

The purpose of the plumed cap became apparent as by its aid he added elaborate flourishes to his bow. Then fixing the bauble upon his curly head, he went away hurriedly, as became one weighted with responsibility; and as became one torn between love and fear, the *jarl's* sister went up the ladder-like stairs with a hand pressed to her heart, and crossing the strange little fur-hung bower, dropped down beside Freya's window to watch as Freya before her had watched.

Higher and higher slanted the long rays, until only the tree-tops knew their golden glory. The horizon became as a band of red fire behind the black network of the woods. The lower that fire burned, the farther the great outside world seemed to fall away from the little world of the tower. As though to make a stand against impending isolation, the foresters drew their circle closer and beaconed it with cheery fires. Over the young wife's vigil crept a spell of awe, so that though she leaned wide-eyed upon the sill she did not see the one for whom she watched when presently he came up a twilit trail, a spear gleaming on his shoulder, Bolverk's brawny bulk looming beside him.

It was he who espied her—her bright head like a star hung low in the gloaming—and slackened his pace to stand looking at her.

Following his friend's gaze, Bolverk spoke with his buoyant laugh: "Small wonder you stare, comrade, at seeing Freya's ghost filling Freya's blue kirtle!"

The song-maker roused himself with a deep breath that was like a sigh. When he moved for ward again, the springiness was gone from his step.

"Would that I did not see the ghost of Freya whenever I looked at my wife!" he said. "Like goblin-bells they start out of space and clang in my ear, the words Erna spoke that night by the tower fire,— 'Freya loved Rolf in spite of all, but it was the effort of doing so that wore her out before half her life was lived.'"

A second time Randvar came to a standstill; and as the sun from the wood, so had the light fled from his face and left it a place of shadowy dread.

"Suppose," he said, "that my quarrel with—the *jarl*—come to no round end one way or the other but, as oftenest happens, drag on and on in uncertainty. . . . Suppose the *jarl's* sister wearing out year after year between these walls of solitude . . . eating into her memory, the murder of her father . . . burning into her eyes, the thing we saw at the pool . . . gnawing at her heart, her fear for me. . . . Suppose it should not be her love that gave way—"

"Nor her life!" Bolverk finished hastily. "Nor her life!"

But the weight did not lift from the Songsmith's bent shoulders. He said slowly: "When grisly thoughts had dwelt long enough in her brother's mind, it was not his body that they killed, but his reason."

Gasping a dread word, Bolverk caught him by the arm. In heavy silence they walked the rest of the distance that lay between them and the cordon of fires.

Giving them greeting and at the same time demanding their news, a score of voices broke in upon their reverie. In a moment, the song-maker was the centre of a cordial group that listened eagerly while he told how the Skraelling chief had received him, and approved boisterously the new trading treaty which the chief had granted to the new colony at the tower.

"No better pleader than you was Njal of Iceland!" growled the veteran in bearskin. "Next spring we shall send to Nidaros a richer ship than ever sailed from Norumbega; and no less a man than you shall stand by the steering-oar."

"Yes! Yes!" the chorus gave jovial approbation, and made a jesting onslaught as though they would have raised him to their shoulders. But his expression grew in grimness as he motioned them back.

"A ship that had a corpse on board would get better luck than one that had me at the steering-oar," he said. "I have told you without deceit that I stand so with most Northmen that my name and the word traitor has the same meaning. Never make the mistake of thinking that I shall let you put me forward where I should draw down hatred and failure on your heads. When you have lent me your weapons to guard my wife, you have done me as great a service as a man can do another, and I have reaped all the good of your love that I can bear. Never can I repay you as it is!"

He broke off abruptly. Perhaps they were glad that he did not wait for them to answer, but leaving them strode on towards the tower. Yet it would have been no unworthy response if they had put into words what spoke from, their hard faces as they watched him gain the firelit archway and take his young bride in his arms. To search with passionate anxiety the eyes she lifted to his, he held her there, forgetful of all the world beside; while her hands betrayed a passionate eagerness to clasp his hands, to cling to his deerskin-sleeve, to feel him safe and whole.

It may be that when life is at its fullest, the need of words falls away like a husk that is shed. By-and-by when the two had gone in to their rude hearth, tongue-speech grew less and less frequent between them, less and less until—like candle-light into sunshine—it faded into the perfect communion of silence.

Bringing the fowl from its bed in the hot ashes, the bread from its birch basket, the wine from its cask, the young mistress of the tower moved to and fro in the firelight. Resting on a fur-heaped bench in the shadow, the young master followed her every motion with worshipful eyes. Sometimes, as their gaze met, the gracious gravity of her demeanour sparkled into a moment's playful mimicry of some pompous servitor they had known in the pageantry of the *jarl's* house, and their laughter, bass and treble, blended in a full chord. Sometimes it was his hand that encountered hers, and closing on it with an inarticulate cry, put it to his lips in place of wine, and pressed it there while for them both Time ceased to be.

And then again, a moment came when for him all jest went out of her service, when to see her waiting before him in Freya's faded robe of blue was a thing he could not bear. Rising, he took horn and trencher from her hands and flung them aside, and almost roughly placed her on the cushion-heaped bench, and placed himself on the cedar mat at her feet.

"One high-seat you shall have, and one thrall!" he said fiercely; and drawing his harp towards him, he played for her as he had never played for himself nor yet for the *jarl* in all the splendour of his feast-hall.

She made but one alteration, stretching out her hand that it might thread his hair as his head leaned against her knee; then with eyes softly closed and lips softly parted, she rested listening.

Floating through Paradise on the wings of the music, she knew nothing of it when the circles of the outlying camp-fires were thrown into commotion as reeds by an incoming wave. Only when Randvar plucked a twanging discord from the harp-strings, and then flung the instrument from him, did she start awake.

One hand stretched behind him to grasp her robe, and one hand thrust across him to clutch his knife-hilt, he had risen to his knee before her. Over his shoulder she saw what he saw—a brass helmet glowing in the firelight where the path gave upon the open, more brass helmets glinting like fire-flies far up the dusk of the trail. Now four figures separated themselves from the throng, and pushing through the wavering rank of foresters, came towerward, two figures in dark robes and one wearing the plumed cap of a courtman and one clad in shining mail.

"Mord—and the Shepherd Priest! Gunnar—Visbur!" the Songsmith told them off mechanically.

The arms Brynhild had locked around his neck tightened as she whispered at his ear: "God be praised, Helvin is not there! Love, if they meant us ill, they would not have fetched Gunnar and the priest, who are our friends."

But Randvar's voice was harsh as he loosened her hands that he might rise. "If they mean us well, why do they come with a troop of armed men at their heels?" Never quitting his grip on his hilt, he strode forward and stood a pace beyond his threshold, awaiting them.

Glancing down at her poor attire, it seemed for an instant as though the *jarl's* sister would have shrunk back into the shadow; and then as one would catch up a deserter she caught herself, and holding her head high, moved forward until she stood at her husband's side.

At sight of the Songsmith, the sentinel of the path cried out earnestly: "We let them through, Rolf's son, only because they pledged you peace. If they have spoken false—"

He did not finish, but it was not needful that he should. Around the ring of hunters, like the light of a moonbeam, sped the glint of steel. And still beyond that, where wood encompassed the open, there passed of a sudden a noiseless stir, as if from every tree-shadow there had glided a lithe and dusky body. Joining soundlessly as shadows blend, the dark mass drew nearer, until here the firelight was reflected in rows of glittering eyes, there through the gloaming gleamed the pale shapes of stone axes uplifted. It is no shame to the courage of Gunnar the Merry that his handsome face blanched as his glance made the circuit. Mord spoke sternly when they came to a halt before the young master of the tower.

"What right have you to speak of peacefulness, Randvar, Rolf's son, that surround yourself with outlaws and savages of the wood, ready to do murder at your bidding?"

Even in the twilight it could be seen how the blood mounted in the Songsmith's brown face, but there was no wavering in his mouth's steady line as he answered.

"I take friendship and help where I find them freest and truest, and I expect evil from the quarter whence evil has risen against me before. Though you come in the name of the *jarl*, to whom you hold me traitor, I shall not yield a whit more. Your blood be on your heads if you heed me not!"

From the gathering circle of foresters came back a sound like an ominous echo; and the murmur was taken up in the wood beyond, till it rose like the roar of the wind in the trees. But all at once Visbur made a long stride forward and held out his huge hand.

"Never look at me with that look on your face comrade!" he said gruffly. "I know now that you were no traitor to Starkad's son, and Rolf's self would not be gladder of the knowledge. Take now my hand as a token that you will accept atonement from me."

The Songsmith and his young wife spoke in one breath: "You know—?"

"From him who alone had the right to tell it," Visbur answered briefly. "While the day was still young, we came upon Starkad's son in the forest near the town, with Olaf's blood yet on him. Because his wits were not in him, he mistook us for Shapes risen to torment him, and stood and shouted his secret at us in defiance. And then his strength went from him; and he fell down to the earth; and death came to him where he fell."

"And it was on your name that he called as he died," the gentle voice of the Shepherd Priest sounded amid the stillness that had spread. "Because I was the first to reach him and raise his head to my breast, it is likely he thought it was you, for he spoke your name in a tone of love; and that was his last breath."

No longer was there steadiness in Randvar's voice as he tried to speak. Of a sudden it broke, and he turned away from the eyes upon him and stood with his face in the shadow, his clinching hand still holding his young wife to his side. What she said softly in his ear—whether of grief for her kin or gratitude for her loved one's safety—none could hear.

Then it was Mord the Grim who spoke with ceremony: "Now the end of it is that Helvin Jarl has been five days dead and five days buried, and we have come to offer the rule to you, Starkad's daughter, who are the next of kin—" He lifted his hand as, turning, Starkad's daughter would have interrupted him, indignantly. "To you and to your husband, who is of all men most beloved by the folk of the new lands. To you two together."

What Brynhild cried out, as she stretched her hands towards them, could not be heard for the acclamations that burst from the listening foresters. Then, drowning even that, rose the clangour of the guardsmen's shields as they pounded on them with their swords.

Once more the Songsmith's lips became unsteady, so that he dared not trust his voice to them; but presently he turned and made the shouting throng a gesture of acceptance of their honour and of thankfulness for their love, and all understood him.

A Viking's Love

and Other Tales of the North

SCHOOLING HER BOW SHE MUST PUT HIM FROM HER HEART AND FORGET HIM

Contents

A Viking's Love	283
The Hostage	292
As the Norns Weave	299
How Thor Recovered His Hammer	312

A Viking's Love

It was long ago, when the world was so young that peace meant little more than a breathing spell between battles at the royal farm of Augvaldsnes, in Norway, King Olaf Haraldsson sat at an Easter feast with his men.

Right and left on either hand the long tables stretched away, cleared of all their bounty, save two lines of brimming ale-horns. Down the middle of the hall fires burned brightly, flushing the delicate faces of the women on the cross-benches, sending the golden light higher—higher—until every shield upon the tapestried wall flashed back an answer. Overhead, through the smoke-holes between the sooty rafters, shone the still white stars.

"So, it may be, the eyes of angels look down upon our earthly pastimes," King Olaf said thoughtfully, and his stern face softened with the satisfaction he had in a scene of such orderly good cheer. Rolling his ale on his tongue, he settled himself to listen to a man who had just risen from a place on the left of the high-seat.

Thorer Sel was the man's name, and he was the bailiff that had this royal farm of Augvaldsnes under his management. As he stood now, a showy figure in the firelight, he would have been good to look at if his eyes had not been shifty and his mouth coarsely overbearing. He smiled jeeringly at the man who had addressed him.

"So you want to know what took place between me and your friend, Sigurd Asbiornsson, do you?" he asked.

"If you will," the man on the bench answered. "I was away on a Viking voyage last summer when it happened."

Next above this man on the bench sat a tall, broad-shouldered young fellow with a frank, comely face and the air of one amiably used to having his own way. He was the son of King Olaf's most powerful vassal, and his name was Erling Erlingsson. Now suddenly he, too, spoke up.

"I, also, would like to hear that story. If it is true, as I have heard it, then are you the only man in the world who has ever made Sigurd Asbiornsson bow his neck."

Thorer Sel threw him a glance over his shoulder.

"I forgot that it would not sit comfortably in your ears," he said. "It had slipped my mind that the Halogalander is your kinsman."

"Kinsman or not, I like to see justice done to men of courage," young Erlingsson answered. "I say, in the presence of everybody, that Sigurd Asbiornsson is one of the bravest men that ever drew sword or breath."

"The story will show," Thorer Sel said mockingly, and began forthwith.

"To start at the beginning, Sigurd Asbiornsson is the man who came down here from the north and bought corn and malt to carry home for the entertaining of his friends, though it was well known to him that because of the bad seasons, King Olaf had forbidden that any meal should be carried out of the south of the country. Dauntless as I am wont, I went down where he had put in under the island for the night and stripped him of his cargo and his fine embroidered sail, and drove him home in disgrace—all in the manner which I will truthfully relate."

"I have seen that you have his sail in your possession," Erling said slowly, "but only he could convince me that you got it without a trick, if you got it against his will."

That was not a bad guess, since the only cause to which the bailiff owed his success was his forethought in providing himself with sixty men, as against Sigurd Asbiornsson's twenty, and in falling upon him at the moment when he and his crew were dressing after a morning swim and stood utterly defenceless against attack. But a guess is only a guess—and no one stood up to confirm it.

"The story will show," sneered Thorer Sel, and proceeded to tell it at great length, with less and less regard for the truth.

He drew it out so long that many of the feasters tired of him and began talking among themselves; but four people continued to listen attentively. One was the Viking who had asked for the tale. Another was Erling, ominously fingering his sword-hilt. A third was a young girl sitting among the matrons on the cross-bench—a beautiful girl who bore her small fair head with brave dignity. The fourth was a strange man in poor attire who had come in unnoticed among the servants that were fetching fresh supplies of ale.

The stranger listened the most keenly of all—it almost seemed as if the bailiff might have left him hanging on the words. Step by step, he was drawn forward until only a space of bare table lay between him and the storyteller.

He was a tall man, with a mighty girth of chest and limb. For all that he wore a shabby hat and held a hayfork in his hand, he did not carry himself like a churl. As he moved from the shadow of the last pillar into the firelight, the girl on the cross-bench stifled an exclamation, and her cheeks went white as the linen before her.

"Astrid, my friend, what ails you?" the housewife beside her asked kindly.

A woman on the matron's other side admonished her with a nudge.

"Have you forgot," she whispered, "that Asbiornsson wooed her before her father married her to Hall the Wealthy? Naturally she would be troubled at hearing him ill-spoken of."

Then both forgot her and their gossip and all else.

"How did Sigurd behave when you unloaded his vessel? "the Viking had just inquired.

And the bailiff had answered brazenly: "When we were discharging the cargo, he bore it tolerably, though not well; but when we took the sail from him, he wept."

They were the last words Thorer Sel spoke on earth. While they were still on his lips, the stranger cleared the table at a bound. There was a flaming of warrior-scarlet from under homespun gray, a hiss of steel, the sound of a blow—and then the whole room seemed turning scarlet, and the head of Thorer Sel rolled on the table before the king.

"Sigurd" the girl on the cross-bench cried piercingly.

"Sigurd!" shouted young Erlingsson, leaping to his feet.

After that, it was hard to tell what anyone said. Pushing forward in obedience to an awful gesture from King Olaf, guards laid hold of Sigurd Asbiornsson and hurried him from the hall, and thralls came running with towels and water and a board. While some took up what lay heavily among the reeds of the floor, others spread fresh linen, and still others removed the bespattered mantle from the king's shoulders. Only in one thing they all acted alike—no man raised his eyes to the king's furious face.

Of a different mettle was Erling Erlingsson. Coming back from the door through which the guards had led his friend, he came straight up to the high-seat.

"Lord," he said, "I will pay the blood-money for your bailiff, so that my kinsman may retain life and limbs. All the rest do according to your pleasure."

King Olaf's voice was very low. It was his way when his rage was highest.

"Is it not a matter of death, Erling, when a man breaks the Easter peace, and breaks it in the king's lodgings, and makes the king's feet his execution-block? Though it may well be that it seems a small matter to you and your father!" His teeth showed through his quietness.

Erling tried his unpractised tongue at entreaty.

"The deed is ill-done, Lord, in so far as it displeases you, though otherwise done excellently well. But though it is so much against your will, yet may I not expect something for my services to you"

After a little, King Olaf said:

"You have made me greatly indebted to you, Erling, but even for your sake I will not break the law nor cast aside my own dignity."

By a gesture he forbade a reply, and spoke on, asking what had been done with the murderer.

"He sits in irons, upon the doorstep, with his guard," Erling said, heavily.

Then he roused himself to ask one thing which he thought might not be denied him.

"Lord, it is a year since I have seen him, and we have been blood-brothers since we were children. Give him into my charge this one night, and I will answer for him in the morning."

After a long time, King Olaf said grimly:

"It is true that to hang a man after sunset is called murder. Take him, then, for the rest of the night. But know for certain that your own life shall pay for it if he escape in any way."

"It must be as you will," Erling answered, and went out of the feasting-hall that but a short while before had seemed to him a place of such good cheer.

Upon the doorstep, ironed hand and foot, Sigurd Asbiornsson sat listening quietly to the excited expostulations of his guard. Now that the broad-brimmed hat had fallen off, it could be seen that there was nothing blood-thirsty in his handsome sun-browned face. Strong-willed and proud and hard, it might be, and yet in some delicate curve of his mouth, some light of his fine gray eyes, lay that which won him, unsought, women's trust and men's love. He looked up with a smile to meet Erling's troubled gaze.

"Why take your failure so much to heart, comrade?" he remonstrated. "I came prepared to pay Olaf's price. Stay here by me that we may at least have tonight together, for I suppose he thinks too much of his wonderful laws to hang me before sunrise."

Nodding, Erling turned and spoke to one of the guards, who caught up a hammer and commenced knocking the chains off the prisoner's limbs with far greater alacrity than he had shown in putting them on.

"What is the meaning of that" Sigurd asked in surprise.

"Olaf has given you into my charge until morning," Erling explained briefly.

For as long as the space between one breath and the next, the prisoner grew tense and alert.

"What pledge did you give for my safety?" he asked quickly.

Less quickly, Erling answered: "My own life."

The half-formed hope faded. Sigurd's mighty frame relaxed.

"I give you thanks," he said, and no more was spoken on the subject.

One by one, the guards drifted back to the ale-horns, and the friends were left alone in the starlit silence of the courtyard. Suddenly, Erling laid hold of the great shoulders before him and shook him fiercely, while at the same time his fingers clung to them in a caress.

"You madman!" he burst out. "Could you not guess that I was going to kill him for you? Olaf dare not slay me—a fine would be the uttermost. What fiend possessed you! Did you imagine Olaf loved you because you had always defied his laws? You madman! Did you not know that I would do it for you?"

"Would that have rubbed out my disgrace, if you had done it for me?" Sigurd asked quietly.

He laid his hands on the other's shoulders, and they stood breast to breast and eye to eye.

"Come, come, kinsman, these are useless words; why waste breath on them? If you knew how Thorer Sel spoke to me that morning—spoke to me before my men!—and how the tale spread northward until churls that had never dared sneer behind my back before, taunted me to my face! No, no, it was the only way to do it, boldly and openly, with everyone looking on. Now I shall leave a clean name behind me. What more could I do if I lived to be a hundred?"

Erling was silent; only, his hands that rested on his friend's shoulders gripped and held them so that marks were left on the flesh, and the two men remained looking into each other's eyes until a mist came between.

Then, without speaking, they freed each other; and Sigurd said quickly:

"One more thing lies on me to do. Will you help me?"

"I trust there is killing in it," Erling said through his teeth.

"It is to get a message to Astrid, Gudbrand's daughter," Sigurd replied.

Erling cried out in amazement: "The wife of Hall the Wealthy!"

"Hall the Wealthy has been dead two seasons."

But Erling exclaimed again: "Gudbrand's daughter! Of whom you could not speak bitter words enough—even though you knew they would reach her ear!"

"I spoke unfairly," Sigurd said, flushing. "She sent me a token that I did not receive—I cannot tell you more. I do not ask now that she should stoop to see me herself, but if she would send some woman who has her confidence—if I could speak my message to her with the certainty that it would come truthfully to Astrid's ear—" His dark face flushed redder and redder in the moonlight, and he did not turn away to hide it. "It is the greatest service you could render me, kinsman," he finished.

Stifling an impatient breath, Erling flung the end of his cloak over his shoulder and turned.

"The sooner the better, then—before they are gone to bed. Wait in the herb-garden, yonder. It is the spot where you will be the least liable to interruption."

Netted around with bare bushes and strewn underfoot with shrivelled leaves, the herb-garden lay in desolation. Yet even here the slender sides of branches showed the swelling hopes of springtime. A thought came to Sigurd of the budding trees at home, and the harvest he would never reap; then he thrust it from him angrily, and strode up and down the pathway, waiting.

Three times the wind rustling through the bushes tricked him. But at last there was the ring of spurs on gravel, and Erling came out of the shadows, followed by a slender figure wrapped from head to foot in a hooded cloak of blue.

Trying to guess which one of Astrid's women the silken folds hid, Sigurd stood gazing at her silently. She halted before him without speaking; but Erling said shortly:

"You have little enough time. I was only able to manage it because Gudbrand is still swilling drink in the hall. The instant I see his torch-bearers, I shall call you."

He disappeared again into the gloom that lay between them and the gate.

Unconsciously, Sigurd's glance must have followed him, for when it came back to the girl, she had answered the question in his mind. The blue hood was thrown back, and the moon shone on a small fair head, upborne with brave dignity, even while the lovely eyes and lips were tremulous.

"Astrid!" he breathed.

She returned his look with the grave steadiness that was a little pathetic in so young a girl.

"For the second time I have lowered the point of my pride to you," she said. "Are you going to make me sorry this time also?"

He began to speak eagerly. It seemed that he would have caught her hands if he had dared.

"Astrid, I was not to blame! I beg you not to believe that I would slight a token from you who have always sat highest in my heart. The churl you gave your rune-ring to—he must have mislaid it, and then feared to give it to me when he found it afterwards. Not until this Spring, when he died and his relation came upon it among his things and brought it to me, did I know that you had sent me a message of love after your father refused to bargain with me. Because I was not in the king's service, Gudbrand was even disrespectful in his treatment of me. And the next month, I heard that you had married Hall. And I had had no farewell from you. What could I think but that you had held me lightly, and lightly let me go? What else could I think?"

"You could have remembered that I was helpless," Astrid answered slowly. "Could I wed you against my father's will? Could I hold back from marrying Hall, though he was in everything what I detested most?"

She steadied her lip in her little white teeth.

"You could have believed in me," she said, "as I would have believed in you. Three seasons we had spoken and feasted and ridden together, and when had you ever found me changeable toward my friends, or greedy after gold? You could have believed in me."

"I ought to have believed," Sigurd said humbly.

His face had grown white, as no man had ever seen it. Even when spurs clanked on the path, he stood before her helplessly.

"I ought to have believed," was all he could say.

Moving a step nearer, she laid her hands upon his breast and looked up at him with a little flickering smile.

"You would have believed—if you had loved me as I loved you," she said.

She touched her finger to his lips, as he would have cried out.

"I do not think it is in your nature to feel much love for a woman, my friend. If you had not loved your own way better than me, would you not have entered the king's service to win me, when only that lay between us? Your land—your chiefship over your men—the freedom to do as you pleased—all those you loved; and what was left over, you gave to me. It was not very much, was it? Yet perhaps it does not matter, since I was so glad to get it."

Though her eyes were misty with tears, she held up her mouth to him bravely.

"I give you thanks for telling me," he whispered softly, when he had kissed her.

As Erling's voice sounded urgently, she drew her hood over her head and was gone.

It was a soberly thoughtful man that was pacing the garden-paths when Erling came back. They walked away the rest of the night in silence, while the moon went on in darkness, and the gray dawn which is neither light nor shadow spread coldly over the sky.

It was this new expression which caught King Olaf's eye, when he and his outlaw faced each other again.

With the first burst of morning sunshine, the king came out of the hall on his way to mass, followed by the highborn people of his household. Blinking laughingly in the dazzle, and drawing in great breaths of the fresh sweet air, the retinue made an odd contrast to the other group waiting on the doorstep—three swarthy thralls testing a coil of rope in their hairy fists, and Sigurd Asbiornsson once more ironed and guarded.

King Olaf stopped abruptly.

"How is it that things which I dislike are always kept before my mind? "he demanded. "Why was he not put to death at sunrise?"

The guard answered that the king had named no definite time, and they feared to misunderstand his will.

"I have seldom heard a poorer excuse," King Olaf returned coldly. But he did not make his will clearer. He remained scrutinising the prisoner with a touch of uncertainty in his strongly marked brows. Fearless, Sigurd Asbiornsson looked, as always, but for the first time that something seemed gone from his boldness which had stirred the king's temper against him.

Olaf smiled slowly as a test came to his mind.

"To please your friends, Sigurd," he said, "I will make you an offer which you can do as you like about accepting. It is the law of the land that a man who kills a servant of the king shall undertake that man's service, if the king will. Would you submit to that law, and undertake the office of bailiff which Thorer Sel had, if I gave you life and safety in return?"

He gathered up his mantle to depart, as he concluded, so sure was he that his offer would be rejected. Of all the throng, from Gudbrand's daughter to Erling, not one believed that it stood any chance of acceptance. They almost ceased to breathe when—slowly—with a flaming face and the stiffness of a pride that was cracking at the joints, Sigurd Asbiornsson bent his head and kissed the king's hand.

Not to save his life could he have spoken. His power of speech did not come back to him until the churchgoers had swept on across the court, and he was left alone with Astrid in his arms.

"Do you believe now that I love you?" he asked, raising her face between his hands.

Then it smote his heart that he should even seem to reproach her, and he finished lightly:

"What does it matter? We will make a jest of it between ourselves. Let the world think me the king's man—we know that I am yours!"

The Hostage

I seek to tell of a Danish hostage, called Valgard the fair, that in his youth was ceded to our great Alfred by the Danish King Guthrum when they two made peace together in the year eight hundred and seventy-eight.

From Denmark young Valgard came to England in the following of Ogmund Monks-bane, who was his elder brother and Guthrum's first war chief; and though no warrior of more accursed memory than this same Ogmund ever fed the ravens, it was known that toward his young brother alone of all living things he showed a human heart. Wherefore those on whom it lay to choose the hostages were swift to name the comely boy as the one pledge that might clinch the Monks-bane's shifty faith. And that nothing might be lacking, they further fixed it in the bond what would be the fate of Valgard and the eleven other hostages if they that gave them should break any part of their oath; and it was this—that the discipline of the Holy Church should take hold of them, and after that they should die a shameful death.

A snared and a savage man was Ogmund Monks-bane when they brought this word to the tent of skins in which he laired; and it saddened him besides that the boy Valgard strove to contend him, saying:

"It will be no hindrance to you, kinsman. Never will you so much as think of me when the battle-lust comes on you. And I shall bear it well."

In our king's will at London, therefore, young Valgard grew into man's estate and, contrary to his expectations, throve mightily, discovering a rare aptitude for gentle accomplishments. And for that his heart was noble as well as brave and he was as *débonaire* as he was comely, the king and the royal household came to love him exceeding well until—as the years went by and the peace held—they scarcely remembered that he might one day stand as a scapegoat for loathsomest crimes against them.

Only Vangard himself never for the span of one candle's burning forgot it. Like poison at the bottom of a honeyed cup it lay behind every honour he achieved. Yet even as he had promised his brother, he bore it well and gallantly enough—until, in the sixth year of his captivity, it fortuned to him to fall in love.

She of whom he become enamoured was a young maid in the queen's service, whose rightful name was Adeleve but whom men called Little Nun both by virtue of the celestial sweetness of her face and because of her being but newly come from a cloister school. And in this cloister they had taught her so much of heaven and so little of earth that whenso her heart was taken by Valgard's brave and *débonaire* ways she knew neither fear nor shame therein, but continued to demean herself with the lovely straightforwardness of an angel or a child. Wherefore Valgard, who was used to women that smiled at him from under heavy lids or drew full red lips into rosebuds of enticement, might not dream that she felt more than friendship. And since in her presence he was always silent and humble as he had been before Our Blessed Lady herself, though elsewhere light speeches sparkled on his lips as bubbles on the clear wine, he wist not for a long time the true name of what he felt.

But one day at that season of the year when the king's household rode often to hunt the wild boar in the woody groves that compassed London round, it happened to Valgard to become separated from the rest and stray alone through still and shadowy glades. There in the solitude, as was ever his unhappy case, his gayety fell away and his forebodings climbed up behind and went with him heavily. Riding thus, it chanced to him to approach the spot where the queen and her maidens tarried and so to come upon the Little Nun herself, that also rode apart, following a brook which sang as it went. Then at last was he made aware of his love, for suddenly it was neither a dislike of death nor any rebellious wish to flee therefrom that possessed him, but solely the dread of being parted from her, which so racked him that he was in very agony.

Now as soon as ever Little Nun perceived that a great trouble was upon him she spoke straight from her heart, though timidly as a child knowing the narrowness of its power, and prayed him to say whether his distress were aught which her love might assuage. When he heard her speak thus sweetly and marked the angelic tenderness of her eyes under her little dove-coloured hood, lo! everything fell clean out of his mind before one almighty longing. Descending from his horse, he took her hands and spoke to her passionately, so:

"Tell me whether you love me. My heart cries out for you with every beat. Must it be as the voice of one calling into emptiness? Tell me that you return my love and my life will be whole though it end tonight."

The Little Nun's face of cloistral paleness flushed deeply like an alabaster vase into which is being poured the red wine of the sacrament, but her crystalline eyes neither fell nor turned aside.

"I love you as much as you love me—and more," she answered softly.

Whereupon he would have caught her in passionate arms, but that even as he reached this pinnacle of bliss it came back to him how he was a doomed man; and he was as one that is cast down from a height and stunned by the fall.

Anon his voice returned, and sinking to his knee he begged her in broken words to forgive the wrong he had done her in gaining her love, that well knew himself to be set aside for shame and dole and apart from the favour of woman.

To which the Little Nun listened as it might be one of God's angels, bending over the golden bar of Heaven, would listen to the wailing in the Pit. And so soon as he paused she spoke with halting breath.

"Alas, could anything so cruel happen? Ah, no! The peace has held six years—the king believes it firm—and every night and morning I will pray to Our Lady to change your brother's heart."

As she said this, her face bloomed again with her hope. But Valgard only bowed his head upon his hands and groaned; for that albeit he had faith in the Virgin, he knew the nature of Ogmund Monks-bane.

Soon after, constraining himself to hardness for her sake, he rose and drew her away and continued to speak with the dullness of one in great pain, schooling her how she must put him from her heart and forget him.

But to that, when she had listened a while with widening eyes, the Little Nun cried out piteously:

"Alas! what then shall I do with my love? It came into being before you called it—it cannot cease at your bidding. Oh, if it be God's will that we shall have a long life together, then God's will be done, but make not a thwarted useless thing out of the love which He has permitted me! Let me give it to you. Even though it be too poor to ease you much, yet let me give it! How else shall I find comfort? "

Suddenly, as their eyes met, she stretched out her hands to him with a little sobbing cry that was half piteous and half pitying. And so drew him back, *malgre* his will, until he had put his arms about her where she sat in the saddle above him, when she gathered his head to her breast and cherished it there, with little soft wordless sounds of comforting.

Thus, for that he was so well-nigh spent with struggling, he leaned a while upon her love. And it heartened him. And he lifted his head, thinking to set burning lips to her sweet mouth.

But even as he thought to do this, something in himself or her checked him, so that he kissed instead her small ministering hands. Wherefore the Little Nun remained unstartled and blessedly trustful, and raising her eyes to the blue heavens of which they seemed so much a part prayed softly to Our Dear Lady to keep true the heart of Ogmund Monks-bane.

The fourth morning after this, the queen's maiden Adeleve was wedded to Valgard the Hostage. And that day at noon did our benignant king and his housewifely queen make a marriage feast for the young pair that both of them held dear. A marriage feast, well-a-way!

It happened to the sweet bride to come to it last and alone, for that she had lingered above to pray once more to her on whom she fixed her faith. Blissfully enough she began the descent of the stairs that cored the massive wall; but ere she reached the foot, where a door gave upon the king's hall, dead was her joy. For this is what befell.

First, a quavering shriek as of an aged woman stabbed by evil tidings; and after that a deathlike stillness. Then the door opened and a girl staggered forth up the stairs, her hands groping before her as her staring eyes had been sightless, the while she moaned over and over the name of her soldier lover.

Though she knew not why, little Adeleve shrank from the groping hands and crept by them down the stairs. Whither rose these words in a man's loud voice:

"—but last week came a load of Danish pirates to the shore, reeking of slaughter and gorged with Irish spoil. And every night thereafter a band of them sat at drink with the Monks-bane, stirring his fighting lust, until—"

Here the voice was lost in the outburst of many voices, till it overleapt them hoarsely to answer a question from the king.

"The two-score English soldiers I named to your grace; besides all the nuns of Saint Helena's that lie stark in their blood—"

Then once again the tumult rose, which now there was no overleaping, and the bride cowering against the wall saw how all heads turned toward him who stood opposite the king in the mockery of gay feasting clothes. And suddenly one called down Christ's curse on the race of Ogmund Monks-bane, and a second echoed the cry. Whereat the other Danish hostages—to show that their hands were clean—took up the shout more fierce than any, and smote Valgard so that he reeled under their fists. And the aged woman whose son had been slain flung her cup of wine in his face.

Thereafter the young wife saw only the figure of her doomed lord upon whom it seemed that the curses descended as a visible blight, withering to ghastliness his fresh beauty and blasting his spirit so that he shrank farther and farther from the damning looks and tongues till he might no longer in any wise endure them, but calling in agony upon his God strove with his hands to stop his sight and his hearing. And when presently he became aware of the Little Nun approaching, he cried out to know whether she also was come to curse him, and bent his arms around his head as against a blow.

But even as he did this, he met the anguished love in her eyes and saw how she was labouring to make of her fragile self a buckler for him against the press of crowding bodies; whereupon he caught hold of her shoulder and held to her as a man sinking into Hell might hold to the robe of an angel. Until brutal hands thrust her one way and dragged him the other.

Now the sentence was that he should die at sunrise, unto which time the Church should have him to chasten. And this sentence our king might not alter, for that he was called the Truth-teller and had sworn to take the atonement of life for any breach of the faith. But this much he granted, out of the pity and love he had toward the young pair, that they might be together when the end drew near. And stranger than betrothal or marriage feast was this vigil of their wedding night!

Strange was all the world now to the Little Nun, since the arch of her Heaven had fallen about her with the destruction of its keystone, which was her faith in the Virgin. As the white dove of the Ark hovering over a changed earth whereon it might see no familiar foothold, she hung falteringly on the threshold of the king's chapel, while the bells tolled the midnight hour, gazing at the group of deathful men looming amid blended smoke and starlight and torch-glare, at the pitiless shining figure of Our Lady above the altar, at him who stood in grim endurance before it, stripped to naked feet and a single garment of horsehair.

When Valgard felt her eyes and turned his set face toward her, she fluttered to him as the dove to the Ark. But no longer to brood or minister; only to cling to him in utter helpless woe of her helpless love. And when it happened to her hand to touch his horsehair shirt where it was wet with the blood of his atonement, she screamed sharply and was like to go wild with weeping over him and lamenting that she might not bear any of his punishment on her own soft flesh. It was he that kneeling on the stones gathered her to his breast and cherished her, speaking to comfort her such words of resignation as no priest's scourge had drawn from him with his life-blood.

Lo! it was so that from the very helplessness of her love he drew his best strength, that he no longer cared anything at all for his own woe but only for lightening hers. When she cried out piteously that she must always fear Christ's Mother now her whole life long, and all the world saving him alone, he spoke with tenderest artfulness, thus:

"For my sake then, heart beloved of my heart! Be brave for my sake—because your tears are the only part of my doom that is heavier than I can bear."

Which was the one plea in all the world that had a meaning for her, so that she tried obediently to choke down her sobs.

Yet which was the easier to bear, her courage or her tears, it were hard to say. When the time of parting came and she had suffered him to loosen her clinging hands and fold them upon her breast and leave her, a little white and shaking figure at the Virgin's feet, it seemed to Valgard looking back that death was easier to him than life, and he pressed with mad haste upon those who went before him to the door.

Now in this *vill* it was that the king's chapel was hollowed out of the wall of the king's hall; wherefore the opening of the door permitted Valgard and those surrounding him to look down into the great dun room wherein our king kept sorrowful vigil with his knights, and to behold also a man that stood before the high-seat with the mud and mire of the road yet besmirching him. Upon whom Valgard's glance fell amazedly for that he knew him to be a Danish thrall and his brother's trusted slave, albeit the Monks-bane had used him so cruelly that some of his features were lacking.

As the door opened, the thrall began speaking, thus, in the dull voice of one who has neither wit nor will but only dogged faithfulness:

"This is the message of Ogmund Monks-bane, that because as soon as he got into his senses again he disliked the thought that he should cause the death of his brother whom he loved, he sends you this atonement."

Saying which, he thrust his hand under his cloak and drew therefrom, by the knotted yellow hair, a bloody head. And the ashen face on the head was the face of Ogmund Monks-bane.

Through stillness, the thrall spoke again. "Do you accept this atonement, king?"

To whom, after a little time has passed, our king answered in a strange voice: "I accept this atonement."

Then, his task being accomplished, the thrall loosed an awful discordant sound of grief; and raising the head between his palms kissed it on either cheek, crying:

"I slew you and I brought you hither because I have never dared go against your will in anything, but even you cannot hinder me from following you now! "

Wherewith he slew himself with the knife he had at his belt. And the sound of his falling body broke the spell, so that the bars of silence were let down and men's voices rushed in like lowing cattle.

Excepting only in the little chapel in the wall. There Valgard stood as a man in a dream, gazing on the dead face of his brother; while the Little Nun, clasping him close, yet lifted awe-filled eyes to Our Lady that thus in her own inscrutable way answered the prayer to keep alive in the nature of an evil man its one good part.

Let us all give thanks that there is such a Lady, and pray that she may harken to us in our need!

As the Norns Weave

There was a man named Thorolf; he was Thrain's son, Eric the White's son, of Norway.

He kept house at Thorolfstede, in the Rangrivervales in Iceland. He was an honourable man, and wealthy in goods. His wife's name was Thorhilda, but she does not come into the story for she died the year after she was married to him. The name of their daughter was Rodny. While she was yet in her childhood, it could be seen that she was going to be fair of face, and her eyes were as blue as the sea where it is deepest.

Lambi was the name of another man, a son of Grim the Easterling. He dwelt in the east dales when he was at home, but he was more often at Thorolf's for the bond of friendship was strong between them. He was a truehearted man, but somewhat soft-tempered. The name of his son was Skapti, and he comes shortly into the story. Now one spring while Rodny was still a child in years, Thorolf took a sickness and died; but before he breathed his last he spoke to Lambi and asked him to see after his daughter and take in hand the care of her goods, and Lambi gave his word to do that.

So Thorolf died and was laid in a cairn in the Rangrivervales, and Lambi came to live at Thorolfstede to see after Rodny and her household. And Skapti, his son, came with him. And so they sat for ten winters, and nothing noteworthy happened.

At the end of that time Rodny was grown up, and the fairest of women to look upon. Some said that she was rather wilful in her temper, but for all that she was one of the best loved of maidens. A fast friend she was, too, and warm-hearted and generous; and the best proof of that is that she never grudged Skapti, Lambi's son, his way about anything.

Skapti was this manner of man. He was so born that one foot was withered and there was a hump on his back, and he never waxed large of frame or sturdy. But in his face he was the most handsome of men, and his hair hung down in long curls of good colour. It was thought that his father's rearing had not bettered his disposition. In order that his spirit should not be humbled by his deformity, Lambi praised his face and his wit and all he did, and begged everyone else to do the same; and the upshot of it was that Skapti thought there was no man like himself for dash and keenness, and was always bragging and boasting, and everyone had to give way to him or have his wrath. He had a shrewd mind, but he was so spiteful that many were afraid of him.

Now a fourth man is named in the story. He was called Hallvard, the son of Asgrim the White. He owned a good homestead in the Laxriverdales, but he lived more on his longship than on land for every spring he went a-sea-roving. He was the most soldier-like of men, and the best skilled in arms; tall in growth, too, and powerful and well-knit. Some said that his wits were rather slow because he lived so much where it was of most importance that hands should be quick; still for all that he was fair-spoken and bountiful, and better liked and more humble than any other man.

It happened one spring that he rode to the Assembly, with all his shipmates at his back. Many great chiefs were there besides, but everyone said that no band was so soldier-like as his; and a group of women that stood near the booths of the Rangrivervale men turned their heads to look after him; and one of them who knew him called out merrily and bade him stop and talk to them.

He got red in his face at that, for his mates were much given to gibes and jeering; still he would not refuse her; so he rode back and got off his horse and greeted her well, and told her all the news she wished to hear. It is told about his dress that it was of red-scarlet and very showy, and he had on his head a gilded helmet that King Sigurd had given him, and his face was brown from the sea-winds.

Now the maiden that stood next to the one that had hailed him was Rodny, and no woman there was as fair as she. She was so clad that she had on a kirtle of a rich blue colour that trailed behind her when she walked, and a silver girdle around her waist. Hallvard could not keep his eyes off her as he talked, until his tongue began to blunder and say the same thing twice over. Rodny kept her feelings better in hand; still it could be seen that she listened eagerly to everything he said, and the colour trembled in her cheeks as the Northern Lights tremble in the sky.

As soon as he got a chance to speak apart with the woman he knew, Hallvard asked her what maiden that might be. The woman told him; and then she managed it so that he should talk alone with Rodny, though the others stood near and spoke among themselves. And they talked together a long time; though sometimes there were silences between them, but neither of them seemed to mind that.

At last Hallvard said: "Many strange wonders have I seen abroad, yet the thing which seems strangest to me I see here in Iceland."

"What is that?" says Rodny.

"It is that a maid like you should be unwed."

"Oh!" says Rodny.

Hallvard said: "It is easily seen that you would be thrown away on any match you should make; yet that would not hinder me from trying my luck if you thought me good enough to ask for you."

She was rather slow in answering that, but at last she spoke in a well-behaved way and said there could be no two minds about that since everyone thought him a man of the greatest mark.

"I might be all that," said Hallvard, "and still not be at all to your mind. I should be glad if you would say that you would have nothing in your heart against such a bargain."

Then Rodny could no longer keep herself altogether in hand, and she began to laugh a little and said that he was hard to deal with, and that perhaps if she should say that she had nothing against the bargain, he might answer that that was too bad because he had no mind to it. But the end of her jesting was that she broke off without finishing, for he got red in his face again, and it could be seen that he was much in earnest.

"I should have thought that the risk as to that lay all on my side," he said, "but now I will say right out that my life will never seem good to me again unless I get you to wife."

Then Rodny answered him well and straightforwardly, and said: "From what I have seen of you so far, I think I could love you well; but you must see my foster-father, Lambi, about it; though it will go as I say in the end."

After that they left off speaking together.

But the next day Hallvard came to Lambi's booth, and all his shipmates with him to show him honour, though they had gibed much when they first heard what he had it in mind to do.

Skapti sat in front of the booth entertaining himself with the antics of a tumbling-girl, that cut capers there while an old man played on a fiddle. The man's name was Kol, and his nickname was Fiddling Kol. Jofried was the name of the girl, and she was Fiddling Kol's daughter. She had on a man's kirtle, and she was well-shaped and not ugly of face, though one could tell by her mouth that she was determined in disposition. They were vagabond folk, that went from house to house and lodged where they could. Skapti always talked with the girl because she had the greatest store of gossip at her tongue's end; while on her side it could be seen that she set a value on every look he gave her.

Hallvard greeted Skapti kindly, and his mates did the same, for when they saw his deformity they thought that there was more than enough that was wanting in his life; and Skapti took their greeting well because it seemed to him that they could not but be envious of the fairness of his face. And so they talked together smoothly, for a while, and Skapti offered to give them his help about their errand—whatever it might be—and sent a man to call Lambi out, when he heard that that was what they wanted; but he himself went back to his sport with the tumbling-girl.

Lambi came out of the booth at once, and gave them a good welcome. After that they fell to talking, and Hallvard asked for Rodny, and added that he had spoken to her about it and the match was not as far from her mind as might have been expected.

Now Lambi had long had it at heart to wed Rodny to his son, and there was no bargain that he would not have been more willing to make than this one. And at the same time he knew that it would be pulling an oar against a strong current to go against Rodny's will. So he held his peace for a while, and after that he answered in this way:

"Every Spring since you have been able to stretch your hand over a sword, Hallvard, you have fared abroad; and for all that we in Iceland can tell, you may have wooed a maiden in every land your ship has touched. It is said that the sea's own fickleness soaks into the bones of them who live on her, and many a man has done such things and been thought no less of. But with Rodny I will not have it so, and these are the terms I lay down. You shall sail abroad as you had the intention to do, and there shall be no betrothal between you; but if you think of her often enough while you are gone so that four times during the summer you send a man out to Iceland to greet her from you, then when you come home in the Autumn the bargain shall be made. But if you do not think of her that often, it is unlikely that she would get any pleasure out of her love even if she were wedded to you, and you shall not get her."

Hallvard said at once: "I agree to those terms. And now let us take witnesses."

So they stood up and shook hands, and the bargain was struck; though Hallvard's friends murmured among themselves and said that such terms ought not to be laid down for a man like Hallvard.

Then Hallvard said: "I only make this condition—that Rodny should give me her word not to betroth herself to any other man while I am gone."

"I have no fault to find with that," said Lambi.

So he sent for Rodny, and she came thither, and with her three women. She spoke to them all well and courteously; and after that she sat down, and Lambi told her all about the bargain and left nothing out.

It could be seen from her way that she thought the terms far too strong. And when she heard what it was that Hallvard wanted of her, she answered without waiting:

"I will promise that, and more besides. I will promise that when his ship comes to land in the Autumn, I will come down half-way between my house and the shore to meet him, that some honour may be done him, as too much has not been shown so far."

Hallvard said that it was honour enough that he got the right to woo her, still he would not fling back the kindness she offered him; and they made a bargain about that also. After that, they bade each other farewell, and Hallvard and his friends rode away to their booth.

Now it must be told how Skapti wearied of his pastime and came in and asked his father what it might be that Hallvard wanted, and Lambi told him of the bargain he had made.

At first it looked as Skapti could not believe it, and then it seemed as if he would never leave off scolding.

"Now," he said, "it is proved true what I have long suspected, that you are a doting old man that no longer knows how to behave with sense, when you thus give away to another man the woman that I have always had it in my own mind to marry."

So he went on, and made it known in every way that he thought he had been wrongfully used.

Then Lambi said: "You take it ill, kinsman, and there is some excuse for you. But now this is to be taken into consideration, that Rodny had set her heart on the man, and his honour is great everywhere."

"His body is great," said Skapti, "as big as a bear's; and he shall yet dance to my wit as a bear dances to a willow pipe."

Then they had many words about it, until they were both wroth; and Lambi said:

"There is no use in troubling oneself about what is done and over, but I see now that my rearing has made you crooked in your temper as well, and limping in your sense."

After that he went away; and Skapti flew into a great rage, so that there was no speaking to him; and he laid saddle on a horse and rode without drawing rein until he came to the booths of the Laxriverdale men.

It happened that Hallvard and his friends were still out of doors; and they were in a merry mood, and drank and made jesting wishes about the bridegroom; and Hallvard wore a joyful face, and took all their jibing blithely.

When Skapti rode up, Hallvard greeted him well and asked him to get down and drink with them. But Skapti began at once to talk in the most ill-tempered way, and the end of his scolding was that he bade Hallvard turn his steps and his thoughts away from Rodny from that time henceforward because he had the intention to wed her himself.

Now in the beginning of his speech it was so that Hallvard looked at him and did not know what to make of him. And in the middle of it, his temper got a little tried. But when he came to the end, Hallvard burst out laughing. And his friends began to laugh, one after the other; and no one took further heed of Skapti, but all went back to their drinking.

It is said that Skapti was so wroth, and had his temper so little in hand, that he wept. Then he went away by himself, aside from other men, and stayed so a long while. After that he rode over the plain until he found Jofried, the tumbling-girl. He talked long and low to her, and no man knew what passed between them. But when they stood up to part, Skapti said this out loud:

"So things shall take this turn, that she shall not come down to meet him when his ship makes land next Fall, nor shall he have courage enough to follow her up in her hall. And then it will be put to proof whether or not I am to be set aside and made game of."

Then the tumbling-girl spoke so as to flatter him, and said that she had never heard a plan that promised to work out better.

Skapti swelled out his chest and said: "Jofried, this is how it is, that when I look at the clods around me it seems as if it were given me to know their every weak spot; and I declare with truth that I can take their life-threads and weave them as the Norns weave, and my judgments are no more to be spoken against than theirs! "

After that, Skapti rode home. But Jofried did as he had bidden her and went down to the shore where Hallvard's ship lay, and prayed Hallvard to give her and her father leave to fare abroad with him that they might show their accomplishments to other audiences and increase their goods.

Hallvard gave them leave; and now the story follows the ship for a while.

Shortly after, they got a fair wind and sailed away to sea. Hallvard stood by the steering-oar, but Jofried sat on the deck at his feet. When they could no longer see the land, Jofried began to weep much and bemoan herself, so that Hallvard asked what was on her mind.

Jofried said: "I would give all I own that I had never come hither; and it will stand me in little stead though I get all the goods in Norway, if by going away I lose my chance of Skapti's love."

Hallvard laughed and said: "I did not know before that Skapti got on so well with women. But tell me who it is that you think is likely to rob you of his heart."

"It is Rodny, Thorolf's daughter," said Jofried. "He has always looked upon her with eyes of love, but now I can see by his manner that his love is at the harvest; and the likelihood is that they will be wedded before we get back." And as she said this, she wept.

But Hallvard looked as if he did not know whether to laugh or get wroth, and at last he said: "I think there is no need for this to look so big in your eyes, messmate. Skapti sets too much store by himself to love anyone who does not love him, and there is little danger that Rodny will ever do that."

"But she will do it," Jofried answered, "for he is the most handsome man that men ever saw; and his hair is as fine as silk; and there is so much of it that it hides his lame back like a cloak of gold."

"He is a little crooked stick with a gilded head," says Hallvard.

"You can call him that if you want to," said Jofried, "but it only proves what I knew before, that you know nothing at all about women; for with a woman, a gilded head counts for more than a great clumsy body like a dancing-bear's."

Now it had happened to Hallvard, each time he came before Rodny, to feel himself very big and clumsy and out of place; so he got red in his face at that, and went away to another part of the ship, and he and Jofried saw little of each other for a time.

But when they had been out three weeks they came to Norway, and sailed into the bay there and made land at the King's Crag. And Hallvard went up to the town, where some trading-booths were, and bought a good gold finger-ring and sent it out to Rodny on a ship that stood ready to sail. Jofried praised the ring much, and Hallvard was so pleased at that that he answered her eagerly and said:

"It is no lie what you say of me, Jofried, that I know little about women; yet this has occurred to me which should also be borne in mind, that Rodny is different from other maidens. I know it for true that she sets great store by weapon-skill and deeds of might, and I tell you for your comfort that she will never give herself away to a man who spends his days kissing the maidservants by the fire."

But Jofried shook her head and answered: "That may well be, master; and yet Rodny is a woman for all that, and all women think alike. And the proof of that is this, that although I am no more than a gangrel woman, I have the same feelings as a maiden reared in a bower; and to me as to them, all other men look like shambling giants when Skapti, Lambi's son, is by."

In this manner she kept on speaking about Skapti's fairness until it seemed to Hallvard as if it could be no otherwise than so; and he got wroth and said that if it went as she foretold, Skapti would not be so handsome of feature after he got through with him. And after that he was very short with her for a while.

Then they sailed from the Bay out into the open sea again; and there they fell in with sea-rovers and a great fight sprung up; and they got the victory, and much goods. Among the spoil there was a necklace of fine gold and the best workmanship; and Hallvard took that for his share, and sent it out to Rodny by a trading-ship that was shaping her course toward Iceland. But before he sent it, he showed it to Jofried and said:

"Do you not think that will get me some favour in her eyes?"

Jofried answered: "Good is the gift, but methinks it would be still better if it were not dumb."

He asked her what she meant by that, and she went on: "I should think anyone could see that when Rodny has hung the necklace around her neck, she will think no further about it; but Skapti will sit by her side and be always speaking so as to flatter and gladden her, and the end will be that he will have all her thoughts; for in the whole of Iceland there is not his equal for a quick wit."

Now Hallvard knew himself for a slow-witted man, so his heart went down at this; and thereafter he took no pleasure in the gifts he sent. And from that day forth he grew very silent, so that men noticed it.

At first no one could guess what was at the bottom of it, but soon Jofried repeated everything that she had told him about Skapti.

All spoke against it, in the beginning; but the end was that they believed her. After that the matter was their daily talk, when Hallvard was not by; and the more they talked, the more wroth they became for his sake. At last they went so far as to go before him, one after the other, and beg him not to stop at the Rangrivervales as he had intended, lest Rodny should break the tryst and make a laughing-stock of them, but to hold his course north to the Laxriverdales and send a man back from there to see how the land lay.

Hallvard listened to them all without speaking, but it was easy to see that each piece of advice left him more sick at heart than before.

And now the days run on until the time comes to turn their faces toward Iceland.

Then one night when the shipmates were drinking under the tents on the forecastle, Hallvard came among them and said:

"I have taken counsel with myself about what you want of me; and though I will not sail past the Rangrivervales as you wish, neither will I ask you to ride up to the trysting-place, as was intended. But we will so manage it that we come to land after sunset, and make a night-camp on the shore; and there we will be that night and the next day. And if it happens that during that time Rodny sends anyone down to us with a bidding, we will ride up to her hall and make the excuse that we could not come before because we had much goods to see to; but if she does not send any welcome down, then—when we have camped on the shore one more night—we will weigh anchor and sail away north."

All said that was a better way than to keep the tryst and run the risk of being laughed at. And now the story goes back to Thorolfstede, and what happened there.

When Hallvard had been away six weeks, a ship came out from Norway and ran into the Rangriver, and a man that was on board came to Thorolfstede and greeted Rodny from Hallvard and gave her the gold finger-ring that Hallvard had sent. And Rodny was glad, and put it on her hand where she could see it all the time that she stood at her loom; and at night the hand that wore it rested under her cheek.

But when the next month had worn away, and that trading-ship came into the river which had on board the necklace that Hallvard had taken from the sea-rovers, Skapti went down to meet her, and sought out Hallvard's man and made him drunk and robbed him of the necklace and threw it into the river. And when the man came into his wits again and saw what had befallen him, he was so frightened that he dared not come near Rodny at all, but fled back to the ship and stayed there while she held her course northward. And Skapti came home and told Rodny that no greeting had been sent.

Rodny was rather cast down at first, for she had made sure that the ship would have some word for her. Still it was not long before she had thought of many good reasons why Hallvard might have been hindered from sending; and she looked at her ring more often than before, and was soon light-hearted again. So another month passes away.

Then a third ship came out from Norway, and on her was one of Hallvard's men that had in his keeping for Rodny a brooch of gold with four silver crosses hanging from it. But Skapti went down to meet him, and then it was the same story over again. The man leapt overboard and swam to a ship that was just pulling out for the east. But Skapti went home and told Rodny that no greetings had come.

At that Rodny held her peace for a long while; and once tears came into her eyes, and that was not her way. But still, when Lambi spoke and said that it began to look as if her lover had forgotten her, she answered quickly and said:

"If he has forgotten me, it is in doing deeds that men will praise; and so it may well be forgiven him. And besides, it will not be long now before he remembers me again." And in this way she answered all who found fault with him, and showed herself big-hearted in everything.

But when the Summer had worn away till it lacked but five weeks of Winter, a fourth ship came out of the east; and Rodny got no greetings that time either, for the man that was bringing a gold arm-ring to her was in such haste to take passage back again that he handed over his charge to Skapti of his own free will, and rowed out to another ship as fast as he could go. And Skapti threw the gift into the sea, and told Rodny the same lie as before.

Then Rodny could no longer speak up for Hallvard, but sat biting her lips in silence, when Lambi spoke against him and said how much better it was to make bargains with men whose lives she knew all about. Men thought that this time her pride was put to a hard trial.

Yet she never spoke any ill words of Hallvard.

And now the time goes on until the last of the days before winter conies. One day at even, Rodny's shepherd came galloping up to the door and said that Hallvard's ship had sailed into the river. Skapti and everyone looked at Rodny; and first her face was as though it were all blood, and then it was as white to look on as the moon.

Skapti thought there was little risk, but that her temper would jump the way he wanted it to, and yet to make sure he spoke up sharp and quick and said:

"Now Hallvard has forgotten much, but one thing I hope he will remember, and that is that he has promised to meet you half-way between your hall and the shore; for you would get the greatest shame if you went down and he was not there."

Then Lambi said: "If you will lean on my counsel, foster-daughter, you will call up your pride and stay at home. Hallvard has broken agreements enough to set you free, and more besides; and it is even as my son says, that mocking tongues will not be wanting to shame you if you keep a tryst that your lover has forgotten."

But Rodny, when she had held her peace for a little, answered them slowly and said: "It is true that Hallvard has seemed to forget me, and that my pride has been sorely tried; and it is no less true that if he gives me fresh cause for anger, I may let my temper go as far as it will. But now you both show how little you guess what love is in a woman's breast, or you would know that while there is any chance at all that he may prove himself guiltless of meaning disrespect toward me, I care no more about mocking-tongues than I do about the blowing of the wind."

After that she went away, and at first Skapti thought matters had taken a bad turn. But shortly he saw that it was unlikely that Hallvard would keep the tryst himself, and that would become a fresh cause of strife between them; and then he was merry again.

Now it must be told how Rodny rode the next morning to the trysting-place, and Lambi and Skapti and ten men with her. And when they got there, there was no one to meet them.

"What did I tell you?" said Skapti.

"It is early yet," replied Rodny; and so they sat for a while.

Then there came the noise of hoofs trampling over brush. But it was only one of Rodny's house-*carles* that had taken horse and come after her to tell her that he had just been up on a high hill that overlooked the river, and there he had seen Hallvard's men camping on the shore, and taking no steps to get ready to ride, but lying about on the sand and amusing themselves with the tumbling-girl.

Rodny made him tell it three times over, and then she was so wroth that no one had ever seen any woman so wroth before. She swung her horse about and was for riding home without a word, when Hallvard came out of the wood before her, red in his face and out of breath because he had come on foot from the shore while his mates thought him sleeping on the ship.

As soon as Skapti saw that, it seemed to him that he had got into a luckless state; and he slipped behind a bush and made off toward the shore to find Jofried and scold her for her great falling-off of wit. But Hallvard went up to Rodny and gave her a joyful greeting; and after a little she welcomed him with both hands.

Then he said: "I see that you dislike my tardiness, and I want to beg off from your wrath; for it is the truth that I came as fast as I could."

Rodny said: "But where are your friends, that you come alone and unattended like a man of no honour?"

Hallvard seemed to find that hard to answer, and he waited a while; but at last he said: "I will tell it just as it is and not lie about it. I did not want my mates along for fear that you would not keep faith with me, and I should be put to shame before them. And now I see that I have behaved like a great fool from the beginning; though the reason is that it seemed so wondrous a thing that you should love a man like me, that I could hardly believe it when you were no longer before my eyes."

At that Rodny was so well pleased that she did not want him to see how much pleased she was, and kept her eyes on her hands where they lay in his. But shortly he spoke again, and then his voice was a little downhearted.

"Though I see," said he, "that you did not like my gifts, since you wear them neither on your neck nor your breast nor your arm. And yet I had hoped that they would please you a little."

"Gifts!" said Rodny. Then he began to ask questions, and it came out that she had never set eyes on the pretty things.

Hallvard was so wroth that it looked for a while as if some man would have to go down before him. But Rodny took it in quite another way.

"It is to me as though I had got the three best gifts in the world," said she. "And I care not a whit what became of the gold so long as you remembered to send it."

With that, she slipped off her horse and put her arms around Hallvard's neck and kissed him; and thereafter their love ran smoothly enough.

And now all that is left to tell is how Skapti came down to the shore and began to scold Jofried, and she answered in this way:

"No more of the blame for this lies on me than on you; for it is proved by this that though you know much of men's weaknesses, you know nothing at all about the strong parts of their natures. And now you may have your choice of two things—either you shall take me to wife and give me equal rights with yourself over your goods, or I shall go to Hallvard and tell him everything about this plan, and then you will have his wrath to bear, and you know as well as I whether you would be able to stand up under that."

Because he thought he knew enough of her to be sure that she would do as she said if he did not give way to her, Skapti took her to wife; though he thought the choice a hard one. They went away into the east dales to live on a homestead that Lambi gave them; and Jofried stood up for her rights in word and deed.

And here we end the story of how the Norns wove.

How Thor Recovered His Hammer

1

As I have told you before, Bilskirner, the palace of Thor the strong-one, was built in his kingdom of Thrudvang, the realm that lay beyond the thunder-clouds. It was the very largest palace that was ever roofed over, for it had five hundred and forty halls beneath its silver dome; and it was so dazzling bright that when people on earth caught a glimpse of it through the clouds, they blinked and said they had seen lightning. In a tremendous hall in the centre of it, Thor spent most of his time when he was not away fighting giants or attending assembly-meetings. There were benches all around the walls for his followers; gleaming weapons hung above them; a fire blazed on the golden hearth; and in the middle of the line of seats the Strong-One had his splendid shining throne or high-seat.

One would have supposed that such a bright place would have been difficult to sleep in, yet here every night, when the feasting was over, the members of the household stretched themselves on the cushioned benches and took their rest; and here, on this particular morning of which I am going to tell you, they all lay sleeping soundly—perhaps even snoring, if the truth were known. Thor leaned back in his high-seat, his red beard tossed up and down by his deep breathing. Loki the Sly-One, who was visiting him, sprawled unconscious among the cushions beside him; even the fire was slumbering and only roused now and then to wink a drowsy red eye down among the embers.

Amid all this peace and comfort, Thor's bushy brows began to frown as though a bad dream were troubling him. You know how proud he was of the hammer that the dwarfs had made for him? He called it The Crusher (*Mjolner*) because nothing could withstand a blow from it; and always while he slept it stood on the floor leaning against the arm of his seat, within easy reach of his hand. Now he dreamed that Thrym, the giant king, had stolen it and borne it away to his stronghold.

He awoke with a start and sat up and looked about him. He was safe in his own hall, surrounded by his own men. It was impossible that anything could have happened. Yet—just to make sure—he put out his hand and felt for The Crusher.

If you will believe me, it really was gone!

The Strong-One uttered such a shout that down on the earth people thought they had heard a thunder-clap. His hair and his beard rose and quivered like a million tiny flames. He bent over and shook the sleeping Sly-One.

"Mark, now, Loki, what I say! What no one knows on earth or in high heaven—my hammer is stolen!"

Loki was instantly awake. He was a very handsome youth and one of the cleverest of all the mighty beings who lived above the clouds. Sometimes he was more clever than honest, which is why I call him the Sly-One. There came a time when he was so wicked that he brought a terrible punishment upon himself. But just now his shrewdness was of great use to Thor.

He answered as soon as he had heard about the dream, "It is likely that you are right and that Thrym is the thief. But it would be unadvisable for you to go to him. You are so fiery that you would kill him before you had learned anything. I will borrow the feather-dress of Freyja the Lovely and do the errand for you."

"I should be very thankful to you," said Thor.

Hastening out, they harnessed to the chariot The-Goat-That-Gnashes-His-Teeth (*Tanngnjost*) and The-Goat-That-Flashes-His-Teeth (*Tanngrisner*) and drove to Folkvang, where Freyja's immense palace (*Sessrymner*) stood. No mansion in the upper world had so many seats for guests as hers; and she was as generous as she was hospitable.

When Thor had told her why they had come, she answered with the sweetest of smiles, "I would give you the dress gladly though it were of gold. Though it were of silver, I would give it to you instantly." And she ordered her attendants to bring it at once from the chest in which it was stored.

Though it was neither of gold nor of silver, yet it was very handsome. It was made of the white and brown plumage of falcons and fitted Loki's graceful body like a glove.

"I only hope no one will think me such a pretty bird that he will catch me and shut me in a cage," the Sly-One laughed, rustling his feathers as you have seen canaries do after a bath.

Then he spread his shining wings and flew out of the window, over the world, on and on. By the time the goats had brought Thor back again to Thrudvang, the magic pinions had carried Loki into the Land of the Giants (*Jotunheim*).

It would almost seem as if Thrym were expecting him, for he had placed himself where he was very easy to find—on a mound in front of the royal cavern. There he sat sunning himself and braiding gold collars for his greyhounds, while half a score of his horses nosed and browsed around him. He was very, very large and very, very old. His long beard and hair glittered like frost, and short glistening hairs grew all over his face and his hands. When Loki alighted before him he did not seem in the least surprised, but looked up with a wicked grin.

"How fare the mighty ones? How fare the elves? Why come you alone to Jotunheim?" he asked.

Loki answered sternly, "Ill fare the mighty ones. Ill fare the elves. Have you concealed the hammer of Thor?"

The giant's grin broadened until the mouth looked like a wide crack across his face. It was evident that he thought he had played a very clever trick. He answered promptly, "I have concealed the hammer of Thor eight lengths beneath the ground. No man brings it back unless he gives me Freyja as my bride."

Freyja the Lovely the bride of such a hoary old monster! Loki burst out laughing. But the giant only turned his back upon him and began talking to his horses and running his huge fingers through their snowy manes. They were all of them as large as hail-clouds. It suddenly occurred to Loki that if one of them should chance to step upon him, there would be very little of him left. There was nothing to do but carry the answer back to Thor. So again he spread the shining wings, leaped into the air, and flew back over the world to Thrudvang.

2

Although he was not long kept waiting, Thor had time to imagine all sorts of unpleasant things—even to fancy that perhaps the Sly-One was playing another of his tricks and would not return at all. The instant Loki in the feather-dress appeared upon the threshold, he called out sternly:

"Have you succeeded in doing your errand? Then give me the message before you sit down. What one tells after he has had time to sit down and think up fibs, is often of little value."

As Loki happened to be acting honestly for once, he felt somewhat aggrieved at this.

"Well have I succeeded in doing my errand," he answered; "Thrym the King of Giants has your hammer. No man brings it back unless he gives him Freyja as bride."

Thor snorted so that his red beard streamed far out, and down on the earth people thought they had seen the fiery northern lights streak across the sky.

"Is it to win her that he has made all this trouble? Ride we to Freyja without delay."

They mounted the chariot, and in an astonishingly short time the lightning-swift goats had drawn them to Folkvang.

Freyja the Lovely sat in her high-seat playing with her wonderful necklace, whose beads sparkled and flashed like water-drops in the sun. When she heard wheels, she guessed that the Strong-One was approaching and came out into the courtyard to meet him.

"I give you good greeting," she said, smiling kindly as Loki flew to her and dropped the feather-dress at her feet.

But she did not smile so sweetly when Thor had reined in the goats before her and told her of the giant's demand.

"Dress yourself, Freyja, in bridal robes," he finished, "together we will ride to Jotunheim."

The Lovely One straightened up so quickly that her hand caught in her necklace and broke it into a shower of sparkling balls.

"Sooner will I die than put on bridal robes for such a monster," she declared.

The Strong-One looked at her in surprise. The hammer was so important to him and to them all that he thought anyone ought to be willing to do anything to recover it.

"It is likely that you will die if I do not get The Crusher back," he said at last. "If the giants should invade the sky, I would have nothing to fight them with and they could get the victory over us."

Freyja answered nothing whatever, but she put back her beautiful shining hair from her beautiful rosy face and looked at him sorrowfully. All at once it occurred to Thor that she was much too lovely to be given to such a wicked old creature. He made only one more very faint attempt.

"I am told for certain that Thrym has got great riches," he said, "he has a herd of all-black oxen and all his cows have gold horns."

Then Freyja stamped her foot.

"I would be a love-sick maid indeed if with you I would ride to Jotunheim!" she said severely. And with that she left them and ran into the house—and I am not sure that she did not close the door pretty hard behind her.

Thor scratched his head thoughtfully.

"Much goes worse than is expected," he said at last. "We will see now what advice my kinsmen have to offer."

Again he puffed and snorted so that the trees on the earth below were stirred and swayed as by a rushing wind.

"Certainly there is going to be a great storm," the earth-people said to each other. And as they heard the chariot-wheels rumbling along above the clouds, they added, "Hark! Do you hear the thunder?"

They must have thought it a very long storm for before he stopped, Thor had driven to almost every palace in the sky. Odin the All-wise Ruler, Balder the Bright, and Heimdal the White One, Tyr, Brage, Vale—he visited each of them. Soon they were all gathered together at their meeting-place on the plains of Ida.

They consulted long and earnestly. At last Heimdal the White One, who had the gift of fore-knowledge, gave them this counsel:

"It is my advice that we play a trick upon the King of the Giants and allow him to believe that we have done as he asked. We will dress Thor in bridal robes and send him to Thrym."

At this, loud laughter went up from the others. You remember that Thor was not only stronger than any man on earth, but he was also mightier than any being in the sky. Imagine dressing him up for a beautiful graceful woman!

"That is cleverly devised!" cried Loki. "With a bridal veil will we hide the red beard, and Thrym shall not know him until the Strong-One has got his hand on his hammer. Then will he know him to his sorrow!"

They all laughed again; but the mighty Thor frowned angrily.

"Never will I submit to it," he growled. "Every living thing would mock at me, should I go dressed in bridal robes."

Perhaps Loki wished to revenge himself on the Strong-One for having spoken so sternly to him when he first brought the message from Jotunheim. Now in his turn he said sternly:

"Be silent, Thor. Stop such talk. Soon will the giants build in the sky if you do not bring your hammer back."

Because he knew this to be true, Thor could say nothing more. He stood frowning and stamping and growling in his beard while they brought Freyja's jewels and her beautiful robes to dress him in.

They put on him a very long gown that trailed about his feet so that he was certain that it would trip him up when he should try to walk. They hung sparkling necklaces around his neck, and placed a bunch of jingling keys at his belt to show that he was a good housekeeper. Broad gold broaches they pinned on his breast, and then they braided his red-gold hair into two beautiful wavy braids.

How the Mighty-One did stamp and fume at all this! And how the others laughed at him! The more they laughed, the angrier he grew—and the angrier he became, the funnier he looked in his bridal robes. The whole vault of the sky echoed and re-echoed with their mirth.

At last he was all dressed and they dropped the bridal veil over his furious face.

Then Loki said, with a slim grimace, that such a lovely bride could not be allowed to travel without at least one serving-maid. So he took the dress of one of Freyja's attendants and put it on himself. As he was young and handsome and with no more beard than either you or I, he made a very pretty waiting-damsel.

He got into the chariot beside Thor, the lightning-swift goats were hitched to the car, and away they went to Jotunheim.

3

The chariot-wheels rumbled like thunder. The-Goat-That-Gnashes-His-Teeth and The-Goat-That-Flashes-His-Teeth struck out fiery sparks from their gold-shod hoofs. So came Loki and the Strong-One into Jotunheim.

While they were yet a long way off, Thrym heard them coming and laughed exultantly:

Much wealth have I!
Many gifts have I!
Freyja, methinks, is all I lack!

... he sang; then he called out to his followers, "Giants, arise and spread the embroidered cloths over the benches. Freyja comes to be my bride."

The servants tumbled over each other in wild excitement. Some covered the seats and the walls with embroidered tapestries. Some strewed fresh straw upon the floor. Others scoured the shields and brought in the tables and set forth the massive golden dishes.

Just as twilight was falling, the chariot thundered into the courtyard.

When he saw Freyja's robes and Freyja's jewels, it never occurred to Thrym to doubt that it was really Freyja under the veil. He took the bride's hand and led her to her seat, laughing exultantly and singing his boastful song:

Much wealth have I!
Many gifts have I!
Freyja, methinks, was all I lacked!

Then he ordered the food to be brought in, and invited everyone to help him keep his wedding-feast.

When they began to eat, it was a wonder that Thor's appetite did not betray him the very first thing. Either he was so hungry that he did not care what they thought, or else he forgot that he was pretending to be a dainty lady. Besides all the cheese and the curds and the honey, he ate seven whole salmon and one whole ox, and after that he drank three barrels of the sweet spicy mead. Loki pinched him under the table as a sign for him to stop, but he only growled in his beard and ate one salmon more.

Thrym's eyes grew as big as milk-bowls.

"Saw I never such a hungry bride!" he exclaimed, pushing back to stare at her. "Saw I never a bride eat so much! Saw I never a maid drink so much mead!"

At that, even Thor was a little alarmed, for if the giant king should discover them before they got the hammer, not only would their plan fail but they would lose their lives into the bargain. He could think of nothing to answer, however, so he sat silent. Lucky was it for him that Loki always had his wits about him.

The Sly-One answered quickly, "Hungry is Freyja, thirsty is Freyja, for nothing has she eaten or drunk for eight days—so much did she long to come to Jotunheim."

Thrym's look of surprise changed to one of complacency.

"Is it so indeed! "he exclaimed, and finished his supper very pleasantly.

But by and by he became so pleased with his bride that he wanted to kiss her. Before Thor could hinder it, he reached out his great hairy hand and pulled at the veil. It slipped aside just enough to disclose Thor's furious, fiery eyes.

The giant king sprang back the whole length of the hall.

"Why are Freyja's eyes so sharp?" he cried. "It seems that fire burns in her eyes."

By this time, the Strong-One was so angry that I think he hardly cared what happened. Lucky was it for all the folk of the sky that Loki was there to answer for him.

The Sly-One spoke up quickly, "Sharp are Freyja's eyes, fiery are Freyja's eyes. She has not slept for eight nights, so much did she long to come to Jotunheim."

"Is it true indeed! "said Thrym, much flattered that his bride had been so eager to come to him. And he came back and sat down beside her and looked at her affectionately.

Finally the time came for the giving of the bridal gifts. An old sister of Thrym came and bowed low before the bride.

"Give from your hand the golden rings if you desire friendship of me," she demanded, "if you desire friendship of me—and love."

Because he was determined that he would never give her anything but a blow, Thor answered nothing whatever. Thrym feared that his bride was offended by the questions he had asked, so he hastened to do something to appease her.

He called to his servants, "Bring me the hammer to please my bride. Place the hammer on the lap of the maid. Wed us together in the name of Var."

Thor's heart laughed within him when he saw his beloved hammer drawn out of its hiding-place and borne toward him. But he sat as stiff as a stick. Until his hand grasped it, there was still danger. Nearer they came with it. Nearer—and all unsuspecting, they laid it upon his knee.

Then at last Thrym learned how the cleverness of the sky-people surpassed his cleverness. Thor's mighty hand closed upon the handle; he threw back the veil; he leaped to his feet. His terrible eyes blazed upon them as his arm flew back to strike.

Once! and Thrym fell dead at his feet. Twice! and the old giantess lay beside her brother. Again and again and again—until the whole race of giants were felled like a forest of towering trees.

Thus came Odin's son again by his hammer.

ALSO FROM LEONAUR
AVAILABLE IN SOFTCOVER OR HARDCOVER WITH DUST JACKET

THE EMPIRE OF THE AIR: 1 *by George Griffiths*—*The Angel of the Revolution*—a rich brew that calls to mind Verne's tales of futuristic wars while being original, visionary, exciting and technologically prescient.

THE EMPIRE OF THE AIR: 2 *by George Griffiths*—*Olga Romanoff or, The Syren of the Skies*—the sequel to *The Angel of the Revolution*—a future Earth in which nation states are given full self determination when the Aerians, the descendants of 'The Brotherhood of Freedom,' who have policed world peace for more than a century, decide they are mature enough to have outgrown war.

THE INTERPLANETARY ADVENTURES OF DR KINNEY *by Homer Eon Flint*—*The Lord of Death, The Queen of Life, The Devolutionist & The Emancipatrix*.

ARCOT, MOREY & WADE *by John W. Campbell, Jr.*—The Complete, Classic Space Opera Series—*The Black Star Passes, Islands of Space, Invaders from the Infinite*.

CHALLENGER & COMPANY *by Arthur Conan Doyle*—The Complete Adventures of Professor Challenger and His Intrepid Team-*The Lost World, The Poison Belt, The Land of Mists, The Disintegration Machine* and *When the World Screamed*.

GARRETT P. SERVISS' SCIENCE FICTION *by Garrett P. Serviss*—Three Interplanetary Adventures including the unauthorised sequel to H. G. Wells' *War of the Worlds-Edison's Conquest of Mars, A Columbus of Space, The Moon Metal*.

JUNK DAY *by Arthur Sellings*—". . . . his finest novel was his last, Junk Day, a post-holocaust tale set in the ruins of his native London and peopled with engrossing character types . . . . perhaps grimmer than his previous work but pointedly more energetic." *The Encyclopedia of Science Fiction*

KIPLING'S SCIENCE FICTION *by Rudyard Kipling*—Science Fiction & Fantasy stories by a Master Storyteller including 'As East As A,B,C' 'With The Night Mail'.

DARKNESS AND DAWN 1—THE VACANT WORLD *by George Allen England*—A Novel of a future New York.

DARKNESS AND DAWN 2—BEYOND THE GREAT OBLIVION *by George Allen England*—The last vestiges of humanity set out across America's devastated landscape in search of their dream.

DARKNESS AND DAWN 3—THE AFTER GLOW *by George Allen England*—Somewhere near the Great Lakes, 1000 years from now. Beneath our planet's surface tribes of near human albino warriors eke out an existence in a hostile environment.

AVAILABLE ONLINE AT **www.leonaur.com**
AND FROM ALL GOOD BOOK STORES

ALSO FROM LEONAUR
AVAILABLE IN SOFTCOVER OR HARDCOVER WITH DUST JACKET

THE COLLECTED SCIENCE FICTION AND FANTASY OF STANLEY G. WEINBAUM 1—INTERPLANETARY ODYSSEYS *by Stanley G. Weinbaum*—Classic Tales of Interplanetary Adventure Including: A Martian Odyssey, its Sequel Valley of Dreams, the Complete 'Ham' Hammond Stories and Others.

THE COLLECTED SCIENCE FICTION AND FANTASY OF STANLEY G. WEINBAUM 2—OTHER EARTHS *by Stanley G. Weinbaum*—Classic Futuristic Tales Including: *Dawn of Flame* & its Sequel The Black Flame, plus The Revolution of 1960 & Others.

THE COLLECTED SCIENCE FICTION AND FANTASY OF STANLEY G. WEINBAUM 3—STRANGE GENIUS *by Stanley G. Weinbaum*—Classic Tales of the Human Mind at Work Including the Complete Novel The New Adam, the 'van Manderpootz' Stories and Others.

THE COLLECTED SCIENCE FICTION AND FANTASY OF STANLEY G. WEINBAUM 4—THE BLACK HEART *by Stanley G. Weinbaum*—Classic Strange Tales Including: the Complete Novel The Dark Other, Plus Proteus Island and Others.

THE COLLECTED SCIENCE FICTION & FANTASY OF JACK LONDON 1—BEFORE ADAM & OTHER STORIES *by Jack London*—included in this Volume Before Adam The Scarlet Plague A Relic of the Pliocene When the World Was Young The Red One Planchette A Thousand Deaths Goliah A Curious Fragment The Rejuvenation of Major Rathbone.

THE COLLECTED SCIENCE FICTION & FANTASY OF JACK LONDON 2—THE IRON HEEL & OTHER STORIES *by Jack London*—included in this Volume The Iron Heel The Enemy of All the World The Shadow and the Flash The Strength of the Strong The Unparalleled Invasion The Dream of Debs.

THE COLLECTED SCIENCE FICTION & FANTASY OF JACK LONDON 3—THE STAR ROVER & OTHER STORIES *by Jack London*—included in this Volume The Star Rover The Minions of Midas The Eternity of Forms The Man With the Gash.

THE CRETAN TEAT *by Brian Aldiss*—The Cretan Teat is a wry and comic novel that interweaves its own fiction with an inner fiction about the discovery of a Byzantine painting of the Mother of the Blessed Virgin Mary suckling the infant Jesus and a fake ikon that becomes an instrument of Nemesis.

AVAILABLE ONLINE AT **www.leonaur.com**
AND FROM ALL GOOD BOOK STORES

ALSO FROM LEONAUR
AVAILABLE IN SOFTCOVER OR HARDCOVER WITH DUST JACKET

THE FIRST BOOK OF AYESHA *by H. Rider Haggard*—Contains *She & Ayesha: the Return of She.*

THE SECOND BOOK OF AYESHA *by H. Rider Haggard*—Contains *She and Allan & Wisdom's Daughter.*

QUATERMAIN: THE COMPLETE ADVENTURES—1 *by H. Rider Haggard*—Contains *King Solomon's Mines & Allan Quatermain.*

QUATERMAIN: THE COMPLETE ADVENTURES—2 *by H. Rider Haggard*—Contains *Allan's Wife, Maiwa's Revenge & Marie.*

QUATERMAIN: THE COMPLETE ADVENTURES—3 *by H. Rider Haggard*—Contains *Child of Storm & Allan and the Holy Flower.*

QUATERMAIN: THE COMPLETE ADVENTURES—4 *by H. Rider Haggard*—Contains *Finished & The Ivory Child.*

QUATERMAIN: THE COMPLETE ADVENTURES—5 *by H. Rider Haggard*—Contains *The Ancient Allan & She and Allan.*

QUATERMAIN: THE COMPLETE ADVENTURES—6 *by H. Rider Haggard*—Contains *Heu-Heu or, the Monster & The Treasure of the Lake.*

QUATERMAIN: THE COMPLETE ADVENTURES—7 *by H. Rider Haggard*—Contains *Allan and the Ice Gods, Four Short Adventures & Nada the Lily.*

TROS OF SAMOTHRACE 1: WOLVES OF THE TIBER *by Talbot Mundy*—55 B.C.--an adventurer set during the Roman invasion of Britain.

TROS OF SAMOTHRACE 2: DRAGONS OF THE NORTH *by Talbot Mundy*—55 B.C. —Caesar plots, Britons war among themselves and the Vikings are coming.

TROS OF SAMOTHRACE 3: SERPENT OF THE WAVES *by Talbot Mundy*—55 B.C.--Caesar is poised to invade Britain—only a grand strategy can foil him!.

TROS OF SAMOTHRACE 4: CITY OF THE EAGLES *by Talbot Mundy*—54 B.C.—Rome—Tros treads in the streets of his sworn enemies!.

TROS OF SAMOTHRACE 5: CLEOPATRA *by Talbot Mundy*—Tros and the Roman Empire turn to the Egypt of the Pharaohs.

TROS OF SAMOTHRACE 6: THE PURPLE PIRATE *by Talbot Mundy*—The epic saga of the ancient world—Tros of Samothrace—draws to a conclusion in this sixth—and final—volume.

AVAILABLE ONLINE AT **www.leonaur.com**
AND FROM ALL GOOD BOOK STORES

Milton Keynes UK
Ingram Content Group UK Ltd.
UKHW030022180324
439604UK00001B/167